THE MAN WHO LOST THE WAR

THE MAN WHO
LOST THE WAR

W. T. TYLER

Copyright © 1980 by W. T. Tyler

ISBN: 978-1-4976-9716-4

Distributed by Open Road Distribution
345 Hudson Street
New York, NY 10014
www.openroadmedia.com

①

For Joan

THE MAN WHO LOST THE WAR

ONE

Early snow fell in the Alps that autumn and blocked the Grand St. Bernard Pass between Switzerland and Italy. There were blizzards along the southern Swiss plain, freezing rain over the meadows of the Piedmont and Lombardy. On the slopes of the Carpathians, Polish herdsmen watched the wolves withdraw with their half-grown cubs to the lower ranges and prepared for an unseasonable winter. By the first week of October a light frost lay over the Berlin Wall, barely two months old. The freeze had cracked its footings and fissured its mortar joints. Technicians from the East German construction industries inspected it in the bitter morning wind, standing huddled in cheap overcoats and machine-made hats, ashamed at what the frost had done to that clumsy, scab-built abomination, a scandal to their trades. They were accompanied by armed units from the East German *Volksarmee*. Across the frontier, in West Berlin, young American platoon leaders from the first US Battle Group watched them suspiciously through binoculars, and afterwards reported their presence, describing them as Russians, probably from the Twentieth Soviet Guards Army. They thought the Reds were searching for weaknesses in the US salient.

In Moscow real Russians worked all day and all night within the Kremlin walls near the old captured Napoleonic guns, trying to complete the new Palace of Congresses in time for the Twenty-second CPSU Party Congress at which Khruschev was expected to deliver a new ultimatum on Berlin. The milky pylons and the slabs of pine-green marble were already mortised in place. Under the skeleton of wooden scaffolding inside, metal salamanders smoked throughout the night to dry the walls so that the platoons of painters and lacquerers could finish their work by October twenty-second.

3

In the basement of the White House carpenters and electricians were working too, expanding the rabbit warren of offices where President Kennedy's newly enlarged National Security Council was working. Tarpaulins and canvas drop-cloths were hung from the doorways to keep down the dust. Senior staffmen moved carefully between sawhorses, acoustical-tile setters, and electricians moving telephone outlets and mysterious ropes of rubber-insulated communications conduit.

New intelligence key words had appeared. New intelligence monitoring systems were beginning to produce a new conceptual consciousness. At the CIA, the DIA, and in the State Department, a few key officials recognized Khruschev's limitations. There was uncertainty in Moscow, despite the ultimatums, despite the recent success at Novaya Zemlya in the Arctic, where a one-hundred-megaton weapon had been tested, despite the reappearance of Soviet power in the Pacific, where Russian ICBM launchings had begun, contrails of frozen crystal feathering as silently as sharks above the reefs of cumulus over the blue-green waters of the northern Pacific. Soviet industrial growth had slowed. Khruschev's liberalization had produced internal strains. The Chinese were hostile. The missile gap had perished as a credible fact, dissolved under the peregrine eye of Samos, the US spy satellite launched in January to replace the U-2 surveillance which had come to an ignominious end over Sverdlovsk. Panning across tundra, white fields, the blue nugget of Lake Aral, the lonely track of the Trans-Siberian, Samos had betrayed an already moribund technology, a scattering of missiles as clumsy and irrelevant as prairie dinosaurs concealed under thatch and greenery too meagre to hide their prodigious obsolescence—reptile brains unable to transform the four-year-old Sputnik head-start into a strategic advantage in the *pax ballistica*.

The Soviet military cartographers knew. They had already begun to change the maps of Estonia and Latvia—shrinking coastlines, falsifying distances, obscuring details . . . like the breath of the hare contracting under the shadow of the droning hawk.

Fog had cruised the Baltic coast of East Germany northeast of Rostock since before dawn but now had begun to lift from the dunes, from the marsh flats, and the sea itself. Nothing was heard but the wind, the shriek of the gulls, and the sweeping of the waves against the beach. Storm clouds were driven like chimeras from the sea, blown through the tops of the pines and stunted cedars, and lost again against the gray overcast. Reefs of paper-thin ice lay in the stiff grasses beyond the slope of sand and shingle. A solitary wagon road wound along the beach between the trees and the dunes and disappeared in the distance.

The two men moved across the dunes, faces bent into the cold. The wind howled as they walked, licking at their ears, lathering the surf to milk and driving the last of the morning fog into the inland meadows. The smaller man struggled to keep up. The wind bit at his coattails and his gum boots hobbled him in ankle-deep drifts of sand. He was winded and stopped at the top of a dune, breathing heavily as he looked out at the infinite expanse of gray beyond him. He was thin but wiry, as small as a jockey. A shadow of beard lay over his bony cheeks like soot on a chimney sweep. A coarse woolen muffler was pulled about his neck; his ears were red from the wind.

"Perishing cold! What'd we come here for?" Bryce shouted towards Strekov, who turned and looked back, his face neutral below the wind-blown blond hair. He was wearing a blue corduroy shooting jacket and gum boots, his gray trousers tucked away at the knees.

"Would you like to go back to the car?" Strekov asked. Bryce shook his head, his eyes searching the beach road suspiciously for the Mosca that had brought them from the safe house that morning. Strekov knew he was still wary. He was troubled, unable to account for it.

"It's easy for you, isn't it?" Bryce shouted when he caught up and they resumed their walk. "Used to this filthy weather, ain't you. Not me. It's a whiskey I need, that's all."

"We'll have a whiskey soon."

"I'm not complaining. You never heard me, did you? Walk these ruddy boots off if I had to. What's that?" He looked out to sea where the lifting fog had revealed a few gray ships inbound to Rostock. They rode high in the swell before they were blasted down again by the hammer of the sea, foam breaking over their bows, blue water disgorging from the icy fathoms below. Strekov saw the fear in Bryce's eyes and knew that whatever else might explain it, it was also irrational. He had begun to despair of learning anything from him.

"An East German fishing fleet," Strekov replied easily.

"No warships—Q-boats? Breaks your bones watching it. Sods, all of them. Living on swill. Brine-sodden rashers and roach meal for grub. Bloody fools."

"They're used to it," Strekov said.

"Who's used to it?" Bryce said viciously. "Bloody sickening, it is. It's what the captain tells the crew when he tells them to fuck off. 'You'll get used to it, lads!' Used to what? Used to getting drowned? Shag him, lads!" he yelled suddenly towards the ships. They sailed on. Bryce stood watching them helplessly.

As the two men moved forward again, Strekov said, "How was London? How did you find it?"

"Rotten. Nothing I couldn't manage, though."

"You were tired of it? You wanted to go someplace else?"

"Who wouldn't if the money's there," Bryce said elusively. He lifted his boot over a piece of driftwood scrolled like a scrimshaw, carved bone-white by the salt wind. His foot came down heavily, smashing it. "More money than this frigging place," he complained bitterly. "Siberia is what it is. Not like Brighton now, is it? As different as chalk and cheese, your sea and mine. Frozen sea. Frozen sand. Call it tundra, they say. Siberia's a rifle shot away . . . where we all get to, eh? Dig your grave with an ice pick. It's money I need. Do you handle the finances? They never paid me enough." He pulled a packet of cigarettes from his pocket.

"We can talk about the money," Strekov said. "Why did you leave London so suddenly?"

"I told them," Bryce said sullenly. "I told Kirilen first night I got here."

"Tell me."

"Money," Bryce said emphatically. "Not enough of it. I couldn't get on. Then they were going to pension me off. I was twenty years in the Forces and the wireless service was going to pension me off. Didn't say a dicky-bird about the work I'd done."

"When did you learn that?"

"The day before I left. I went to the pension office, see. Wanted to see what the future might give me. Then I'd been under the doctor with my nerves, see. Sick as a dog."

"You went to the pension office?"

"The day I left."

Strekov stopped. "You told Kirilen that you were thinking about going to the pension office. You didn't tell him you'd gone."

"Maybe I forgot," Bryce said. "Don't get smart. Don't get pushy, see. I'd shut up now and you'd never get another word."

Strekov let it pass. He walked on, studying the sand at his feet. "What else would you want beside money?"

"Just money. A flat too. A place to work. Once a Marconi man, always a Marconi man. I'd work. I never said anything different, did I?" He sucked at the cigarette hidden in his cupped fingers. "Does Kirilen work for you or do you work for him?" he asked slyly.

"We work together." Strekov watched the inhaled smoke dissolve the suspicion in the small, spade-shaped face, filling the undernourished body with warmth and light, like gas expanding in a beaker. The smell of the cigarette reminded Strekov of England again—and of light, too, in the darkest of collieries, in damp pubs among pints and bitters, in sweltering movie houses with fog on the streets outside, in lifts lowering to the floors of Welsh mines, among dustbins, frozen canals, and piled scrap iron, in the cold back yards of Birmingham, below yellow chaffinches in plaster medallions hanging over rain-rotted flock wallpaper, and wind disintegrating ceilings in Notting Hill, blowing through the sawtooth slag heaps, over the gummy lino in Cheapside grocery shops, among trodden parsley and smashed quinceberries, blowing embers nursed by old soldiers with black teeth and orange fingers on the pier at Brighton.

This was Bryce's world as well and Strekov knew it. There were few in Moscow who did.

"You were frightened in London," Strekov said. "That was it, wasn't it?"

The eyes showed the fear momentarily as they looked away but then dimmed and were empty as they contemplated the infinity of the gray sea beyond the beach. "Not frightened," Bryce answered softly. "It was dodgy but I wasn't frightened. Not me. But I'm finished now. All the ruckus they're raising in London. Couldn't manage London now, could I? They'd nick me in a flash. Coppers swarming over me like a widow's broom over a street turd quick as me feet found the pitch. A nutcase, they'd say—drowned in class hatred. Dirt to them, I am now—common as dirt. No, I couldn't manage."

"But others can, is that it?" Strekov said quietly, looking out to sea as he recognized again what made Bryce unique. He wondered how well Moscow understood that. Bryce had stopped in his tracks. Strekov looked back.

"I didn't say that!" Bryce shouted. "Never. You can't make me, see!" He was terrified. "Make you what?" Strekov asked, surprised.

"You're trying to trap me, you are!" Bryce cried. He was livid.

"I'm trying to understand why you left London so suddenly," Strekov said patiently. "This is important to us. Moscow wants to know. If something has gone wrong, we want to know that as quickly as possible."

"I told Kirilen. I told him—the first night!"

"You told Kirilen you'd been betrayed. Betrayed by whom? Now you say it was the money, that there wasn't enough money. Was that what you meant by betrayed—that your handler in London wasn't giving you enough money?"

"Wouldn't give me the drippings from his nose," Bryce remembered bitterly. "It was dodgy, what I was doing," he continued sullenly. "Then there was my nerves, see. I told Kirilen, that first night. Had a bottle of rum, too. Too much, maybe. Just talking, I was. That first night with Kirilen. Just blathering, see. Nowt wrong in talking now, is there? Fair been bathing in rum too, see." It was a scullion's voice taking refuge in its class: a sort of stage Cockney more cunning than Strekov expected from someone of Bryce's meager gifts.

Strekov's gray eyes puzzled out a line of combers as he walked, listening to Bryce's dissembling voice at his shoulder. The white-capped combers moved like sea serpents towards the beach as the wind picked up.

Bryce wasn't a code clerk. When he'd been recruited in Berlin eighteen months earlier, he'd been working in the pouch room, with only limited access to classified documents. He was still angry about his recall from the British embassy in Moscow, where the KGB had had its first contacts with him. In Berlin, Bryce's sole value was in providing information on visiting British intelligence officers and the gossip of the mission family, much of it malicious, some of it misleading. An ex-serviceman and wireless operator with the RAF before he joined the diplomatic wireless service, he had shown an enlisted man's misperception of the sexual life of his superiors. Much that he'd identified as promiscuous was not; much that he found aberrant was merely eccentric. His professional problems, like his insights, were rooted in his class. In Berlin he'd had trouble with his supervisors, was often rowdy, sometimes drunk, and constantly in debt. After eighteen months he'd been reassigned to the UK at the Diplomatic Wireless Station at Hanslope Park outside London. A month after his return his handler from the Soviet mission contacted him and told him to buy a Hallicrafters radio and install it in his newly purchased detached house in the suburbs. He gave him the money for the radio. A month later Bryce bought the radio and installed it in his attic. At the second meeting with his Soviet handler he was provided with two crystals and a high-speed keying device. Three weeks later Bryce had fled.

The radio hadn't yet been placed in service, and Bryce had received no further instructions from his handler. He'd emptied his bank accounts, left the crystal and antenna loop, together with the high-speed keying device, in a locker at Liverpool Station. He'd taken the train to Harwich, where he'd boarded a boat for Holland. Once he was on the continent, his behavior proved as inexplicable as before. He spent two drunken days in his Copenhagen hotel before getting in touch with his Soviet contact, who knew nothing about Bryce's flight. The following day the Soviet intelligence officer gave him an accommodation passport and a plane ticket to Warsaw. At the airport Bryce changed his mind and asked to be sent to East Berlin instead. He claimed he had a German fiancée in East Berlin and that they'd planned to be married. Bryce drove to Gedser on the coast in a rented car and caught the ferry to Warnemunde in East Germany. Kirilen had been sent from Soviet intelligence headquarters at Karlshorst to meet him. The address of Bryce's East German fiancée was a false one. Kirilen escorted Bryce to a safe house in the country, where his debriefing commenced. The first night Bryce told Kirilen that he had been betrayed in London. The following morning he denied it, as he also denied giving the Soviet contact in Copenhagen the address of his East German girl friend in Berlin. Two nights later he slipped away from the safe house. The guards found him in the woods near the main gate. He told Kirilen that he was on his way to the pub in the village. Kirilen thought Bryce was attempting to escape from the house and return to Warnemunde. Apart from concluding that Bryce was terrified and a hopeless alcoholic as well, Kirilen could make no sense of his story. From Moscow, Orlov had asked Strekov to fly in from London to interrogate him.

"Did your handler in Berlin talk to you about money?" Strekov said, searching the beach road ahead of them for the car. "Did he promise you more than you received?"

"He gave for what he got," Bryce answered. "Boris was his name. Boris and Vasily. They worked together. Easy to get on with. Treated me like a perishing nursemaid. Anything I wanted. Booze, fags, a bit of crumpet now and then. German lasses, too, they were. Not tarts. Young ones. Not those old trots you pick up on the streets." He lit another cigarette and shivered from the cold.

"You wanted to marry one of them?"

Bryce nodded. "Always after me, she was. Wanted me to get her to England," he added proudly. "Make her a good home there. What'd I be to her in England with all those nobs around? All that money everywhere?" He looked towards Strekov. "What would she see in me then?"

"What would she see?" Strekov stopped and looked back.

"What those embassy wives used to see," Bryce said without malice. "Socks on a rooster, lad. Lifting up shit." Bryce looked away over the dunes. Strekov wasn't sure he understood.

"Why did you leave from Liverpool?" he asked, still studying Bryce's averted eyes. They were calm, even tranquil.

"Liverpool," Bryce remembered. He nodded and they moved on. "Those were my instructions. Have to follow instructions, don't we? Same as you do."

"Why did you change your mind then and not go to Warsaw?"

"I thought maybe I could talk to Boris again. Boris and Vasily." He followed along after Strekov, head down. "Who's number one?" he asked again. "You or Kirilen?"

"We work together."

"The same section?"

"Different sections. You said you were sick in London. You said your nerves were bad. Why was that?"

"Worried. Thought it was my liver. Thought I had cancer. Lost four stone in a week. Then London didn't suit me anymore. I couldn't stick it. Not just my work, see. Everyone's on the grab these days—out for number one. Me, I wanted peace and quiet. What I always wanted—the country life. I've studied life up, see. I knew what I wanted and it waren't London. Be your own guv'ner, that's my style."

He looked towards Strekov, the slyness back in his voice again. Strekov pitied him so much for his cowardice and deceit that he hardly had the courage to look at him.

"You had done nothing for us in London," Strekov said. "You hadn't used the radio. You hadn't received your instructions. What had changed since Berlin? You'd done nothing in London."

"Kept dead mum about it, didn't I? Dead mum about everything. But London's no place for a workingman like me. You see that. Then there's the bombs. All them bombs. Nuclear bombs. Reading about it every day. Bloody sickening it is, how the Yanks come in with their airplanes and submarines full of bombs, and the government won't do owt about it. Blow us all up, see."

"And that worried you?"

"Worried me sick," he pleaded. "Worried me to death, it did. Hear them in Hyde Park all the time. Ban-the-Bombers. It's coming to that one day. Wipe out London in a flash, they would—"

Strekov stopped. "And so you left," he said simply. "Left because you were sick, frightened, and poorly paid. You ran away just because of those things and when you got here, you tried to run away again. Do you expect us to believe that?"

"Bible oath," Bryce muttered.

"You're lying."

"Leave me be!" Bryce cried miserably. "I told you. Driving me loony with your filthy questions! Not a fucking word more! Nothing, see!"

"You're safe now. Don't you understand that. No one can reach you here. No one. I promise you that. But if something frightened you, I must know what it is. I can't help you like this."

"Look!" Bryce pleaded, flinging up his hands.

"It's not possible that you believe someone is after you here, is it?" Strekov asked. "That you believe someone has followed you?"

Bryce was holding out his hands. "See these hands," he entreated. "I could find a dory! I could row all the way to Harwich with these hands if I'd the mind to. Only I wouldn't, see! Not for what they've done to me. Pension me off after thirty years. Not just me, either. Not for what they did to me. My old dad. My mum, too. Four years on the toby in the great slump and he never got right by it. Killed him, they did. Poisoned his heart with money! Killed me mum, too. Do you think I could forget that? Do you think I could? Killed Mary, too. Lovely Mary. Bonny young Mary. Dead in Merseyside during May week, 1941. Burned to death, see. Burned in a tenement fire the Jerry bombs didn't even touch. Lit up the whole sky, they say. Ferocious!" He trotted after Strekov. "Ferocious it was too, because it burned me own heart to a cinder when it cooked her own dear soul. Ask Boris. Ask Carlos, back in Moscow. We talked about it. Ask him."

"What do you want now?" Strekov said wearily, wanting only to be rid of Bryce's tireless voice.

"Peace and quiet, that's all," Bryce answered. "No one blackguarding me fore and aft when I've had too many pints in the evening. No one cursing the fire out when I mash me some tea in the wireless room. A spot of turf I can call me own. Get reeling drunk when I've a mind—"

His voice rambled on. The thunder of the sea roared in their ears and drove Bryce's words away as Strekov moved down the dune and onto the exposed beach, Bryce at his heels. The changing contours of the sand had uncovered a rusty tank trap, like the twisted vertebra of some long-extinct animal. They climbed the last dune and saw the muddy Mosca in the distance. The Russian driver was holding a pair of binoculars in his gauntleted hands and looking north where a single Soviet trawler pounded westward in the spray, inbound to Warnemunde.

It was rye weather in the Rappahannock, rye and quail weather, and nothing in East or West Berlin gave Plummer much pleasure these wet autumn days. He had an early evening appointment at the East German Planning Commission on Leipzigerstrasse. When he found his Opel on the street outside and splashed towards West Berlin, a few armored cars were still prowling the boulevards after the four o'clock gunfire. At the intersections squads of Vopos reinforced with *Grenz-polizei* units were checking documents. The wind hammered through the tramwire, chasing a few Baltic snow flurries through the icy halos of lamplight. A skirmish line of Vopos was turning back automobile traffic near the Potzdammerplatz, but Plummer sneaked over a few blocks, jogged down a cobbled alley, and swung back from the north, his approach hidden by a pair of Soviet T-55 tanks near the check-point. The Soviet tank crews stood in their turrets, looking toward a few mobile searchlights that were strobing over a field of rubble and a blasted brick apartment building, its roof collapsed, its sashes black-ened by fire.

Two red-faced Vopos wearing gray-green forage caps stood near the door to the control shack. Plummer walked by them and pushed his identity documents through the slot inside. He heard a field tele-phone being cranked up, then someone at the PBX switchboard, ring-ing up the East German internal security office. One of the Vopos pulled on his overcoat, looked out the window at Plummer's Opel and back at his companion. *"Gottverdammter Engländer,"* he said.

Plummer heard him. "Say what?" he said, turning.

"Nein," the other Vopo said. He pushed his companion towards the door. *"Nein."*

Plummer watched them through the window and a few minutes later saw a car wheel past the tanks and into the compound. He heard the doors slam, heard footsteps across the gravel, and saw a torchbeam flicker across the windshield of his Opel, then move against his West Berlin license plate. The torchlight went out and he heard the footsteps retreat towards the rear of the control shack. A moment later the door opened behind the wooden partition. More voices now, quieter than the others. The telephone was cranked up again. Plummer lit a cigarette and stood looking out into the darkness. A beading of light snow mixed with rain lay across his windshield. He was still standing there when the clerk pushed open the window and called to him: "How did you come from Leipzigerstrasse?"

"I drove."

"Traffic was closed off from Leipzigerstrasse."

"Not the way I came." The German looked at him blankly, at the wiry brown hair and the ginger-brown eyes, the old raglan with the collar pulled up, the shoulders dark with rain. Still studying Plummer, he picked up the telephone and, while he waited, moved his eyes to the passport photograph and the photograph in the West German identity document. Two Germans in dark hats and overcoats stood in the bright room behind him, watching Plummer silently. The clerk spoke into the telephone, moved his eyes to Plummer's face, and nodded. He hung up.

"You're American," he said in English, pushing the documents back across the counter. "The next time you should obey the militia." He reached forward to close the window. "There's no traffic tonight, not here. Everything is closed down in this sector. But you can drive through. Drive quickly." The window shut and Plummer was alone in the control shack.

He drove forward across the brilliantly lit security strip and into West Berlin. He left his Opel outside the West Berlin control point. When he returned to his car, he looked back across the roadbed and into the Zone. The barricade was down and two Soviet T-55 tanks had racheted forward to the edge of the tank barrier. The sedan was gone. Ahead, across the road from the West German control point three figures stood under the security lights near a British Ford, talking to the MP captain and looking east into the darkness. When Plummer started his engine, one of the men crossed the road in the beam of his headlights and motioned for him to shut it off. He was a German, a light heavyweight with goat shoulders and a tightly buttoned black raincoat. He bent towards the window, his hands in his pockets. "We want to talk with you," he said.

"I've got an appointment," Plummer said. "I'm late."

The German had a square, muscular face and oily black hair. He looked over Plummer's shoulder and into the back seat, then turned and walked to the back of the Opel and looked at the license plate. When he came back to the window, he said, "You see nothing in East Berlin?"

"Nothing."

He examined Plummer steadily, his hands still in his pockets. "It's been closed since five o'clock. Since after the gunfire." When Plummer didn't answer, he said, "Let me see your passport."

"They just looked at my passport inside."

"So we look again." He took the passport and crossed the road towards the other two men. They talked together for a few minutes and crossed the road to Plummer's car. One was wearing a storm coat with a fur collar and was hatless. The other wore a dark-blue overcoat and a fur hat.

"The East Germans let you through?" asked the man in the storm coat. He was an American.

"They usually do," Plummer said.

"You could save us a little time if you helped us out," the American said. He took Plummer's passport and studied it under the blue-white glare of the security lights. He was in his late forties, with a smooth blond face that was beginning to thicken in the jowls and an exaggerated ease that privilege and good breeding had carefully cultivated over the years, but not yet beyond the point of condescension. The graying blond hair was fine and flaxen under the security lights, but too long for his collar. It curled against his temples and neck, like the feathers of a Westminster spaniel. He was wearing a tweed jacket under the unbuttoned coat. The wool tie was also British, like the vowels in the accent, but he was as American as the Yale Club, and Plummer had known dozens like him. "You're American?" he asked.

Plummer blew on his hands, his ears stinging from the cold. The third man moved forward. He was English. "Look here," he protested.

15

"We don't have all bloody night." The wind bit his breath from his lips, snapping it out across the darkness. A black astrakhan hat sat on his head.

"Neither do I," Plummer said. "What's the passport say?"

"It's an American passport," the German said.

"So what does that make me?" Plummer asked.

"What'd you see in East Berlin?" the American said.

"I've got ten thousand pounds of British oil at Treptow," Plummer answered. "What do you want me to see?"

"The wheels of commerce, is it?" the Englishman said. "Ruddy Shylocks—"

"It pays your salary," Plummer said.

"Your own too, I'll wager. Handsomely, I should imagine. Not above that now, are we?"

"You saw nothing, then?" the American interrupted.

"Nothing."

"You have a depot in Treptow?"

"Something like that."

"You do business in the Zone?" the American asked.

Plummer didn't answer.

"*Schnauze*," the German muttered. "Maybe we take him inside." He shifted on his heels, one gloved fist pressing the leather palm of the other hand, chest high across the tightly buttoned raincoat.

"What's the name of your firm?" the American continued.

"BIL," Plummer replied. "British International Lubricants."

"Do you know it?" the American asked the Englishman. "What do you think?"

"Never heard of it," the Englishman scoffed. "Never."

"He's never heard of it," the American repeated.

"Ask him if he's ever heard of tough shit," Plummer said.

"Look here!" the Englishman shouted.

"*Schnauze*," the German muttered.

"Why don't I handle it," the American suggested, moving closer to the car window. "You two go ahead. Maybe the MP's have picked up something." When the German and the Englishman crossed the road to the English Ford, the American returned Plummer's passport

16

through the window. He took a card from a leather card case and handed it to Plummer. "My name's Peter Templeman," he said easily. "The Brits don't like that very much. Neither do we."

Plummer looked at the card. It read:

Peter R. Templeman
First Secretary of Embassy

"I thought the embassy was in Bonn," Plummer said.

"It's an old card," Templeman smiled. "From Paris."

"What is it the British don't like?" Plummer asked, squinting up through the rain.

"Bad manners. Shysters bootlegging strategic stuff into the Zone. We don't like it very much, either." He leaned closer to the window. "Maybe we can talk about it some time. You don't want to lose your export licenses, do you?"

Plummer looked at the smooth, blond face. "What do you do, Templeman," he said, throwing the card on the dashboard, "sign them up when they climb over the Wall or just take them cold turkey, ass hanging out, right off the streets?"

"It's all right what I do, sport," Templeman said. "What the hell do you know."

Plummer started the engine. "Nothing," he said. "Just stay out of my hair."

"Do you know who you're talking to?"

"Sure I know who I'm talking to," Plummer said. "A squire on the New Frontier. Someone from the zoo over at Dahlem, looking for assets to help him run his rabbits out of the Zone. Forget it."

"I'll forget it all right—"

"Do that," Plummer said, moving the Opel into gear. "Do us both a favor." The car moved forward into West Berlin and Templeman followed it for a few steps, watching it disappear.

A cold rain was still falling when Plummer and Elizabeth Davidson left her apartment in Charlottenburg and drove towards Wilmandorf. "You're angry," she said. "You are—still."

"I was late," Plummer said.

"Perhaps it's the rain," she said. "I don't wonder that you're anxious to escape Berlin for a few days."

"Rostock's no escape," Plummer said. "Do I look anxious?"

"No, but you never do, do you?" Her face was turned away, her legs drawn up on the seat of the Opel where she sat sideways, watching the cars splash past. A Mercedes slammed on its brakes ahead of them, bathing her in sudden fire, and Plummer moved into the other lane. He had missed dinner with her at her apartment and they had had drinks instead. "Driving in Berlin petrifies me," she said, her hand lifted in reflex towards the dashboard. "Especially rainy nights. It didn't matter at first. Now it does."

She was English, slim and cool faced, with dark eyes closely set behind a long aquiline nose. Her hair was dark blond, tied in a brown velvet ribbon at the back of her neck. They had met again in Berlin after five years. She treated him like an old friend, an elderly uncle returned from the antipodes after a long absence. They hadn't talked about the past.

"Why don't you forget the recital and we can go someplace else?" Plummer said.

"That would be lovely but I promised."

"Promised who?"

"The Gwenhoggs. You remember them, I'm sure. From Vienna. He was with the embassy." She turned and looked at him.

"I remember."

"I told them you were here. They were pleased. Was it all right?" She smiled as she watched him. Plummer turned and looked at her. "You *do* keep to yourself, don't you?"

"I keep busy," he said.

"Is it the same thing?" She put her head back. "This is a lovely car. You're still as negligent as ever, aren't you?" She looked at the dusty dashboard, the dog-eared road maps in the door pouch beside her, and the ruptured upholstery along the door frame. "Still careless in the same way. Do you still call it economy?" She lifted her head suddenly with the recollection. "What happened to your Porsche—the one you abused so terribly in Vienna?"

"I got rid of it when I left. I thought you didn't want to talk about Vienna."

"I don't," she said. "I should be very cross if I did. Does it annoy you so?" She rested her head back against the seat again, looking out from beneath her long lashes at the roadbed ahead. The streetlamps moved across her face, amber and blue-white, the raindrops on the windshield cobwebbing her brow and cheeks.

"You're too tired to go to any recital," he said.

She smiled again. "The drink made me sleepy. When I'm sleepy, I'm relaxed. When I'm that way, nothing annoys me, not even hypocrisy. Not even my own. So perhaps we should talk about Vienna."

"It was cold," he said.

"Very cold. Very cold and very lonely. I shan't forget it. Have you been back recently?"

"No, not recently."

"You still travel, though."

"Not very much anymore. What are they playing at the concert?"

"It's a recital. Scarlatti, I believe."

"Is that why it's in a church?"

"You can't tempt me," she said. "I promised the Gwenhoggs." She closed her eyes. "If you go to London soon, I shall give you a list. Some shopping. When will that be?"

"Maybe in a couple of weeks. After Rostock."

"Rostock sounds very far away."

"It's because you're sleepy and it's raining. A recital is no damned good on a night like this."

She only smiled, her eyes still closed. After a moment she said, "You gave me a keen look. I distinctly felt it."

"Why don't you forget about the recital," he said. "You can come with me. Afterwards we could go to Rostock."

"That would be splendid. We could go very quickly," she said sleepily. "Without telling anyone. Just go. And then when we tired of Rostock, we could go to your house in Spain. We could take a herring boat." Her eyes were still closed. "It would be lovely."

"We'll do it, then," he said.

She didn't answer. After a minute, she said: "Are you happy, David?"

"Not much. Are you?"

"It's such a silly question, isn't it? Why did you ask me that the other night? Why did you ask me if I was happy?"

He turned to look at her. "Maybe I wanted to know. Maybe I didn't think you were."

After a moment she stirred and sat up, opening her eyes and looking out the windshield. "Don't make it difficult for us to see each other. Don't remind me of what is past. I should hate it terribly if you did. Is that selfish of me?"

"No, it's not selfish," he said. He didn't know what he was saying.

He turned the car towards the chapel near the corner. "Perfect," she said. "I am on time after all." She sat forward and pulled up her coat. "It was splendid. I did enjoy it. You're not angry, are you?"

"No. I'm not angry."

"I must run. Do call me again."

"I will. Watch the puddle." She slipped out the door and ran across the pavement towards the chapel doors. She turned back and waved. Through the windshield he watched her join two figures standing near the entryway where they had been waiting for her, and then they went inside.

Plummer drove back through the rainy streets to his flat in Kreuzberg. It was a drafty, top-floor flat that had once been a painter's studio. Standing under the skylight, he could look through the gallery of windows and into the decay of East Berlin's Friedrichshain across the canal. He could see the rear stoops of the flats, could watch the bundled children of the East German factory workers as they left for school in the morning, and watch their blue-faced mothers hanging up laundry afterwards. With a Zeiss lens he could count the paint scabs on the old window frames or the bubbles in the ancient, hand-drawn panes. The flat was cheap and anonymous, located in a West Berlin working-class section where he was as anonymous as the people he lived among, where he could leave in the early morning silence or return after midnight without attracting attention. It was a neighborhood where the fruits and vegetables were cheap and overripe, where people worked all day or all night and sometimes disappeared without explanation, where curiosity was as extinct as the sounds of spring rustling in the Tiergarten after the long, ugly winter of 1945.

TWO

Bugger the reports officer!" Templeman shouted, borrowing a locution from the British diplomatic circuit where he spent many of his bachelor hours in Berlin these days. "Bugger him—bugger *all* of them!"

He slashed his riding crop across his desk and his middle-aged secretary nearly spilled the morning coffee; but no matter. He held in his other hand a draft telegram which she'd sneaked into his inbox the evening before but which he'd just read. He also had a hangover. His brain was starved of oxygen and dehydration had defoliated his arterial tree. The morning light was as cold as seawater across the CIA desks there at Dahlem sector in West Berlin, leaking into closets and chilly offices where safes were being unlocked, vacuum tins of American coffee popped open for the percolators, cable files fragrant with ink and copy fluid were being clasped in steel bands and green-jacketed portfolios labeled TOP SECRET NO FOREIGN DISSEM for circulation among the operations officers.

The draft telegram Templeman had dictated three days earlier had been returned from the reports officer, brutally condensed. The spelling of a few of the Russian names had been corrected. So had the conclusions. Three paragraphs of exposition had vanished. Because the Soviet emigré organization Templeman had been following had less of a constituency among his Washington readers in the US intelligence community these days, the CIA officer who'd reviewed his draft had suggested that it be sent by diplomatic pouch rather than cable. "Good Christ!" Templeman shouted. "Does he realize how long it took me to get this frigging stuff?" It was a rhetorical question. Templeman's secretary had already vanished through the door. He flung the draft on the desk, grabbed a red grease-pencil, and scribbled an obscenity across the first page. Satisfied, he tore the draft in two, wrote *Burn* across the first page, and threw it in his out-box. He sank down into his chair.

He was still a stranger to Berlin. He'd been there only a month after almost ten years' absence. Times had changed—his own no less than the Agency's. He had only six years to go until retirement unless he slipped badly. Anything was possible.

On the wall behind the brown leather chairs and the walnut coffee table was an oilskin map of Berlin in polychrome, ten years old now, but Templeman's predecessor had kept it up to date, and so had Templeman, who'd marked with a red grease-pencil on the plastic overlay the saw-toothed salient of the Berlin Wall, built only just before his return.

On the wall behind the desk was a rough-grained photograph under glass showing a man standing in the cockpit of a thirty-foot sailing ketch near Cowes on the Isle of Wight during the Admiralty Cup series. The August sun flashing from the Solent had bleached the blondish hair white, but it was Templeman, leaner and more the master of his fate, enjoying one of his blue-water days. Flanking the photographs were his diplomatic commissions from Paris, Trieste, Beirut, and Bern, where he'd been accredited under diplomatic cover. Those were better days too, especially Bern, where he'd run a covert operation into the Zone funded at a little less than three hundred thousand dollars a year. Not as sexy as the operations at Bad Wiessee and Kaufbeuren which carried into the Soviet Union itself, but you had better control, the perks were superior—far from the muck-and-mud of the displaced-persons camps where the Bad Wiessee cadres were recruited—and the results weren't as tragic. In Bern he'd had his own organization, an office paneled in larch with a stone fireplace, and a private villa in the suburbs. The ski slopes were empty those years, the dollar was as sovereign as Caesar's gold from the Urals to the Cornwall coast, and on cold afternoons you could have a whiskey at your desk before locking up. The Agency was smaller, informality encouraged, and bureaucratic rule hadn't yet replaced the privileges of private initiative.

But not these days. Templeman picked up the telephone and spoke to his secretary in the outer office. He told her that he'd sent out a

Cromwell Thatcher, hunched over a bowl of borscht, a wad of rye bread in his fingers as he listened to his table partner who sat opposite, long legs folded, his vegetable plate pushed aside, puffing intermittently on a crusted pipe. He must be English, Templeman thought—the sky-blue socks and the down-at-the-heel librarian's shoes. A dirty plaid scarf was knotted around his neck. Shingles of crinkly hair sprang up from his head like broken lyre strings. His long, translucent fingers plied the air, as white as communion candles, embellishing a point of doctrine. Marxist theologians, both of them, bending over their vegetarians' plates and trading textual lint, erasure rubbings, parchment paint, a spot of medieval gold here and there, together with a few nosehairs in the bargain, like a pair of weak-eyed Talmudists. Thatcher was one of Dahlem's resident Soviet experts, prodigious in memory, awesome in his conceptual powers, but hopelessly inept in the things mothers taught—finding a wife, changing his ties or his wash-and-wear suits with the season, mixing a decent drink.

Thatcher might know something about British International Lubricants and its operation in East Berlin, Templeman reminded himself. Or about KGB operations in Rostock. He was halfway through his chop when Harry Dunstan dropped into the chair opposite. His young companion had disappeared into the ladies room. His face was damp, his chestnut hair curled over his collar. He was five years older than Templeman, which made him fifty-three or fifty-four. Yet he still played squash three times a week.

"Alone today?" Dunstan queried, breathing heavily, as if he'd just come from the squash court. "Bad for the digestion, Temp. Can't have that, now, can we?" Most of Dunstan's questions were rhetorical. Templeman thought they came from his reluctance to share his private life with others. His brown eyes roamed the room restlessly.

"What's happening? Anything new?" Templeman asked.

"Not a bloody thing. Strange feeling in the air, though. Don't know what it is. Something's up, I'd say. Two meetings scrubbed this week. Everyone's lying low. Don't know why. They say London's the same way. We've a group here, you know. They came in from London two days ago. Say they can't get a wing in the air. No lift—no lift at all."

"It's not about the Bryce disappearance, is it?"

"Bryce?" Dunstan laughed softly. "A mongrel if you ask me. No, not that. Everyone's waiting. Don't know what the deuce they're waiting for. Scuppered us—scuppered us all, I'd say. Like swimming in treacle. I wish Khruschev would get on with it, whatever the bloody hell he's up to. I suppose it's the Party Congress. Has everyone guessing. Don't know whether we'll get a peace treaty or a bomb down our stockings, down the stack. On a bad patch—"

Templeman said, "What about this Bryce business?"

Dunstan's eyes wandered the darkened room. "The press is a bloody liar," he said softly. "He wasn't a cipher clerk at all. Head over heels in debt, they say. Probably left some bit of crumpet in the Zone, poor bastard. He was here last year, by the way. Worked in the pouch room, stuffing bags. Repaired my wireless once. Did a bloody good job. I gave him a bottle of rum."

"Bryce was here?"

Dunstan didn't turn. "Eleven months," he said. "Moscow before that. He'd been a Marconi man in the RAF. Cyprus, I think. I offered him two bob and all he wanted was a bottle of rum. Poor bugger."

"I didn't realize he had been here," Templeman said.

"You wouldn't," Dunstan said. He looked towards the entrance to the lady's lounge. "What can you buy for a bottle of rum these days?" he asked. "What's Khruschev up to?" he continued. "You chaps must have a feel for it."

"Maybe a peace treaty," Templeman suggested, pushing his plate aside. "I don't understand about Bryce."

Dunstan didn't seem to hear. "Small beer," he muttered finally. "Isn't that your man over there?"

Templeman followed his gaze across the room. "Thatcher, you mean? Who's he talking to?"

"One of our Soviet gurus," Dunstan said. "Came in last month. What are they talking about, the Party Congress?"

"Probably."

"Sod them," Dunstan said. He sat aggressively forward, elbow on one knee, his astrakhan hat in his hand. "I rang you up yesterday. You remember the chap at the checkpoint the other night? Plummer?" He sat back and looked at his watch. "I talked to one of our lads in the commercial section. He told me about British International Lubricants. They're doing business in East Berlin, supplying custom lubricants to the East Germans. The East German fishing fleet, a few light industries. They opened an office here two months ago. This chap Plummer is their man. It's a small firm. The name stuck in my mind. Have you talked to him?"

"Not yet."

"You might want to talk to our commercial section," Dunstan suggested, getting to his feet. Across the room Dunstan's pink-cheeked secretary had returned to the table and was picking up her coat. "Don't forget the bash tonight," he said. "Eight o'clock. Cheerio."

Templeman finished his bottle of wine alone. Cromwell Thatcher's luncheon companion had also departed and Thatcher was sitting alone, reading a magazine, when Templeman leaned over his table on the way out.

"Not the agenda for the Party Congress you've got there, is it?" Templeman inquired. "I've been looking for a copy."

Thatcher stared up at him silently, his eyes a precocious schoolboy's blue behind the tortoise-shell glasses. Templeman screwed his head about and read the title on the cover. It was a Royal Astronomical Society catalogue, a listing of ninety-megacycle emissions from Alpha Centauri. Good God, Templeman thought. Radioastronomy too? Thatcher, his expression unchanged, turned the cover in his hand, trying to identify the reason for Templeman's stupefaction. Templeman tapped him on the shoulder and fled, his headache roaring back.

Darkness had fallen beyond the draped windows when Templeman finally met with the station chief in the latter's office. The room smelled of cigar smoke. Dinner music was playing on the small radio on the bookshelf behind the desk. The station chief turned in his swivel chair, looking again at the penciled draft on the yellow legal pad in front of him. He fingered it reflectively, still turning a few phrases over in his mind. He finally put it aside and lifted his eyes. "So you're worried about your tracer?" He was a quiet man, tall and gray haired, with gentle manners and civilized tastes.

"Not worried. Just curious," Templeman said. He sank down in the green leather chair next to the desk. The room was in darkness except for the desk lamp. Most of the staff had gone home. "They didn't tell me we'd had a response." It was chilly in the room, a coldness Templeman couldn't identify. He didn't know the station chief. He'd been in Berlin for two months; Templeman didn't know the man at all.

"That was my fault. I should have told you. I apologize," the station chief said quietly. "We're to leave him alone," he resumed in the same gracious tone. "No contact. No contact at all."

Templeman sat forward. "Plummer? You mean this guy David Plummer?"

"Is that his name? I didn't know." The music lifted into the room again. His eyes didn't leave Templeman's face.

"Who's he working for?"

The station chief didn't answer.

"Was it Washington or London?" Templeman asked.

The station chief took off his glasses and rubbed his eyes. When he put the glasses on again, his eyes were suddenly colorless, neutral, like the ice of a winter pond. "I think we'd better leave it at that."

"Don't they want to know anything more from our end?"

"No."

"And that's all!"

"That's all."

"Just how sensitive is this, anyway?" Templeman said hotly. "How do they expect—"

"I didn't say it was sensitive. I simply don't want to hear his name again . . . in this room, in your own office, or in this building. Not from you, not from anyone else. I think that's clear, isn't it?"

By nine o'clock Harry Dunstan's house in Wilmersdorf was as crowded as an airdrome pub on weathered-in night: socked-in diplomats, rum-soaked attachés and intelligence officers from the British services, visiting English border resident officers from the hinterlands, a few guests from London, from the Foreign Office, or MI6, some business-men, a few journalists, a handful of German liaison types, and a few Americans, like Templeman. It was cold outside. The temperature had dropped ten degrees since three o'clock. Eager hands had overbuilt the fire in the huge stone fireplace. The orange flames sent torrid breaths out across the low-ceilinged room beyond, warming the bibblers in the doorway to the dining room, sun porch, and study as well, where someone was hammering on an old upright piano and a group of ex-soldiers turned diplomat had joined the military men in singing a few raucous choruses from the screw-them-all World War II songfests from Plymouth, Southampton, or Piccadilly on embarkation eve:

Shag them all,
Shag them all—
Springtime, summer and fall:
Turnip-shaped maidens
      who give themselves airs;
Dewey-eyed virgins
      in silk underwear.
Stroke them up!
Stroke them down!
Every young trollop in town—

A few British NCO's from the stadium were handling the drinks—light German lagers, Dutch beer, Double Diamond pints, gin, whiskey, vodka, and rum at the bars; no bourbon, sorry, but brandy if you like, sherry too. On the freezing patio outside the French doors to the dining room, two British NCO's in North Sea weather gear were roasting skewers of lamb, beef, and kidney. Baskets of chips were frying in the kitchen, where meat pies had been cooking since noon; and Dunstan's Bavarian cook was mixing vats of onion-and-bean salad. The entire melee was being supervised by Dunstan's young calf-eyed secretary. She was in and out of the kitchen, drink in one hand, cigarette in the other; she was one of the reasons Catherine Dunstan had taken the children and fled to London a month earlier, semihysterical, ready for analysis, therapy, or a divorce. It was bedlam.

In a cushioned, dimly lit corner of the living room far from the fire, a few British diplomats were listening in annoyance to a slightly drunk British-naturalized journalist berate HMG for its present paralysis. Radio GDR from East Berlin had carried a report that a British businessman had been arrested in Rostock that morning and charged with spying. It was a lie, of course. How could the East Germans believe such swill? Who in East Berlin or Moscow who knew anything about HMG or the British services could attribute to them the courage or the will to send a spy into Rostock? The moral bankruptcy in London was complete. Who had permitted the East Germans to build the Wall, if not the British and the Americans? Yet the East German state radio could still talk as though London was still part of the Cold War. Nonsense!

"What awful rubbish," Compton-Bofers complained. Then, in a louder voice: "What the hell do you mean by that?" He was standing near Templeman, addressing the Polish-born journalist. Compton-Bofers was tall and raw boned, with a squire's feudal haircut—no sideburns, just a dark thatch of coarse brown hair beginning to gray. He'd just left the group of vocalists at the piano and his face was still flushed.

The journalist didn't hear.

"Give them a bloody good bollocking, that's what he's saying," Dunstan muttered. Hugh de la Beresford Perse was there too, thin and still blond-haired, despite his forty-two years. His eyes were ice-blue. Both Compton-Bofers and Beresford Perse had sailed with Peter Templeman at Cowes years earlier and they all shared a tailor on London's Old Burlington Street. They were both in their forties, but looked younger, like Dunstan. They were public-school lads who'd never aged—mischievous, murderous, and secure, with some unrequited cunning still left in their hearts after their youthful service during the war.

"He's saying that there's no one in Rostock," de la Beresford Perse summarized. "That this poor chap's just a ghost."

"Who's a ghost?" Templeman asked, having joined the conversation late.

"We all are," Dunstan replied. "Even you, Temp. Temp's a ghost too."

"But it's not the Americans he's talking about," Compton-Bofers said, still indignant.

"Who?" a British diplomat asked. The circle had broken up now and was fracturing off in a dozen directions.

"That chap there, the short one," Dunstan said, nodding towards the journalist, who was following someone towards the bar.

"What was he saying?"

"That we've wasted our youth," Dunstan replied.

"I daresay we should do something," Beresford Perse said sleepily.

"You've gone gray and threadbare," Compton-Bofers said, looking at Dunstan. "That's what he was saying. Old men dreaming over port and walnuts, propped up amongst the horsehair cushions." He was still angry.

"I shouldn't wonder, poor sod," Dunstan said. "He buried his family in Poland as I recall. Jewish, isn't he, Temp?"

"I don't know him," Templeman said. "But I imagine so."

"I suppose he's bought property here," Beresford Perse said. "Worried sick he'll lose it."

"A race of screaming bores," Compton-Bofers said. "The bloody cheek!"

"Maybe we ought to bring this chap out, whoever he is," Perse suggested.

"What chap?" Dunstan asked.

"The one in Rostock."

"Have you lads been up to something in the Baltic?" asked a middle-aged British diplomat.

"The point was that the report had no substance at all," the other diplomat interposed. "That it had no substance—and yet the GDR believed it. Wasn't that the point?"

"But if they believe it, then there's an obligation on our part to bring him out," Beresford Perse said. "You see, don't you. It's really quite simple."

"But it's a tissue of lies."

"But what isn't, these days?" Perse continued with an innocent smile. "What isn't? When something is believed, then it doesn't matter awfully whether it's true or not, does it? I think perhaps we should do something. Where are the gels, Dunny? I haven't seen much, Dunny. Is this the best you have to offer?"

Dunstan said, "I think maybe the Admiralty would be good for a Q-boat. Fetch him off the beach. What do you think?" He looked at Compton-Bofers. "I think we could manage that, don't you?"

"We'd have to bring the Admiralty and Sir Percy around. I daresay Compton could manage that quite well," Perse said.

"Sorry," Compton-Bofers said, turning. "Manage what?"

"A Q-boat to pick up this chap the East Germans arrested," Beresford Perse said.

"One of ours, is he? Don't know him, do I?"

"I'm not sure, as a matter of fact," Beresford Perse said. "No one seems to know him. Do you have his name by any chance, Dunny?"

"Whose name?"

"The chap at Rostock, the one the East German services picked up. Look here, we'll really have to be of a single mind on this if we're to do anything at all."

"What happened to your atlas?" Compton-Bofers asked Dunstan. "The Baltic coast? Rostock? Didn't we put a few chaps on he beach at Rugen some years back—over the dunes one night?"

"I think we did, as a matter of fact," Dunstan said, smiling with the recollection.

"Dunny burned his atlases the day they suspended the Baltic operation," Perse remembered. "Then we went to Whites to sober up."

"Probably a Danish herring fisherman," Templeman speculated aloud.

"Who?" Compton-Bofers asked.

"This man the East Germans arrested."

"One of yours then, eh?" Beresford Perse turned with a smile. "Do you much go in for that sort of things these days?"

The two British diplomats looked on in growing bewilderment.

"Look here, Temp," Compton-Bofers said. "You chaps haven't put someone ashore at Rostock or Rugen, have you? You're on our turf, old man."

"But if he's a herring fisherman, so much the better," de la Beresford Perse said. "That would be splendid, wouldn't it?"

Templeman had turned to watch a honey-haired blonde leave the crowd at the bar and drift along the bookcases, pretending to study Dunstan's library. She was alone.

"Are you serious?" one of the British diplomats cried finally. "Are you actually serious? A Q-boat! The Admiralty! In this atmosphere! You've taken leave of your senses, all of you! It was a lie—a tissue of lies!"

"I imagine that we'd be infinitely more serious if we had an atlas at hand," Compton-Bofers muttered, eying the blonde himself.

"Did you say 'tissue of lies'?" Bereford Perse asked solicitously, turning to the diplomat. "That's a bit emphatic, isn't it, old boy?"

"Temp, you old soak!" Compton-Bofers called as Templeman tried to sidle away on the sly. "Leave off. Leave off this instant! We haven't pronounced yet."

"If it was on the wireless, then it's bound to be believed," Dunstan explained. "Once the blood is up, there's no escaping it. Anything that's believed has some truth to it. Isn't that the pronouncement?" He looked at Compton-Bofers. "That's completely logical, so it's not a lie at all."

"Quite," Beresford Perse said, still following the blonde.

"So we're all dead keen to help that chap, whoever he is," Dunstan continued. "That's really the sense of it."

"But you haven't the *faintest* idea who this chap is," the diplomat cried in exasperation. "You don't have the slightest shred of evidence that one of your people was even involved."

Compton-Bofers, de la Beresford Perse, and Dunstan stood looking at him reprovingly, their faces mirroring a single disappointment.

"Are you serious?" Compton-Bofers asked.

"Well, if you feel that way about it," Dunstan said calmly, "then what's the use. What's the use at all."

The three turned away.

"What's the name of that blond gel, Dunny?" Beresford Perse asked. "The one near the bookcase."

Templeman had known Dunstan, Compton-Bofers, and de la Beresford Perse in London during the late forties and early fifties. He had had a speaking acquaintanceship with Dunstan in Cairo during the war, when Dunstan was with MO4. Compton-Bofers and de la Beresford Perse were with Special Operations in the Balkans and Middle East, in and out of Cairo on leave, for training, debriefings, or on special assignment. Templeman had known neither of them during

34

his six months in Egypt in 1943, but he had heard stories about them. Everyone had.

Compton-Bofers and de la Beresford Perse had led separate commando units in the Balkans—in Greece and Yugoslavia. Later they moved to Libya and Sicily, then Italy and the Low Countries. They commanded assassination teams targeted against German and Italian staff officers—demolition units, well-poisoners in the African desert, typhus or diphtheria vectors at German and Italian encampments, garroters and knife-men along the defensive perimeters of the German and Italian reserve units dug in along the collapsing Axis front in the Middle East. They killed Germans, Italians, Greeks, Albanians, and Yugoslavs as efficiently as the snipe, blackgame, and golden plover Templeman had hunted with them in Northumberland during his London years.

On Crete, Compton-Bofers had machine-gunned a German panzer general and two of his corps commanders at a seaside villa during a predawn strategy session over brandy and cigars, then escaped out the bedroom window over the cliffs on a scaling ladder to the rubber boat below while the general's staff aides and bodyguard were running in confusion through the terraced gardens, away from the sea, firing indiscriminately through the darkness. In Yugoslavia, de la Beresford Perse had led a team of Serbian guerrillas for almost eighteen months— blowing bridges, tunnels, and ammunition depots when they weren't pursuing de la Beresford Perse's own preference: ambushing German staff cars on the narrow mountain roads. One snowy evening on a pine-covered mountainside in Slovenia they surprised three companies of German paratroopers that had been dropped in to search them out, cutting them down in their tracks with automatic weapons fire. The handful that escaped they tracked until dawn. They bayoneted them in their sleeping bags, still silvered with the fall of fresh snow. The German paratroopers slept in two-men sleeping bags. Three of the sleeping Germans they left untouched during the massacre. When they awakened in the cold dawn light, the bodies of their comrades stiff at their sides, the three were lost and alone. They huddled around a fresh fire, searching their maps. The partisans watched them through the falling snow. When the three Germans, still undecided as to which direction to set out, showed no signs of leaving, de la Beresford Perse's men grew restless and uneasy. They shot them where they squatted, under the pine boughs.

Following the war Compton-Bofers joined British intelligence and was assigned to Ostend, Belgium, where he searched for German prisoners-of-war who'd served on the Russian front and might be recruited for operations in the Baltic: dropped along the coast in Estonia and Latvia with the help of Q-boats from the Admiralty. Dunstan and de la Beresford had followed in time. The three were in London during Templeman's posting to the UK as a CIA liaison officer with British intelligence. They kept uncommon hours, disappeared for weeks or months at a time, lived riotously on their return, and nearly wrecked Templeman's liver, bank account, and marriage. Compton-Bofers, Dunstan, and de la Beresford Perse had all come from the same background—the same schools, the same clubs, the same country houses. They had all done the same things during the war, a war without moral limit, which had claimed their consciences, their promise, and their youth; and which had abandoned them afterwards in a postwar society where decency mattered again. In disappearing one by one back into the world of British intelligence, they had rediscovered themselves in a war in which moral absolutes had vanished once again. It was the only world they knew.

One winter in London Templeman had helped Compton-Bofers celebrate the anniversary of the capture of an Italian general in Sicily ten years earlier. The old general was dead by then but Beresford Perse had managed to track down one of his nephews who was working in the locomotive yards at Turin. He brought him to London for the anniversary dinner. The young man spoke no English but remembered the liberation of his mountain village by British troops. Invitations of a rather vague description were printed. The dinner was held at de la Beresford Perse's club. Compton-Bofers knew nothing about the celebration until he walked into the private dining room. Drinks were being served. The dead general's sword, tunic, and pistol case were displayed on a table inside the door, together with a photograph from the Admiralty archives showing the fishing vessel on which Compton-Bofers had spirited the general away from Sicily to the DE waiting off the coast. Compton-Bofers had misgivings about the accuracy of the photograph. He thought the fishing vessel a trifle small; but Dunstan had done the ferret work in the dusty Admiralty basement and insisted that it was the same vessel. A few olive faces were hiding among the stinking fishing nets, among them, Dunstan claimed, that of the kidnapped general. Compton-Bofers noted a sinister face hiding in the darkest recesses of the hold and admitted that it might have been the face of the old general, a man known not for his ferocity but for his cowardice. It didn't matter.

When the dinner commenced, the introductory remarks were in Arabic, provided by an Arabist who'd served on the staff at SOE headquarters in Cairo. Both Compton-Bofers and de la Beresford Perse had a passing familiarity with the language, but the introductions were intended to recapture the mood of the times. It was Cairo in 1940. Included among the guests were old colleagues, commandos, pilots from the RAF, Admiralty officers, and intelligence officers. Some had been persuaded to wear their suntans, an embellishment which delayed the start of the dinner by ten minutes or so when the club doorman refused to admit a dark-skinned guest in more bizarre attire. He was an old Sudanese waiter from the Semiramis hotel in Cairo whom Dunstan had found in London, living on a pension. He wore a tarboosh and a pair of Sudanese slippers. The Italian embassy in London was represented by an aging counselor of embassy who'd arrived out of curiosity from a diplomatic reception in May-fair. He'd been unable to ascertain the purpose of the celebration, even after his seating, and there were few in his vicinity who could clarify it for him. In the middle of the presentation speech, as all of the dead general's possessions were being heaped in front of the speechless nephew at the head table—sword, pistol case, medals, brandy flask, a pair of red-and-white pajamas, a tasseled nightcap—the Italian counselor suddenly divined the purpose of the celebration. "*Scusi,*" he muttered, and walked out.

The nephew was drunk when he was lifted to his feet to deliver his response. The tasseled nightcap was on his head, fixed there by the boisterous revelers nearby; the sword dangled from one shoulder, the gilt tunic from another (Beresford Perse had found them in an East London theatrical-supply house). His speech was in Italian. No one knew what he was saying. Toasts were exchanged. More brandy followed. By the time the hired car had returned him to the Dorchester, he was in a stupor. At three o'clock that morning as Dunstan and de la Beresford Perse were celebrating their *coup de théâtre* in the study of Compton-Bofers's house in Kensington with a few of their colleagues, Compton-Bofers wondered aloud if the nephew had truly appreciated the magnitude of their problems in kidnapping the Italian general in Sicily so many years ago, or the old man's humiliation in surrendering in his pajamas to a group of black-faced English commandos. Dunstan suggested that the nephew hadn't the foggiest idea of what had gone on that night. Someone proposed that they teach him and reenact the whole episode the same night in London.

"Take him from his hotel!" Compton-Bofers bellowed. "By God, you're right! Are we game?"

"Fetch the burnt cork, Dunny!" Beresford Perse agreed, pulling off his tie.

Templeman's Jaguar sedan was parked at the curb. It was the vehicle they were bound to commandeer. He slipped from the house as inconspicuously as possible and drove off at high speed towards the safety of his own detached house on the other side of Kensington, leaving his overcoat behind. When he recovered it the following day, Mary Compton-Bofers told him that the whole drunken affair had ended quietly in the nearby streets when Dunstan had driven his dangerously overloaded MG over a curb and blown out a tire.

There were other incidents. Templeman remembered Compton-Bofers tottering drunkenly through the Strand, Perse and himself in tow, searching for some obscure address where an equally obscure acquaintance once lived—an Oxford classics tutor turned vagabond, Templeman guessed. Compton-Bofers was paraphrasing Suetonius and mumbling to himself about spare flagons of port and brandy, a coal fire going somewhere, recitations of Ovid or Petronius filling the air: "And all on six hundred pounds a year!" he hectored them drunkenly as they failed to keep pace. "Six hundred pounds! Six hundred! Can you fathom that? Oh, the shame of it! The shame!"

Or de la Beresford Perse at a reception for a visiting French diplomatic delegation, quietly drunk, identifying himself to an inquisitive

French vice-minister as Sir Thomas Urquehart, the translator of Rabelais into fustian and author of*Bottom Views of English Gentry.*

"He poisoned the wells at Tobruk," the French military attaché muttered to a guest as Beresford Perse moved away, leaving Templeman speechless on the spot. "The same chap," Templeman heard him say.

Or Dunstan leaving Chelsea with two tarts in tow, discovered two hours later by Templeman in his own house, a tart in each bedroom and both wearing Edna Templeman's nightgowns—she, thank God, in Paris—while Dunstan sat drunkenly at the kitchen table with one of Edna's canasta decks, trying to decide his next move. "Look here, Temp old man. I mean it's decent of you to come. Splendid. That's the answer, isn't it? Of course it is. I mean what do you fancy tonight? Do you want looks, personality, or a rousing good romp? Which one would you fancy?"

"This isn't quite what I had in mind," Elizabeth Davidson said to Plummer as they moved through the small entry hall inside the front door. A quartet of drinkers sat on the lower steps of the front staircase. Others gathered in the doorway to the living room. "Rather difficult putting quarts in pint pots, isn't it?" she added as they squeezed past. A fire was roaring in the fireplace. Someone was playing the piano in a nearby room. "How romantic," she said, looking up at him.

"It was your idea," said Plummer.

"Don't remind me. It was a horrid one. We'll only stay a minute. But I promised."

They pushed towards the front where a few British mess-men were serving drinks across the walnut bar. The bar was wet and filled with empty glasses. "A double vermouth," she said. "With gin, please."

Plummer said, "That makes it a double martini. Forget the gin." The barman looked at Plummer and back at Elizabeth.

"Ignore him," she told him. "You're not to be intimidated."

"Not bloody likely," the barman said. "Vermouth it is."

"Rostock! Are you chaps still talking about Rostock? You're mad—all of you!" The voice came from behind Plummer. Elizabeth looked past him, lifted herself on her toes, and peered over his shoulder.

"Rostock," she repeated in reflex as she looked past him, her slim face as open as a girl's, innocent of everything except her curiosity. "They're not talking about you, are they?"

"They're your mob, not mine," Plummer said, watching her face. Someone moved past him and he saw her expression change.

"So we did come," she said with a smile.

"Splendid," the man replied, "really splendid. I was dead sure you wouldn't—not after all this time. Bloody madhouse, isn't it?" He looked up at Plummer.

"This is David Plummer," Elizabeth said.

"Hullo," Dunstan said. Plummer recognized the Englishman he had seen at the checkpoint with Templeman. But he saw nothing in Dunstan's eyes. The Englishman was more interested in Elizabeth Davidson. He turned back to her almost immediately.

"I am sorry we're late," she said.

"But you're not late at all," Dunstan said. "Not at all. Have drinks, do you? Good. You don't enjoy parties, they say. Not true, is it?" Dunstan laughed suddenly, seeing Elizabeth's expression. His eyes hadn't left her face. "Gave yourself away, did you?" He laughed again and glanced at Plummer.

"I'm sure I didn't," Elizabeth said. "I can't think you mean to be rude." She was smiling again, looking at Plummer. "Perhaps I was severely taught." Plummer caught the mischief in her eyes. Dunstan didn't know what to think.

"Sorry about the noise," he said.

"I think someone's trying to get your attention," she said to Dunstan, looking beyond his shoulder at the blonde calling to him from the doorway.

"Sorry." He put his drink down. "Another crisis, I suppose. Excuse me."

"We'll manage," Elizabeth said as he turned away. He hadn't heard. "Strange man," she said when he'd gone. "He's mad about parties. Do you think I offended him?"

"No."

"Good. Shall we find someplace quiet? It's terribly noisy here."

He followed her through the crowd.

"What's the alternative these days?" someone was asking. "I'm afraid I haven't a clue."

"The *Pax Americana,* quite obviously," a second voice responded. "Watch my drink, old boy," he added as Plummer joggled his arm in passing.

"What awful rubbish," Compton-Bofers complained. "You're talking cock, Perse."

"Is he serious?" asked a woman's voice.

"He's being deliberately offensive," an Englishman suggested.

Beresford Perse said, "I'm not being deliberately offensive at all. I merely said that Americans prefer fascism to anything else. Ask Temp. It's ridiculously simple. Why should that be offensive? Fascism has a much greater tolerance for vulgarity, is infinitely more efficient, and shows a far greater respect for money."

"Is he serious?" the woman asked.

Plummer followed Elizabeth through the crowd. She stopped a few steps beyond, her passage blocked. "It's ghastly," she said. "I can't seem to move." Plummer slipped past her, took her arm, and drew her after him. He found his way to the darkened sunporch. The piano player and the chorus had retired. The phonograph was playing quietly and a few younger couples were dancing in the shadows. The wind blew against the dark windows. Elizabeth found a quiet corner near the windows and stood with her back to the casement, pushing away the light strands of hair from her cheeks and forehead as she gazed out through the twilight towards the crowded, smcky room beyond. "This is much better," she sighed. "I rather like quiet corners."

Plummer said, "Is that what you came for?"

"Do you mind it so awfully?" She searched his face. "We needn't stay very long. It's simply that Dunstan has asked me to drop by so many times. I couldn't refuse again and still be civil to him."

"It's all right."

"He's a friend of the Gwenhoggs. Quite a different type from Peter but they're friends." She looked out through the doorway. "They're all absolutely different, aren't they? What do you suppose they do?"

"I don't know."

"I'm sure I don't either. We can stay and be unnoticed, can't we?" She smiled for a moment, pushing her hair back further from her face. Her face and neck seemed even slimmer. "It's not quite our world, is it?"

"Not quite."

"I've never liked crowds. Do you remember?"

"I remember." For a woman as lovely as she, there was an unusual vein of modesty, a lack of confidence or a vulnerability which he'd never been able to account for. He remembered it again, looking at her face.

"How about dancing?" he said.

"I'm very rusty."

"So am I."

"The music is nice, isn't it?" She looked towards the two couples, smiling for a minute as she watched them. She turned and put her drink on the windowsill behind her. "Why not?" she said. "Would you like to try it? It might be fun."

He put down his glass. They moved out onto the sun-porch floor, but a moment later the music stopped. She held his hand as she waited for one of the couples to change the record. When they did the music was much too fast and a few other couples moved quickly out onto the floor. Elizabeth led Plummer by the hand back to the window. She picked up her drink again.

"Not your speed?" he asked.

"I don't think so," she smiled, looking back at the dancers crowding the small, darkened sunporch floor. "Is it yours?"

"You never know until you try it."

"She's here someplace," a woman's voice erupted from nearby. "I'm sure I saw her. Of course, here she is." Plummer turned and saw Peggy Gwenhogg moving towards them. "There you are, pet," she said to Elizabeth. "We've been searching all over for you. We thought you'd vanished. You remember Alan, I'm sure." Compton-Bofers stood behind Peggy Gwenhogg, looking down at Elizabeth.

"Peggy told me you were here. It's been years," he said.

"Indeed, it has," Elizabeth said.

"You've grown up a bit," Compton-Bofers said. "I remember the pony cart." He looked at Plummer and nodded, still smiling affectionately.

42

"This is Mr. Plummer," Elizabeth said.

"I suppose she was fifteen when I last saw her," Compton-Bofers explained. "Hullo."

"Elizabeth stayed with us in Vienna," Peggy Gwenhogg reminded Plummer, smiling herself. "How good to see you again." She was a thin, nervous woman in her late thirties wearing a plain black dress, and a strand of pearls about her throat. "That was nineteen fifty-seven I believe." She looked at Elizabeth. "Wasn't it fifty-seven?"

"Don't remind me," Elizabeth said.

"You were in Vienna?" Compton-Bofers asked her in surprise.

"Nineteen fifty-six and nineteen fifty-seven," Elizabeth said.

"She was at Pullendorf during the Hungarian business. The refugee camp there. It was dreadful," Peggy added.

"But that's not why you're in Berlin, is it?" Compton-Bofers interrupted.

"What?" Elizabeth asked curiously.

"Refugees," Compton-Bofers replied. Suddenly, it seemed to make sense to him. "My God," he laughed. "You're not in that racket, are you?"

"Racket?" Elizabeth inquired coolly.

"The refugee game. Are you serious? Refugees?" He turned in disbelief towards Peggy and then back to Elizabeth. "Who with— The Friends of the Tate? The Daughters of the Pytchley Hunt?" Compton-Bofers threw his head back and laughed.

"Don't be rude," Peggy Gwenhogg said. "Elizabeth is with the UN. She's been with the UN for years. *Pro bono publico.*" She sipped her drink to hide her small, clever smile.

"But I can't believe it," Compton-Bofers said. "You doing refugee work? With those bags, those sods—"

"I'm afraid it's true," Elizabeth said calmly. "Is that typical of the Foreign Office point of view, by the way?"

"I don't think you'll find Alan typical of anything these days," Peggy said soothingly.

"I don't suppose you're with the UN, too, are you?" Compton-Bofers asked Plummer, who was watching Elizabeth. He'd seen the anger in her eyes.

"Not recently," he said, putting his drink down. "Why don't we dance?" he suggested to Elizabeth.

"That's a perfectly lovely idea," Peggy said.

"Mind you, I've nothing against the UN," Compton-Bofers said. "It manages nicely in its own way."

"But it's never been your way, is that it?" Peggy intruded. Elizabeth was looking off across the crowded dance floor, her mind a thousand miles away.

"What about the dance?" Plummer reminded her.

Her glass was empty. She looked at it thoughtfully, as if unable to break the spell of whatever recollection she found there. Then she lifted her head. "Would you get me a drink?" she asked Plummer.

Peggy Gwenhogg followed Plummer towards the bar. The crowd had begun to thin. A fat Englishman was telling rowdy stories to a group near the bar. "It's rather a coincidence, you meeting Elizabeth again after all these years," Peggy said, struggling to catch up with him. "How long has it been?"

"Five years, I suppose. Five or six."

"Have you just come?"

"A few months ago."

"And you didn't know she was here?"

"Not until a few weeks ago."

"You must have been surprised."

"Pretty surprised."

"I suppose you met again through mutual friends. At the American mission?"

"As a matter of fact, I saw her on the street." They stood at the bar. "What would you like?" he asked.

"Whiskey, please, but very light." She opened her purse and took out a cigarette. She searched unsuccessfully for a match. Plummer lit the cigarette for her. "We thought you'd left Europe permanently," she said as she exhaled, gazing up through the smoke towards Plummer. Her eyes were a clear, brittle blue. "Elizabeth had assumed the same thing, hadn't she?"

"I think so."

"Berlin can be rather sterile without friends, don't you think?" She

44

stood next to him, a bony, unattractive woman—an incorrigible med-
dler in whom vitality had survived a childless, loveless marriage in the
shape of a rapacious curiosity. "I suppose you lead a rather active life
here. Are you in business?"

"Still in business. What else is there?"

"She's engaged now, you know," she said suddenly.

"I know." He handed her the drink. "He's a friend of yours, is he?"

He thought it was the question she had wanted him to ask and
watched her nod in relief. "A very old friend, as a matter of fact. He
entered the diplomatic service with Peter. He's in in Brussels now. Jim
Buxton. Do you know him?" Plummer shook his head. "I suppose that
does make us a bit possessive, doesn't it?" Peggy continued, watching
Plummer's eyes.

But he was looking beyond, towards the darkened sun-porch.

When they returned, Elizabeth was dancing with a middle-aged
Englishman with an erect carriage and silver-gray hair. They were doing a fox trot. The dance floor about them was nearly deserted. A few
younger couples were still dancing and their movements were more in
tempo with the music. They were doing the frug. Peter Gwenhogg had
joined Compton-Bofers and the two men stood talking. "You remember David Plummer, dear," Peggy said.

"Of course," her husband said with a smile. "How are you?"

"Fine, thanks," Plummer said. "How about yourself?" Peter Gwenhogg was short and overweight, with gray hair, a gray moustache, and
wet brown eyes.

"Who's Elizabeth dancing with?" Peggy asked.

"I haven't the foggiest," her husband said.

"Leeby!" Compton-Bofers said suddenly. "That was it, by God! *Leeby!*"

"What on earth are you talking about?" Peggy asked.

"Elizabeth's name. I knew I'd remember. Martin called her that. *Leeby.* She'd be furious."

"Fancy that," Peter Gwenhogg said. "That's quite like Martin."

"Martin was her only brother," Peggy said to Plummer, who nodded. He was fifteen years older than Elizabeth and had been killed on
Crete early in the war.

"She had shockingly bad manners, even then," Compton-Bofers

45

remembered. "She couldn't have been ten years old at the time but I remember she hammered Martin's rook gun to smithereens one weekend after we'd been potting snipe."

"That strikes me as quite civilized," Peggy said.

"She absolutely despised guns. A headstrong little gel as I recall. I'm sure that's what Martin called her—*Leeby*. I shall ask her." Compton-Bofers swallowed his drink.

"I shouldn't if I were you," Peggy said. "She doesn't talk of Martin. I should be careful about mentioning him."

Compton-Bofers turned. "That was over twenty years ago." He was shocked. "Are you sure?"

"Quite sure."

"Compton, you sot!" A voice called from the doorway. "The car is here."

"Damn," Compton-Bofers muttered, putting aside his glass. "There's no time these days, no time at all." He looked at his watch. "We must talk, Peter. I'll ring you up. You, too, Peggy. Where are we off to, I wonder? Good-bye now."

He moved off to join de la Beresford Perse and Templeman, who were waiting beyond the door, their coats on.

"It is late, isn't it?" Peter Gwenhogg said.

"I wonder where they're going?" Peggy said, watching them cross the room. When she turned back again, she noticed Plummer, who was watching the three men as they stood talking to Dunstan. "You're awfully quiet," she said. "You knew Compton before?"

"No," Plummer said, turning.

"He was quite a figure in his time," Peggy said.

"Weren't we all," her husband added. His glass was empty, too. "Shall we have a dance and then nip off? It is late."

"Thanks awfully, but I couldn't, pet. Not in these shoes. The song is nice, though."

Elizabeth joined them, out of breath. The dance floor was deserted. She leaned against Plummer as she bent to adjust her pumps. "Couldn't what?" she asked.

"Peter has just asked me to dance."

"Don't be silly, Peggy. Dance—do. The music is lovely."

"Who were you dancing with?" Peggy asked.

"A perfectly charming colonel who has just come from Cyprus and is quite homesick." A few couples moved out on the floor and Elizabeth turned to watch them.

"Shall we?" Peter Gwenhogg asked his wife.

"It's a splendid idea but I think we'd better go find poor Mr. Dunstan, don't you? I'm not even sure he knows we're here."

Plummer and Elizabeth watched them go. "I'm suddenly very sleepy," she said after a moment. The few couples who had been dancing were moving away through the door. The phonograph was still playing.

"Do you want to go?" he asked her.

"In a minute," she said. "The music is lovely, don't you think?" Her face was very tired. She picked up her drink and held it to her lips as she listened to the music.

"Maybe we can dance now," he said.

"That's sweet of you. Do you really want to?"

"Maybe I'm homesick, too."

"You're teasing me." She turned and put her drink on the windowsill. They moved out onto the floor and she turned towards him, arms raised, her head lifted, her eyes watching his own.

It was the first time he had held her in over five years. She came into his arms easily, her forehead against his cheek, relaxed in his embrace. They moved in time to the music, not speaking, neither able to see the other's eyes. It was easier that way. But after a few minutes he felt her self-consciousness return. Her movements grew more awkward and he stopped and looked down. She stopped too.

"We're all alone," she said. The floor was deserted again.

"Maybe it's time to go."

"Maybe it is."

"I'll get the coats." As he turned and led her across the room, he saw Peggy Gwenhogg and Harry Dunstan standing just beyond the door, watching them.

The rain had stopped and the wind had died down. Clouds drifted across the cold winter moon. A few cars slid by them on the streets.

The heater wasn't working too well but she didn't seem to notice, burrowed deeply in her coat as she was. He thought she was sleeping until he turned and looked at her face in the passing glow of a streetlight and saw the silver crescents of her eyes brooding out through the windshield at the empty street ahead of them. "I thought you were sleeping," he said.

"No."

"Thinking, maybe."

"Not really."

"How old is he?" he asked after a minute.

"Who?" She turned sleepily.

"This guy in Brussels you're engaged to. Paxton."

"Buxton," she corrected. "Was that deliberate?"

"No. Buxton, then. How old is he?"

She stirred as if to sit up, but merely shifted her position. "Forty-five or forty-six, I imagine."

"That's ten years older than you," Plummer said.

"It is, rather. But that's sometimes an advantage." Her voice was far away.

"Like when?" She didn't answer. "Like when he's sixty-five and collecting his pension?"

He saw her smile. "I think we're rather talking at cross-purposes," she said.

After a minute Plummer said: "Is he part of that mob back there?"

"At Dunstan's you mean? He's a diplomat. Very good company. Very understanding."

"Has he been married before?"

"As a matter of fact he has." She sat up for a moment. "It's chilly in here." Plummer turned up the heater. He pulled his raglan from the seat beside him with his right hand and lifted it over her knees. She brought the coat up further, covering her arms and shoulders. They drove in silence. "This is quite comfy," she said. Her eyes were shut.

"Don't go to sleep."

"Why?" She didn't turn.

"You'll be home soon."

"No, I won't," she smiled, her eyes still closed, arms and shoulders huddled under the raglan. "Home is in Kent."

She was sleeping when Plummer drove up the curved driveway in front of the apartment house and parked the car under the overhang. He opened the car door and leaned in, but she didn't stir; her head was fallen to one side, her body curled under the coat. He called her name. She opened her eyes and looked up at him quietly. She didn't move, gazing up at him as if he were a stranger again. Finally she said sleepily:

"You've come back. How long will it be this time? A week? Two weeks?" She closed her eyes and let her head fall to one side. "I thought we were in Austria," she said softly. "I thought we'd driven back to Pullendorf in the Porsche. It was Sunday night. It was snowing. I could hear the snow chains on the tires. I could hear you talking about Virginia and the Rappahannock and it was lovely. But then I remembered that this wasn't Austria at all. It was Berlin and a terrible man was following us. This is Berlin, isn't it?" She sat up and looked out at the old street and the midnight silence gleaming across the cold tile and the sterile glass doors of the apartment-house lobby. The foyer was empty. The doors to the elevator were open. "Yes," she murmured, still half asleep. "I was right." She gave him back his raglan. "Why are we here?" she asked again, standing in the cold driveway and shivering for a minute, still looking into the empty lobby.

"You live here," he said. "You're home."

She turned and looked at him. "You. Why are you here?"

"Business," he told her, taking her arm. "I told you."

She stood gazing at him sleepily. He had told her before. Now she was only half awake. He knew she didn't believe him.

THREE

Darkness was an hour away but already the evening twilight had encroached from the surrounding woods and moved against the tall stone manor house in the clearing. The lamps were lit. Strekov stood at the high window, looking out across the lawn. On the desk behind him were two thick dossiers which had been brought to him by courier from Karlshorst that day. He had spent the afternoon reading them. They described the KGB's first contacts with Bryce in Moscow three years earlier and his recruitment in Berlin nearly two years ago. Kirilen knocked at the door and Strekov turned from the window. Kirilen was a short, moon-faced Russian with tinted spectacles. He wore an ill-fitting gray worsted suit which Strekov supposed had been purchased in East Berlin. Even his shoes were new, their luster almost garish, if not vulgar, their seams unbroken, as if they'd just been taken from a shop-window dummy. The two men scarcely knew each other. Kirilen was nervous in Strekov's presence, even deferential. Strekov suspected that the young man had mishandled the Bryce debriefing but in ways which still weren't clear to him. Berlin was his first posting in Eastern Europe. He had never been out of the Soviet Union before and his success in East Berlin would determine whether he would ever go again.

Kirilen gave Strekov a telegram which he'd just received from the communications clerk in the *referentura* section on the third floor. It was from Moscow. Strekov read it, initialed it, and gave it back to him. "Is there an answer?" Kirilen asked uncertainly. The telegram was captioned *Most Urgent* and bore the indicator *From Orlov for Strekov*.

"Not tonight." When Kirilen looked at the text again dubiously, Strekov said, "Tomorrow is soon enough. Sit down for a minute. I want to go over a few things."

Kirilen sat on the plush sofa near the fireplace. Strekov moved to the desk nearby where the lamp was burning. He stood over the desk, searching among his notes for the questions he had scrawled there that afternoon. Rain dripped from the eaves and smeared the glass windowpanes beyond the desk, darkening the sky over the treetops. In the cold fireplace behind him lay the ashes of a recent woodfire. The smell of the wet ashes had filled the room that long afternoon, reminding Strekov of another winter, more recent than his own exhaustion told him was possible. Then he banished it from his mind.

"That first evening here," he began, sitting down at the desk, "Bryce told you he'd been betrayed. Were those the words he used—'betrayed'?"

Kirilen stared at him silently, trying to guess his meaning. "Yes," he said finally. "Those were his exact words."

"What did it mean to you?"

Again Kirilen waited. His lips seemed to move but he caught himself. His shirt collar was too tight, Strekov noticed. In his impatience to outfit himself for his East Berlin posting he had settled for what was available. Vanity had triumphed over comfort, Strekov thought, watching Kirilen's eyes behind the tinted spectacles. "To me it meant that he'd been discovered."

Strekov had assumed as much. "That's not the same as betrayed, is it?" he asked quietly.

"Isn't it?" Kirilen asked, encouraged by Strekov's tone. "The results would be the same."

"So you understood the distinction," Strekov replied.

But Kirilen was still cautious. "I'm not sure I do. I don't know. What I mean to say was that it seemed he was in danger."

"So you thought merely that he was in danger. What did you tell him?"

"That we would look into it. I told him that if he had been discovered in London, we would know about it in time. I told him that it couldn't be kept from us."

"Betrayal," Strekov reminded him. "He didn't say that he'd been discovered. He said that he'd been betrayed."

"You're correct. Yes. He said betrayed." Beads of perspiration stood out on Kirilen's forehead.

The house was overheated. Strekov had stripped off his jacket and tie and had been working in his shirtsleeves during the long afternoon. He watched Kirilen's face silently. It was an important distinction. He wondered if Kirilen had chosen the word as carelessly as he had chosen the new shirt. "It's important," he said quietly.

"I agree that it is," Kirilen acknowledged.

"But however you interpreted it at the time, it seemed to you that the British had found out about Bryce and were after him."

"Yes. He was terrified. That was my conclusion."

"That he was terrified or that the British were after him?"

Kirilen was confused for a minute. But Strekov smiled and when he did, Kirilen thought that he was merely playing with words. "I didn't make that distinction," he said with a laugh.

"It's an important one to make," Strekov told him, looking at his notes again. He was serious but he knew that Kirilen could not sense it. He was a simple, conscientious young man. What Strekov had learned would never again be taught; what Kirilen knew Strekov could never again learn. They were a generation apart.

"Tell me," Strekov began again. "What did you talk about the night Bryce attempted to escape?"

"I didn't talk to him that night. We talked in the afternoon."

"What did you talk about?"

"I told him that we still hadn't any word about his"—Kirilen hesitated uncomfortably—"about his betrayal. I said that the British seemed as perplexed as anyone else and that our sources seemed to think the British government was completely confused by the whole affair."

Something pulled at Strekov's mind for a moment. He sat forward and wrote down, word for word, what Kirilen had just said. "So you told him that he was wrong, that the British weren't looking for him at all."

Again Kirilen was slow in responding. Again Strekov thought he caught the movement of Kirilen's lips. Then he realized why Kirilen was so slow: he was repeating Strekov's question to himself as he considered his reply.

"Yes. That was what I told him," Kirilen agreed finally.

"Did you talk about anything else?"

"I told him that his handler in London had left quietly and had returned to Moscow. I also told him that we were expecting his report within a few hours."

"His handler's report from Moscow?" Strekov asked.

"Yes. We got it the following morning."

Strekov had read the report in East Berlin the morning before he had left for Rostock. It was the report by Bryce's handler to Orlov that had convinced Moscow to send him to Rostock. Bryce's handler in London had been unable to shed any light on Bryce's disappearance.

"But Bryce tried to escape that night," Strekov said.

"Yes," Kirilen said. "The same night."

Strekov nodded. "How was he when you found him? What was his condition?"

"He was very drunk. But he was terrified. I'm convinced of that. Still terrified."

"Do you think he believed the British might have sent someone after him, that someone had followed him to East Germany?"

Kirilen's eyes widened in surprise. "No, not at all. I'd have said that was impossible."

"Impossible?" Strekov conjectured quietly, turning toward the dark windows. Night had fallen. The mist was in the trees. "Impossible?" he asked again. "If not the British, then someone else."

Kirilen sat silently watching Strekov. "This Bryce isn't a serious man," he said finally. Strekov wasn't surprised. He'd known that was what Kirilen thought from the beginning.

"To someone he is serious." Far away in Moscow, Orlov had understood that. No one else had.

"It would be suicide to pursue him here," Kirilen said. When Strekov didn't answer, he asked: "Is that what you believe?"

"I don't know what I believe. His terror is real. The rest needn't be. But the fear is genuine."

Kirilen left. Strekov sat at the desk, puzzling over the words he had written during their conversation. They meant nothing to him now. He would look at them again in the morning. It was after seven. The room had grown chilly. He pulled on his coat and lit the fire in the grate, then squatted on the stone hearth and watched the flames sweep through the bark and dry tinder in the fireplace, exploding its dry, fragrant heat into the cool mustiness of the room. The old lodge was silent. The sea wind stirred through the tall pine trees at the edge of the woods. The rain had stopped. For a moment he'd forgotten where he was. He was thinking of his own dacha then, of how the the wind blew through the pine trees and how deep the snows had been during his last visit. Something in the room reminded him of the dacha and he stood up slowly, looking around as he tried to remember. But he couldn't find it and so he stood silently in front of the fire, looking down into the flames, resting his arms against the crude mantelpiece whose rough-hewn flanks still held the cuneiform of the adze that had shaped them.

He was still standing there when the orderly knocked at the door and told him that his supper was waiting for him in the small dining room. He picked up the two thick folios which had been brought to him from Karlshorst and took them with him to read over his solitary dinner.

Bryce had first come to their attention a few months after his arrival in Moscow. He was in his middle forties, a peculiar, solitary little man, as errant as a mongrel, idling sideways through Komsomolsky Square on a crowded autumn evening, standing quietly in the Leningrad or Varoslavl terminals as if they were Buckminster Abbey, watching the arrivals from Central Asia, buying flowers along Leningradsky Prospekt or three-kopek raspberry sodas for the children in Gorsky Park, or sitting contentedly on a bench along the Embankment in the fading autumn light. With the arrival of winter he bought a fur hat, a Russian grammar, and a few notebooks. During his spare time, he sat for hours in the reading room of the Lenin Library, copying out Russian phrases. On Sundays he made his rounds of the public parks and museums. The Pushkin was his favorite. His holiday routine varied in other respects, but once a week, as regular as clockwork, he managed to take time out from his duties at the British embassy to visit the Pushkin.

Bryce. They were patient. When Bryce was reassigned to West Berlin, contact was reestablished. In West Berlin the young Soviet intelligence officer who restored contact had at his disposal resources far more lavish than those available in Moscow—women, whiskey, cars, furniture. Within a year Bryce had begun supplying him with information on a regular basis. Then he had been posted to London with the promise of more to come. A few months later he'd fled in terror. Why? No one knew. Once arrived in East Germany, he'd tried to flee again, back to Denmark. Why? No one knew.

The room had grown chilly. Strekov sat at the desk, the lamp still lit, but he had stopped reading. The files were shut on the blotter in front of him. It was close to midnight. He sat for a long time looking at the dossiers, still sprawled in the chair, his long legs stretched out in front of him. The fire had gone out.

Bryce had said he'd been betrayed. Who had betrayed him? There was only one answer to that. His Soviet handler. If he had fled London in fear of arrest, why had he tried to flee from East Germany that night they had found him hiding in the woods?

Strekov sat up and searched among his notes for the few sentences he had scrawled there during his talk with Kirilen. He read them again and for the second time that day the answer that had eluded them all surfaced in his mind again. *I told him that we still hadn't any word about his betrayal,* Kirilen had said. *I said that the British seemed as perplexed as anyone else and that our sources thought the British confused about the whole affair.*

Sources? Strekov asked himself. What sources? And how had Bryce reacted to that? He sat for a moment, looking at the dark window at his side. Bryce had tried to escape the same night.

Kirilen was asleep in his small bedroom on the second floor. Strekov waited a few minutes and went down the hall and climbed the stairs to the *referentura* section on the top floor. The *referentura* section was brightly lit, brighter by several intensities than the floors below. The code clerk bolted the steel door behind Strekov, took back the two dossiers, and said he had a few telegrams. Strekov waited in the larger room as the code clerk disappeared into the radio room. At a table in the corner a small, powerfully built man sat reading a newspaper and drinking a glass of hot tea. He had thick shoulders and pale eyes, almost yellow in the intense light. The lump of nose in his square face was only a stump of flesh nipped out of the cold dough of his face; a prognathic bulge of bone and lip lay beneath it; and his skull was covered with a plush of dirty yellow hair. He had arrived with Strekov from Karlshorst to investigate the Bryce defection and would escort Bryce to Moscow if the KGB Center or Strekov so ordered him. Now he was awaiting instructions. He lifted his head towards Strekov, who shook his head in turn. "No," he said, "nothing new," and the Uzbek sat looking at Strekov silently and after a few seconds went back to his newspaper. It was a German paper from Frankfurt and the Uzbek was looking at the pictures.

The telegrams the code clerk brought for Strekov were from Karlshorst. They were routine. One reported the departure of a group of British intelligence officers from West Berlin, where they had been visiting for over a week. They had returned to London. Another described the arrangements underway for the Kaliningrad fleet visit to Rostock only a few days away. The final telegram aroused Strekov's interest. It was a routine report, obtained from the East German security services, listing the names and schedules of visiting foreign diplomats, officials, and businessmen for the coming week. Some would be conducting business in East Berlin; others would be touring in East Germany. Department IV of the*Hauptabteilungen* had alerted its detachments in the field to their presence. A few of the foreigners were under close surveillance controlled from East German headquarters. A few would be the responsibility of the local SSD detachment.

One of the names on the telegram caught Strekov's eye. It was a name Strekov knew. Was it a coincidence? There was nothing in the East German report or the KGB comment that suggested the East German intelligence service or the KGB knew him as well.

"What is it?" the Russian code clerk asked. The Uzbek lifted his head from the table nearby and looked towards Strekov, who sat silently studying the telegram. His first impulse was to send a telegram to Karlshorst and to Moscow, calling attention to the American's name and recounting what he knew of him. But he hesitated, without knowing why, and handed the telegrams back to the code clerk.

"Nothing," he said, getting to his feet.

On his way back down the narrow stairs to his room the moment of indecision annoyed him. Ten years ago he would have reacted differently. Probably it's not the same man, he thought. He tried to put it out of his mind. He had come to Rostock at Orlov's instructions to talk to Bryce. Neither Orlov nor Karlshorst would understand his recollection of operational matters unless it somehow related to the Bryce affair.

Were the two related? Was this the same man he remembered from Prague so many years ago? Neither explained his hesitation or his lack of resolve in the *referentura* section when he had seen the name in the telegram. He went to bed, depressed and uneasy.

Strekov had a late lunch alone in the dimly lit dining room, his folder of notes spread out on the table in front of him. He sat under a pair of polished staghorns and a brace of eighteenth-century hunting rifles with flared silver barrels as large as gramophone horns. He was served by a sleepy young military orderly wearing a bloused white shirt with full sleeves and soft leather boots. Strekov had almost finished his meal when three Russian military officers entered the dining room from the military annex. They wore army trousers and boots but had taken off their woolen blouses and replaced them with loose-fitting cotton shirts. One was carrying a bottle of Polish vodka. Before they took their places at the table that had been set for them, they circled the room, carrying their glasses and looking at the hunting trophies that hung on the darkly paneled walls. There were two stag heads, the head of a boar, and, atop the cabinet, a stuffed fox. The stuffed fox was as old as the manor house. Wads of old sawdust leaked from his chest cavity; one glass eye hung from its socket by a rusty wire. Strekov lifted his head and watched the three Russian officers standing in front of the cabinet. Around the hips of the Russian colonel hung an empty bandolier, its pockets designed to hold shotgun shells. The three men had come to hunt the old reserve around the manor house.

It was late in the afternoon when Strekov pulled his coat on and left. The wind had come up and blew through the tops of the trees, tapping a loose shutter near the corner of the house. The wind tasted of snow. He went down the path through the pine trees to the low-roofed stone building that lay in the woods at the foot of the hill. Iron bars covered the small windows. On a patch of bare earth near the door to the old stable two Russian youths crouched over the remains of a wood fire, blowing into the mound of ashes. A tin plate of uncooked potatoes, lean meat, and quarters of cabbage lay in the dirt beside them near a smoke-blackened enamel pot. The seams of their leather boots were ripped, the soles warped with age, the heels missing. Their filthy seamen's jackets hung over a wooden sawhorse nearby. Despite the cold both of the youths were dressed in thin cotton undershirts. Their heads had recently been shaved and their skins had the cold bluish glare of congealed lard. Strekov spoke to the two Letts. They lifted their chapped faces from the bed of ashes and stared at him. With their shaved heads, their dirty rags with the smell of the kennel, and their pale eyes as blue as snowflakes, they looked like a pair of mute, hairless dogs from whose line intelligence had long ago been bred out in search of some other attribute. They were illiterate Russian seamen who had murdered a German grocer after raping his wife. Sentenced to twenty years hard labor by a military court, they were awaiting transfer to the Soviet Union to serve out their sentences. The Russian guard sat inside, a rifle across his knee, watching them through the open door. At the table nearby a Russian corporal was filling the kerosene lanterns from a metal pail.

Bryce was sitting alone in his stone cell, looking towards the small barred window. He turned when Strekov entered but the nod of recognition was as dim as the October light which already was beginning to fade and would leave the room in full shadow within the hour. His dirty hair sprouted in tufts from his head; he was hollow-eyed and still unshaven. Strekov took the small bottle of brandy from his coat and put it on the table. "Booze, eh," Bryce whispered hoarsely in a voice that had lost its resonance. "Won't last here." There was a small bruise high on his right cheek and his eye was partially discolored. A second bruise was visible low on his jaw. On the table in front of him were an ashtray and a water tumbler, but no cigarettes.

"Where are the cigarettes I sent you this morning?" Strekov asked.

Bryce hesitated evasively. He licked his dry lips and said finally: "Sojurs. Took the fucking lot."

"They're not soldiers," Strekov replied. He left the cell and went back along the stone corridor to the orderly room. He spoke to the Russian guard and went out into the yard. The two Letts were crouched on their knees in the dirt blowing into the embers which had begun to flare up against the blackened pot. He crossed to the pile of stovewood near the wooden saw-horses where their jackets hung and picked up a faggot of cordwood. He crossed back to the fire and squatted down on his heels. "Cigarettes," he said quietly. The two Letts lifted their heads simultaneously from the fire and stared at him. Their eyelashes and cheeks were white with the blown ash of the fire. "Cigarettes," Strekov repeated.

They watched him without moving, still on their hands and knees, looking at the faggot of cordwood which he held in his left hand, watching as he reached forward with his right hand and took a quarter of uncooked potato from the tin pot, studied it silently, wiped the ash on his trouser knee, and put it in his mouth. They watched him chew it slowly, looking out over the hillside, watched him turn aside and spit the potato into the dirt, then take a second quarter also, chew it as solemnly as the first, then spit it out into the dirt also. They watched him with growing uneasiness, breaths suspended, heads moving in unison as the hand moved to the pot and back again, looking on like two dogs at a campfire, watching potato, cabbage, and lean meat disappear only to be spat out into the dirt again; and finally the shorter Lett arose with a cry and scampered towards the lean-to built against the rear wall of the stable, and rummaged frantically among their pallets of rag, fur, and greased paper. He brought out the carton of cigarettes they'd taken from Bryce that morning following the altercation in his cell.

Bryce acknowledged the return of the cigarettes with a nod. He sat forward, opened one package, and lit a cigarette. "Nice kip this is," he said, eyes roaming the room. "A winder. A bed. Blankets. Even a kip house fire outside."

"Kip?"

"Jail, you might say. Now smokes and booze." He opened the bottle of brandy.

"It's not a jail," Strekov said, moving a stool closer to the table where Bryce sat.

"You'd best tell that scum outside that—them sojurs. Stinking with dirt, them two. Fair been bathing in shit if you ast me. Not a tongue in their heads. Where's Kirilen?"

"He's here."

"Yer number one, ain't you?" Bryce said. He smiled uneasily. "Haven't seen hide nor hair of him. It was you all along, wasn't it?"

"Kirilen thinks you tried to escape not long after you arrived here," Strekov said. "Is that true?"

"What else did he tell you? Speaks English like a bleeding Packy lawyer. Din't understand a word he said. Did he say escape?" Bryce laughed falsely. "Me? Never. That's cock, see. Where'd I escape to, eh? Did he answer that? Shove me inside and I'd never get out."

"You mean they'd arrest you?" Strekov asked.

"Nick me in a flash," Bryce muttered, wiping his wet chin. He put the glass down carefully and pulled his handkerchief from his pocket. He looked at the small notebook Strekov had pulled from his coat and was studying. "What's that?" he demanded.

Strekov didn't lift his eyes. "You didn't try to escape, then?"

"That's a lie! Going for a stroll, you might say. Taking the air. I'm always off to the woods when I get the chance. Ever been to Whipsnade Zoo? Used to spend my afternoons there, me and Mary."

"What did you do at the British mission in West Berlin?"

"Pouch room."

"You didn't represent yourself as a code clerk?"

"Never. Not me. I was working in the pouch room, stuffing bags. Got reeling drunk one night and they took me off the communications watch. No more wireless work for three months. Boris knew about it. Boris and Vasily both. They were a lovely pair. Do you know them?"

"No," Strekov said.

"What's in that book there?" he asked again. "What Kirilen said?"

"Some of it. It's a difficult problem, isn't it? It's difficult to remember what has been said. It's difficult to keep the details in order." Strekov put the notebook away.

"You've talked to Boris?"

"No." Strekov got to his feet. "They gave you money?"

"Generous, those two. Both of them. Had money to spend. Not like some of those buggers with our own services."

"They paid most of your expenses in Berlin?"

"Most of 'em. What if they did? They got as much as they gave."

"What did you give them? Copies of cables? Dispatches?"

"Never had to open a bleeding bag for them," Bryce said. "Maybe a telegram now and then. Listening devices. Bugs, you call them. That was what I was doing—putting them where they'd do the most good. They didn't always work but that wasn't my fault. Then I used to do a little repair work on the side—fixing someone's wireless or gramophone. Sometimes they'd give me the key to their flat if they were going away for the weekend. When I had enough time, I could wire up a flat like a bleeding Christmas tree. Father Christmas, I was," Bryce smiled in recollection. "Even got a bug in the back seat of the Minister's Humber one evening. Maybe it's still there." He emptied his glass, then filled it again. "Talk to Boris," he continued. "Ask him about it. I told them about the visitors we had coming in, the diplomats from the FO, the intelligence blokes from SIS in London who used to come in from time to time on special projects, the communications watches we'd set up, what frequencies we'd be monitoring. It was important. All of it."

"Why did you do it?"

"Do what?" Bryce asked in irritation.

"Why did you work with Boris and Vasily? You couldn't make up your mind when we talked to you in Moscow. What made Berlin so different? Was it just the money?"

"I'm no hypocrite," Bryce said, lighting another cigarette. "Not me. I'm not out for number one. Not all the time. The principle of it, you might say. Boris and me used to talk about it. Being on the right side of things. He helped open my eyes, you could say. I saw things the way they were . . . right down to the muck of things, bottom and all. I saw where I'd been a coward all those years, see. Living in my own dirty cellar, lice and all, and pretending I belonged upstairs, where the good life was. There I was, cursing the Establishment and doing nowt about it, not lifting my hand. I'd studied life up, see. Money and the system.

Poisoned my life, they did. Treated me like dirt, too, them nobs at the mission in Berlin. Scum to them, I was. Just scum—"

"Why did you think you'd be arrested?" Strekov asked. He moved towards the window, his back to Bryce. "You'd just bought the radio in London. You hadn't made any transmissions. You hadn't received any instructions and you didn't know what your mission was to be. Why did you think you'd be arrested?" He stood at the window, looking out over the cold hillside where darkness had begun to fall.

"It was a feeling I had," Bryce mumbled. "Eyes in the back of me head sometimes."

"Who was your handler in London? What was his name?"

Bryce hesitated. "Josef," he said finally.

Strekov turned back towards the table. "Was he like Boris and Vasily?"

"Gave himself airs," Bryce answered grudgingly. "Tight fisted too. I told you before—wouldn't hardly give you the drippings from his nose."

"How many times did you meet with him?"

Bryce hesitated again, studying Strekov's face. "Three times."

"Where?"

"First time at Paddington station. After that, in Chelsea . . . a pub there. Last time in Ealing. That's when he gave me the crystal."

"Did you ever complain to him? Did you ever argue?"

"Never. We hit it off, you might say. But Josef wasn't like Boris. Too bloody serious. Cold as a fish, he was."

"London isn't Berlin, either," Strekov said. "Did you trust him?"

"Had to, didn't I?" Bryce laughed awkwardly. "It was me and him."

"Did you have any close friends in London, men you could talk to, the way you talked to Boris? At the diplomatic wireless station, for example?"

"Not bloody likely. Trying to pension me off, they was."

"How about relatives, old friends?"

"No one. Who would I talk to anyway? About what? I told you, everyone's on the grab these days, trying to get theirs. Nark you in a flash if they thought there was a bob in it for them. Rotten it is—the whole bleeding system."

"So there was no one you could trust?"

"Said so, din't I?" Bryce muttered sullenly. "What are you pecking at my bit of muck for? What's in it for you?"

Strekov got up from the stool and went to the window again. "Just a few questions more. Tell me, what does 'betrayed' mean to you?"

"Betrayed?" He looked towards Strekov. "Betrayed?"

"What does it mean to you?"

"I dunno. A chum, a friend . . . he turns you in." He stared at Strekov's face, searching for a clue.

Strekov came back to the table and sat down on the stool. "Did you ever see Boris after you returned to London?"

"Boris?" Bryce repeated in mystification, still searching Strekov's face. "Boris? No. He wasn't there, was he?"

"Did you ever see him?"

"No," Bryce answered. "Was he in London?"

"Would it have made a difference?"

"Maybe. Look, what is it you're asking me?"

"I want to know who you thought betrayed you," Strekov said. "It was Josef, wasn't it?"

"I didn't say that," Bryce cried. "I didn't—"

"You told Kirilen you'd been betrayed. You were talking about Josef, weren't you?"

"*Never!* I was just talking, see. Just blathering. I had a filthy crossing from Gedser. Then this bloke puts me to talking and gives me a bottle of rum."

"What happened in London?" Strekov continued. "Was it something you read about in the diplomatic wireless traffic? Something you learned about from your friends there? Or was it something you saw?"

"Nothing happened!"

"Something happened," Strekov repeated. "Something happened which made you believe Josef was in contact with British intelligence. Wasn't that it?"

"I don't want to know!" Bryce cried savagely, rising from his chair. "Not a word, not another fucking word!"

"Was it in the telegraphic traffic you were reading? Was it talked about at Hanslope Park? Or was it something else?"

"I told you! Not another word."

"It's too late," Strekov said. "Something happened in London which convinced you that Josef had betrayed you to British intelligence. You lost your head, emptied your bank accounts, and took the boat from Harwich, spent a few drunken days in Copenhagen. You changed your mind about going to Moscow by way of Warsaw and came to Rostock instead. Why? When you talked to Kirilen the first night, you didn't mention Josef straightaway. You talked in generalities instead. Why? I don't know. Perhaps you thought you had a commodity no one else had, that you knew something no one else knew, and that men like Boris might appreciate that. Perhaps for the first time in your life you thought you were in possession of something unique, something for which you could ask any price you wished, and which men like Boris would willingly pay. You didn't think Kirilen was such a man," Strekov added. "You were right. He isn't."

"That's cock!" Bryce shouted. "You don't know what yer saying."

"You thought Josef was in touch with British intelligence," Strekov continued. "How did you know? The cable traffic at Hanslope Park? Did you read it there? Or was it something else?"

"Nothing! Nothing else! I swear—"

Strekov shook his head. "It had to be something else. Something personal. Something not shared with anyone. Something you could identify in a way no one else could. What would it be?" He kept his eyes on Bryce's face. The cheeks were pale, the mouth half open; the untidy grain of beard made the jaw seem even weaker. The small eyes were as bright as nail heads in the dissolving light of the room. "You'd been in Berlin. You watched the visitors from London come and go. You knew their names and their faces as well. You knew who worked with British intelligence, who was with the Foreign Office, who worked in the Cabinet Secretariat, who in the Permanent Under Secretary's office. You knew who was important and who wasn't. You passed this information on to Boris when they arrived in West Berlin, however anonymously they might have come. So that gave you an advantage. When you left Berlin and went back to London, you had a good sense of the operational structure of British intelligence concerning East German or Soviet affairs. If Josef had been in contact with such men, you might have been able to identify them. In addition you had a curiosity about such people. You repaired their radios, pried into their personal lives, looked into their flats when they were off on holiday and you'd promised to look at a balky gramophone. You may have examined their wardrobes, their liquor cabinets, even read their mail. You passed on the gossip about their personal lives to Boris or Vasily."

Bryce's eyes hadn't left Strekov's face.

"When you returned to London, perhaps that curiosity continued. You could still read about them—in the *Times* or someplace else," Strekov continued calmly. "You knew more about them than you could ever convey. One day you suddenly discovered that one of these men was in clandestine contact with Josef in London. Josef was working for them, he had betrayed you. He was being paid for his services in the same way that Boris and Vasily had paid for yours. He was an agent for British intelligence. You ran. It wasn't until you reached East Germany that you realized—Kirilen told you that British intelligence knew nothing about your disappearance. He told you that our 'sources' had told him as much."

"Shut up!" Bryce shouted. "You bastard! Shut up, do you hear! They'll kill me! You too! Both of us!"

Strekov nodded. "It was what you always feared, wasn't it? Those not part of your world, those too highly placed to feel what you had felt. Those who could only be hypocrites, playing out their murderous games—"

Bryce sprang towards the door, knocking over the chair, but Strekov was too quick. He reached it first and slammed it shut. Bryce backed away. "You bastard!" he cried. "You *knew*. All this fucking time! Keep away from me! Don't come near me, you bloody Judas!" He stumbled backwards across the room. "You knew. It was you that done it! Right from the beginning."

Strekov returned to his stool. "Did you think it was your own private war?" he said. "To satisfy you and no one else? Did you think others weren't involved too?"

"Not another fucking word! I want to talk to Boris, see! Boris or Vasily! You're mixed up with them—high and mighty like they are! They sent you! Where's Kirilen? What'd you do with him?"

The room was almost in darkness. Strekov lifted the kerosene lantern to the table and lit it. "Who was it you saw?" he asked, blowing out the match. "What happened in London?"

Bryce didn't move, the lantern light lifting his small face from the darkness, his thin body hidden in the shadows against the stone wall. Strekov knew what he feared. He had blundered into a world he'd hardly known existed except as an abstraction.

"I don't want to know," he pleaded. "Never. I didn't see anything. Not a bloody thing." His voice had grown hoarse. Now it died to a whisper. "It's a bloody nightmare, that's what it is. Just say I'm a bloke that got in the wrong door and wants to ease out again, no harm done. Live and let live. You can tell them that, can't you? Back into the mob with me, the way I came. Mum's the word, see. Tear up half of Europe looking for me, he would. Say the word. They don't have to know, do they? You could tell them that."

He crept forward out of the shadows, the bright eyes riveted to Strekov's face. "Mum's the word," he pleaded. "Just the two of us, talking like this. Say it's over. You don't want to know. Just tell your headquarters I'm tired of it, wore out, rubbed to the bone. Peace and quiet, that's all I want. Bible oath." He slipped into the chair opposite Strekov, his voice only a whisper. "Mum's the word," he breathed. "Just say it's all right."

Strekov watched him silently, his elbows folded across the table. Bryce sat unmoving, like a penitent schoolboy, and Strekov felt his exhaustion, his humiliation and helplessness, as surely as if they were his own. He nodded finally. "Mum's the word," he conceded, shifting his weight to bring the notebook from his pocket. He tore out a single page and put it on the table. He brought his pen from his pocket and pushed it across the table with the slip of paper. "Give me his name," he said quietly. "Josef is now in Moscow. It's a simple matter to send a telegram and ask about his activities those last few days before you left London—who he saw. Who he talked with. It would be better if it came from you. If I'm going to help you, this is where we must begin."

Bryce, watching Strekov's face, didn't move. He sat for a long time looking at the piece of paper. At last he lifted his eyes, studied Strekov's face for a final time, and looked back down as he wrote.

Strekov knew then that a terrible mistake had been made, one of those grotesque errors of timing or judgment. If there were those among Strekov's colleagues in the KGB power establishment who were privy to his recruitment, they were men like Orlov, not in East Germany but in Moscow, buried away in the anonymous silence of the old building on Dzerzhinskay Street. It was likely that even Josef didn't know whom he was contacting that night.

Strekov lifted his eyes, examining Bryce's face in the lamplight. He understood Bryce's terror. It was as real to him as the sleepless, unshaven face watching him hopefully from across the table. "How did it happen?" Strekov asked. "Where did you see this man?"

Bryce didn't answer. Strekov waited. Bryce's eyes were on the slip of paper in his hand. Strekov finally leaned forward and, taking the paper, held it against the glass chimney of the lantern, moved it to the top, and let it catch the flame. It burned quickly, flaring up in his hand, and he dropped the ash to the stone floor and ground the embers under his foot. "How did it happen?" he asked again.

Bryce took a breath and began. He had dodged into Paddington station on a stormy autumn night to escape the rain. He had been searching for an address in the neighborhood, a hired-car agency that rented automobiles by the month, but hadn't been able to find it. He was on his way to the phone booths at the far end of the station when he thought he saw a familiar face in the crowd. For a moment he couldn't identify him. By the time he placed him, he had disappeared. It was Josef. Bryce trailed along in the direction Josef had been moving but after a few minutes thought he might have been mistaken. He gave up the chase and turned back towards the phone booths. He found the hired-car agency in the telephone book, wrote down the address, and crossed to the newspaper stand on the other side of the station to pick up an evening newspaper. The vendor went inside to get change. Waiting for him, Bryce looked through the glass windows of the small bookstore and saw Josef. He was standing at one of the bookshelves at the rear, his face in full silhouette. He was talking to a taller man whose back was turned. Bryce saw the taller man nod once or twice, replace the book on the shelf, and pick up another. Josef continued to talk. Suddenly the man turned, a book in his hands, still studying the pages as he listened. Bryce's blood froze. He recognized him immediately. He had spent a week in West Berlin on three occasions during Bryce's posting. He was a senior official with Special Intelligence Services who was close to the Home Secretary and the Cabinet Secretariat.

Bryce fled without waiting for his change. He thought that he had been betrayed. Swept along by the crowd, he didn't look back. He hailed a taxi in the rain outside. It wasn't until he reached Chelsea that he began to breathe easier. He didn't return home that night but took a room in Bayswater. Late the following morning he returned to his house, packed a bag, took down the antenna, and locked the radio in a trunk in the basement. The same afternoon he left London for Harwich. When he reached Copenhagen two days later, his panic had eased. For the first time he recognized the enormity of his discovery. Wandering the streets of Copenhagen and listening to the babble of foreign tongues, watching the girls and the housewives as he sat on the park benches, or drinking in the hotel bar as he studied the tourists, he recognized something of his own uniqueness—that he knew what none of them knew, what no living soul east of the Channel knew: an unknown Russian in London named Josef was a double agent, employed by British intelligence.

He spent two days in Copenhagen considering his predicament. For the first time since that initial approach in the Pushkin Museum in Moscow or its aftermath with Boris and Vasily in West Berlin, he had discovered his own rarity—something not to be explained by his position at the Embassy in Moscow or his access to the bag room in West Berlin or the offices and flats of the British diplomats posted to the Stadium, but something else, something special.

He spent two additional drunken days in Copenhagen enjoying his newly discovered power. When his bewildered Soviet contact proposed that Bryce fly to Warsaw and on to Moscow, he was wary. Moscow wasn't West Berlin. He wasn't ready to yield his advantage— not yet. He wanted to see Boris and Vasily in Berlin. Could official cables or dispatches tell the tale that he intended to tell them himself in Berlin? Kirilen met him at Warnemunde and brought him to Rostock instead. He was disappointed at first. After the first five minutes in the car with Kirilen, he'd known that Kirilen wasn't the man to share his secret with. He didn't talk about what he'd seen at Paddington that first day. By the time the key had turned in the lock the first night, he'd guessed that he'd surrendered too much in coming to East Germany. He knew that Josef's involvement with the British official was the only negotiable asset he had left. He continued to stall. Kirilen grew more bewildered. Two nights later Kirilen told him that their sources in British intelligence were as puzzled about his abrupt departure as everyone else. It had taken some time for Kirilen's reassurances to sink in.

So they didn't know. What sources? Sources like him? He thought about it for a minute. Why was he here, then? What had he seen after all? He was confused. Could he doubt what he had seen with his own two eyes?

Something else, then. Kirilen, Josef, everyone else—not knowing what the truth was. Why? Something he didn't know either? *Sources?* Not like him, then—couldn't be. What did he know? He sat rigidly on the stool, alone with the bottle of rum Kirilen had returned from his confiscated suitcase, remembering the figure in the bookshop at Paddington, the face suddenly turned. Josef was talking. He listened, the two figures in the glass window framed in his mind's eye. What were they talking about? Betraying *him?* Impossible. And suddenly he knew, his breath suddenly failing, his spine as cold as ice.

He had been wrong from the beginning. The Englishman was Moscow's man. He was the double agent, not Josef.

The cigarette fell from his fingers and he sat on the cot. Bryce had never been convinced such men existed, except as comic parodies of their class. He heard the words of Russian down the stone corridor where the guards were talking. He couldn't move. He sat frozen, looking at the autumn moon, saw it framed in the small rectangle of window as it hovered over the earth, as tranquil and mysterious as he'd ever seen it, this finite mirror of the universe riding out its perfection in the night sky for all the world to see: lovers, children, jailbirds, murderers, Packies, nobs, swanks, and Borneo apes. This perfect sphere whose ash-strewn, cuspy flanks and blue-gray plains deny nothing— virgin, harlot, barren goddess, or prodigal queen of God-knows-what, but still there, for all eyes to see—nobler, more regal and chaste than he'd ever seen it before, telling Bryce of another order somewhere beyond, and watching it that night in the cell he knew that he was going to die.

Later that night Bryce had tried to escape. They found him in the woods near the main guard gate.

It was dark when Strekov returned to the manor house in the clearing and climbed the stairs to the third floor. In the brightly lit *referentura* section he drafted a telegram to Orlov in Moscow. The Uzbek sat at the end of the table, his sleepy eyes studying a month-old newspaper from Moscow, a glass of tea at his elbow. The telegram took a long time to compose. He told Orlov what he had learned from Bryce and described the meeting at Paddington station. He included the Englishman's name and closed by recommending Bryce's immediate evacuation to Moscow by the first available military transport. He suggested that he accompany him. The telegram was sent to Moscow through Orlov's own headquarters channel. No one else would see it.

After Strekov passed the message to the communications officer for encryption, he read over the telegrams that had been received that day. At the back of the file were the telegrams he'd already seen. He studied them quietly. The American's name was still there. He was en route to Rostock. Was it only a coincidence? Would the American services have known about Bryce, known what not even the British knew? Were the Americans searching for the identity of the Englishman Bryce had recognized that rainy night in Paddington station? How would they have made the connection, guessed what not even the KGB could guess?

He got to his feet wearily, returned the file to the code clerk, and went down to his study on the first floor. The kindling in the stone fireplace was slow to take the flame. He stood watching the fire, weary from groping with the riddles his answers couldn't solve. He was depressed without knowing why. Was it his conversation with Bryce or his own isolation from the Center in Moscow, from what Orlov or the others on Dzerzhinskay Street knew? How important was this Englishman? Ten years earlier, after his return to Moscow from Prague, he might have known. He'd been working with Orlov then, reorganizing the European and UK Divisions. Late one evening in his office on Dzerzhinskay Street, Orlov had mentioned someone in passing. "We would have lost him except for the Americans," Orlov had said. In his hand was a twenty-year-old NKVD report from Berlin. Scrawled in purple-black ink along the margin were the words *Is he English? Who is this man?* The report had been found in one of Orlov's personal files which his secretary was retiring and had brought to him for guidance. It was from prewar Berlin. "It was the Americans who gave him back to us," Orlov added. "After the war." He gave the report back to his secretary and told him to burn it. "They've been looking for him ever since. He's a killer. But twenty or thirty years from now he'll be sitting in his club in London, mumbling through his claret about the dreadful Americans—how they'd prolonged the Cold War for two decades, how they would have blown the world to smithereens if Fuchs and Portecorvo hadn't given Moscow the bomb, how fascist the Americans had become for our having it."

At the time Strekov hadn't understood what he was talking about. In some ways he understood even less now.

Kirilen knocked at the door and came in. "Did you learn anything new?" He'd just returned from the *referentura* section and had heard that a high-precedence message had gone out.

"I talked to him," Strekov said, rubbing his eyes. "That's enough for now."

By mid-afternoon the following day Strekov still hadn't received a reply to his telegram. He couldn't understand Orlov's delay. After a third visit to the *referentura* section he returned to his room below, pulled on an old jacket and his gum boots, and went out the side door.

It was difficult walking in the gum boots. He crossed through a dense stand of pines where ropes of old snow lay twisted among the crevices, roots, and racks along the periphery, and where the earth within was carpeted with a copper-colored blanket of old pine needles that gave up a soft aromatic dust as he walked. Beyond the pine woods he entered a sloping meadow, crossed thirty yards down the slope through the leaning grass, and stopped suddenly, head lifted. Fifty yards beyond, a large red fox stood motionless near the woods on the far side of the meadow, head raised towards a few old apple trees. His ears were pricked, his nose lifted suspiciously into the wind that blew up the slope towards Strekov. Perhaps in the late summer there had been rabbits or partridges there, crouched in the wet grass, foraging for windblown apples. Strekov saw nothing under the trees except a few wormy boughs lying in the grass.

He watched the fox, who stood motionless on the far side of the meadow, gazing towards the apple trees. Then with a slow movement of his head, he turned and looked at Strekov. The wind lifted the hair from Strekov's forehead as it moved through the trees. Strekov, looking still at the fox, held his breath, his heart beating rapidly, the blood beginning to pound at his temples. Then the fox turned and trotted towards the woods. His tufted ears were pricked forward. He gave Strekov one last look before he vanished into the undergrowth along the tree line. Strekov stood rooted to the spot. After a moment he released the breath from his lungs, still gazing dumbly towards the undergrowth where the fox had disappeared. At that moment in the cold chill of the winter woods, he thought it was the most magnificent animal he had ever seen.

He crossed the meadow in the opposite direction and plunged into the trees. A quarter of a mile beyond he crossed an abandoned logging road choked with young saplings and fallen tree trunks. A mile beyond the trees thinned and the road climbed to a higher meadow, steeper than the first. It looked out over the distant hills, which retreated endlessly, like the waves on a frozen sea, towards the Polish border. He followed the road up the meadow and down again, through the forest. Twenty minutes later he turned into the final curve of the road and thirty yards beyond saw the wire fence interdicting the old track. The road vanished beyond the fenceline in a tangle of undergrowth. He turned back. Like a dusty baroque frame the wire fence had broken the illusion of space and of solitude—the expectation that the woods and the rolling hills were as limitless as his own Siberian woodlands, where distances were measured by time itself, by a day's journey; and where, at nightfall, travelers turned aside to the huts and cottages that leaked their smoky yellow light to the snow outside, and were fetched in to warm themselves by cherry-red stoves and kerosene cookers, by porcelain hearths where the hares were skinned and roasting, where wet buskins steamed in front of the fire and the wind howled beyond the window, moaning of the conspiracies of the season, of nature boundless and interminable.

An hour later Strekov climbed the hillside where he had seen the fox and looked back over the woods. Darkness was falling. It had begun to snow, at first a dry flutter against the dried grass of the hillside meadow, stinging his cold face and covering his shoulders with fine dry pellets, then more heavily as the wind eased. He crossed the field in the growing darkness, hands deep in his pockets. Lifting his head he saw the tall gray building looming ahead of him through the falling snow. He had forgotten it for a few hours, but now he moved towards it, his footsteps visible in the light gauze that had already silvered the hillside and the flagstones of the old courtyard. High overhead the small yellow window of the*referentura* section was still lit.

On the third floor the code clerk gave him the cable traffic that had accumulated during the afternoon. There was no reply to his telegram of the previous day. He had dinner alone in the small dining room. It was deserted. Afterwards he returned to his room. An hour later he descended to the first floor, carrying a book and a small tablet, and went into the wooden-beamed library next to the main foyer. It was still snowing outside. He turned on the lamp and coaxed to life the small mound of ashes in the stone fireplace. When the coals ignited he added a few split logs and pulled his chair closer to the fire. He lifted his head from time to time as he read, listening to the sound of the wind in the chimney, and at the window behind his chair. Outside the snow was still falling. He saw it move obliquely against the security lamps at the perimeter of the driveway, falling softly into the meadow and woods beyond.

He was reading and didn't hear the Uzbek when he entered, moving like a shadow across the firelit room. He circled Strekov's chair—cautious, predatory, almost feline, like a cat stalking the hearthside where the hunting dogs slept. He pulled a stool from the shadows and settled down at the far end of the hearth. Strekov lifted his head and looked at the hard muscular face, the plush of yellow hair, and the curious eyes. He was holding a pickled egg in one hand. In the other was a small tumbler of cognac. His face had a sleepy, conclusive look. Strekov was still searching its meaning when the door burst open.

Three Russian army officers stood in the bright light of the foyer, stamping their wet boots against the oak floor, as noisy as schoolboys as they shook the snow from their quilted parkas. Snow clung like rime to the fur beaks of their caps. Two still carried their shotguns on leather slings. The third cradled the broken breech of the shotgun across his waist with one arm; with the other he held the rear leg of the dead fox. The thick winter pelt was still wet with fresh snow, which spilled an irregular gray line across the polished floor. From the crushed skull flopping at the officer's heels the dark tongue leaked drops of fresh blood, each drop as quick as the life pounding quietly in Strekov's heart and chest.

He gazed at the dead fox. Then his eyes caught something else as they followed the trail of gray water to the front door and back again to the broken body. The firelight blazing at his back picked up the track beyond the boots of the Russian officers and brought it into the room with him, as silently as a ghost. The track moved through the open door and across the cold floor towards the firelight and the small stool at the end of the hearth. Strekov sat in silence, the book in his lap, looking at the Uzbek's shoes. The snow had melted by now and lay in small gray pools under his soles and heels.

He left the book in his chair and climbed to the third floor. The code clerk was expecting him. He had Orlov's cable in his hand when he opened the iron door. It had come an hour earlier. On the cover sheet he saw the Uzbek's initials where he had acknowledged receipt a few minutes after delivery. Even as Strekov signed, he knew what Orlov's message had been. He lifted the cover sheet, glanced at the text, and then turned and ran back down the stairs.

He found his jacket in his room below and moved out the side door and into the falling snow. The night was silent; the snowflakes clung to his hair and cheeks. He found the path through the woods and raced towards the stone stable. The snow had blanketed the bare earth at the end of the old building. It covered the mound of ashes where the two prisoners had built their fire. The single light burned over the small door at the end of the stable. The lean-to nearby was empty, its carpet of rags, burlap, and filthy furs scattered over with a light frosting of snow. He stood for a moment in the cold silence and then a sound came to him from the woods. Lifting his head he saw the gleam of lantern-light deep in the woods and heard the pick striking through the iron earth, then the ring of the axe that followed, slashing through the knotted pine roots and into the hard clay beneath the humus and loam of the forest floor.

The stone corridor was dark. The small guardroom inside the door was empty. He struck a match, found a lantern and lit it, and moved down the corridor. On the stone floor outside Bryce's cell his lantern showed the burlap bagging, the small lengths of rope, and the wooden wheelbarrow. The door was open. He moved the lantern forward and found the empty cot, the wooden table with its tin ashtray, and the cold stub of candle. The lantern was gone. He stepped on something. Dropping the lantern to his knee he saw a torn shirt near his foot. Bryce's cap lay off to his left. He lifted the lantern higher until the flickering light reached the far wall. He moved it slowly to his left towards the mound of shadow in the corner. Two bare feet showed cold and yellow in the lantern light. Bryce's body lay broken in the shadows where the Uzbek's final violence had carried it, head twisted upwards in death, one eye glaring fixedly at the lantern light from the shattered brow and skull. It seemed to look at Strekov. He lowered the lantern to the floor and knelt for a moment. He was still kneeling there when he heard the Uzbek's light tread in the corridor outside and saw him standing in the doorway with his lantern.

The Letts came scampering back through the trees like wild dogs, their hairless faces bright with perspiration, hands and feet stained with raw earth. The two Russian soldiers followed them silently. Bryce's shoes, tied together by their laces, dangled around the neck of one of the Letts. The other wore Bryce's winter mackinaw. They rollicked into the stable yard, but when they saw Strekov standing in the doorway, they dropped their shovel and pick and fled back to the leanto, where they remained crouched until Strekov had climbed the hill to the safe house.

The snow had stopped. Strekov stood at his window on the second floor, watching the lights from the kitchen below reflected against the snow. His head ached and he wondered if his fever was returning, if his posting to East Germany and his missions in the West weren't premature after his recent convalescence. But it was the dacha he was thinking of, of winter nights like these, and he wondered when he would be able to find it again. It was the only place where he had known peace. It wasn't like the KGB dachas near Moscow or at Gorky. This was his own. Before his posting to Prague over ten years earlier he'd found an abandoned woodcutter's hut near the banks of the Dniepr less than a day's journey from Kiev. From this he'd built the dacha. It was surrounded by dense green woods during the spring and summer, by snow in winter, with a wild orchard on one side and a small patch of strawberries on the other. Less than a mile away was the Dniepr, reached by a footpath which began at the front steps and led through the woods to a small jetty, where he kept a skiff.

Standing at the window and looking out at the fresh snowfall, he could smell the small parlor of the dacha and its lingering woodsmoke, the dampness from the river, his moldering books, the light bamboo fishing rods in the small larch cabinet, the oil from his shotgun and boots. He remembered the tactile pleasure of taking one of the books from the bookcase near his chair next to the tile stove, the reassurance of turning the pages and reading words long forgotten—remembered the mushroomy smell of the damp pages left uncut during his long winters abroad, remembered sitting there in the chair near the stove, waiting for his wife to bring the steaming tea from the old samovar and sit across from him, the firelight touching her slim face.

When he was a schoolboy tired of physics, mathematics, or history, he'd written verses in secret; and that first winter at the dacha he'd begun to write verses again. In the back of a German paperback edition of Gogol he'd brought his wife from Vienna, he wrote a poem in pencil—a simple, foolish poem describing the pleasure of picking up one of his books from his bookcase and of returning to the same low-ceilinged parlor after a year's absence and sitting in the same armchair still redolent with the woodsmoke of past winters, reading words he hadn't remembered since they were last together.

What was Orlov protecting in London?

He and his wife had a small flat in Moscow overlooking Novodeviche monastery near the university and there were books there, too—lining the unpainted pine shelves in the small living room, the hall, and the bedroom. From the top shelf of the hall bookcase his wife had hung—securing it by the weight of some books—a strip of colorful Kazakh cloth, to which she had pinned his medals. In the bookcase in the study she'd propped the first pictures of their two sons where he could easily find them when he lifted his head from the plain wooden table in front of the window. But his work in Moscow wasn't like the work at the dacha. He'd written no poems at the flat near Novodeviche monastery. Instead they were in the paperback books at the dacha, hidden away from prying eyes in the end pages, their letters carved in the damp paper like a schoolboy's initials carved in the green bark of a birch when the sap had begun to flow. He and his wife were alone there. He remembered the morning sunlight bathing the rain-mottled walls of the small bedroom under the roof, her slim arms stretched towards the log rafters as she awoke. He remembered the way the gnats and wood moths moved against his face as they walked together barefooted down the weed-choked path in the green summer light to bathe together in the river.

"Why is it you don't write more here?" she asked him one day at the flat in Moscow. "So that I could find them—in the backs of your books when you're gone?"

He hadn't answered. It was the same month she'd forced him to admit that he was with the KGB, not the diplomatic service. "Now I understand," she told him when she learned the truth. "Because *they're* here. Because your work is here. Because you despise it as much as I do."

"They?" he had asked.

"*Beshniki,*" she breathed contemptuously. She meant the KGB. It hadn't occurred to Strekov until then that his work in Moscow might have been responsible.

It was very far away now. In Moscow the year following her death, he'd been assigned to the KGB's first Directorate and had fallen ill. He returned alone to the dacha during his convalescence. Orlov had urged him to go elsewhere—to the spas on the Black Sea, to the Caucasus, to Sochi. But Strekov had refused. In his fever he had thought of nothing but his dead wife and the dacha. Snow and rain had fallen continuously during his week there but the ice had begun to thaw on the river and he knew spring would come soon. One night he had left the chair in front of the fire where he'd been sleeping, awakened suddenly when the wind flung open the front door. He was sure she had returned. Still half asleep, with the wind and cold rain sweeping across the parlor, he had tried to find her. He searched the kitchen and the bedroom, the small loft over the parlor, still feverish; but it was only when he stood in the cold rain outside and looked back through the small window into the room, looked at the solitary chair where he had been sitting, that he understood she was gone. Only her language books were left. The rain continued to fall in the woods outside and he rebuilt the fire. He wrote a few lines in the back of her English grammar, still heartbroken at his discovery:

> Now it is April and the trees are wet
> And gleaming upon the altars of the dead;
> And I from dreaming find sleep's eyes are set
> Agape with copper pennies in your stead.
> I can remember everything you said.

The following night a freeze came and the ice thrashed in the trees along the river. Still feverish, Strekov sat in front of the dying fire long after midnight and wrote other words in turn. In the cold, bitter light of morning, he had read them again from the endleaf of the book, but was no longer sure of what they meant. She would have known.

He leaned forward, his forehead touching the cold glass as he stared out into the newly fallen snow. He heard the voices from the kitchen below. They were Russian voices, as homesick as he might once have been on a cold and snowy Baltic night. A few of the Russian officers may have drunk too much, but it didn't matter. They'd eaten and hunted well; and tomorrow would be returning to their regiments:

> You are covered with snow, O Russia:
> Over your shrouded, icebound body
> The cold winds breathe a funeral dirge.

FOUR

The locomotive crashed against its frozen couplings, hesitated, and creaked forward out of the East Berlin train sheds into the cold gray morning. The coach was airless and dry, pewter light leaking through the double panes and flooding the tattered lime-green carpeting, the worn brass fittings, and the polished wood of the bench where Plummer sat alone. The windows and undercarriages began to rattle as the train left East Berlin, gathering speed, and turned north. A few East German bureaucrats and a handful of soldiers sat on the benches nearby, watching the monotony of landscape that rolled across the window—bored, silent, and ruminative, like a jury at a bankruptcy litigation. Across the aisle an old man with a soot-pitted face was asleep, wrapped in a tattered *Wehrmacht* overcoat. His white head slid back and forth across the chilly pane as the train swayed along the track. In the seat ahead of him two young East German nurses in dark-blue coats were playing cards.

The train lumbered across the Brandenburg plain, through the scrub pine and the stubbled grain fields, past the collapsed outbuildings and the flocks of decayed stables and farms, past the weathered monuments to East German collectivization that littered the silent landscape like wild sheep abandoned to forage. Plummer watched the dark clouds push across the tops of the trees and through the standing pines. Driven from the north, the clouds were dark with snow. The narrow streets and stations of the villages were deserted; the countryside beyond, empty. The train moved into the low hills of the lake country, rattling over bridges and crossings, across frozen meadows where tatters of last week's snow still lay in the woods like a winding sheet. Crusts of snow clung to the bottom of the ditches and nestled in the stiff grass along the ballast bed.

Two delays north of Neubrandenburg left them an hour behind schedule. Drawn to a sudden stop south of Rostock, the train stood on a siding for thirty minutes, waiting in solitude near a frozen field where yarns of old snow wound through the furrows of an abandoned cornfield. A few hundred yards away stood a whitewashed stone stable with a silver-gray roof. A rusty hayrake stood beneath a row of poplar trees at the end of a collapsing stone fence. A man in a cracked leather jacket with fleece at the collar crossed through the open stable doors and into the yard. Through the open doors Plummer saw a mound of coals in a forge bed where another German was shoeing a horse. A thin thread of smoke climbed from the stone chimney and into the gray sky. When the German in the fleece jacket recrossed the yard and shut the stable door behind him, Plummer sat back, listening to the quiver of steam in the brake lines and the monotonous rattle of steel plate. After a few minutes he heard the Berlin-bound train streaking towards them in the distance. The Germans stirred as the first sounds reached them—first a meteoric pulse along the rails and then a secondary fibrillation that trembled through the inert iron of the wheels. It exploded a moment later with a savagery that shook the windows and doors as it raced by, leaving them vibrant and transfixed with its rush of energy, like summer leaves in the shock of an electrical storm.

They stood near the windows, looking out. Plummer watched the long, low flatcars flash by, saw a ribbon of identical squat shapes lashed to their decks under frozen tarpaulins, identified the masked gun barrels and tank turrets, watched the multiple frames of a single unchanging image flicker past the gray lens of window beyond, then saw the slatted freight cars replace the flat cars with their cargo of concealed armaments still in pine and cosmoline, still as cold as a slab ice from the holds and decks of the Soviet freighters that had brought them down through the icy seas of the Gulf of Leningrad and into the Baltic.

He lit a cigarette and over the match flame watched the final ice-covered gondola cars flash by. Behind them was the military caboose with bundled East German soldiers in military parkas. Suddenly the window was empty. Plummer looked away, in the other direction, towards the stone stable where the doors were still closed. The beading of smoke had thickened; a few gouts of ash and cinder erupted into the gray sky as the blacksmith fired his forge below. The old coach jerked suddenly, wrenched from its vacuum, and began to inch out of the siding. Plummer sat in its gathering motion, looking silently at the snowswept fields. He had counted fourteen T-54 Soviet tanks, eight T-55's, three Soviet ZSU-5-2 self-propelled guns, and a few heavy trucks, but the freight cars were different: 82mm rocket launchers, maybe—Simonov carbines, Kalashnikov assault rifles, ten to a crate at 110 pounds and still in grease. In Prague the tank and gun counts had interested them less than the factory markings: factory and serial number, any irregularities in the die or hammerer's stroke—*Get under the canvas and find them in the dark—numbers, letters, anything that can tell us where the Soviets were making them. Ryazan? Tula? The tank works at Kursk?* In Prague he'd found a young oiler in the military arsenal who'd enjoyed the work. He rubbed gravestones on his holidays.

He looked across the frozen fields, the stubbled grain rows, and the fencerows beyond. It was autumn in the Rappahannock, quail and dove weather still; and the recollection brought a familiar ache to his bones. *What did it matter anymore? It was time to go home.* Thirty minutes later the train entered Rostock.

Herr Kohler from the East German Planning Commission was waiting for him on the station platform. His driver took Plummer's suitcase. "How was your trip?" Kohler asked. He was a small man with deep-set black eyes, a finely chiseled face, and a neatly trimmed Zouave beard. He looked like a Marxist academician, which he was. He'd studied in Moscow, had a passion for doctrinal dialogue, and an economist's belief in his own infallibility. To Plummer he was nothing more than a pint-sized nuisance, but he treated him with the same caution he'd treat any accountant sent by headquarters to audit his books.

"Not bad. How was yours?"

"You found many things to interest you, I suppose."

"Not much. The train was two hours late."

Kohler considered Plummer's reply without answering. Plummer watched Kohler's black beard working as they followed the driver back to the car. He knew that like most East Germans or Russians he had known, Kohler considered his remark a veiled indictment of the GDR. When they sat back in the rear seat of the Russian-built Volga, Kohler said, "I suppose the trains in America are quite different."

"I wouldn't know," Plummer said, looking out the window at the gray streets of Rostock. "I haven't been on an American train in years. They're quicker ways these days."

The hotel was a tall, old-fashioned hostelry on a side street near the center of Rostock. A district meeting was in progress and on the felt mat near the elevators were the words *Welcome SED District Delegations.* The lobby and lounge were full of party members and civil servants in from the hinterlands—rural Marxist orthodoxy, grim and whey-faced, a little threadbare, with a hint of Protestant righteousness to their parsimony. It was that kind of hotel—decent, puritanical, and cheap, where the menu, like the service, was slight and inconsequential, the help morose and unaggressive, and where the official expense account might cover rooms, meals, and maybe laundry; but few tips and no indiscretions.

"Is this an American passport?" the desk clerk asked Kohler.

"That's right," Plummer said.

Kohler said, "The formalities have already been completed." Plummer watched the eyes of the desk clerk as they moved from Kohler to the German driver and back to him. The desk clerk took a key from the drawer at his waist and passed it across the counter. For someone who hadn't known a moment earlier whether Plummer was an American or an East German official, like his hosts, the desk clerk showed a remarkable prescience in choosing the right key. Plummer knew what kind of room it would be—in the middle of the corridor with empty rooms on both sides, wired up like a Christmas tree. But it didn't matter; he was here to do their work, not his.

He spent the remainder of the afternoon looking at warehouses near the railyards and the docks along the Warnow River which the Pankow government might make available to his firm. The following morning he gave Kohler his recommendation. The remainder of his morning was free. He found a guidebook at a bookstore near the hotel, dawdled about the center of the city for an hour, and by ten thirty was rubbernecking through a small seventeenth-century chapel. He followed a group of Danish tourists through the interior, but left them and went out the rear door, crossed through an old graveyard, and found the rear gate. An old man in a dark coat was digging up dead shrubbery at the rear of the graveyard. He lifted his head and shouted towards Plummer, who ignored him, let himself out the rear gate, and tomcatted up the empty street away from the center of Rostock. The rain had begun to fall again, carried by the same wind that brought the smell of saltwater to the wet streets near his hotel. Gulls dipped over the sloping roofs of the bargeboard houses on the hillside below. He found a tramline a few blocks beyond and swung aboard; it returned him to the center of the city. By then he had already achieved his purpose. The car that had followed him to the old chapel had reappeared, trailing after him as he walked up the tramline and waited at the stop. There were two men in the car. One was the driver who had picked him up at the station the previous day.

On the same gray, windy day with rain slashing in softly from the Baltic, Plummer watched the launching of an East German factory ship fifteen kilometers from Rostock. The fishing vessel wasn't outfitted yet, but the hull was already streaked with rust. Six months would pass before it went to sea, but when it did the steering and hydraulic system, valves and turbines, winches and deck cranes would be lubricated from Plummer's East German inventories.

Before the ship slid down the rails, a half dozen rain-coated figures had splashed up the wooden steps and across the platform in front of him. Kohler sat beside him, huddled in a wet black raincoat. The speeches were interminable. Most of the speakers were senior officials from East Berlin. Some were local party dignitaries. A tall, skull-faced woman was awarded a labor ribbon by the District Party Secretary. A Soviet admiral was the guest of honor. He was the commander of the Kaliningrad fleet. Surrounding him was a phalanx of Soviet diplomats, attachés, and advisers from the Russian mission in East Berlin. Plummer studied their faces one by one as he listened to the speeches.

"We, the workers and people of the GDR, are proud of being inseparably linked forever with the Soviet people and its glorious navy. . . ." The speaker had turned to address the commander of the Kaliningrad fleet. Plummer looked out to sea. Far in the distance a freighter was hull down on the horizon, steaming towards the estuary. He watched it crawl towards the Soviet Kaliningrad fleet, trailing a wisp of smoke. Except for the gulls dipping in the chill air, the ship was the only moving creature on the seamless expanse of sea and sky. The shipyard smelled of fish. Rain, sea, polished raincoats, and wet faces, the greasy planking at his feet, the smoking breaths around him—all stank of fish. Even the black freighter that now hung on the horizon, like a fly on a kitchen wall, seemed to be drawn inexorably towards this convocation by the ubiquitous smell of dead fish.

The speeches were concluded; the vessel launched. It thundered from the slide with a roar and sent a gigantic cascade of spray out over the estuary. A military band played "March of the Black Sea Fleets." The Soviet admiral got to his feet and began to applaud. The audience joined him.

A reception for the Kaliningrad fleet was held afterward in an old stucco building near the main gate. The reception rooms were crowded, the floors wet, the ceiling gray with cigarette smoke. Along one wall was a bank of windows looking out over the estuary; along another a group of German waitresses in smocks and aprons were serving the guests from buffet tables crowded with dishes of smoked fish, ham, sausage, cavier, and eels in sauce. The reception line was beginning to disintegrate when Kohler and Plummer entered but the Kaliningrad admiral turned from his heaped plate and shook both their hands briefly. They moved down the rug and into the crowd. Kohler said, "I understand that one day he will be a minister of the Soviet Republics." He wiped his greasy hand with his handkerchief.

"What's he going to do then?" Plummer asked, looking out over the heads of the Germans and Russians nearby, searching for the bar. "Send for you to hold his finger bowl?" He saw the bar and pushed towards it. A barman gave him a lager and he continued on to the rear of the room. The windows looked out on a small garden enclosed by a concrete wall. Beyond the wall lay the Baltic estuary. A tile stove stood in one corner near the windows, its bed of coals whipped to a fierce orange by the sea wind at the flue. The woman who had won the labor ribbon stood talking to an owl-faced German in a raincoat. Three Russians were eating and drinking noisily. Their faces were red, their hair in disarray, their tight coats wrinkled and damp, as if just taken from a sea locker. A large tiger cat stretched lazily on an old chair near the stove, watching them with quiet yellow eyes.

"Mr. Plummer," said a voice from nearby. Plummer turned. A tall man in a dark coat held a glass towards him. His eyes were cool, as colorless as seawater. He had high cheekbones, like a Slav, and dark blond hair. "It's Scotch," Strekov said, the glass still extended. "Your preference, I believe."

"Thanks, but I'm drinking beer." Plummer studied the face again. "I don't think we've met."

"My name is Wulf," Strekov said. He put the whiskey aside. "Did you enjoy the ceremonies?" he asked in German.

Plummer replied in English. "Not in this weather."

Still in German, Strekov said, "It's no worse than London, is it?"

"In London only a damn idiot makes speeches in the rain." A photographer standing on a chair nearby snapped a photograph of the Kaliningrad fleet captain standing with the captain of the East German fishing fleet. Two more pictures were taken. Another group assembled; more pictures followed. Plummer turned away from the magnesium glare of the flashbulb. One of the Russians nearby dumped the cat from its chair and stood on the seat to toast Soviet-German solidarity.

After the toast Strekov said, "You didn't drink."

"Habit." Plummer raised his glass. *"Prosit."*

"Prosit," Strekov said. He drank and put the glass aside. "How long will you be in Rostock?" He had returned to German again.

"Maybe another day. Maybe not. Which ministry are you with?"

"Ministerium für Staatssicherheit," Strekov replied.

"State security," Plummer repeated. He had guessed as much but was surprised at the casualness with which the fact had been admitted. "Protecting the Kaliningrad fleet?"

Strekov didn't smile. "I'd prefer to speak German, if you don't mind. Your German is very good."

"My English is better. Why give up an advantage?"

"Is that why you're here?" Strekov asked. "To find the advantage? To use it if you can?"

"I sell oil," Plummer said. "That's my advantage, too. The East Germans need oil."

"Just to sell oil," Strekov said. "You've been in East Germany before, haven't you?" He still spoke in German.

"A few years ago. Not long after the war."

"When would that have been?"

"Forty-eight or forty-nine. Over ten years ago."

"So you've been in Europe a long time."

"Long enough."

"Selling lubricants?" Strekov asked. "Selling oil, as you call it?"

"Other things too. Engineering equipment, tool and die machines."

Strekov seemed to smile. "Other things, yes," he nodded, looking across the room. "Perhaps we can talk about it some time." He moved to go, but turned back. "At what hotel are you staying?"

Plummer told him. Strekov nodded, as if he'd forgotten. He moved away through the crowd. At the front of the room some of the East German and Soviet officials were leaving.

Kohler and Plummer drove back to Rostock in the twilight. The streets were quiet and a cold fog had crept up from the river. The streetlamps gleamed through the mist. They passed a small bus on a side street near the hotel. Plummer leaned forward to read the dim panel of light above the windshield. "It's not a military bus," Kohler said dryly. The bus was taking workers to an East German fishing vessel that would sail before midnight for the Atlantic fishing grounds. Kohler continued to watch Plummer's face, still amused at himself. Plummer didn't reply.

He was chilled to the bone. He took a hot bath and sat in the tub for a long time, letting the hot water bring the life back to his bones. He dressed and went down to the lobby. The East German delegates to the SED District Convention were assembling in the foyer, awaiting transportation to an official reception and banquet given by the municipality. Plummer had a whiskey in the bar, which was almost deserted. He read the Rostock paper. At nine o'clock he climbed the stairs to the restaurant on the mezzanine and found a table next to the window. Like the bar, the dining room was nearly empty. He ordered another drink. An old man and a small boy came into the dining room from the kitchen, both carrying armloads of dried wood. They built a pyramid of faggots in the stone fireplace. The wood looked as if it might have been gathered from the sea marsh and dried slowly in the summer sun. After a few minutes the flames began to fill the dim room with their orange light, with the smell of pine, of tar and resin. Plummer was finishing his drink when two men came into the restaurant from the lobby. One took a table at the end of the room. The second crossed to Plummer's table at the window. "I thought you might be here," he said in German. Lifting his head, Plummer recognized the same man he'd seen at the reception that afternoon. "Do you mind if I sit down?"

"Be my guest," said Plummer in English. "I was just looking at the menu."

"Try the fish," Strekov said. "The fish is very good." He beckoned to the waitress and ordered a drink for himself. Plummer ordered the fish. Strekov was wearing a dark-blue suit and a dark tie with white polka dots. His pale hair was damp and neatly combed. For a moment it seemed to Plummer that he might be anyone—a West German banker, a Swedish diplomat, or an Austrian lawyer. There were few frontiers in Europe which could give assurance against that kind of anonymity. His English had been learned in practice, not by rote, and it gave him a self-assurance few Germans had. He offered Plummer a cigarette from a thin silver case. "So you came here to sell oil and nothing else," Strekov said.

"That's all," Plummer said. "What do your people tell you?"

"People?"

"State security. *Ministerium für Staatssichereit.* Isn't that what you told me?"

Strekov sat back in his chair. "Where *did* you learn German?" he asked.

"Here and there."

"It's good," Strekov said. "Your German is very good. You come directly to the point. Very direct. Not at all academic. As functional as a canal. Carrying business, that's all. Just business. Never flooding its banks, never rising too high, never picking up stray chickens and cats on the way. Straight to the port. The language of a practical man." Strekov smiled and his face suddenly lost its blankness.

Plummer said, "Maybe I've just got a small vocabulary."

"Maybe," Strekov replied. When he spoke again, he spoke in German: "You've been a long time in Europe."

"You said that this afternoon."

"So I did. But that only means I've been thinking about it, doesn't it?"

"Maybe. Who do you work for in state security? Which division? Recruitment?"

"The European sections."

"Following businessmen from the West. English. American." Plummer looked around the room indifferently.

"There are few American businessmen in the GDR," Strekov reminded him.

"You scared them off."

"But not you, is that it?"

"Give me a few weeks more."

"A few weeks, yes. What will a few more weeks give you?"

"Maybe a lubricant agreement with the German Democratic Republic," Plummer said. "Maybe not."

"Commerce again," Strekov said. "Is that what has kept you in Europe all of this time? Just commerce, nothing more?"

"Something like that," Plummer said. The waitress brought his plate. The fish looked undercooked. "Where do you work?" Plummer asked as he tasted the wine she poured for him. It was as flat as old cider. "Rostock or Berlin?"

"It doesn't matter," Strekov replied. "In Berlin they believe you came for other reasons."

"What reasons?"

"To create problems."

"East Germany has enough problems," Plummer said. "Why would I want to create more?" He sliced a morsel of fish from the bone. "Where did this fish come from?"

"It's from the Baltic," Strekov said, watching him. "You've been on the Baltic, haven't you?"

"No."

"The Rhine?" Strekov asked. "The Danube?"

"Vienna?" Plummer tasted the fish. "Not recently. You said problems. What problems?"

"Political problems."

"I came here to sell oil. If the GDR doesn't need oil, they can tell me that—invite me out. I couldn't care less."

"Selling oil, yes. But what does that create except problems—political problems. Dissension among allies."

"You'll have to drive that one by me again," Plummer said in English.

Strekov's face was blank. "I don't understand," Plummer explained in German.

"Dissension among socialist allies," Strekov said.

"You mean the Russians won't like it?"

"I mean it compromises socialist solidarity."

"I know what you mean," Plummer said, interrupting Strekov. "Socialist solidarity. Is that what your internal security people believe? That sounds like the sort of rubber bone you throw your security cops before you lock them up for the night. What is socialist solidarity if it doesn't give you what you need?" He took another bite of the fish. "I didn't come here for that."

"What did you come here for?"

Plummer pushed his plate away. "To find out what you do with the potato peels the Russians send you. Now I know. To make the formaldehyde that embalmed this fish."

Strekov said, "What the state security services believe is very simple. They believe that you're here to undermine East Germany's relations with the Soviet Union. Trade with the West has that effect. It could erode socialist solidarity. It could poison German-Soviet relations."

Plummer lit a cigarette. "You've been to the Soviet Union, have you?"

"That's beside the point."

"If you haven't been there, maybe you know others who have. Maybe someone from the Planning Commission, like Kohler. Someone from the Ministry of Trade—a delegation to Moscow, buying up Soviet plants for East Germany. On the cheap." He refilled his wine glass. "Tool and die mills for Karl-Marx-Stadt, drill presses for Cottbus, cement kilns, drop forges, diesel locomotives. You've seen that happen, have you?" Strekov didn't answer. The wind blew against the window. The bluish-gray lights from Rostock glimmered in the distance. "What have the Russians given you?" Plummer asked. "What's this socialist solidarity worth, anyway?"

"It's worth much more than cement kilns," Strekov said.

"What have they given you? What have you gotten out of it? Nothing. Not a kopeck, not a cog-tooth, not a mustard seed. Nothing." Plummer laughed. Strekov was annoyed.

"I asked you to speak German."

"All right. German, then. What are you worried about? Me selling oil to East Germany? A few thousand tons of custom lubricants? Christ! The Russians have bled your country white. They've tied you to the barn, raped you in your grave, and then dug you up every spring to let you carry their maypole while they celebrate your liberation, and you're worried about me selling oil? They've pumped your life out by the billions—eighteen billion in sixteen years—and left you with this miserable, flyblown little country in death heaves, and you've got the nerve to sit there and tell me I'm trying to poison your relations with Moscow? What relations? The one between the knife and the carcass, the block and the cleaver? If we're going to talk, let's make it sensible. Otherwise I don't have anything to say." Plummer folded his napkin carefully and put it next to the wine glass. His glass was empty. "Sorry, but that's it."

"Such talk isn't likely to be appreciated," Strekov said quietly. "Either here or in the Planning Commission. Or anyplace else in East Germany."

"Then why don't we forget it."

Plummer got to his feet. He wasn't sure that this man who called himself Wulf would forget it. His face puzzled him. There was a quality to it that repelled him, and now, as they left each other outside the restaurant, he identified it again. It was a face that seemed to deny the human element, that expressed a sort of isolation that in banishing doubt or uncertainty, banished everything else as well. It was a look assumed by most searchers after truth or absolutes, the vacuum that infinity leaves behind when it terrorizes the temporal world. Some priests had it; so did most anarchists; so did men left too long at sea in open boats. Plummer didn't know how to account for it, but it troubled him as he climbed the stairs to his dark hotel room. He didn't think Wulf was the kind of man who would easily forget.

Plummer left Rostock for East Berlin on the one o'clock train. Fifty miles south the rain vanished but the weather was colder. When a crack of sunshine broke through the clouds and bathed the wintry countryside, Kohler brought out a bottle of plum brandy and they had a drink. Afterwards Kohler lay sprawled on a seat nearby, reading a copy of *Ostsee-Zeitung* from Rostock. When the train stopped at Neubrandenburg, Plummer climbed from the coach and walked down the platform towards the station. Kohler followed him on his short legs. The clouds were beginning to clear; patches of blue sky were visible. A team of uniformed East German workmen with long-handled brooms and mops splashed cold water across the soot-streaked windows of the coaches. At the foot of the steps of a private car further along the track, a few Russians stood smoking and talking.

"Who are your friends?" Plummer said as they passed down the tracks. "How come they rate their own private coach?" Kohler didn't answer. He was more concerned with avoiding the flying spray and the standing puddles left by the wash crews.

When they were out of hearing of the Russians, Kohler looked back at the coaches. "Why must they do it in full daylight. Don't they know there are visitors inside?" One of the wash crews was soaping a window of the Russian-occupied coach. "I'm ashamed of our railroads," he sighed after a moment. "Men are flying about in space. Soon they will sputnik themselves to the moon, while we Germans are still traveling in this nineteenth-century abomination."

Plummer agreed. "The Russians did this to your railroads when they dismantled them," he said. "Like everything else in this country. They've dragged your carcass halfway to Asia to mulch their own putrid heavy industry, and you let them do it."

Kohler stopped. "That's unacceptable," he said coolly. "It's one thing for the party to practice self-criticism. It's quite another for a stranger to do so. Why do you insist on such provocations? Do you think they go unnoticed? Do you think they go unreported? Are you trying to provoke me? Are you?"

Plummer was too hungry to argue. "Why don't you try provoking your ass on down the tracks a little," he said in English. "See if we can't get a sausage or two before the whole thing takes off again." He looked back at Kohler. "C'mon," he called. "Don't make a federal case of it."

They found a sausage seller near the station. As they walked back to the coach, Kohler said, "You are too careless with what you say. You must be more discreet."

When the train reached Berlin, Kohler was asleep on the seat. Plummer sat looking out the window, where he had been sitting for over two hours. The clouds had returned. High overhead in the late afternoon sun the vapor trails from a pair of Russian MiG-21's scrolled the dying sunlight like a pair of silken filaments as they patrolled the air corridors into the city. Then the train was engulfed in angry shadow, brick and stone reverberating with the racket of the wheels as they entered East Berlin.

That same evening Plummer telephoned Elizabeth Davidson from his office in West Berlin. The old German woman who answered the phone told him that she had gone to Geneva for a week or ten days.

The Tuesday night following her return from Geneva, she drove into East Berlin with some diplomat friends to see a performance of *The Magic Flute* at the East German State Opera. Tanks and troop carriers were positioned along Unter den Linden. There were barricades in the Potzdammerplatz. Driving back through the checkpoint with her friends, she was overcome by the lunacy of her predicament. She couldn't reconcile the music that still stirred in her mind with what she saw in the streets around her. Was she the only one who recognized it? Her friends chattered on.

Few of them had predicted the Wall. No one would predict what

would follow. The Wall stood in the cold gray light, as ugly and obscene as any other prison or factory wall, built to keep men in and
everything else out. In the grim winter light it was slashed with rain,
scabbed with a few ulcers of slapdash mortar, and strung with oxi-
dizing twists of barbed wire that made her think of tetanus or lots
strewn with weeds and rusting tin, brickbats and broken bottles—lots
seen wherever men worked hopelessly and then returned home to
dwellings just as wretched. These lots appeared wherever the shabby
abutments of industrial growth and decay hid: below the back stoops
and working-class laundries of Brussels, Dusseldorf, or Merseyside,
behind the jetting steam and cinders of trains clattering through the
backstreet squalor of Milan, Antwerp, or her own London.

The rain concealed everything from her, past as well as future.
Her engagement and her coming marriage gave no relief. She seldom
thought of either, except consciously, like the birthdays or anniver-
saries of distant relatives. He seemed less a fiancé than an old family
friend, and she remembered his existence the way she would that of
an elderly uncle or cousin. There were his children as well—the girl
was twelve; the boy nine. She hadn't yet defined a relationship with
them. The marriage would be a small family affair in the spring, a time
convenient to both careers and the childrens' holidays. She hadn't yet
decided to relinquish her own career. He hadn't pressed her. She suspected his indulgence would prove to be temporary. She didn't think
about it. She knew only that marriage was less a new beginning for her
than the end of something else, something half defined—a promise or
possibility. She was unable to think beyond it. Like the rain, it hid her
life from her.

Friday night she couldn't get the car to start. She had worked all
day and was late to a diplomatic reception. *Oh dear God,* she thought
miserably, her head resting suddenly on the steering wheel. The battery was dead. She was helpless, alone in the cold car in the rainy
courtyard, no boots or umbrella, everyone else gone, the guard already
beginning to lock the front gates. For the first time in two years in
Berlin she yielded to her helplessness—the tanks in the Potsdammer-
platz, the relentless rain, the misty streets, the sterile convenience of
her engagement, and the frightening banality of her life—terrorized

by the mechanical trivia to which she was hostage and which might suddenly go awry: a missed reception, balky ignitions, a dead battery, or a locked gate. She wept silently, her head fallen against the wheel. A gust of raindrops flooded the windshield; the rain hammered the metal roof. The deluge made her angry.

When the rain eased, she slipped from the car and plunged out into the downpour. She went through the pedestrian gate and out into the street. Three blocks away she found a taxi stand. Ten minutes later a taxi came by. She was soaked to the skin.

In her flat she took a hot bath, slipped into an old bathrobe, and dried her hair in front of the fire. She heard the phone ring but refused to answer it. Ten minutes later it rang again. She turned on the wireless. The BBC was playing Sibelius but she heard nothing. In the utter negation of her will she found a certain amount of strength. She would attend no more receptions, drive no more obstinate motorcars, demand nothing of herself except what her own resources could supply. She would tell Jim Buxton in Brussels that she was returning the engagement ring. Looking at the ring and then into the firelight, she heard the music again. It was Sibelius still, moving through her.

The days grew colder. The November wind dried the streets and swept the gutters, piling damp leaves, old newspapers, and lottery tickets in the blank alleys and abandoned U-bahn entrances amputated by the Wall. Ice fractured the ponds of the lake country and the cold drove south. The smell of winter was suddenly in the air again.

One cold morning she attended a small wedding at an old chapel on Rankestrasse. The bride was a young East German girl who had fled to West Berlin the previous winter and had worked in the medical unit at the refugee camp at Marienfelde. The bridegroom was a young German medical student. To Elizabeth both looked terribly young; so did the handful of young German students gathered around her on the hard wooden benches. She was suddenly conscious of her own age—not yet thirty-six—and her isolation in the lonely pew near the rear of the chapel. A few middle-aged Germans finally joined her. A few rays of late morning sunshine fell through the prisms of glass in the ornate gothic windows high to her right. The splintered light left a sourceless finger of pure red, yellow, and blue on the edge of the hard oak bench nearby. For those few minutes in the old chapel Berlin wasn't only tanks and guns, weapons carriers, and the frosty jet contrails high overhead where the sunlight gilded their icy molecules to platinum, but something else too, that you could discover if you looked closely enough among scrolled organ lofts and in the altarwork as well, among the wooden benches and balustrades too, where the sudden morning light discovered in the deeply polished wood all manner of medieval merriment—lyres and acorns, griffins, wood nymphs, and bounding does.

Two days later David Plummer appeared at the front door of her apartment. It was after seven. She had just returned from her office and had taken off her pumps to warm her feet in front of the fire that burned beyond the brass fender. Her scarf was still around her neck. "Maybe your phone's permanently off the hook," Plummer said. "I tried a couple of times. Nothing seemed to work."

"I just came in," she said. "Did you ring me here?"

"Last week a couple of times," he said, still standing in the hall. "I was on my way to a cold dinner someplace. It doesn't make much difference when you're on your own. I was wondering if you had any plans?"

They had a drink in front of the fire and afterward he sat in the kitchen while she made an omelette and a salad. He'd been to Rostock earlier, and had just returned from Cottbus in East Germany. He asked her about her trip to Geneva and they talked about it over dinner.

"It's much too early for winter, isn't it?" she asked him when they returned to the living room. It was after ten o'clock. The wind moaned against the windows; the fire had almost gone out. She put her head back against the couch, looking at the coals in the brazier, listening to the wind. He stood at the edge of the rug. It was late. There was no reason for him to stay. She understood his uncertainty and sat up. "Do sit down. Please," she said.

"You're tired."

"I'm not at all tired, I'm quite contented. Come sit down."

It was after eleven when he retrieved his coat from the hall closet. They hadn't talked about Vienna but it was on Plummer's mind. She'd known as much since they'd sat at the small table in the kitchen during dinner. Now she knew that it was coming, but she didn't want to face it. "It's new, isn't it?" she said as he pulled on the coat.

"What's new?" He was so clumsily honest that she was embarrassed for a moment.

"Your raincoat. Isn't it new?"

He looked down at the stiff folds of the new raglan. "Maybe a little," he said. His old raglan had disappeared from a West German restaurant a week earlier; someone had taken it in place of a frayed overcoat. But it wasn't the coat he was thinking about. "Just one thing," he said finally as they stood at the door. He looked out into the empty hall and then back at her. "Are you okay? Everything all right?"

"You're very inquisitive," she said. "You asked me the same question a month ago."

"Maybe I did."

"I suppose I am," she said. "What about you?"

"Happy? Not much." He watched her expression but it didn't change. "Is anyone these days?"

"Some are, I suppose."

"Guys like Buxton, you mean."

"I think so."

He was still watching her eyes. He nodded finally, and opened the door. He had seen nothing in her face. Then he turned back. "Where are you going to be on Sunday?"

"Here."

"Maybe we could take a drive."

"That would be lovely," she said.

"You look very pleased with yourself, I must say," Peggy Gwenhogg remarked when Elizabeth opened her apartment door. Peggy had returned from a diplomatic lunch and had dropped her husband at the British mission afterwards. She was at loose ends. She pulled off her gloves in the front foyer. Elizabeth had been cleaning brass and copper in the kitchen. "Someone must have called you from Brussels," Peggy said.

"I'm afraid not."

"Something must have happened. I can see it in your face. Are you alone?" Peggy turned suddenly and then peered into the living room.

"Quite alone. It's the weather," Elizabeth said. "It was perfect this morning. I took a walk."

"Only a walk?" She looked at Elizabeth dubiously. "We looked for you at the Duncan's. It was a dreadful dinner. Perfectly atrocious. You must have been prescient."

"I wasn't invited, as a matter of fact."

"Weren't invited? How horrid of Sarah. You were here?"

"An old friend stopped by. We had a lovely evening."

"Who was it?" Elizabeth could smell the wine from the diplomatic lunch.

"David—David Plummer."

"Good Lord," Peggy groaned.

"It was quite pleasant, actually."

"Did he kiss you?"

Elizabeth looked at her in astonishment, half angry, half embarrassed. "Kiss me? Don't be silly."

"He was always mad about you. Or didn't you condescend to notice." Peggy poured a small brandy carelessly at the sideboard and sat down with her glass. "I never cared for him," she continued. "Never. Not for anything he said or did. I simply never cared for him. I'm quite aware that others think him clever. I don't. He's simply a brute. He behaved atrociously in Vienna, disappearing the way he did. I don't understand how anyone could forgive him for that. I once saw him again—long after you left. I think it was at a restaurant. A hotel or restaurant. He was sitting at a table with a group of rowdy Austrians. Two of the women were drunk. I wouldn't have noticed him except for the noise. I had the impression that he thought you were married at the time. I don't recall but I believe he mentioned it."

"Why should he have thought that?"

"I haven't the slightest idea." She emptied her glass and returned to the sideboard. "I'm sure Peter thinks him a rough-and-ready chap. I think he's a rogue. Why on earth is he now in Berlin? You're quite right. I should be wary of him. They say he walks through the Wall like Banquo's ghost. Harry Dunstan told me as much the other evening. As if it didn't exist. You really shouldn't encourage him, pet." She sighed and put the glass stopper back in the brandy bottle and returned to the couch. "Tell me—tell me more about your plans. Is Jim coming here for the holidays or are you going to Brussels?"

The East German Ministry of Trade had provided Plummer with an old warehouse at Treptow in East Berlin. It was a crumbling eighteenth-century building that had survived the blitz, with a brown stucco front, scrolled wooden tracery under the eaves, and a steep tile roof. When the emperor's flag had flown over the portico of the Imperial Palace on Unter den Linden, the building had been occupied by a brewery, but the vats were a hundred years gone—their staves beaten into carriage springs or pickle barrels—when the *Wehrmacht* crossed into Poland in 1939. The building was abandoned until the East German Ministry of Trade reopened it to store the drums of English lubricants brought by canal from Plummer's oil depot in West Berlin.

The warehouse office was on a second-floor balcony reached by a set of narrow wooden stairs from the warehouse below. An iron stove stood on a piece of tin plate inside the door. Nearby was the desk belonging to the Ministry of Trade bookkeeper. The warehouse foreman was an elderly East German named Munch, a sixty-five-year-old ex-*Panzerschütze* who'd crossed into the Ukraine with the German invasion in 1939 and had lost two fingers from his right hand in a grenade explosion. He'd been unemployed for two years when the East German ministry assigned him to the Treptow warehouse. During the first several weeks after Plummer had opened the warehouse and the first shipments of lubricants hadn't yet arrived from the UK, Munch had found work of his own to relieve his boredom. He had rebuilt the old steps to the gallery, scoured the ancient pine floors of the old office, and found a tea kettle and hot plate in a nearby junkshop. He'd added a few wooden chairs to the office furniture, including a small card table at the rear of the office, and concealed it from the bookkeeper's desk by a muslin curtain hanging on a length of carpenter's twine. In the wooden boxes outside the front windows Munch and a few of the older warehousemen kept lager and tinned milk. Geraniums had once bloomed there but until the reoccupation of the warehouse the boxes had been empty, lined with an ancient black dust that might have settled from the incendiary storms of Berlin's last days in 1945, a litter of dry leaves as powdery as old tobacco, and a few dead bugs. Plummer sometimes shared their lager at noontime, when the older men played cards at the small table behind the curtain. The younger men stayed in the warehouse below, and the old *Wehrmacht* veterans, like Munch, encouraged their exclusion. A few were informers, like the bookkeeper.

Plummer was alone in the second-floor office that evening. He'd been working for over two hours on the shipping consignments to be sent out to Cottbus and Karl-Marx-Stadt the following day. He was preparing to leave when he heard the bell ring from the dark warehouse below. The sound surprised him. He thought at first that Munch or the bookkeeper had forgotten something. He lifted his head from his desk but heard nothing. He thought he'd been mistaken. A few minutes later the bell rang a second time. It was an old bronze bell, hanging from a cast-iron arm inside the alley door, rung by a new chain that Munch had scavenged from somewhere and had fitted through the channel above the door so it could be rung from the alley. He didn't move for a moment, but remained seated at his desk. There was no mistake this time. He took a flashlight from his desk and went down the steps and across the dark warehouse. The alley was empty. At the corner a figure passed under the yellow glow of lamplight, climbing away from the canal along the street that intersected the alley. He disappeared in the darkness.

Plummer stood in the dark alley, listening. The air was cold and the night silence brought the sounds of the river nearer—the slap of black water, an engine burrowing through the channel, a truck moving in low gear from a nearby warehouse. He saw no one; he heard nothing nearby. A car droned suddenly out of the mist and its headlights illuminated the drifting shrouds of fog rising from the canal, but the ruby tail moved into view and he knew that the car had turned the other way.

Munch had hung the bell chain too high to be reached by the children in the neighborhood. Plummer bobbed the flashlight against the hanging chain. It was still swaying. He slid the beam along the brick wall and the paving stones below. He saw nothing. He moved forward towards his Opel, parked twenty feet beyond against the rear wall of the warehouse, probing the shadows as he walked, but still he found nothing. When he reached the car, he looked under the chassis, and then tried the door on the driver's side. It was still locked. Looking through the window he saw something on the front seat, under the steering wheel. He thought it was a package at first, but when he lifted the flashlight, he recognized his own missing raglan, taken from a West Berlin restaurant two weeks earlier. It lay neatly folded on the driver's seat, as if the laundry woman had just left it there, still warm from the charcoal iron.

It was after nine o'clock when he reached his flat in Kreuzberg in West Berlin. He locked the door and turned on the lamp in the living room and looked at the raglan. He explored the pockets and the lining but found nothing. Holding it up, he began again. It was only then that he realized what was different about the coat. The buttons had been changed. The original leather buttons were gone. In their place were five cloth-covered metal buttons mounted on the same pins that had held the original buttons. They were cheap buttons, probably East European in origin; the workmanship was shoddy. On the back of one of the buttons a ring of tobacco-colored glue stained the edge of the beige fabric where it had been glued to the flange. But it may have been something more than just shoddy workmanship. He removed one button from the metal cotter pin and scraped at the glue with his penknife. It was still pliable. He scraped some more, holding the button under the lamplight, and saw the glint of a machine-tooled circumference under the fabric. He knew then that the buttons were hollow.

Plummer brought a small toolbox from the back of the kitchen closet. He pried each button free of its metal pin, judged their relative weights, and put aside the two lightest. He took a small screwdriver from his tool kit and pushed the shaft through the metal eye soldered to the back of one button. Holding the front of the button against his palm, he tried to turn the flange. It wouldn't turn. Using a pair of pliers, he gripped the eye more powerfully and tried to rotate it counterclockwise. When he finally broke its purchase, the flange turned easily. There were six full rotations in all. When he lifted the flange, the cavity within was as finely tooled as a Swiss watch. Inside was a packet wrapped in optical tissue. It contained fifteen negative prints taken with a miniature camera. Thirty additional prints were contained in two other buttons. The rest were empty.

He had nothing in the flat with which he could read the prints. He replaced the buttons and wrapped the prints in a square of cigarette foil and put them in his wallet. Then he mixed a drink and turned off the light. He sat in the old armchair, looking out through the dormer windows towards the bluish lights of East Berlin. He made no attempt to guess the contents of the films. The contents didn't interest him. He was more troubled by the theft of his raglan in West Berlin and its reappearance in East Berlin. It was more the design. A cache of films dropped anonymously in his Opel while it was parked on an East German street wouldn't have troubled him at all. He would have thrown the films into the nearest storm sewer without a second thought. But the reappearance of the raglan in East Berlin after its disappearance in the West implied more than a mere seizing of opportunity. Cranks or crackpots might have a single opportunity, whether in the alleyway outside the Treptow warehouse or on the boulevard near the East German Planning Commission on Leipzigerstrasse. Cranks could be written off, but not someone who knew his movements both in East and West Berlin.

It was after eleven when he went to bed. He didn't sleep well. The day dawned bleak and raw, the streets were deserted, and Kreuzberg looked as bleak as Battery Park under a January dawn. He left the apartment and drove to the port area near his depot in West Berlin. Newspapers blew across the cobblestones in front of the Opel. He prowled the quays along the canal listening to the sounds of sluggish engines coughing, to the somnolent slap of dirty water, the morning sounds gliding out of the mist, the catarrhal noises of the day's beginning. He stood in the blowing mist, looking out over the waters of the canal. In midchannel a tug loomed suddenly out of the fog. He could see the silhouettes of the deck crew, aft of the wheel-house, moving the lines and hawsers forward as the tug veered towards the quay.

Reassured, he watched the tug glide forward, white water boiling from beneath the stern. He heard the voices of the crew, watched as the bow slipped lightly alongside the quay without contact, then saw the deckhands spring forward to the dock, no movement lost, and loop the hawsers around the old standing timbers.

He stood for a moment in the mist, the films forgotten, and then turned and went back toward his car.

"I was thinking about nineteen forty-eight," Elizabeth said that evening in the small restaurant near the Grunewald. "When I was living in Montmartre. I had a tiny flat, brutally cold, but marvelous windows. I was just eighteen. Does that seem possible?" With her blond hair drawn behind her ears, without makeup, she looked like a schoolgirl again as Plummer listened.

"Anything's possible," he said.

"Are you quite sure of that?"

"Sometimes." He didn't want to talk. He only wanted to hear her voice.

"You're not sure at all," she said. Her face was partially in shadow but the candlelight was caught in her eyes. They were darker now, not gray-blue at all. Her elbows were on the table, her hands resting along her neck, the tips of her fingers touching her hair. "You're pretending."

"No, I'm not." She didn't answer for a moment, dropping her eyes. "Tell me about Paris," he said.

"I told you once." She smiled. "I was a failure. It was bitterly cold. A beastly winter but I enjoyed it. Still, I was a failure. As a student, a dilettante, even a bohemian. I was something of a prig as well. When I told my father that June that I'd decided to stay on—to study medicine in Paris, that my eight months had taught me absolutely nothing except for that—he fetched me back to England. We had a spitting row. I never went back." She lowered her head towards the candle flame. "Quite sensibly, as I realized later. But at the time I thought my life was over. I could never have studied medicine. I was nineteen at the time. But I never think about that summer without thinking of how very different everything might have been if I'd gone back to Paris that autumn." She turned her head and looked out over the room. "A missed opportunity," she said. "I know how absurd it was at the time. But I shall always think of it that way. Everything might have been different."

"Berlin, too," Plummer said.

"Yes," she said with a smile. "Berlin, too. Isn't it extraordinary how we feel capable of changing everything else as well. At that age, I mean. I suppose it's the promise most of all, isn't it?"

He was watching her throat. Her ivory skin was no dimmer now than it had been five years ago in Vienna. "The promise is some of it," he said awkwardly.

"And innocence the rest of it?"

He didn't know what to say. She had always been better at words than he. When he had left her that cold morning five years ago at the Pullendorf refugee camp outside Vienna, she had slipped a copy of St. Exupéry in his dop kit. He had found it the following evening in Brussels. He'd sat up to one o'clock in the morning in his hotel room, reading it as painstakingly as a college freshman reading his first philosophy text. Whatever the message conveyed in the book, he hadn't recognized it at the time. After the accident and his months of convalescence at Walter Reed in Washington, he had found the book among the possessions retrieved from his smashed luggage. He had read it again. He still had the book with him.

"Maybe some of it," he said finally.

"Where were you at that age?" she asked, watching his eyes. "Did you feel the same way?"

Plummer laughed and shook his head. She insisted, leaning forward into the candlelight. "But you must tell me," she begged, her hands folded in front of her. "Please—you must."

"When I was nineteen, I was a junior in the engineering school at VPI in Blacksburg, Virginia. It was 1941. That autumn I drove a 1931 Model A Ford northward to join the Canadian Air Force in Montreal, rooster-tailing along the back roads, through the orchards and foothills, following the Shenandoah, then north into Pennsylvania and New York. I'd never been there before. In upstate New York I sold the Model A to a dairy farmer looking at secondhand cars in a local Ford lot, and caught the bus into Montreal. The Canadian Air Force recruiting officer told me to come back in three months. I had already sold the car, withdrawn from the university, and mailed a letter to my father—a doctor in Virginia—telling him my decision. So I enlisted in the Canadian Army instead. Three months later I was outward bound from Halifax aboard a Canadian troop transport."

The Atlantic crossing was the longest and most difficult journey he had ever made in his life, but in retrospect he remembered it as little more than an excursion compared to when he had left Elizabeth Davidson that foggy morning at Pullendorf and driven back to Vienna.

"So it might have been different," she said, watching his face. "You might have done something quite different. Did your father want you to study medicine?"

"We didn't talk about it much," he said. "I have an older brother who's a doctor. A surgeon. That sort of turned things around for me. He knew what he wanted from the beginning."

"And you didn't?" She was still leaning forward.

"It was my Model A Ford," he said.

"Was it innocence," she suggested, "or was it romance? I wouldn't have suspected that of you."

Plummer nodded. "A long time ago."

"Lost opportunities?"

Plummer laughed without answering. Looking at her he knew he wouldn't have changed anything.

The night air was cold and bracing. They left the curb near the restaurant and crossed the road to Plummer's Opel. A light mist lay over the windshield. "Are there stars?" she asked, standing in the empty street and staring skyward. Plummer stopped with her, looking into the night sky. A car pulled from the street nearby and drove past the restaurant. Both moved towards the Opel. Neither looked at the passing car. Plummer unlocked the door and opened it for her, then crossed in front of his car to the driver's side. She leaned across the seat and unlocked the door. He slid behind the wheel and started the engine. The windows were misty. He switched on the headlights and then the windshield wipers. When he did, he saw the small oilskin pouch lying on the dashboard beyond the steering wheel. He had never seen it before. He sat looking at the pouch as the engine idled and the windshield wipers ticked across the glass. It hadn't been there when they'd left the car on the street almost two hours earlier.

When he opened the tobacco pouch in his apartment that night, he found a fistful of fresh tobacco and two packages of book matches from an East German hotel. There was nothing hidden in the lining of the pouch or among the crumbs of fresh tobacco. The books of matches were different. The metal staple that fastened the match cover to the pasteboard of matches was loose. With the end of a screwdriver he pried the metal staple from below the striking strip. Concealed within the double pasteboards of one book of matches he found a single negative print, the same size as the prints he had found in the hollow buttons.

He did nothing for two days. On the third night he went to bed after midnight, restless and uneasy, still undecided as to what he would do. He awoke a few hours later and sat upright in bed. He thought that he had heard something at the front door. Looking from his bed into the small hallway, he saw the glow of the living-room lamp against the floor. The living-room lamp was lit. Not moving, he lay thrust forward on his elbows, looking into the hall and knowing as surely as he knew that he had extinguished the light two hours earlier that someone was sitting in the living room, waiting for him. He continued to listen. Finally he rolled from the bed, pulled on his trousers, and silently moved into the hall. He waited in the darkness, still listening, and heard nothing. Moving forward, he looked into the living room. The lamp was lit on the small table next to the old American armchair near the windows. The chair was empty. There was no one in the room. On the arm of the chair were a whiskey glass and ashtray where he had left them over two hours ago. The air still smelled of the stale cigarette smoke. The front door was still locked. He opened it and looked into the front hall, but the hall was empty, the stairwell silent. He locked the door and went back into the living room and turned off the table lamp. Standing in the darkness again, he looked about silently as his eyes readjusted to the darkness. He crossed to the window and looked down into the empty street. He searched the sidewalk, the parked cars, and the dark doorways. Nothing moved. Looking into the street from the high window above, he remembered other nights like this, other streets, and other cities. He knew that whatever had happened that night, whether it was his own imagination or something else, his privacy was quietly being taken from him. He didn't know who was responsible, but he knew it was happening. It was as if his own past was returning, and someone in the darkness below was waiting for him to remember it. He didn't know why anyone should want him to remember a past he had tried to put behind him, but he guessed that it would be used against him. Already Berlin had begun to change. It had changed a lot since four o'clock that afternoon when he came through the Wall from Treptow. It was like Prague and Vienna now. He remembered how gradually the change had come as privacy was denied, a sort of lurking uneasiness at first which grew more constant as pressure was increased, surveillance stepped up, and harassment begun. One was isolated, as he had been isolated in Prague, but never alone. The uneasiness gave way to fear and finally terror when the invasion was complete. It was the sort of fear that comes to the brain of the hare as he realizes that the darkness into which he has escaped within his burrow is suddenly as close as his own breath and growing smaller. Neither darkness nor anonymity would protect him in Berlin.

Plummer had the films with him the following morning when he left his flat. Early in the afternoon he drove to the library at West Berlin University. In the card catalogue he located an American scientific periodical whose back copies were printed on microfilm. The librarian showed him to a small carrel behind the stairway, turned on the filmstrip machine, and left the film strips on the desk. After she shut the door, Plummer brought his own microfilms from the envelope in his pocket, mounted them between two plastic sheets, and studied each in the film reader. The lens didn't give Plummer the magnification he would have preferred, but the resolution was good enough to supply a few tentative answers. With eighteen of the films resolution didn't matter. Plummer wouldn't have known what they described even if he'd had the original documents. They looked like prints from a crystallography text, a schematic of Fourier molecule projections, positioning the atoms. The legends and symbols meant nothing to him, being far too complex for his own engineering background. He guessed that a few of the other films described Soviet weapons deliveries to Russian and East German units near Zossen, Oranienburg, and Bernau. The typewritten text was in German. A few frames in the series were incomprehensible. The final film baffled him for a few minutes. It was the film he'd retrieved from the tobacco pouch the night before. At the top of the film was a title cut from the page of a Berlin guidebook. Below it was the description of three locations in East Berlin, also scissored from the pages of a guidebook. Accompanying the description were more precise instructions for locating specific physical objects at those locations: a park bench, lamppost, doorway, and mailbox. Listed also was a sequence of dates. It was the description of deaddrops in East Berlin to be used over the coming two-month period.

Plummer slid the other films into the envelope and put it in his coat pocket. The list of deaddrops he returned to his wallet. He assumed that both films had been supplied from the same source, but he wasn't convinced this was so. For the moment caution persuaded him to deal with them separately.

It was late. He drove to Charlottenburg and left his car near the stone fountain in the old courtyard. Below a wrought-iron balcony on the second floor of the old stone building, a pair of weathered stone griffins held between them a stone escutcheon. From the flagstaff the pastiche banner of the international refugee organization hung like a frozen tea towel.

"I have to go to London," Plummer told Elizabeth in her corner office. She was puzzled, standing inside the door.

"When—today?"

"I'm on my way to the airport." She was still puzzled. Plummer felt foolish. He hadn't wanted her to misunderstand, to think he would go away abruptly without telling her. They were to have dinner together the following evening. Now he had provoked her suspicions, recalled old memories of Vienna. What had he been trying to do these last weeks except put those memories to rest? "I thought maybe I could bring you something from London," he added.

"That's sweet of you. Would you like some tea?"

He had two hours before his plane left. "If you've got time," he said.

"Of course." She took his raglan, stood holding it for a moment, mystified. "But you found it," she said with a small cry, smiling with delight. "You didn't lose it at all."

FIVE

Phil Chambers was in his late fifties, short and overweight, with a jowlish face, sad brown eyes, and a rumpled demeanor some mistook for insouciance. They were mistaken. He had a single object in life, a single passion, and in its pursuit he was as calculating as a Jesuit priest. He was an American intelligence officer and a specialist in Soviet affairs. He had spent most of the postwar years in Eastern Europe or along its periphery; and now, nearing retirement, with a chronic heart condition, he sometimes pondered the cost of his commitment—what its ultimate consequences might be, what he had gained or lost, whether there might not be among his years a generation that would one day betray the emaciation, like the malformed rings from the years the tree had grown under blight that would sputter queerly in the burning.

He passed the afternoon at the Foreign Office in London, closeted in a shabby little third room with an elderly British diplomat who was being debriefed following his retirement in Budapest. The room was musty and dimly lit. On an old bookcase near the window was a pot of anemic-looking plant life. Chambers couldn't understand how it had survived. If it was as old as it looked, there was something sinister about its metabolism or root structure. Apart from the plant, the room had the proper Foreign Office smell—monkish, decaying, redolent with shabby respectability and down-at-the-heel gentility, like the banistered offices of an old New England textile mill that had lost its markets. The diplomat they were listening to was a shell of a man, all dust and ashes, decayed from within, like so many other diplomats Chambers remembered who'd never received a post of their own. He knew very little about the Soviet Union or Rumania.

Like most diplomats he attached exaggerated importance to the flotsam of knowledge he had acquired. Now he had digressed and was describing Rumanian wine-pressing hydraulics. Chambers listened, looking again at the purplish-green plant whose thin, waxen leaves spilled down over the bookcase and dipped perilously close to the teapot which stood on the water-ringed table. Could one suppose it fed on tea leaves and tannic acid in the light of the moon?

The British intelligence officer from SIS finally brought the briefing to a close. Chambers stood up and pocketed his small notebook. "Quite an odd-looking plant," the Brit said when the diplomat whose office they had been using began tidying up the chairs. "I don't think I've ever seen one like it."

"Sumatra," the young Englishman replied, moving a chair back to the wall. "I believe it's Sumatra. Sumatra or Ceylon. Alan Compton-Bofers owns it. God knows I wish he'd come claim it. Consumes insects, I'm told."

"You're not serious?" the British intelligence officer said.

The name seemed to bring the retiring diplomat alive. "Where is Compton these days?" he asked, lighting his pipe. "Not on the Baltic still, is he?" He stood wagging the match, standing in the middle of the floor. Chambers looked at him silently—at the gray skin, the long graying hair, and the rabbity teeth clamped on the pipestem. Still on the Baltic? The man was a fool. Was Beria still in the Kremlin?

"In London," the younger man said.

"What about Hugh Perse?"

"He's here too, I believe," the intelligence officer said. He turned to Chambers. "I'll take you down."

They descended in the clattering iron lift. Chambers stared at his shoes thoughtfully. Then he watched the floors slide by. "Waste of time," the Brit said when they reached the main floor. "I'll know better next time. Sorry."

"It doesn't matter. I didn't realize Compton-Bofers ever had an East European desk," he said as they went through the lobby. "Was that his old office?"

"I think so. I think he had it for a year."

"Forty-nine or fifty?" Chambers raised his head.

"I can't be certain. After the war. Do you have a car?"

"It's outside. Thanks again."

In 1949 Alan Compton-Bofers had thrown a drink in Roger Cornelius's face at the Savoy, Chambers remembered, searching the street for his car. Chambers had been at Roger's elbow when it happened, brought back from Vienna to London for the annual chief-of-station meeting. Until that evening at the Savoy, Phil Chambers had never laid eyes on Compton-Bofers, although he'd heard his name. Roger Cornelius was an old friend, first at Harvard, later in the OSS, now in the Agency. At the time of the incident Cornelius was running an operation out of West Germany targeted against the Soviet Union. He was training Ukrainians, Moldavians, Estonians, and Letts recruited out of the displaced-persons camps. They were trained at Bad Wiessee and Kaufbeuren in Bavaria, equipped with PH-4 and PH-6 radios, and then dropped by night along the Latvian coast, in the Moldavian forests near Naliboki or in the Carpathians near Lvov. It was an American operation. Cornelius had been dropped into Yugoslavia with the OSS during the war. He'd expected the postwar sweepings from the cellars and cattle sheds of Europe to be as successful but they weren't. They lost everyone they sent in. Cornelius had almost resigned after that failure. He knew that Roger had blamed the Brits. He wasn't sure that was justified.

But he'd never liked Compton-Bofers since that incident. He considered him a bully, hot tempered and unreliable. Washington felt the same way. The Agency had denied him direct access to CIA intelligence reports for over ten years. As the CIA liaison officer with British intelligence in London, Chambers had maintained the embargo, even though he recognized that others in SIS were sharing access to their own materials with Compton-Bofers.

It didn't matter. The principle did, and it was the principle Chambers was protecting—the principle of a common decency, a common commitment, a common code. Those who violated it, like Compton-Bofers, they would continue to isolate. Those who violated it in more murderous ways, like the man who had betrayed the Bad Wiessee operation, they would destroy, as ruthlessly as the Russians had slaughtered the Moldavians, Letts, and Ukrainians hanging in harness in the forests of Naliboki after their night drops out of Frankfurt. But to destroy him, they had to find him. It had been ten years now. They were still searching.

In his office at the embassy on Grosvenor Square, Chambers took off his wet raincoat and stood behind his desk, looking at the telephone messages. One was from his wife. He put the call through himself as his secretary brought him a file of outgoing telegrams awaiting his signature. He spoke to his wife briefly and then got to his feet and took his raincoat from his rack. His secretary stood looking at him. With a sigh he returned to the desk and sat down and read through the cables. As he read, she brought the medicine bottle from her drawer, dropped a few teaspoons in half a glass of water, and left it at his elbow. He drank it mechanically and then put it aside. When he finished signing the telegrams, he pulled on his raincoat and left the office. "No calls," he said as he went by her desk. "I'll be at home but no calls. Tell the duty officer that."

It was after six when Chambers arrived at the red-brick house in Kensington. A visitor was waiting in the book-lined study, his wet raglan lying across the chair inside the door. A coal fire was burning on the hearth and Eva Chambers was sitting in her chair next to the fire, an old photograph album across her knees. Her hair was almost white. Her face was finely boned, with dark eyebrows.

For a moment Chambers didn't recognize him. His face was half hidden in the shadows, but when he stepped out from behind Eva Chambers's chair, Phil Chambers laughed and extended his hand. "David," he said. "My God, David. When I called Eva I couldn't believe it."

"He hasn't changed," Eva said, looking up at Plummer from her chair. She was smiling. She had been showing Plummer old pictures from Prague and Vienna. Both of her two daughters were married now. A wedding picture was on the mantel.

"Who wants to change?" Plummer said.

"We didn't know you were still in Europe," Eva said. "He came in today from Berlin," she told her husband, rising to go. "I'll leave you two."

The two men had a drink in the study. "I'd heard you were in Berlin," Chambers said quietly. "We had a tracer a while ago from Dahlem. Someone wanted to know who you were."

"Templeman," Plummer said. "I met him once in Paris years back. I don't think he remembered."

"He didn't. He asked Washington to look you up for them. He asked us, too. What happened?"

"He spotted me one night at the Checkpoint and wanted to know how I came through. Everything else was closed down. I told him to bark off. He was a little pissed."

"I don't blame him," Chambers said evenly. "Selling oil to the East Germans. I wouldn't have expected it. What's your formula—oil today, computers tomorrow?" He put his drink aside and moved the firescreen forward to poke at the cinders. "Is that what they built the Wall for, to let people like you in? What you're doing doesn't make any sense. The East Germans are using you. They don't want a lubricant agreement with the British. They just want to cover some short-term oil shortages that they got caught with because of poor planning. When the shortages are covered, they'll throw you out." He sat back in his chair. Plummer didn't attempt to reply. Chambers said, "Until I saw the tracer, I thought you'd gone back to the US."

"Doing what?"

Chambers thought about it. "A number of things. You've got an engineering degree still—"

"It's obsolete."

"We're all getting obsolete. Talent is never obsolete. Neither is self-pity." He looked towards Plummer, who didn't reply. When Chambers spoke again, his voice was milder: and Plummer knew that he was trying to apologize. "There are other things you might do. You have experience few people have. You've known things few people have known." Chambers's hair was nearly white in the firelight. His face was tired, almost drawn. "You could share that experience. You could teach others."

"Which others? Rand or Brookings?" he replied. "One of those think tanks where you sit on eggs all day for the Agency or DOD?" Plummer laughed and got to his feet. He refilled his glass. "Then write a book? My books don't write."

"None of our books write," Chambers said, lifting his head to look at Plummer. "How did you get mixed up with this BIL organization? The British oil company?"

"They needed an engineer—bilingual, German and English. Someone who could read a blueprint and disassemble a lathe."

"It's nonsense. Washington didn't like it. Roger Cornelius was disturbed. He called me up the date the tracer came in and wanted to know what I knew about it."

It had been almost five years since Plummer had resigned. He had almost forgotten Roger Cornelius's name. "I thought Roger would have retired by now," Plummer said. "You, too."

Chambers turned back to the fire. After a moment he nodded. "I've thought about it," he said. A gust of wind brought rain against the window. He didn't move his head. "I suppose I'm too frightened to. After twenty years, thirty years, that's the price you've paid. Who are we going to leave things to—the Brits? The French? If you don't do it, who will? That's what you keep asking yourself. Halfwits like Peter Templeman in Berlin? I don't suppose you can lead the sort of life we've led and not become frightened by it. I saw a friend of mine last summer in Maine. He's retired now. He won't do anything—won't fly, won't drive on the freeways, won't even take the subway. He sails his boat. That's all. He knows too well how our society works—how shallow are its pretensions of competence. Something may go wrong. We trust our lives to illiterate radar mechanics, to bored enlisted men on the Dew Line, to leaky gas lines under the pavement, to irresponsible juveniles in overpowered cars on the freeways our taxes pay for, to Congressional Know-Nothings who run for reelection every two years. That's what he told me. It came as something of a surprise. I haven't lived in the United States for over a decade. But I know what he meant—that he was the final victim of his own professional pride, that aside from himself, nothing is safe anymore. Certainly I'd like to retire. So would Eva. I'd like to get away from diplomacy and fools, from neurotics and paper mills, boors at dinner parties who know what Khruschev is up to, to professional America-haters at British receptions, to the murderers and liars who masquerade as world socialists, to the ugly little minds that live in East Berlin or Budapest and who teach their victims that anyone with more money in their pockets than their bankrupt economies can provide is an Enemy of the People, that any nation which has achieved more military power than Moscow is by definition fascist."

Chambers lifted the drink to his lips. Afterwards he sat back in his chair and stared. He said, "You're helping them. Those are the people you're helping. In helping them, you're helping Moscow as well." There was no anger in his voice, just the pleadings of advancing middle age. "I'm sorry, David. I didn't mean to begin like this. But I wanted you to know how I felt. I don't think you came to London to hear that."

Plummer took the envelope of films from his pocket and gave them to him. Chambers slipped on his glasses, studied the contents of the envelope, and sat back. "Where did you get this?"

Plummer told him he'd gotten them in Berlin. He was vague about details. He didn't know their source. "Probably a paper mill," Chambers muttered, putting the envelope in his coat pocket. Berlin was notorious for its intelligence fabricators, for the printing and filming of impressive-looking technical apocrypha, ingeniously faked. Chambers said he would look at them. It might take ten days or two weeks. "Did he ask for money?" Chambers wondered.

Plummer said he hadn't.

"Entrapment, then," Chambers concluded. Plummer's face told him nothing. "You're not worried about entrapment?"

"I'd thought about it," Plummer said.

"Are there more to come?"

Plummer didn't answer. The microfilm listing the East Berlin deaddrops was still in his pocket. "I doubt it."

Chambers said, "Probably a paper mill, then. Are you staying for dinner? Maybe Eva will consent to one more drink." Chambers got to his feet and was already lifting the top of the ice bucket.

Plummer said he had to go. He was booked on an early-morning plane from Heathrow to West Berlin. When he left Chambers's house he was troubled and angry. He had allowed himself to be lectured like a schoolboy. He despised the bureaucracy, whatever his respect for Phil Chambers, and knew that once a man had brought his personal affairs to official attention, he had set in motion a train of events whose results were usually painful, always inexorable, and frequently disastrous. Even if he managed to outwit the iron law of the bureaucracy, he could seldom escape humiliation. Yet he had just surrendered to official curiosity packets of microfilm which common sense told him he should have burned in the iron grate of his flat in Kreuzberg or thrown into the Spree.

The rain had stopped and a dim yellow fog drifted through the streets. He walked for blocks through the cold mist before he remembered he should be looking for a taxi. He felt stupid and thick witted, like a drunk hauled into domestic court before the eyes of his children and neighbors. His face burned from the two whiskeys he had drunk with Phil Chambers. He had declined the dinner invitation but had no place else to go. What was he running from if not their curiosity? He let two taxis splash rainwater over his trousers before he moved to the center of the road and hauled down a third.

His hotel was on the fringes of Chelsea. It was an old residential hotel with white tile floors in the lobby, like a Turkish bath, a refrigerator case with soft drinks and ale and a derelict iron-caged lift that rattled and wheezed its way to the third floor. His room was unheated and stank with the cold. In front of the double windows looking down into the street was a black horsehide sofa. On the rain-mottled walls between the windows was a faded green engraving of St. Paul's. Stuck between the frame and the wall was a rattan carpet flogger.

"Bleddy cold in here," the Pakistani bellboy said when he brought up the pitcher of ice. He moved the towel to his arm and watched Plummer prying the cork from a bottle of whiskey. "You'd enjoy her, sir. A nice piece."

He was the same bellboy who had brought Plummer up in the lift that afternoon, when he'd offered him the prostitute's service for the first time. "What's she look like?" Plummer asked.

"A lovely piece," the bellboy said. Plummer looked at the thin, dark face, the carefully arranged mop of violet-black hair, and the soiled waistcoat that was six inches short in the sleeves. It was dirtier than the towel.

"How old is she?"

The Pakistani was less sure about that, but he had a tradesman's quickness. "Your age, sir."

Plummer poured out two fingers and recapped the bottle. "How old is that?"

The Pakistani hesitated. "Twenty-four," he guessed.

Plummer opened the door. "Beat it," he said. "Go peddle your rugs."

In Italy, Plummer's armored recce unit had been bushwhacked by the First German SS Panzers as it crossed a rain-swollen river. Plummer had been the only survivor. Working his way by night back towards his own lines, he'd been captured by a First SS Panzer patrol. It had happened three days following his twentieth birthday.

The First SS Panzer *Oberleutnant* at the road junction behind the German lines had kept Plummer segregated from the other Allied prisoners. He was taken further north and kept manacled in a rock quarry with six other prisoners from the First Canadians. On the tenth day they put all seven prisoners in the back of a truck, still manacled, and moved them northward. The following night the convoy was joined by more trucks bringing prisoners from the Anzio beachhead. At dawn the American Rangers from the First and Third Ranger Battalions ambushed at Anzio were segregated from the regular infantry prisoners. The Rangers were manacled, like the prisoners from the Canadian First, and put aboard trucks in Plummer's convoy; the other Allied prisoners were taken to the rail junction and loaded on a prisoner-of-war train. Two nights later the convoy arrived at a small camp in the Alban Hills below Rome. In the caves were other English and American prisoners from the more elite or specialized units to the south. Some had just arrived; others had been there for weeks.

Plummer was kept in one of the caves for twenty-six days. Accordion wire was strung across the mouths of the caves and, beyond the wire, guards from the Third German Panzer Grenadiers sat behind .30 caliber machine guns in their sandbagged emplacements at the edge of the escarpment. The prisoners were given a single ration once a day, moldy biscuit and rice. There was no tea or coffee; no water for shaving. Once a day an Italian unit in the village below brought up two mules with jerry cans of water. Each prisoner was allowed to fill his cup once; if he had no cup, he used his tin plate or his hands. A few Brits from the British VI Corps were commandos who had been at Dieppe. They thought they were going to be shot. They joked about it with the Italians across the barbed wire when they brought up the mules. The Italians said nothing because of the Germans at their back, but from their eyes they could tell that the Italians believed it, too.

The caves were filthy. They were lice- and rat-ridden; there was no sanitation, no sunlight. "Nothing but smoke and shit," a Canadian from Saskatoon complained every morning when he crept out of his pallet. One of the Canadians remembered that a company of Germans from the First SS Panzers had been massacred on the banks of the Po after they'd been taken prisoner by a battalion of Poles. He thought the Third German Grenadiers would make retribution.

On the twenty-seventh night the Germans brought up mobile searchlights which played over the entrances of the caves from the road below. The prisoners were routed out of the caves one at a time. The Germans took away their shoes and marched them, as blind as bats, down the trail in the glare of the searchlights. Trucks were waiting below. They were moved again to the north that night, past the bombed-out villages, the olive groves, and the unplowed fields, bone-white in the moonlight; and at dawn the trucks rattled into the suburbs of Rome itself. In the chill dawn darkness they were assembled near the trucks, their shoes were returned, and they were tied together with ropes at the waist. They waited for four hours, bearded, filthy and half starved, still as blind as bats as the sun climbed into the bright Roman sky. High cirrus moved in a thin herringbone overhead; the stone fountains brimmed with crystal water in the white sunlight. At eleven o'clock they began their march, all sixty of them, tied together like wild dogs, led by a regiment of spotless German infantry from the Third Panzer Grenadiers. Ahead of them two German sound trucks summoned the Roman street rabble along the Corso Vittorio Emanuele, from the Tiber to the Piazza Venezia:

Questi soldati sono i vostri liberatori! These are your liberators, people of Rome! These are the Allied elite—the vanguard, the conquerors!

The Italians on the curbs whistled and jeered. Those on the balconies threw down garbage and chamberpots on their filthy yokel heads.

This scum! These maggots and vermin are your liberators! The vanguard!

The crowds along the pavement mauled them from the sidewalk. They spat, threw stones, gouged them with umbrellas and fingernails. Two street urchins knocked down the young English lieutenant and kicked blood from his face before they could lift him to his feet again. The German grenadiers sat in their troop carriers ahead of them, knee to knee, resplendent in olive green, impassive as gargoyles under their beaked helmets.

Six, seven, eight miles of blood, garbage, insanity, and shit, but a cordon of fresh grenadiers protected the trucks where they finally took refuge, lying exhausted against the floorboards, poisoned by carbon monoxide and their own vomit as the trucks rolled north again, canvas drawn. They bivouacked in the late afternoon and sprawled in the grass near an abandoned gristmill, its tiles half gone, water trickling from a spring somewhere under the mosses, the sunlight beginning to fade. The Germans brought their medics up and dressed the wounds. A field kitchen was set up in the olive trees behind the mill. While the German grenadiers brought them hot soup, bread, tea, and chocolate, the German Panzer *Oberst* passed the word that those who wanted to bathe could do so in the small springhouse nearby before the trucks took them to the railhead where they were to be put aboard a northbound troop train. Cigarette rations were distributed. It was over.

The German Panzer *Oberst* stood in the center of the old mill, surrounded by his aides. He was small and doll-like in his olive green whipcords, one polished bootleg lifted to the fallen grist wheel as his eyes searched the shadows under the falcon-beak of visor. Some of the prisoners were already smoking; others were still eating their chocolate. Their faces were bearded, like Plummer's; their hair matted with filth, like his own. A chaff as old as Carthage drifted with the German corpsmen as they squatted on their heels with bottles of alcohol, bandages, swabs, and salt tablets, still tending the wounded. The Panzer *Oberst* stood motionless, looking out through the oblique shafts of sunlight falling through the open roof and the white-dusted olive trees. He took off his hat and wiped the perspiration from his brow. The leather had cut into the white flesh of his forehead. An aide called for a cup of water and he drank it, head lifting slowly. A warm wind moved across the hillside and stirred the green leaves. An airplane droned faintly in the distance, moving in and out of silence.

Plummer stared out across the somnolent Italian hillside, looking at the glossy sky, the sunlight, the steep Roman hills, trying to see what the Panzer *Oberst* had seen. He saw only the pastoral silence, the sun as bright as enamel on the hills, and the white roads. He saw its golden brilliance melted down into ingots, golden threads, Flemish tapestries, and quattrocento paint cans, saw its golden landscapes and its timeless dreams of privilege and power, understood what the *Oberst* understood.

The *Oberst*'s aides saw him sliding weakly through the dust behind the gristmill, a bearded Virginia youth in the tattered khaki-woolens of the First Canadians intent on killing their commander. The *Oberst* saw him, too. His eyes were shiny at first, then puzzled, perhaps even hurt. He stepped away from the gristmill, his gauntleted hand fumbling abstractedly with his black leather pistol case. When Plummer gathered his knees under him, the German corporal was already standing behind him. He flogged him once, twice, then a third time with his rifle butt as the *Oberst* turned away.

In France, Plummer had escaped from the prison train. A French farmer had found him in his fields, still dizzy from his head wound. He had told him that he would fetch a doctor. Instead he told the Germans. After Plummer was recaptured, he was hospitalized for a month and sent to Oflag 4C, Castle Colditz, a prison for British and Canadian officers. In time he'd escaped from Castle Colditz as well. An excellent candidate.

In the autumn of 1947 David Plummer was in Prague, where he represented some half-dozen American machinery firms in Czechoslovakia, Hungary, and Austria. He'd gone back to the US immediately after the war, collected his mechanical-engineering degree, and joined two other ex-GI's in buying up surplus military construction and industrial equipment from military depots, shipyards, and warehouses along the East Coast. When the domestic market for second-hand machinery grew sluggish, Plummer went to Europe. He found a brisk demand for any kind of construction equipment in Western and Central Europe. He made his headquarters in Prague rather than Vienna because Prague intrigued him, its medieval mysteries no less than the prospect of Czech economic recovery. He liked the Czechs and had spent two years as a German prisoner-of-war at Castle Colditz. His dislike of both Germans and Austrians had died hard. A Czech farm family had given him succor for two weeks in a potato cellar after his final escape from Colditz; he had found no help among the Germans.

Phil Chambers was also in Prague. Phil was twenty years older, had a Harvard law degree, two small daughters, and a lovely wife who played the harpsichord and collected baroque musical instruments. They had a comfortable bohemian apartment in the Old City while Chambers was studying for a doctorate in international law at Charles University. Plummer thought them both dilettantes. He had nothing in common with them and disliked their patronizing interest in his welfare, as well as their curiosity about his private life. He was going with a dark-eyed Slovakian girl at the time, a young Marxist named Nadia whom he'd met at the university where he was taking a few courses in economics. She considered herself a revolutionary. She was small and hot tempered, with almond eyes, stiff black hair which she cut herself with a pair of scissors, and a small, button nose. She seldom wore hose, and never lipstick. She was doing her best to convert Plummer, who had never met an intellect as energetic as hers, a voice which could hector him so mercilessly one day and yet apologize so eloquently the next.

At a Christmas party at the Chambers's flat that December, Plummer met for the first time some of the Chambers's friends. Nadia was with him. There were Americans from the embassy, a few diplomats, some liberal professors and journalists, a few priests, and even a handful of Marxist parliamentarians. Plummer and Nadia listened silently as the guests debated the future of Europe, an Austrian peace treaty, the Marshall Plan, and the restoration of Czech polity.

Plummer was skeptical. More accustomed to the smoky industrial suburbs of Prague where he installed die presses and lathes, to the hostility of shop stewards or the communist action committees in the plants, Plummer was less optimistic about Czechoslovakia's future. He thought their hopes unrealistic, their salon talk as ephemeral as the tinsel-strewn cedar boughs in the corner, or the thick Christmas candles melting down on the buffet boards of the Old City apartment.

The Chamberses were aggressive hosts, keeping glasses filled, the canapé trays circulating, turkeys carved, the boards heavy with meat and grog. They seemed to know a little about everything. They quoted Tacitus for the professors, Ronsardian fragments for the musicians, St. Jerome for the tippling priests, Trotsky for the journalists. So it went on amid smoked ham and turkey, clouds of steaming sack, mulled wine, and brandied puddings. There were two phonographs playing simultaneously from opposite ends of the apartment. In the living room they listened to the Agnus Dei from the High Renaissance; in the small study where many of the Americans were gathered someone was playing Jo Stafford and "White Christmas" on a small portable phonograph. Plummer had wandered into the small study long enough to see it wasn't for him. A drunken blond secretary from the embassy was sitting on the floor, sipping a rum-and-coke while she waited to play her Stan Kenton record. Someone asked him how many commies were in the living room. A young American diplomat wearing a tattersall vest gave him his card.

Plummer remembered that evening more than any other that winter because he had known it wouldn't last, that the following Christmas would find them in different countries, different circumstances. It ended in the cold predawn darkness. The last of the guests staggered off, Plummer and Nadia among them, while from the open windows overhead the Chamberses serenaded them with the sounds of the "Nachtwächter":

> Last Ihn Hern und last euch sagn
> der Hammer der hat neyne geschlagen

Walking through the cold streets with Nadia, towards her flat, Plummer was depressed. She hardly spoke. It was now Christmas Day. He had drunk too much and heard too much. Lying next to her in the small, overquilted bed under the dormer, he knew that the talk, the music, and his own infatuation were no more proof against the anarchy gathering in the streets outside than the coruscations of frost on her small window panes were proof against the morning light.

The *putsch* came two months later. Plummer had been right. He stood and watched the communist-armed workers' militia trudge through the cold, breaths steaming in the thin bitter air. He knew that for many in Prague a world had been smashed, not to be repaired again in their lifetime. For him it didn't matter. A man beyond politics, a solitary whom the war had made brutal in some ways, devious in others, he was still contemptuous enough of history and the illusions of permanence or of sacrifice to think that the revolution in Prague would no more affect him than it would the dogs in the Old City or the dray horses that brought winter produce to market there. He knew that the *putsch* wouldn't change how he thought or felt. He was still too embittered by the war to believe that politics or history could ever recover its capacity to alter or transform his life.

The same evening he was on his way again, slipping through the deserted streets of the Old City on his way to Nadia's flat. But at the top of the blue-tiled stairway the door was locked. She didn't answer his knock. A fellow student on the floor below told Plummer that he had marched that day with the students who had intercepted the communists on their way to the parliament. Some of the students were clubbed; others, shot. He hadn't seen Nadia. Some said that she had marched with the communist action committees. Plummer searched for her the following day at the university. No one had seen her. Some of the students he talked to confirmed that she had marched with the communists that day. He searched the hospitals. After the third week her possessions were taken from her flat and returned to her mother in Bratislava. In April, Plummer finally gave up the search.

That June, Plummer took the train to Vienna to look for a new freight forwarder in Austria. He stayed at the same small pension near Mariahilferstrasse where he always stayed. On the evening of the second day someone knocked at his door. In the hall outside stood Phil Chambers. He and his wife had left Prague after the coup four months earlier. He asked Plummer to join him for dinner the following day.

Phil Chambers wasn't the same man Plummer remembered from Prague. He was less voluble, more intense, with a cynicism Plummer hadn't recognized in Prague. There had always been a rumpled carelessness to Chambers—the wrinkled gabardine suits, the pebble-grained calf or cordovan shoes warped by rain or slushy pavements, the oxford-cloth shirts with the odd thread along the collar, or the baggy flannels with their pleats gone. Plummer saw none of this that evening in Vienna.

The Chambers apartment was an expensive one. Plummer wasn't surprised. They stood with drinks at the french doors, looking out into the warm Viennese twilight and watching the old couples return from the parks. The flowers were already in bloom along the neatly graveled paths. Cars drifted through the boulevards with their headlights already on.

They talked at first about the *putsch* the previous February. Chambers said he wasn't surprised at the coup. He claimed that he'd known as early as October that the communists would attempt it. He recalled a conversation the Czech Comintern rep had had with Beria in Berlin the previous autumn. He said Benes had been warned in December and again in January that a coup was being prepared. Plummer listened. The names didn't interest him. He was annoyed that Chambers might believe they would. After a little while Chambers began talking about some of his friends in Prague. He knew who had been jailed, who released, and who shot. Then he mentioned Nadia.

"You knew she was a communist, didn't you?" Chambers asked.

No, Plummer was tempted to say. "We talked about it," he replied instead.

"Have you heard from her?"

"That's not your problem, is it?"

"She's in Moscow," Chambers continued. "On a student exchange program. Probably planned for some time. She led a student cell at the university. What about freshening your drink?" He picked up Plummer's glass.

Plummer didn't know what to say. He remembered her throat and mouth, the long brown skirt she wore, how she would sit on the edge of the bed, the skirt drawn back over her thighs, how carefully she unfastened the buttons at her waist, how he would begin on the bottom buttons of her blouse while she began with the top button, her arms lifted. There were always too many quilts on the bed, too many books on the bedside table. Scattered about the small room were the ceramic ashtrays she had stolen from a few of the more fashionable Prague hotels. Once, at a bookstall in the Old City, she had spent all of her money on a copy of Rilke and had to go without lunch for two days. One gray Sunday evening after a long, sullen afternoon punctuated by bitter arguments, tears, recriminations, and suicidal despair about her future, she had taken him to mass at an old cathedral nearby. Afterwards they had gone to dinner and spent all their money.

This was the Nadia Plummer remembered. He knew that Chambers didn't know her at all. Plummer said little during dinner; he was anxious to leave. He knew that nothing Chambers could say to him would be of any consequence.

But Chambers knew something of Plummer's background as well. He knew that he'd joined the Canadian army at Montreal before he finished college, that he'd fought in Italy with the First Canadian Division before his armored recce unit had been overrun by the First SS Panzers, that he'd been taken prisoner.

"That doesn't interest me very much," Plummer said. They were sitting in the study after dinner. A silver coffee service and a pair of brandy snifters sat on the coffee table in front of them.

"Your career? You had a good record. No one could have done more."

"Forget it," Plummer said. "What are you doing in Vienna? What's this all about?"

Plummer was irritated. Chambers knew it; he had expected it, even if he hadn't fully calculated the depth of the reaction. Italy was not his favorite subject.

"It's a long story," Chambers said with relief. After he'd left the OSS, he'd returned to his New York law practice, but was restless and bored. When the new Central Intelligence Group was established, he went to Washington, where he had helped draft the new national security act. When the interim group became the CIA, Chambers had already chosen his terrain. He was sent to Prague.

The 1948 coup had robbed him of what few intelligence assets he'd acquired in Prague. Now he needed help. He offered Plummer a job with the Agency in Vienna.

Plummer refused. He told Chambers he knew nothing about the CIA, knew nothing about its operations or its goals, and had made a vow after the war never again to associate himself with any military group, government bureaucracy, or anything else which pretended to represent a national purpose. Chambers told him he could be trained in sixty days. Plummer said he couldn't take the time. Chambers said he could be trained in the Bavarian Algau—at Bad Wiessee or some other camp. Again Plummer refused. Chambers asked him to think about it. They could talk about it the next time he was in Vienna.

Prague changed in the months that followed. A new class emerged to take over the management of the Czech economy. Many of them were Russian trained. Plummer's import licenses were delayed or lost when they weren't denied outright. One autumn afternoon the Ministry of Finance refused to approve a foreign-exchange transfer for a shipment of lathes awaiting delivery from Antwerp. It was the fourth denial in as many weeks. Plummer had had enough. He told his office staff that he was closing his Prague office. He flew to East Berlin and offered the lathes to the East German Ministry of Light Industry. The East Germans were interested. They gave him a car and a driver while the Ministry of Light Industry negotiated with the Ministry of Planning.

Standing in the ruins of East Berlin one day and looking across fields of rubble, of brick dust, and collapsed factory walls where Soviet railroad cranes were still lifting from the wreckage whatever machinery could be salvaged for the Soviet factories in Smolensk, Kharkov, or Stalingrad, Plummer knew that Czechoslovakia still had time. He watched a line of gondola cars shunt eastward on the tracks. The East German driver stopped the car on an overpass so he could get a better view. The gondola cars were filled with copper wire, old telephone cable, generators, and dynamos awash in a bilge of rusty water. Following the gondolas were flatcars piled with old scrap iron and rusty reinforcing-rods, much of it torn from the underground bunkers of Berlin during demolition. Boulders of concrete still clung like broken teeth to the old iron. The East German driver told him the train was bound for the Soviet Union. "Reparations," he muttered. Plummer had no words to give it. A Danish journalist staying at the same hotel had seen the same thing. "What is Russia after all," he said to Plummer in the bar that evening. "—*le néant*. The nothingness." Plummer thought of something which devoured its own dead.

The East German Ministry of Finance approved the sale and Plummer was paid in US dollars through a Swiss bank. When he returned to Prague, he withdrew all of his equipment tenders and his foreign-exchange requests. He made plans to leave Prague and open an office in Vienna. Two days later he was summoned to the Ministry of Trade. He met with a vice-minister in an ornate office on the third floor. With the vice-minister was a senior official from the Ministry of Finance and a Soviet advisor from the foreign-exchange section. The Russian was in his late fifties, white eyed behind his pebble-lensed spectacles. On his worsted knee he held a gray-green dossier in which had been assembled all of Plummer's foreign-exchange requests during the previous four months—those disapproved, those missing, those delayed. All had been reexamined and approved.

The vice-minister made a few mistakes with Plummer that evening. He carelessly introduced the Soviet adviser in the foreign-exchange division as a Czech. Plummer knew he was a Russian. He had been told as much by a clerk at the Ministry not long after the Russian's arrival; other clerks had since confirmed it. The presence of the Russian at the meeting told Plummer that he had been the one responsible for the disapprovals of his import licenses and foreign-exchange requests, something he had long suspected. The Czech vice-minister also displayed some greater curiosity about the recent transaction in East Germany than Plummer had expected. He was interested in details. Were the lathes Plummer had sold to the GDR on the embargo list? If so, how had Plummer managed it? Didn't he risk jeopardizing his export licenses in the West—in the US and the UK—by doing business in the GDR?

Within a few minutes it was obvious what the Czechs wanted. Frightened by the prospect of a Western embargo of strategic goods and technology to Czechoslovakia, they were beginning to explore ways in which they might run any such blockade. They believed Plummer might be useful to them. Nothing was made explicit during that first meeting. No mention was made of a possible trade embargo. Plummer was simply encouraged to maintain his office in Prague. His foreign-exchange requests and his import licenses were returned to him.

That night they offered to fund a revolving account through a Swiss bank which Plummer would draw upon in purchasing Western strategic goods and technology. The goods would be transshipped through Austria to Czechoslovakia; Plummer's Vienna office would manage the documentation; and his fees would be drawn down from the Swiss account, avoiding Czech foreign-exchange restrictions.

Plummer wasn't certain the Ministry of Finance would accept the proposal. He was surprised when he was summoned to the Ministry of Trade a week later and informed that the Czech government had agreed to his offer. Plummer returned to Vienna to lease warehouse space and open an office. He hired an accountant, a secretary, and a warehouseman. He also had a meeting with Chambers. Afterward Plummer flew to Zurich, where he spent two days with Roger Cornelius. It was Roger who officially welcomed Plummer aboard.

Plummer gave himself one to two years in Prague—no more. Chambers was more optimistic, expecting an East European Counter-Reformation. Both were wrong. In 1951, when the Czechs abolished all foreign commercial agencies in Prague, Plummer read the handwriting on the wall and prepared to leave. The Korean War was at its height, bloody and indecisive; Cold War tensions had polarized Europe; anti-American sentiment was endemic in the ministerial bureaucracies; and the state trading apparatus had found other suppliers in Europe willing to violate the Western embargo and transship US and Western strategic goods to the Soviet bloc. Soviet and Czech surveillance of Plummer's movements in Prague also increased. His freedom of movement was taken from him. By that time he had built up a small intelligence network in Czechoslovakia, with assets in the Ministries of Interior, Defense, and Foreign Affairs. Prior to 1951 Soviet and Czech surveillance patterns had reflected the vagaries of Czech internal developments—a new team of Soviet advisers with the Czech internal security services, new Czech officers recently returned from their training in Moscow, or internal divisions in the Politburo. After the nationalization of trade the pattern changed. Surveillance was intensified.

Three days after the announcement Plummer was unexpectedly given a six months' extension of the closure order. He hadn't asked for it. The Ministry official told him that the extension had been granted in recognition of his unfulfilled obligations. Other Western commercial agents, also with unfulfilled contracts, weren't given the same reprieve, although some had requested it. In Vienna, Chambers was suspicious. At the time Plummer was working on an operation targeted against a Soviet KGB officer who was a senior adviser to the Czech Ministry of Interior. The Russian had a mistress, a Czech woman whose husband was abroad, attached to a Czech embassy in Western Europe. She was a secretary in the Soviet liaison section of the Ministry of Interior. From Washington, Roger Cornelius had instructed Plummer to try to recruit the woman. Plummer wasn't enthusiastic. He couldn't identify a single reason why the woman might be recruited; but Cornelius, recently returned to Agency headquarters after the disasters of Bad Wiessee and the Lvov and Naliboki drops, was adamant. Plummer had made a preliminary approach to the woman through one of his assets in the Ministry of Interior when the Czechs suddenly banished all commercial agencies. For Chambers the decision provided an excuse to suspend the recruitment of the Czech woman. For Cornelius, however, it was a reason to speed it up. A few days later the Ministry mysteriously gave Plummer a six months' reprieve. The same week his office staff was informed that their work permits were suspended. The staff were replaced with clerks and bookkeepers from the state trading apparatus. All of them had been recruited by the Ministry of Interior.

Chambers thought that the Soviets might have gotten wind of the operation targeted against one of their own officers and were biding their time until Plummer committed himself. Cornelius was convinced that the operation hadn't been compromised, and that the Soviets were trying to intimidate Plummer. The Czech woman was again approached by Plummer's agent in the Ministry. When she reluctantly agreed to another meeting, Plummer's man was encouraged. She suggested that the meeting be held in Ostrava, rather than Prague, and asked that she meet directly with the man who was interested in her cooperation and who had promised to resettle her in Western Europe—in France, Belgium, or the Netherlands—in exchange for her help. Plummer declined to meet with her. Instead he sent his agent, equipped with a Belgian passport with her photograph on the identity page, a passbook from an Antwerp Bank made out in her name with a sizeable bank balance on deposit, together with a photograph of a Czech diplomat and his wife standing on the Champs Elysées in Paris. The Czech diplomat was well known to the Ministry of Interior; he had defected in Paris the previous winter.

The Czech woman was upset when Plummer's agent arrived alone. She grew increasingly nervous as the conversation continued. They were sitting at a table near the door of a small restaurant in Ostrava. She could hardly force herself to look at the documents. Abruptly she decided to leave. In the street outside the two had an argument. She accused Plummer's agent of deceiving her, claimed that she had been followed to Ostrava from Prague, and that the whole affair was a ruse, designed by the Russians to discredit her with her Russian lover. She was almost hysterical. Plummer's agent tried to calm her. A policeman had heard the argument and interceded. The woman claimed that he'd tried to annoy her. Plummer's agent fled and the policeman gave chase. The policeman was joined by a small Czech-built sedan which had been parked up the street from the restaurant. In an alley nearby Plummer's agent resisted arrest. He had a gun; shots were fired; he was wounded in the exchange. He died four hours later on the operating table of an understaffed local hospital. Two Czech security officers and a Soviet liaison officer were waiting outside the operating room, their interrogations incomplete. The Czech woman was arrested the same evening. Two days later she told the Czech and Soviet officials the whole story.

Plummer learned of the agent's death a day later. That week in Prague the prowling Soviet-built Volgas and the Czech Skodas were more conspicuous. He saw them when he got into his car outside his flat in the morning, when he left his office or went to a restaurant in the evening, or stood in line for a cinema or theater ticket. And afterwards, sitting inside, he would find them there as well—in the theater or restaurant, just a few tables away. He recognized their suits, their shoes and topcoats, and in time their faces as well. There were Russians among them, even more conspicuous than the Czechs.

As the weeks passed, they grew more audacious. He was going with a young secretary from the British embassy at the time. She was newly arrived in Prague. They had no privacy. She was uncomfortable at first, and finally frightened. One night they were stopped on a dark street and forced to stand outside in the cold while the Czechs in the Skoda examined their documents, their currency, and finally the car. They were kept waiting for forty-five minutes on the dark street. They had missed the movie. She asked him to take her home instead. He knew then that Cornelius had been right. If they'd been unsuccessful in their efforts to link him to the Czech civil servant in a plot to suborn a senior Soviet intelligence officer in Prague, they still had the power to intimidate him. Perhaps they were still suspicious. Probably they were waiting for Plummer to betray himself. He grew accustomed to the Russians, whom he disliked the most. He thought they were newly arrived from Moscow, their blood up, their appetites whetted by their first sight of the enemy, an American who was indifferent to their presence and unmoved by their self-importance. He saw the curiosity in their faces as they studied his shoes, his suits, or overcoat, as they contemplated his English car, as they watched him pay a bar bill or a restaurant check, as he bought meat or vegetables in the shops. He saw the contempt in their faces as they grew accustomed to his habits and bored with the monotony of his routine. He despised them for making him conscious of himself and the privileges he enjoyed—his money, his food and drink, his women. But he despised them most for the superiority of their belief that these material things were identical with his own existence.

He gave no sign that he recognized their faces or their individuality. *Le néant,* the Danish journalist had told him that day in East Berlin. He never deviated from the habits of almost four years in Prague, never betrayed by a turn of the head, a lifting of the eyes, or a quickening of his pace in the street that he knew they were there. He looked through them as he looked through the glass windows of the Prague shops, searching for the quickness of life beyond.

One afternoon he read in *Rude Pravo* that a security court in Ostrava had sentenced the Czech surgeon who had operated on the mortally wounded civil servant to six years at hard labor. He concluded that the state had closed its case on the Ostrava affair. The same week the furniture in a neighboring flat was carried down the narrow stairs of the apartment house and left on the sidewalk below. Winter had come. A few snow-flakes drifted down from the gray skies. Plummer stood on the street outside, looking at the furniture. The following week the flat on the other side of his own was also evacuated. Both remained unoccupied. The neighbors on the first and second floors never spoke to him again. Late one night as he stood on the hall landing and searched his pockets for his door key, he heard the creak of a floorboard from one of the empty flats. He stood listening. He didn't hear it again. It was quiet, deathly quiet, the sort of silence that acoustical engineers know nothing about—not silence so much as the suspension of animate life—the sort predators glide through. Plummer knew then that they were in the apartment itself.

He found two concealed microphones in his flat and thought there were more. He left them in place. He had nothing to hide. His clandestine life was over by then, his agents silenced or fled, his freedom of action surrendered. Prague was over.

He realized then that whatever their original strategy had been, it had failed. They wanted him out of Prague, not merely because their plans for entrapment had gone awry, but because he was an American on Soviet terrain, because his continued presence was a denial of their self-respect, a reproach to their dignity, a challenge to their malice. He found his front tires slashed one morning and patched the tubes. When the distributor was ripped from the engine block a week later, he replaced it. When the new distributor cap was smashed, he sold the car. When they broke into his apartment and ripped the books from the shelves, the suits and linen from the closet, and emptied the medicine cabinet on the bathroom floor, he took the morning off and cleaned up the mess. When it happened a second time, he moved to a downtown hotel. He denied the potency of their threat by ignoring it, but at the expense of his own anger and at the price of reducing the physical dimensions of his world in Prague to a nutshell. He knew his limitations. Perhaps they did, too.

One afternoon as he was leaving the front steps of the hotel for the taxi that was waiting at the curb, a man jostled him. Plummer was late for an appointment. When he reached the door of the taxi, he was jostled a second time, and someone tried to enter the rear door of the taxi ahead of him. Plummer saw his face and recognized a small, blond-haired Russian from one of the surveillance teams. Plummer seized his shoulders and thrust him aside easily. Entangled in his own feet as he tried to regain his balance, the Russian fell heavily to the sidewalk. The taxi driver left the front seat and came around to the curb. The hotel doorman left the front steps and tried to help the Russian to his feet. The Russian refused his help, his angry eyes fixed on Plummer instead. He lifted himself to one knee, wiped his nose, hesitated as he measured the distance between them, and then with a fierce grunt lunged blindly towards Plummer, like a sprinter coming out of his blocks. Plummer slid aside, stunned him across the skull in passing, grabbed a handful of limp yellow hair, slammed it face first into the iron doorpost of the taxi, caught the collapsing body on the recoil and lifted it a second time, legs dangling, and flung it back across the pavement. As the Russian lay in a heap against the steps of the hotel, two Czech security agents left their sedan, which was parked up the street. A policeman saw the crowd which had gathered and blew his whistle. Plummer was arrested on the spot.

He spent twenty-one days in a Prague prison. When he appeared for his trial on the twenty-second day, he was wearing the same clothes he had been wearing when he was arrested. His hair had grown; so had his beard. He had lost thirty pounds. At ten thirty he was taken into the courtroom, still in handcuffs. He was sentenced to two years at hard labor but the sentence was suspended. He was deported instead, put aboard a Vienna-bound train the same evening, still in handcuffs. Two Czech police officials accompanied him to the frontier, where they removed the handcuffs, returned Plummer's passport and a single piece of luggage.

So after five years Plummer left Czechoslovakia with little more in his kitbag than when he'd arrived in 1947—a footloose ex-GI with a few books in his luggage, a shaving kit under his arm, and a few naive Yankee ideas about helping Czechoslovakia recover its industrial self-respect. His Prague agency would have paid the bills while he searched for clues about the future, the meaning of the past, why history treated its innocents so shabbily. He thought that the ancient lecture halls and the medieval libraries of Charles University might have had something to say about survival—about turning back the tides of Tartars, Turks, Slavs and Saxons, Magyars and Germans, too. And if them, why not the Russians as well; why not himself? If the past was intelligible, why not the future? But he was no closer to finding that answer than when he'd arrived in Prague five years earlier.

It was after midnight when the train entered the Südbahnhof in Vienna. Chambers was waiting on the street outside. When Plummer left the station, Chambers didn't recognize him. It had been ten months since they last met. Plummer's thick, dark hair was uncut and gathered in a dirty flocculence of terrier's wool at his neck and temples. He had shaved the beard in the train lavatory after he had crossed the frontier, but his clothes were loose and ill fitting. The dark tieless shirt he wore was buttoned at the neck and was almost the same color as the cheap worsted suit he wore under the overcoat. Both were unpressed. He wore a pair of workman's high-topped shoes with light neoprene soles. Chambers thought he recognized the gait and slipped from the back seat.

"David?" he called. Plummer turned from the door of the taxi. In that moment Chambers recognized how completely the five years in Prague had changed Plummer. He was ethnically and culturally invisible, a man come from the industrial and working-class slums of middle Europe, a man who might have been anyone. His colleagues were right. There were few frontiers in Europe secure against that kind of anonymity. Even the eyes, which were cold, stubborn, and skeptical, refused Chambers recognition for a minute in the dim light of the street.

"What do you want?" Plummer asked in German.

"It's me," Chambers said, coming out of the shadows. "I've got a car."

"I'll talk to you tomorrow. Fuck you, Chambers, I'm tired. Where were the lawyers you promised? I want to get some sleep." Then he got into the taxi and drove off.

When they met the following day, Plummer was undecided about his future. He talked about leaving Europe. He still had his small agency in Vienna and there was enough business on the books to keep him active for a few months while he made up his mind, but beyond that he wasn't certain what he would do. Chambers told him the Agency was interested in retaining his services. He encouraged Plummer to stay in Vienna.

The first month in Vienna, Plummer changed his flat three times. He had difficulty sleeping. He was wary on the streets, uneasy in crowds, and convinced that he was being followed. One week after he returned from a trip to Antwerp, he discovered that someone had forced the lock on his front door. The concierge told him he'd been searching for a gas leak and Plummer hadn't left him the key. Plummer thought he was lying. He moved out the following day. He took another flat and the same afternoon changed the lock, ripping out the old bolt and installing a heavy bronze double-bolt lock. When finally mortised in place, it gleamed with the solvency of a pauper's tooth across the third-floor twilight. When he discovered that the box in which the lock had come contained only a single key and that the duplicate key listed on the parts list was missing, he thought the omission deliberate. That night he slept in the living room, watching the door. He would awake suddenly, lifting his head from the divan, and look toward the door, trying to recover his vision in the darkness, trying to identify the outline of the door and the bronze tooth of the new lock. But the door was either open or wasn't there at all and he would lie on the divan looking into the hall, smelling the cold septic smell of the Prague streets. Then he would waken, lean forward, and see the squint of cat's eye where the lock was, or see the winter moon, or the pale glow of the streetlamp as it traced the silver paneling of the door, and he'd know that he had been dreaming. But he was never sure. He was never sure that it was the Austrian moon he was seeing, filtering down through the smoky windows, or if the new lock wasn't a tiny moon itself, shining across a frozen Moravian lake, whether the cold glaze of moonlight wasn't reflected from some baroque doorway in the Old

City in Prague where he had a deaddrop hidden under the broken plaster beneath the mailboxes. He was still Prague's prisoner.

"You could go to Bonn or Frankfurt," Chambers said late one evening in Plummer's flat. "Maybe Berlin. Roger would like for you to stay here."

"Doing what?" Plummer said. The flat was chilly, almost frigid. He knelt to light the gas in the fireplace. Afterwards he carried his suitcase into the bedroom. Chambers waited. The room was used as an office as well as a sitting room. In an alcove next to the curtainless window an old typewriter stood on a small oak table. On the floor beneath were several cardboard boxes filled with shipping manifests, files, and equipment catalogues. In front of the grate was an overstuffed divan. Next to it was a wooden table and a small armchair. On the table were an empty cognac bottle and two unwashed glasses.

"Working out of Vienna," Chambers said when Plummer returned.

"I want a drink," Plummer said. "What about you? Scotch or rye—just water."

"Scotch. Water is fine." Plummer went into the kitchen and Chambers moved towards the fire. Plummer was as elusive as he had been since his return to Vienna. At the end of the mantel was a small short-wave radio in a steel-gray case with stainless-steel fittings. Chambers turned the radio on, fixed the band spreader, and moved the dial to a Vienna station. Plummer returned with the glasses, gave one to Chambers, and heard the music. "Habit," Chambers said. The radio in Chambers office was always turned on. The sound smothered conversational details.

"Trotsky called it the perfect thing for a prison," Plummer said. "You people have made it something else. I can't listen to the bloody thing anymore."

"Turn it off, then."

Plummer moved to the window and stood looking down into the street. Both men still wore their overcoats. "What's Roger Cornelius got in mind?"

"He wants to put you to work," Chambers said. "He wants to talk to you about it."

"Where?"

"London."

"Christ," Plummer complained.

"He thinks you need a change of scenery. He doesn't think you're doing yourself much good like this."

"How does he know what old whores I sleep with?" Plummer said. He stood in front of the fire, an ox of a man, as hostile and remote as he'd been the first time Chambers had talked to him. "If he wants to talk, let him come here."

Chambers was looking instead at the fire. The lining was ripped from Plummer's overcoat. Chambers had noticed it as he climbed the stairs. Now the sleazy fabric took flame from the heat of the fire and began to burn. Plummer turned, looked at the small flame, ripped away the burning edge, and then took the coat off, tore out the rest of the lining, and threw it into the fireplace. He put the coat back on. "It's always London with Cornelius, isn't it? Always someplace else. Let him come here."

"You'll talk to him?" Chambers was aware then he didn't know Plummer at all.

"Sure I'll talk to him. What the hell have I got to lose? What have you got to lose sitting there pretending you don't know it?"

Roger Cornelius spent a week in Vienna, talking to Plummer. Roger said the talks went well. Plummer expanded his office in Vienna, hired an additional bookkeeper and a second warehouseman. He traveled often. In time the old memories were just another part of the past. Of all the Americans in Austria or Germany at the time, Plummer proved the most durable because he was the most elusive, the most enigmatic, the most anonymous—because he hated the most. No one really knew him; few ever talked to him; he had no friends. The few Americans in the embassy who occasionally met him disliked him. They knew him only as a solitary American engineer who'd lost his Czech commercial agency, who'd spent some time in jail and had been deported; yet who continued to sell US and Western strategic goods to Soviet bloc destinations in defiance of the embargo. They knew his office was in the old warehouse section of Vienna and that he kept a depot nearby, that his secretary and warehousemen were as reclusive as he, refusing to cooperate with those officials who sometimes arrived to investigate reports that Plummer had violated his US and UK export privileges.

Phil Chambers and Roger Cornelius knew more. It had been Phil Chambers's idea, not Roger's—identifying the role in which Plummer's experience and hostility could finally find release. Roger Cornelius had sold Plummer the idea, but it was Plummer himself who perfected it—the American predator at Vienna's Cold War transit station, stalking the Soviet and East European quarry as he himself had once been stalked, often prowling the airports and the train stations from the east, the Austrian backroads, and the snowswept fields near the Hungarian and Czech frontiers where the infiltrators came over the border; watching the Soviet and East European missions for a suspicious arrival, a questionable diplomatic passport, or a covert departure; leaving a metallic-blue Porsche, with its sheen gone to a lichen-gray, to weather in the snow and mizzle of the Vienna airport while he disappeared somewhere else on the continent—a Bonn hotel room, a bench near the Hotel Metropole in Brussels, a New York-bound flight from Paris, a little bookstore on Charlotte Street, Holborn, in London on a gray afternoon, the fog creeping in, taxis sluicing by outside from the train station or the bus terminal, even to the iron gates of the Soviet mission at Highgate.

He was still in Vienna in 1956 when the Hungarian revolution erupted and he met Elizabeth Davidson. He'd found her on the road twenty miles outside Vienna on the Sunday afternoon of her arrival from Geneva. A cold steady rain had been falling most of the day and Plummer was alone in his muddy Porsche, droning along the winding roads, through broken woods and sloping windswept meadows, horneting between winter pasturage and black streams, his mind blank to everything but the tick of the wipers and the rhythm of the narrow ribbon of road ahead of him. He'd soared over a rise and down through a tunnel of trees into a sixty-degree turn. He almost missed her. She was standing on the shoulder of road a little beyond, flagging his car with a red tartan scarf. He saw her face as he flashed past—a lovely face, miles from nowhere, half-smiling at her helplessness, half frightened by his speed. He slammed on the brakes in reflex, sending the Porsche drifting into a long, looping spin which ended seventy yards down the rain-slick asphalt with the snout of the Porsche pointed like a compass needle back towards the lonely figure who stood under the towering trees.

"How well you managed that," she said apologetically when he got out of the car. Her blond hair was wet with the rain; a few muddy pennies, thrown by the lorries that had lumbered blindly past her in the rain, clung to her brown hose and camel's hair coat. "I was afraid that you'd have an accident." Her voice was calm, perfectly modulated. The long nose and the graceful jaw seemed to him typical of a certain monotony of English inbreeding, as prized in English daughters as in greyhounds or racehorses, but as he grew accustomed to her face in those first few hours, he realized that it was the smile that made the face seem longer, as her voice had made her seem distant, part of that puzzling conspiracy of grace, innocence, and power that had captivated him from the very beginning. The broken-down UN station wagon was a dozen yards away, hood-up under the trees where it had been abandoned by the Austrian driver who'd trudged ahead to find a telephone.

Plummer put her bags in his Porsche while she left a note for the driver. She was on her way to the Hungarian refugee camp recently opened near Pullendorf. Plummer was on his way to the refugee camp at Traiskirchen, with Pullendorf to follow later that evening; but with Elizabeth Davidson beside him in the Porsche, he changed his mind and drove through to Pullendorf. It was dark when they arrived. He introduced her to the camp administrator, who was too harried to remember her name, and too harassed by his office staff to give her more than a few minutes of his time. He was on his way to a meeting in Vienna with the Ministry of Interior. One of the office staff led them through the rain to the small tack room which had been assigned to her Austrian staff as an office. The tack room was cold and dark. The Austrian lit a lantern and reminded her that she was a day early. They hadn't expected her until the following afternoon. He wasn't sure he could find accommodations at this late hour. He'd ask the camp custodian to try to find a room in the staff quarters. He wasn't optimistic.

She apologized for the inconvenience. When the clerk left, she picked up the lantern and said she wanted to see something of the camp. He tramped with her through the rain while she inspected the crumbling brick and frame barracks where the Hungarian refugees were being quartered, bivouacked like the DP's Plummer remembered from an earlier day. She was shocked at the gutted interiors of those buildings not yet occupied, but said nothing. The floors and walls still wore the gangrene of Soviet troop infestation from a few years earlier. They stood on a broken porch. Rain mixed with sleet was pelting the standing pools beyond, pounding the black mud and geysering from the broken gutters down across the windows and onto the bales of straw piled beneath. A few Hungarians were foraging through the damp straw, filling mattress covers with clumps of straw torn from the bales.

Elizabeth Davidson asked him what they were doing. Plummer told them they were filling their mattresses for the night. She looked at him in disbelief. "When you're on the run, you sleep where you drop," he told her irritably, discovering her innocence. The wind brought the cold rain to their faces. The lights in the nearby barracks dimmed and went out. Plummer told her the generator had broken down. He led her across the darkened grounds to the tack room. Inside, the Austrian camp custodian was waiting. He told Elizabeth that her room wouldn't be ready until the following day and suggested she find a room at the inn in the village nearby. She told him that she intended to stay in the tack room. When the camp custodian left, Plummer followed him out into the rain. Standing under the overhang of a nearby barracks, he gave him an Austrian bank note and told him to get a room empty for her. When the custodian seemed skeptical, Plummer gave him another bank note. Afterward he took her bags from the Porsche and carried them into the tack room. She opened one of the suitcases and took out a small umbrella.

"I don't suppose you've got a raincoat, do you?" Plummer asked. "Maybe some rubber boots or a poncho?"

She had no vehicle, no overshoes, no boots, no heavy clothing, no rain slicker, no tinned food, and no whiskey. She didn't even have a flannel nightgown. Her German was classical but slow, learned over a

decade earlier at an Irish boarding school, taught her by a French spin-
ster whose father had died at the Battle of the Marne and who despised
the Boche thereafter. Her French was better but not much help with
the Hungarian peasantry. Plummer thought Geneva had been out of
its mind to send her.

They sat together over hot soup and sandwiches in the mess hall,
sitting alone at one of the tables reserved for administrative staff. Three
tables away sat a few of her colleagues from the other refugee agencies.
There were a few Frenchmen, a few Belgian priests, two elderly Dutch
women with bobbed hair, a bearded Jew, a nut-munching couple from
New Zealand, and a palsied Italian count from the Knights of Mal-
ta. They looked to Plummer like a congregation of vegetarian quoit
throwers, fruit-juice addicts, or cranks waiting for their annual jamboree to begin. He watched them ignore Elizabeth Davidson. Even
if she had known who they were, she wouldn't have understood why
they resented her presence, which dimmed like June sunshine the secret, underground pallor of their own ministries.

She sipped her tea and ruminated—tired, still a little damp, discouraged too, but trying to conceal it. In her quiet voice she told him
that dislocations were always tedious. She hadn't been too keen on
Geneva either at first, but had learned to adapt. Plummer was in his
thirties and she a few years younger, but she seemed much younger.
She might have been born the year the Germans shelled Almeria, the
year of the Reichstag fire, or the day Hitler entered Vienna. She could
have been sitting in a pony hack in Kent the day Plummer crossed into
Canada and enlisted in the Canadian army. He felt as old as Diogenes'
bunions.

"I shan't be discouraged," she told him quietly. "When you understand what a beastly time these people have had of it, then it rather
stiffens one's determination to do what one can. Naturally, beginnings
are inevitably difficult and poorly managed, even chaotic. But that
shouldn't discourage one. Don't you agree?"

"Sure," Plummer said. What could he tell her? He knew she was
neither seeking advice nor trading confidences. She would have said
the same thing to anyone who asked. It was her public tone that depressed him. He thought refugee work was a mug's game. The camp

had been open a month and was as screwed up now as it had been the first day. He thought she would have known that. If she'd known that, she would have known it wasn't going to get any better, either.

They walked back to the tack room and he built a fire in the iron stove and left her there, already late to an early-evening appointment with the camp security officer. Plummer was searching for Soviet infiltrators at Pullendorf, Eisenstadt, Lutzmannburg, and Traiskirchen. Some were Hungarians; others, mixed nationalities. A few were Russian. Plummer spent an hour with the camp security officer, examining identity documents and searching the lists of newly arrived refugees. Nothing had changed since his last visit. When he returned to the Porsche outside the tack room, the lantern was still lit and Elizabeth still inside. The stove was cold again; the fire had gone out. She stood aside mutely and let Plummer take charge. He found some old newspapers in the trunk of the Porsche and tried to rebuild the fire. There was no kindling. What he needed was a gallon of gasoline. He was tired, cold, and wanted a drink. She handed him broomstraws, dried leaves, and a few hemp strings she'd found on the floor, like a Girl Guide on her first outing. Plummer found a stool, smashed it to kindling on the stone steps, and nursed the fire to life. She watched him silently. Plummer didn't know what she was thinking. The old Austrian returned with Plummer's bank notes. A Hungarian was already settled in her room for the night and refused to budge until the following day. Plummer took one of the bank notes back and returned the other to the custodian.

"I don't understand," Elizabeth said. "Did you give him money?"

"He did me a favor last week," Plummer lied. The custodian left and Plummer followed him out into the rain. Plummer asked him about the Hungarian. The custodian told him that he was a petty Hungarian police official from Koszeg, a small Hungarian village near the frontier. He'd arrived with a group of refugees two weeks earlier and had made his services available to the Austrian security officers, identifying former party members and security thugs now seeking refuge in Austria. He had occupied the room a week earlier on a temporary basis and was reluctant to give it up. He was well provisioned in the small room and had been drinking lager during the rainy afternoon while his countrymen struggled outside in the cold. He was as indifferent to their misery as he was contemptuous of the few bank notes the custodian had offered him. As an ex-policeman and extortionist, he also had a reputation to protect.

"What's the room number?" Plummer asked. The old custodian told him. Plummer went into the tack room and got the flashlight. "I'll be back in a minute," he told her. She followed him.

"Wait. Please wait." She came running after the light. "What is it?"

"You wanted a room, didn't you?"

"Yes, but I understand it's occupied."

"A little misunderstanding." He crossed the grounds towards the administrative barracks while she ran after him. The custodian brought up the rear. "Maybe you'd better wait here," he told her outside the door. Before she could catch her breath, he was gone again, through the door and up the steps. He was already at the end of the corridor when she reached the top of the steps, and pushing his way into a room at the right.

Inside the room an Austrian clerk was playing solitaire at a small table near the window as Plummer entered. He lifted his eyes, recognized the face, and immediately picked up his hat and coat. Plummer moved aside to let him pass. The Hungarian police official was inclined to protest. He was sitting in a small chair, listening to Radio Budapest on the wireless, a thickset man with dark hair and dark, restless eyes.

Standing blindly in the corridor beyond, Elizabeth heard a violent sound that rocked the matchstick walls and floor. The door quivered convulsively and burst open. A moment later a thickset figure exploded through the door and smashed into the wall. She saw him crumple sideways to his knees, lift himself in agonized protest, feebly claw the wall for support, and finally turn. She saw Plummer come forward effortlessly, without a sound, and when the terrified Hungarian raised one limp hand and then the other in capitulation, she watched Plummer, still moving, drop his shoulder and hit the man belt-high below the protesting hands in a terrifying, evil way in which she'd never seen anyone struck in her life. The blow seemed to paralyze her own body as well, crushing the breath from her lungs. She turned and fled.

When Plummer joined her in the tack room thirty minutes later and told her the room was ready, she didn't look at him. She stood at the potbellied stove, the coat still over her shoulders, feeding twigs and dried leaves to the dying flames. "I couldn't possibly stay there," she said finally. Her face was calm when she turned. "I'm making tea," she said coolly. "You're welcome to a cup of tea if you like."

"What are you going to do?"

"I'll stay here." Near the stove was a cot and a few blankets left by the camp custodian. "Would you like some tea?"

"Thanks but I've got whiskey in the car."

"I'm not surprised," she said. It was the first word she'd uttered all day which conveyed anything other than a polite or public acknowledgment of Plummer's existence.

"Surprised at what?"

"I'm not surprised you've got whiskey in the car. Isn't that what you said? But I'd much prefer a cup of tea just now."

"Maybe that's your problem."

"Sorry?"

"Forget it." The raglan was wet on Plummer's shoulders, his right hand still stung from the Hungarian's belt buckle. His feet were cold, and he very much wanted the whiskey he'd denied himself since darkness had fallen. "You'll need some coal if you want that kettle to boil." He picked up the scuttle from the corner. "A gallon of gasoline wouldn't hurt either. A tank truck might help this whole freaking camp."

"Arson, too?" she asked calmly, lifting her eyes. "Are you really so vindictive?"

He went out into the darkness and found the coal dump behind the boiler house, filled the scuttle, and returned and built up the fire. When the kettle boiled, she fixed tea and began to prepare a bed on the cot. She had no sheets and no pillow. Icy draughts swirled across the littered floor. He watched her silently as she folded the blankets over the cot, and moved the cot itself a few times to take best advantage of the stove and yet escape the trickle of rain water that leaked from the tin roof. At last he put aside his tea cup and stood up. "You can't stay here," he said. "So forget it."

She didn't answer.

Encouraged, he picked up her bags. "I intend to remain here," she said.

"You'll get pneumonia. It's getting colder, the fire will go out, and there's no hot water."

"Please put my luggage down. I'll manage."

"Sure. Like you roll out a pallet, chink a joint, and bake a cherry pie. Only not here and not tonight."

"I haven't the slightest idea what you're talking about."

"I'll take you to the village. There's an inn." Plummer's breath showed on the chill air of the room. She seemed to hesitate.

"I'd quite forgotten about the inn," she admitted. She wasn't too enthusiastic, but Plummer hadn't expected her to be. He didn't know why he cared.

He drove her to the village, where he found a room in the same inn where he was staying. She disappeared into her room and didn't join him for a late dinner. He ate alone, sat for a long time in front of the fire with a whiskey. When he got up to replenish it, the bar was closed. There was a bottle of whiskey in his luggage but he went to bed instead.

He awoke early the following morning, ate breakfast alone in the dining room, and was out in the courtyard, scraping the ice from the windshield of the Porsche, when she came down the stone steps, her breath blossoming in the cold clear air. Ice hung from the trees and shrubbery, from eaves and downspouts, and festooned the electric wires. A warmer mist blanketed the surrounding countryside, hiding roofs and trees, spires and fencerows. A few Mercedes trucks rolled by cautiously on the road beyond, their foglights on.

She stood looking out over the crystal landscape. "An ice storm," she said finally. "I didn't realize. It's quite lovely, isn't it?"

Plummer didn't look up from the windshield. "Tough on the titmice," he said. "Border crossers, too." He didn't look at her. He didn't care anymore. He guessed what she thought of him and his kind of carelessness. There was nothing in his repertoire that could change that. He drove her back to Pullendorf and carried her bags into the tack room. She followed him back across the frozen mud to the car.

"I'd quite forgotten about my room," she apologized. "They told me at the desk this morning that my account had been settled."

"Don't worry about it," he said, slipping behind the wheel.

"That's very kind of you, but I insist." She stood near the door, fumbling with her purse.

"That's too familiar for you, is it?" Plummer asked.

She looked at him blankly. "I beg your pardon."

"I mean paying for a woman's room and not settling up afterward." He squinted up at her slim face framed against the gunmetal sky, and smiled suddenly because of her surprise, because she was lovely and watching her gave him pleasure, because she was the sort of woman who belonged to another world, so remote that it gave him pain, and because for that reason he doubted he'd ever see her again.

"That didn't occur to me," she said calmly.

"It wouldn't," he said.

In the weeks that followed he saw her at a distance during his occasional trips to Pullendorf. He strayed away from her office in the tack room. Once he saw her sitting alone in the staff canteen when he stopped for a cup of coffee. His back was to her as he stood at the counter. He didn't turn. He didn't know whether she'd seen him or not. The same week he saw her on the gravel path ahead of him, walking with two old women, and turned away, crossing a muddy field to avoid her. A few days later he couldn't avoid her. It was late in the afternoon and he'd driven down from Vienna to talk to an old man who worked in the Hungarian security offices in Budapest. After the interview a garrulous old Czech artillery officer stopped him on the path outside the Nissen hut and told him he and his Hungarian wife were going to Canada. A few minutes later Elizabeth came around the side of the building. She hesitated for a moment and finally joined them. It was bitter cold and spitting snow. After the old Czech left, she said "I take it you've been quite busy."

"A little. How about you?"

"Terribly. It's quite cold, isn't it?"

"Not bad." She was hatless, her face stung by the wind. She was wearing a twill coat with a fleece collar, heavy cotton stockings, and leather boots.

"I was about to fix some tea," she said. "Would you care for a cup?"

He thought she had something on her mind. They walked back towards her office. "How terribly clever of you to speak Czech," she said after a moment. "I believe that was Czech, wasn't it?"

Plummer said it was. "I'm very much impressed," she continued.

"Don't be," Plummer said.

"Why?" She stopped on the path.

"There are maybe five thousand refugees in this camp," he said. "Most of them lie in five languages."

She didn't answer. At the tack room her staff had departed for the day. She put the tea kettle on. "Was your family Czech?" she asked, bringing cups from her desk drawer.

Plummer said they weren't. He told her he'd lived in Prague for a while. "Is that an English assumption?" he asked her.

"Which?" She brought out a tin of butter cookies.

"Your assumption. That if it's not Greek, Latin, or French, it must be ancestry. If it didn't come in with the cultural baggage, it must have come in steerage, like a Yiddish grandmother."

She lifted her eyes from the kettle. "You are rather suspicious, aren't you?"

Plummer didn't reply. The kettle was boiling. She poured out the cups, brought out the cream and sugar, and put the butter cookies on a plate. They sat in front of the old iron stove and drank the tea. Plummer was still waiting for whatever it was that was on her mind. After a few minutes she said, "I suppose one has to cultivate a certain skepticism of mind here. I find it quite fatiguing. A middle-aged Hungarian proposed to me today. I was interviewing him and he proposed. He was a chemist in Budapest. He had his own shop." She dusted the cookie crumbs from her fingers and passed the plate to him. "He wants very badly to go to London and he was quite sure that he wouldn't qualify. He was practically in tears. It was quite touching as a matter of fact." She got up and brought the tea kettle from the stove.

"What'd you tell him?" Plummer asked.

She took his cup. "I told him I was quite flattered but that I didn't think it was necessary. I was quite sure we could resettle him in London. He seemed reassured. We didn't finish the interview. He's to return tomorrow. How does one interview someone from whom one has just received a proposal of marriage the day before? I'm sure I don't know."

"Is that what you meant about skepticism?"

"I suppose so. But I said skepticism, not cynicism. I've lived with skepticism all of my life. My father is a nonbeliever. But he was never cynical about the beliefs of others. Quite the contrary. Which are you?"

"I don't know." He was studying her face.

"I'm sure most of us don't know," she said. "Although cynicism sustains the illusion that we do. I see it in the staff here. Many of them are terribly bitter about the expectations of the refugees. Almost cruel in many ways, as if those who've escaped over the border did so purely for the material advantages it would bring." She turned and looked out the window. "A sort of mental exhaustion, I suppose," she continued quietly. "Moral exhaustion too, I imagine, if you believe in that sort of thing."

"Do you?"

She didn't answer right away. "I think I do," she resumed then. Her face was perfectly calm. "It's terribly old-fashioned, I'm told. An exhaustion that depletes one, the way some farmland has been depleted. The soil is still there but something has gone out of it, some nourishment that is essential. Perhaps we don't even know what it is. I suppose that was the lesson of my father. He required ten years or so to recover from the trench wars of France. It was 1928 or so before he recovered. Neurasthenia, they called it. As a child I thought it was catching—that one went to a chemist's shop for medicine to treat it. I don't believe the word is very much used these days. I'm not even sure we'd recognize its meaning." She got to her feet. "Is it used in America?"

"I don't think so."

He got to his feet too and carried his cup to her desk. It was dark outside. She put the tea cups in a BOAC flight bag, picked up her coat, and found her scarf in one sleeve. He took the coat and held it for her. She slipped into the coat and pulled the BOAC bag over her shoulder. "What does 'chink a joint' mean?" she asked as they went out into the cold.

"Chink a joint?"

"You used the expression the other evening. I'm not at all sure I've ever heard it before."

Plummer told her it meant putting mud or clay between the logs of a cabin. Most of the log cabins of rural Virginia were chinked with clay. He said he had such a cabin himself, on a piece of mountain property his uncle had left him. He used it when he hunted turkey and quail in the autumn. They walked up the path towards his car.

"I've known very few Americans," she said. "None, as a matter of fact." She lifted her face towards him. "It's quite a new experience for me. But so is everything else."

"I think you'll manage," he said.

"Do you? I wasn't at all sure that first day. I was petrified, as a matter of fact. When courage fails, you're the first to know. It never occurs to you that others fail to recognize that. I was completely distraught that first afternoon. You were quite firm. You made me quite angry with myself. I don't think I should have managed otherwise."

"You would have managed."

"That's very kind," she said.

Driving back to Vienna that night, Plummer wasn't at all sure of what she had said. The more he thought about it, the more confused he was. With women, like everything else, he seldom planned his strategies. He took his opportunities as they occurred. Too much conscious thought frustrated spontaneity, which alone could guarantee success. But watching her face and throat, listening to her voice, and hearing her words, whatever else they might have meant, told him only one thing: He wanted to get her into bed. Getting her into bed would change everything else—her casual pretensions, the affectation of manners, even the modulation of her voice. And afterward he would look back and understand what no one else could understand. He would know it each time she entered a room. He would know it from the way she entered it, the way she picked up a glass, the way she raised her eyebrows or laughed among strangers, and then looked at him afterward. He would know what she knew, what she was, and the words wouldn't matter.

It snowed that week. A Soviet diplomat in Vienna defected and Plummer flew with him to Frankfurt in a military aircraft. When he finally returned to Vienna, ten days had passed. The following Monday he drove down to Pullendorf. Elizabeth was sitting alone in the staff canteen when he came in to drink a cup of coffee. A group of refugee officials were sitting at their customary table, ten feet away, talking loudly. Elizabeth was writing a letter. It was mid-afternoon and a pale sunshine lay over the snow outside; the sky was a pale blue; the wind was bitterly cold. It was the time of day that Plummer despised—too late to believe in the day's possibilities; too early for a drink.

"You're back," she said, lifting her head.

He sat down on the bench opposite her. "Not working this afternoon?"

"I'm caught up temporarily. Are you keen on languages?"

"Not particularly. Why?"

"I'm thinking about learning Hungarian. Is it difficult?"

"I don't know. Who wants to teach you?"

"A Hungarian priest." She hesitated, still watching him expectantly. "How did you know?"

"A lucky guess. What happened to your chemist friend?"

"He's on his way to London by now, I expect."

"Did you give him some references?"

"As a matter of fact I did." She put her writing paper back in the flowered stationery box and moved it aside. "It seemed the least I could do."

"You mean after you humiliated him by refusing his proposal. That's a fair trade-off. Did he let you keep the ring?"

She laughed and Plummer saw the flush rise to her cheeks and eyes. "No, he didn't do that," she said, dropping her eyes for a minute. Plummer smiled as he watched her. He hadn't seen a woman blush in years.

He took her to dinner at the old inn in the village. It was the first time she'd left the refugee camp since her arrival. The moon was out. She was silent as they drove over the dark roads towards the inn. "You've been in Europe a long time, haven't you," she said finally. She was looking at the winding road ahead of them. He was watching the road and the moon over the trees. Plummer looked at her and knew she hadn't been watching the moon at all.

"Pretty long, I guess. Why?"

"I think I can see it," she said. That was all she said.

The restaurant at the inn was almost deserted. They sat in a small alcove off the main dining room. There were two white candles on the table. The wind blew against the casement at his back and from time to time she watched the full moon over his shoulder. Plummer had two whiskeys and she drank a vermouth. They talked about the refugee camp at Pullendorf, her administrative problems, the remoteness of events in Budapest, in London, and Washington as well. He discovered how well she remembered things he had mentioned previously, remarks that he had forgotten.

"You mentioned cultural baggage once," she said. "I wasn't sure what you meant. Where is your home in America?"

"Virginia," he said. He saw the glint of recognition in her eyes. "Not English Virginia—not the Tidewater. Way back yonder—coon and cider country. Back in the mountains."

She still wasn't sure she understood. "And your ancestry? Were they English?"

"English. Scotch-Irish."

She was pleased. "And you intend to go back?"

"Soon enough."

"I'm sure that there are other things you want to do," she said. "More direct things. It's obvious you don't care for bureaucratic solutions."

She waited. Watching the quiet eyes, Plummer told her that he was an engineer and had once thought about teaching technical trades, maybe in Africa, maybe the Middle East. It was a conventional lie, but Plummer lied easily that way, not for himself but for others, like an analyst or physician finding the placebos an anxious patient might require—something to make a long painful night more bearable, to make familiar the nameless abstractions that terrorized loneliness, to put a putty nose on Grand Guignol or a wax moustache on the faceless corpses that bloomed before dawn from leaky radiator cocks in rented rooms. The gift accounted for some of his success in Prague, and in Vienna too. But it was a lie, nothing more. He wanted to reassure her. But that night at the inn it seemed to him an especially damning lie because except for her voice, the thoughtful tilt of her head, there was nothing in the darkness, nothing at all.

That night was the beginning. If it wasn't the intimacy which Plummer had expected, it offered the promise of more to come. He saw her twice a week during his trips to Pullendorf from Vienna. He helped her with her more difficult interrogations, watched over the work of her Austrian staff, and brought with him what she needed from Vienna. He carried mail for her—letters to friends in Geneva, Rome and London, to Cut Hill, Surrey, and Fairwarp, Sussex, among others—names he never forgot. He brought back with him rations, flashlight batteries, lampwicks, Kleenex, *Die Welt,* the *Times* or *Guardian,* tins of tea, cocoa, and pots of marmalade. Some of the camp officials assumed in time that he was part of her staff; others knew better; while some made assumptions of their own. If she knew about these assumptions, they didn't bother her. She knew he was in close contact with a few senior security officials at the camp, but she never asked what he did or why he came so regularly. He thought it characteristic at first, part of her background—her manners, her seclusion from laborious detail, her innocence in discussing international politics, in which she had no serious interest at all. Decency, good sense, and compassion were all that mattered to her. He saw it in her smile, heard it in her words, and recognized it in her silence when something troubled her. She believed in the basic order of things, the rationality of events; and her assurance was as much a part of her breeding or her background as it was of her intelligence. It was an assurance which was centuries old. Plummer didn't understand it.

Occasionally for the weekend they drove to Vienna, where they would have dinner together, and go to a movie or a concert. She would stay with a British couple at the embassy, the Gwenhoggs, and when Plummer would return her to the Gwenhogg flat Peggy Gwenhogg would be sitting up, waiting for her, knitting or reading a book, usually listening to the wireless, her drink on the table nearby, eager to discuss the latest catastrophes on the continent, the news from London, or the latest gossip from the embassy family in Vienna. Peggy Gwenhogg was unable to place Plummer in the American embassy community in Vienna. Her curiosity was relentless. She imagined that she'd met him once at a diplomatic reception. She couldn't recall which. He gave her little help.

Returning Elizabeth to Pullendorf following their second weekend in Vienna, Plummer considered his situation. He was still waiting for his opportunities. If she enjoyed his company, he had seen nothing to suggest that she wanted anything more than moral support, or the opportunity to escape from time to time from her physical and mental isolation at the refugee camp. It was snowing. She slept most of the way, her head bobbing against his shoulder with the motion of the car. The snow fell more heavily, drifting down through the beams of the Porsche. The car was warm. There was nothing ahead of them but snow and silence and he wanted to fade off the roadbed and into some deep featherbed of ditch, wake her gently, and fetch the bottle of cognac from the glove compartment, tell her that they were snowbound. He began to slow down as the snowflakes grew thicker, searching the darkness ahead of him for a convenient curve. He thought she was still sleeping.

Then he heard her voice, as clear as a bell, felt the weight lift from his shoulder, and knew she hadn't been sleeping at all. "Extraordinary," she said, sitting forward for a minute as she rearranged her feet under her.

"What's extraordinary?" He thought she must have guessed his intentions.

"Americans have such extraordinary mobility, don't they? Here we are, on an Austrian road, just having left Vienna, and it could just as well be Lapland, with the snow outside. And you're an American. Don't you find that extraordinary?"

"If I hadn't driven this road before, I might."

"Your ancestry is English, though. Do you think that might account for it?"

"I dunno. Should it?"

"I'm not quite sure. The English have a remarkable capacity for appearing in strange places. Actually, I was thinking of Lapland. Or Antarctica. Or Finland. It's quite lovely, thinking about it." She put her head back, gazing out through the windshield at the falling snow. After a moment she said, "Have you ever been back?"

"Back where?"

"To England. Your family came from England. Have you ever been back?"

"Occasionally," he said. What could he tell her? He knew Paddington, Shoreditch, and Uxbridge Road, Ealing. He knew Rye Lane, Peckham; and Tyneham Road, Battersea. He didn't think she knew them at all. He knew Hammersmith and Coventry Street, Piccadilly; Lennox Gardens, where the Soviets had a drop; a flat on Barking Road in East Ham they sometimes used. He knew Knightsbridge, a pub on a corner where he'd once waited for six hours for a surveillance relief team from MI6 travel control. He knew Bayswater and the Underground, how their couriers went for it, as quick as a rat down a rope; he knew the smoke and chill of Liverpool, Heathrow on murky winter nights when you were never sure you'd get off the ground. He knew all of this, but it wasn't what she knew; and he told her no—no, he'd never really been back, never traveled Devon or Dorset, never seen Somerset, never climbed the fells of North Yorkshire.

"Rough and ready chaps, were they?" she asked, her face turned towards him, smiling at his silence as if she'd caught his mood, comfortable in the drowsy warmth of the car, at the sight of the snow floating beyond the window, and the sound of it crunching like old leather under the tires of the Porsche.

He didn't get her into bed that night or the next. He didn't even try. He knew what the costs would be if he were to try and fail. He knew her that well by then.

He was absent from Vienna the following week. He returned on Saturday afternoon and drove south from Vienna through the gathering dusk. He couldn't find Elizabeth Davidson at first. Her office door was unlocked; a fire was burning in the iron stove; and the rucksack he'd brought her from Vienna two weeks earlier—full of tinned fruit, canned soup, nuts, and assorted victuals—was on the floor near the stove. He went out into the darkness, searching for her. Four buildings away an angry crowd had gathered outside a temporary wooden barracks where the newly arrived refugees were being housed. Some of the Hungarians were carrying lanterns, others bedslats and stakes. The mood was ugly. A few of the younger Hungarians, gathered near the front steps, tried to push their way into the building but were blocked by a group of older men. Elizabeth was with them. Plummer asked someone nearby what was happening. A young Hungarian couple told him that two young law students from Budapest had discovered that a Hungarian refugee who had crossed the border that day with his wife and child had worked with the secret police in Budapest. He was sitting inside on a wooden stool, facing his accusers—a small, gray-haired man, wearing a black rain-slicker. His wife and child stood close by. Plummer tried to move forward, but at that moment the crowd at the foot of the steps broke past the cordon of older men and burst through the front door. Elizabeth disappeared from sight and a moment later Plummer saw her again. A stout Hungarian woman in a black dress had seized her wrists and was holding her away from the surging mob. Inside the barracks the mob dragged the gray-haired Hungarian from his stool and beat him savagely while his wife and child watched helplessly. When the camp security police arrived, it was all over. The clerk was dragged unconscious to the front door and thrown down the wooden steps. One of his assailants was wearing his black rain-slicker.

Plummer went back to the tack room when he saw Elizabeth talking to one of the security officials. He hung up his coat and turned up the lantern. He was rooting quietly through the rucksack when Elizabeth returned. He lifted his head and read her cold, angry face, didn't move for an instant, but didn't say anything either. He quietly resumed his rooting. She stood near the door.

Peanuts, sure. Canned peaches, cashews, beef stock, and marmalade. What else? He read the labels in the lantern light as he dug deeper and finally found the olives he was searching for.

"I saw you," she said. "You were there." He didn't deny it and opened the can of olives instead. "You didn't lift a finger." The door was still open. The wind stirred outside, scattering chaff across the cold floor. A few dark shapes moved by on the gravel path. He walked past her and shut the door. "Can't you say anything?" she cried.

"What do you want me to say?"

"It's beastly what you're doing. You don't care."

"About what?"

"Those people out there."

"Maybe it's my neurasthenia," he said.

"How selfish of you to remember that and nothing else!" she said. "You don't care—you're indifferent. You're brutal—the same way that awful mob was brutal. You let that poor man be beaten unmercifully. You stood there, you simply stood there and did nothing!" He had never seen her so angry.

"What was I suppose to do about it?" he asked.

"You could have helped. You could have at least tried to help."

"Sure. Cracked a few skulls. What would that get you? Nothing. A trip to the infirmary—feet first in the welcome wagon. I've been there. Anyway, they said he was with the Hungarian security police. Do you know what the AKA used to do with its prisoners?"

"I don't need to know. It's beside the point."

"Sure it's beside the point. You weren't there. What's that prove?"

"Whatever he might have done in the past, he's here now! He's here—in Austria, in a civilized country! Not Budapest, but here. Here with his wife and children. That's what he came to escape."

"You can't escape it," he said. "It's too late for him."

"It's not too late. Never. It's never too late."

"Okay, it's not too late. She's not a widow yet, either."

"A widow! Is that the only thing that matters? Is murder the only thing that matters? Didn't you see how he was beaten? It was terrifying—and no one lifted a finger! No one." He didn't answer. "Don't you understand how close they came to killing him?"

"Close only counts in horseshoes and hand grenades," Plummer said. "Close never won the derby, either. He's still in the starting gate with Maybe and Hope So pulling his ears."

"And I suppose that's all that matters. What about his wife and child, standing there, seeing what happened! I despise tyranny as much as anyone, but I despise cruelty, too! Malicious, mindless cruelty—"

"Then take away their soup ration tonight," he said. "Get your camp entertainment committee together. Break out the ax handles and the paper hats. Rap a few skulls. Smash a few teeth."

"That's not what I want!"

"Then what do you want?" he said. She was still angry, but he was just tired. He wasn't angry at all.

"Something sensible from you," she cried. "Don't you understand? Something decent—anger, charity even, compassion. Something just, something that has some feeling, some decency to it!"

He took her hands and brought her towards him, into the lamp-light, and studied the red marks left by the Hungarian woman's ringed fingers. He could still see the gauntlet of crimson at the wrist bone. "No scars, no broken bones," he said. "Do you want a drink or not?"

"No," she murmured, her face flushed. "I don't know." She shook her head stubbornly. "Don't ask—please."

"Nothing comes easily for you tonight, does it?"

"No. But only because you make absolutely no sense to me some-times."

"Maybe it's an ethnic block." He let her hands go.

"That has nothing to do with it." She remained motionless, her face lifted, her eyes raised defiantly.

"Maybe I should have helped. Maybe I should have tried. Maybe I'm sorry I didn't." He didn't know what else to say.

"Why?" she replied instantly. "Why should you apologize when you so obviously don't care?"

"I said help. I didn't say care. Maybe I'm just fed up with them. With refugees, professional paupers. Fruit juicers and creeping Jesuses. Most of those people out there are bastards."

"They've suffered!" she cried.

"So what? What's that prove? Who hasn't, anyway? And if they have, who cares? Are they any better for it? Hell no. They're just bigger bastards, that's all. What about a drink?" He found the glasses and brought the whiskey and vermouth to the table. She sank down on the chair.

"Didn't you hear what I said? They've suffered." He poured the vermouth into the glass and handed it to her.

"They got out, didn't they?" he said, picking up the whiskey bottle. "They're here—not someplace else. What's suffering got to do with it, anyway? If they're here, does that mean they've suffered the most? What about the others—the ones suffering in place? What about the ones that didn't have the money to get out? What about the ones who are suffering for no reason at all, just for being what they are? Not Hungarians, not Catholics, not exiles, not Jews, not anything. Just people. What about them? What about the ones with no place to go, no borders to cross, no bureaucrats or church charities or Catholic or Zionist politicians to plead their case, no UN office to give them blankets and hot soup, a new passport, a steamship ticket to New York or Halifax or Haifa. No fresh new start in life. What about them? Who the hell's going to resettle them? Not the ballet dancers or the right-wing politicians, the poets or the piccolo players. Just the people. What church is going to take them in? Where's their ethnic or confessional lobby in Washington or London? Who gives a rat's ass about them? No one. No one at all. Not you, not me, not the Hungarian lobby, the Armenian lobby, the Catholic charity lobby, the Greek lobby, the Zionist lobby. No one. Well, I'm fed up with them. Why should I give a goddamn about a handful of Hungarians, Catholics, or Jews because they're Catholics or Jews? Because they've just crossed a border. Well, I don't give a damn about them. To hell with them. To hell with all of them."

She watched him as he spoke. He didn't look at her. He was filling the stove instead. "You surely don't mean that," she said hopelessly.

"Okay then, let's forget it." She thought he was relieved for a moment, not at all anxious to talk any more about it.

"I want to know how you feel. Don't you understand that?"

"I just told you how I feel. You don't like it so you want me to tell you something else. So why don't we forget it."

"Is it that they didn't fight?" she asked suddenly.

"Fight where?"

"In Hungary. Is it that they gave up too easily, that they should have remained and fought?" He didn't answer. She said, "I'm sure they tried."

"What are you looking for excuses for?"

"I'm not. Truly, I'm not." She watched him helplessly, saw him look at her, and then bring a chair nearer the iron stove. She moved from her chair to the wooden stool nearby. "Did you fight back?"

He turned and looked at her. "Where?"

"Wherever it was." Her head was tilted, her eyes clear, her face expectant, as innocent as a schoolgirl's.

"Let's forget it," he suggested.

"Stop saying that. I want to understand. You're so difficult to talk to sometimes. You're impossible."

"So why don't we forget it, then?"

"You say that so easily, don't you. 'It doesn't matter' or 'something like that,' 'sure,' 'knock it off' or something equally dimwitted. It's maddening."

"Now who's mad?"

"I am—but I should be, shouldn't I? You make it impossible for me sometimes. And if I can't talk to you, who can I talk to?" She turned her head away. The room was silent.

Plummer waited. After a few minutes he said, "All right. Maybe I'm not too careful with what I say. No, I don't like this camp. I told you why. I don't like the jerks that run it, but I can't do much about that, either. I care how you feel, that's all."

"And it makes you angry?"

"Not angry," he said. "I'm not mad about anything."

"But you do get angry. I see it constantly—how cross you are. I see it in the way you speak to the staff, to the clerks. The way you look at the refugees. As if they were all loathsome, all liars—all so deceitful." She sat on the stool, her legs out, chin lifted, looking down through her long lashes at her hands resting on her thighs. She didn't move. "And then tonight," she began again, "when that family needed your help, you did nothing. You weren't angry and yet I was. I was angry and you did nothing. Why weren't you angry? I don't understand," she murmured. "What do you know that I don't know? What do you see that I don't see?" He watched her without speaking, looking at the silhouette of her face, the slumped shoulders, and the long legs. She was as far away as Sussex or Surrey now, as the darkened fields of Kent—snow drifting down across the English countryside, heaping against hedges, woods, and chapel windows, drifting across lanes and collapsing stone walls—remembering some trust, some anthem from childhood that would come with the first breath of candle flame at vespers and whose words she knew even before she understood their meaning. But now, she didn't know, and Plummer saw the mystery in her face as she tried to understand. Watching her, he knew at last that he had no business being in the room with her, no business at all, and that she would break his heart or her own in the end. There was nothing either of them could do to change that. She dropped her head. "I'm so tired, so confused. I don't know. I don't understand why you're here. When you say there are people who suffer for no reason at all, you're right. It's true. Of course it's true. It's so terrifying when you think about it. It's so much easier to do something for those whose pain is obvious. Perhaps there are selfish motives involved—self-interest, vanity, ethnic pride. Perhaps it is morally vicious at times or even arrogant. Certainly there are those for whom we can do nothing. We recognize that helplessness, yes. Our weakness, too. Yes, of course I agree. But should that prevent me from doing what I can?" She turned her head and looked at him. "Should it? Tell me, please."

"No," he said. He didn't know what else to say. He heard the angry breath from the stove, each clinker seized in its own heat, heard each blade of grass moving against the wooden door at the rear, each whispered creak from every timber as the wind blew, and knew that despite everything else, he loved her.

"Is that how you feel?" she asked. "Tell me if I'm wrong. I want to know. I must know. Tell me—" Her voice was only a whisper, barely raising above the wind, her face lifted, her eyes searching for his.

"No," he said. "You're not wrong."

He stayed in the village that night, didn't sleep well, and drove to Traiskirchen the following morning. It was Sunday. Early in the afternoon he returned to Pullendorf, where she was waiting for him. They drove south into Burgenland under blowing snow clouds and had lunch at a remote inn. After lunch they continued driving because neither wanted to return to their separate lives—Plummer to a Monday morning departure from Vienna, Elizabeth to an early evening camp security committee meeting at Pullendorf. The day was gray and cold. Gusts drove seeds of snow against the windshield. Neither mentioned the incident of the previous day. Plummer was troubled. Nothing mattered except her being next to him in the car. When the time came to leave her once again, he didn't know what he would do. An hour later Plummer parked the car on a rise beneath a pair of oak trees and they climbed a broken fence. From a hillside a quarter of a mile away he showed her the salient of Hungarian border curving westward into Austria in the distance. The rolling, dun-colored fields were broken by a few hedgerows, by spruce blue with shadow, and by corrugated fields now gone to wild grass. The hillside beyond the trees where they stood was heaped with mounds of autumn hay, darkening under winter thatch, where the mower and hay rakes had abandoned them to the weather. She stood next to him under the tree, lifting herself on tiptoe to follow his sweeping arm, trying to see the small Hungarian border post where a curl of woodsmoke lifted from the chimney two hundred yards beyond the frontier.

"But I can't see," she said. "Are you sure it's there?" He lifted her higher, her blond hair billowing across her forehead. "Yes. There it is. With the smoke too. Just a puff. How absolutely perfect. Tea, do you suppose? Do you suppose it's tea-time?"

He brought her back to earth, his gloved hands steadying her uncertain elbows, her fingers gripping his wrists, her hair loose in the wind. "But they must see us. Haven't they? Shouldn't we run?" But they didn't run and he brought her back down against him. Her cheeks and mouth were cold as he kissed her. She didn't move. Her eyes were closed. It was the quietest face he had ever known, the most gentle. When she finally opened her eyes, she put her head against his chest, hiding her face, with nothing to say. Instead, she untangled her hair with her fingers, groping for the brown barrette that had come loose. "What are you thinking?" she asked him quietly, her face still down.

"Nothing much. Just thinking." She looked away, out over the hillside. He felt her stiffen.

"Look," she said. She was looking towards the Porsche parked a quarter of a mile away along the road. A Volkswagen bus had stopped behind it. A few passengers descended to the road and stood along the fence. Some carried binoculars; others held cameras. They were dressed in black. "Who are they?"

Plummer watched the figures along the fence and saw the wind lift their vestments and capes. They were priests and nuns from a Catholic charity. "We'd better run for it," he said.

"Run? But why?"

"Fruit juicers," he said. "Beef tea and hymn books. Let's beat it." He grabbed her hand and they bounded away from the road and down the slope, sliding through the wet grass and flying out across the open pasture, until she could run no more and they collapsed together across a mound of wet grass. They lay face down across its dark thatching which still smelled of summer, catching their breaths. After a while Plummer sat up and she did too, both looking at the dark, racing clouds, cold snow in their faces, no longer smiling. They sat there for a long time, searching the sky and the Hungarian frontier. She pulled the grass from her hair. After a while they heard the sound of a motor starting up. The bus droned away in the distance. He got up and took her hand and pulled her gently to her feet. The day was ending.

They walked in silence back across the hillside, through the trees, and out across the meadow beyond. He helped her over the fence and she turned without speaking, looking back across the rolling hillside towards the Hungarian frontier. The guard hut was hidden beyond the trees. She stood motionless, searching for the plume of smoke and the dark clumps of cedar, for the piled hay mounds and the hillside where they had stood. All were beginning to merge now in the gathering twilight.

He released the handbrake and the car rolled forward from the crown of the hill. His face was wet, her face too. Blades of grass stuck to her hair, to her scarf, to her pile coat and the white knitted sweater beneath. The car drifted along the shoulder of the road, but he didn't turn on the engine. She kneeled in the leather seat, her back to the dash, wiping her face with her handkerchief. He let the car drift to a stop.

"Who's kidding who?" he asked. "Where are we going anyway?"

She didn't answer. The sleet fluttered through the stiff grass of the fencerow and against the cold metal of the hood. He brought her shoulders against him. She came easily, lying across his chest, her knees folded awkwardly, watching him quietly. Still she didn't speak, her eyes open, examining his face as she listened to the sound of the sleet against the roof. He could feel her heart beating. He kissed her and her face came against his, as quietly as before. Afterwards she put her head against his shoulder, and they sat there for a long time, not speaking, not saying anything, watching the darkness fall. A car droned past, its headlights sweeping across the windows and filling the car with its harsh light. After it passed, she lifted herself, straightened her sweater and coat, and sank back into the seat beside him. They drove back to Pullendorf.

"How long will it be this time?" she asked him as they stood on the wooden porch of the old building.

"Next Saturday. Maybe we could go someplace, do something different. I'd like to take a week off."

She nodded as if she understood. "A week then," she said.

Chambers told him that he was being sent to London for a special operation. He would be gone for two months, Chambers said, and should plan to leave the last week of December. Plummer said he'd think it over, that he had plans of his own.

He drove down to Pullendorf late Saturday afternoon. She was expecting him. She wanted to take a walk before dinner. They walked together out the rear gate, down the frozen lane between the sheltering trees, and across the saddleback of open hillside where the winter sunlight was beginning to fade, spilling across the hills to the west like molten metal from the furnace of black clouds massed to the north and northwest. She was hatless, a long green scarf wound around her neck, wearing a heavy white cable-knit sweater under her coat.

"My father wanted to know if you were an American of advanced tendencies," she told him on the hillside. "I wrote that I'd met an American. He's known so few."

"What did you tell him?"

"I said I didn't think so."

"He's worried about you?"

"Possibly." She asked him where he had spent the previous Christmas. He told her Vienna, but he wasn't sure.

"What about you?" he asked.

She'd spent last Christmas with an elderly aunt in Kent. Her aunt lived alone with a housekeeper and nurse, had never married, had never found the time to surrender her pride, her garden, her self-reliance, her financial independence. Each year she found renewal with the coming of the Advent—gifts at the end of the year, Christmas cards, New Year's greetings. Tidying up her sums, she'd told Elizabeth—parsing her accounts to the last shilling. With friends, with relatives, with God. And last year the summing up had been even more final because she knew the end was near. There was nothing to be left over or unaccounted for. The yellowing letters were to be consumed in the fire, the coin-silver fruit knives tied off in felt gloves, the library sent to her father's school, furniture for nephews and nieces, china for cousins, a pious sum for the postman, a silver service for the vicar's wife, an African violet for her surgeon's housekeeper, and two herring for the fisherman's cat. Elizabeth smiled. Canceled to the last tuppence, she told Plummer—like a Georgian poetess, annihilated to the last quatrain. Perhaps last Christmas had been a lesson; she'd joined the UN after that, deciding she needed a change.

He helped her over a fence. She stopped, looking back at him.

"Don't tell me you didn't have other opportunities," he said.

"The conventional ones, yes. But not what I wanted." He leaned across the broken fence, arms folded, watching her face. The sky was growing darker. Soon her presence would only be a shadow where she stood—face and figure both. A few farmhouses with lights at their windows glimmered to the north. Dogs were barking in the woods and there was a frosty ring around the moon, but no, it wouldn't last. Clouds were sneaking in, all over Europe. "Does that surprise you?" she asked.

"No."

"You haven't said a word."

"Thinking."

"Just thinking?"

"Listening."

"What are you thinking about?"

"Advanced tendencies," he said.

"But you weren't." She knew his voice by then, knew its registry, knew its moods. She studied his face in the moonlight, beginning to smile. "But what are you thinking about?"

"A week is a long time," he said. "I missed you."

"I missed you, too. I was quite miserable."

"You wouldn't say that if I were on the other side of this fence."

"I would."

"No, you wouldn't."

"I would."

"You think I can't get over this stile as fast as you can get back to the farmhouse?" The stile was only a few steps away. He could see her face clearly now—the long nose and jaw, the eyes rimmed with silver in the frosty air.

"What farmhouse?" Her head was lifted towards him, and she hadn't turned to look.

"The one over there—where the dogs are—through the trees."

"There's no farm there. There's nothing there." She straightened, facing him stubbornly, even after he'd vaulted the stile and was standing next to her. She remained still, head back, face cold, candle of nose even colder, as Plummer kissed her. After she caught her breath, she said, "You don't frighten me anymore. I've found you out. I have."

He stayed for a week at the remote inn where they had lunched that snowy afternoon. She stayed with him. During their last nights together in Austria they lay in the darkness with the moon hidden over Burgenland under a thick cloud cover, listening to the wind battering shutters, roof tiles, and three limbs; listening to the midnight rain slamming in hard gusts against the dormer window, the black panes reflecting the red glow of the tile stove in the corner of the room. Radio Luxembourg sometimes on the battery radio to protect their solitude; Cole Porter and then a Rodgers and Hart medley before the notes wandered off, fractured into quartertones and then dopplering off like dwarfs into the ionosphere before she found the BBC and William Byrd, Thomas Tallis, and even Purcell and Handel for the Advent, leaning across him in the dim glow of the radio panel, her breasts bracing the chill of the room, her long body as warm and as quiet as his. They listened to the wind, to the rain harden into sleet, sometimes to the whisk of snow breathing against the window, carrying them together into dawn against the stiff cold shingle of morning. Even before the light gathered dimly to the east, she'd be awake, waiting for the light to come, knowing by then how many days they had left, how long it would be before they would be separated again. She had never had a lover. There were things Plummer wanted her to know. His mouth tasted of her mouth, his skin of her skin, her fragrance lay mixed with the salts of his own body; but her silence worried him.

"Elizabeth—you asleep?"

"No."

"Listen. I want to tell you something—"

"Shhh. Dawn is coming."

"OK, but listen—"

"Shhh—"

Naked against him, lying as softly as a mouse, her English maidenhood come down to this, surrendered under borrowed blankets and sheets at an inn she'd never have the courage to enter again without him, she was stronger than he was those dark mornings. She required no words—nothing at all. Their last ten days together were also their first, a new beginning, and she had no words for it. Frost hardened on the spires and turrets of Vienna; the winter sun was a mercury fog over the Alps as they awoke together in the twilight, dressed together near the warm stove, her hair tumbling over her face as she sat drawing on stockings, skirt, and blouse, already ready before he was to face that annihilating cold beyond the front door of the inn, the metal dawn sky, the icy interior of the Porsche which took the breath from their bodies as he drove her back to Pullendorf each morning to begin her day.

Neither had planned it that way, but that's the way miracles happen, she had told him. Once it had begun, both knew that they would never be reconciled to its interruption, however temporary that might be: the morning light which would finally separate them, maybe for the four weeks Plummer had predicted, maybe for the two months she had conceded secretly (but no longer, dear God—*no longer*).

He was outward-bound from Schwechat airport in Vienna the same night, bound for Brussels, stalking a mysterious diplomat who'd arrived from Prague the previous day, a man who'd met surreptitiously with a Soviet intelligence officer from the Soviet mission on Reisnerstrasse a few hours after his arrival at the Südbahnhof, and afterwards booked passage to Brussels and London.

Austrian stewardesses, as plump as milkmaids, sauntered up and down the amber-lit aisles of the airplane; businessmen too, folded copies of *Die Welt* under their reading lamps; ceremonial whiskeys, white-cuffed pilseners on the open trays, shivering under the foil-pounding stresses of the Alpine blasts rising from storms below. His quarry was small, powerfully built, like a circus acrobat. He had a powerful neck, pitted with acne scars; a few blond hairs grew over the clean white collar. Watching him from a few seats away, Plummer remembered Prague and thought he was Russian.

The soft xylophone of the seatbelt sign went on. Aisle lights blinking on as he wakened, the sleepy roar of the engines beyond the window telling him how far he'd traveled. He looked around, searching for her. He found himself among strangers. He saw the shifting beige curtains of the galley where she'd been standing a moment earlier, a harsh, metallic brightness beyond. His mind soared backwards, but the engines still carried him away, and in that moment he discovered how deeply he despised his life, despised those surrounding him, despised it all with a loathing which brought a beading of sweat to his neck and arms, fear to his paralyzed brain.

The anonymous diplomat went on to London, where MI6 travel control took over the surveillance. On the evening of his third day in London, Plummer wrote out his resignation. It was in his coat pocket when he boarded the plane for Brussels, his quarry already seated in the cabin. By then Washington had concluded that the diplomat wasn't what he represented himself to be, that he was an intelligence officer, probably a Russian, perhaps someone from technical services who was making his last trip to Western Europe. The man checked into a Brussels hotel, spent the first day shopping, and that night tried to pick up a Belgian girl in the hotel cocktail lounge. The following morning he rebooked his airline reservations to give himself two additional days in Brussels. He spent the afternoon shopping again—clothes, woman's lingerie, and Western-made electrical appliances he could carry in his suitcase. They decided to take him.

Plummer was in the CIA station chief's office when they told him. The letter of resignation was still in his pocket together with his plane ticket back to Vienna. "They want it to look voluntary," the station chief said. "The Belgians prefer it that way. Do you think he'll go voluntarily?" An airplane was standing by ready to take the diplomat to Frankfurt.

Plummer said he didn't think he would. There was fog in the streets. He and the station chief met with the abduction team to talk about the options. After the meeting was over, he stood in the empty room. He no longer knew himself. He stood looking at the half-finished whiskey-and-water in his hand, trying to recognize what he saw there. When he did, he didn't move. He was still there when the technician returned with the floor plan of a Brussel's pension.

It was close to midnight when they got the call.

The pension was a tall, four-story building blackened by soot and rain from the railroad tracks a block away. Twenty yards to the west the cul-de-sac ended in a flight of broken steps which climbed to the boulevard beyond. There was no lift in the old building. The narrow stairs were lit by a naked bulb at each landing. Memories of old cooking smells lived in the bottom of the stairwell. More recent ones were settling to join them from the flats above—frying margarine, bubbling cabbage, the six-hour simmer of stew meat. On the second floor landing a door was ajar. A man's drunken voice came scraping through the silence. Plummer softened his tread and moved on. In the twilight of the top-floor landing under the skylight, the American stood against the railing, his gloved hands on the banister in front of him. The light from the stairwell below only partially lifted the Irish face from the basalt of surrounding shadow.

The woman who opened the door was tall and horse-faced, with reddish hair swept back. She was heavily rouged. Her claret-colored bathrobe stank of stale beer and French tobacco. She examined Plummer's face, looked past him towards the American and the two technicians behind him, and moved sideways with relief. She nodded towards the door at the far end of the room. Plummer crossed it, stood listening, and finally turned, his eyes searching the walls, the furniture, and the worn rug under his feet. Somewhere down the corridor to his left a refrigerator compressor creaked away, a bedspring whined, a woman groaned in her sleep. It was almost midnight. His eyes found the light fixture in the center of the ceiling. He listened to the whispers from beyond the door, eyes lifted to follow the old exposed electrical conduit from the ceiling fixture through the shadows and down the opposite wall where the woman, the American, and the two technicians stood watching him silently. The voices were fading from the room beyond. All he could hear was the mindless commotion of the compressor, devouring the silence. He nodded and the other American leaned forward and turned off the green-globed lamp. Plummer waited, his left hand on the doorknob, his right hand resting lightly against the paneling of the door. Then he flung the door open, moving forward as his right hand found the light switch.

The muscular Russian on the bed leaped like a goat from the shock of light, bounding half naked towards the chair where his clothes hung; but Plummer stopped him in mid-flight. With his fist, like a wrecking ball on a chain swung backward across his path, he ripped the Russian's face upwards and whipsawed his stockinged feet out from under him. He fell heavily, his skull cracking the frame of the bed. Before he recovered, Plummer, with his knee against the Russian's chest, slammed his head against the floor and, locking his forearm against his throat, immobilized the bullet-shaped head.

On the bed above, the naked Belgian girl shrank slowly away, dragging a faded yellow bedspread with her as she crabbed backward. When her thin shoulders touched the wall, she slumped off, like a terrified child, holding up the spread to cover her spindly nakedness, staring at Plummer with wide, henna-rimmed eyes. "Get out," he told her. She slid away eagerly, rolling across the bed and rising at its foot to flee across the room, still dragging the spread with her.

The American stood looking over Plummer's shoulder at the Russian's face. It was tightly muscled, glistening like raw bone in the overhead light. The Russian stared coldly at the ceiling. He had dirty blond hair, closely cropped, pale blue eyes, and the neck and shoulder muscles of a gymnast. He didn't look at Plummer.

Plummer told him in German that they wanted to talk to him, someplace quiet, away from Brussels.

The Russian didn't move. He was still dazed. The technician came into the room carrying a small black bag. He kneeled down beside Plummer, opened his bag, and took out the syringe. The Russian struggled briefly, trying to lift his head, but it was no good. His arm jerked as the needle found the vein, but the second technician was holding the arm by then. After three minutes he was unconscious. They brought the canvas body bag and rolled him into it. Within five minutes the room was empty. Plummer was the last to leave. The Belgian girl was crying as the American led her down the darkened stairwell.

By the time the C-54 was airborne for Frankfurt, it was almost three o'clock in the morning. Plummer had remained behind.

"Phil thought you'd want to go along," the station chief said as they drove back to Plummer's hotel. "He was surprised when I told him."

"I'll tell him myself tomorrow," Plummer said.

"What do you think of our people? Not bad. They say you chaps in Vienna are the real pros."

"It went well," Plummer said, not thinking of Brussels, or the operation at all. "I'll tell Phil that."

The fog was heavy in the streets the following morning. Plummer's flight for Vienna originated in London and overflew Brussels because of the groundfog. He waited at the airport until noon, but couldn't get a booking. He finally gave up and made reservations for the following day and rented a car at the airport, but he didn't return to Brussels. Instead he drove south to Mons and parked the car and walked along the canal under the trees. The day was raw and cold. An old man was sitting on the stones, holding a long roach pole, a crust of bread and an apple on the knapsack beside him. Plummer stood and watched. When the old man turned and looked up at him, he walked away. He didn't want to talk. His mind was empty. He couldn't think about anything.

The following morning the streets were still foggy in that dense, spectral way of Brussels in midwinter. The pale glow of the arc lights filtered through the fog at street corners. Bundled shadows moved along the streets; trucks were unloading in front of unlighted shops; and yellow lights had begun to flicker on from the flats above. It was six o'clock when he left his hotel. The windshield of the rented car was covered with a curtain of ice as thick as boiler plate. He'd chipped the ice from the left side of the windshield and, as he drove away, had only a narrow vector of vision ahead of him. It didn't seem to matter. The streets were empty. He'd always driven too fast and he was driving too fast that morning when he skidded through an intersection and realized that the steering was erratic. At the next straightaway he accelerated, driving the small car forward to test the linkage at the next corner, but he entered the cobbled square faster than he'd intended. When the diesel truck, with a second van in tandem, rumbled like a locomotive out of the side street, he knew he couldn't avoid it. The brakes were useless against the ice-slick cobblestones. The car spun violently, Plummer still gearing down, but he was doing fifty when he smashed into the rear of the truck and was flung across the intersection like a ripped biscuit tin. The shattered metal shell climbed the curb on the far side of the dark square, careened off a lamppost, and crumpled against a brick apartment house, inert finally under a fine curtain of mortar dust.

For three hours they worked with acetylene torches and hacksaws to remove Plummer from the mangled chassis of the car. His skull was fractured, his left arm and shoulder smashed, his hip broken. His bloody, unconscious face looked like death itself to the bundled Belgian shopkeepers, mechanics, and firemen who watched under a graying winter sky as his body was brought forward, inch by inch, out onto the pavement.

He spent two months in a Belgian hospital. They thought at first that he wouldn't live; then that he wouldn't walk. He was seldom conscious for more than a few hours at a time. When the crisis had passed, he was evacuated to Bethesda Hospital near Washington. From his coat pocket they had retrieved the letter of resignation written in London,

bloody and cryptic. For many at the Agency, the letter and the accident were linked. Roger Cornelius believed they were and he came to
see Plummer.

It was early May. Visiting hours were over. Plummer had fallen
asleep after dinner and awoke to find the room in semi-darkness,
Roger standing awkwardly near the bed, as gray as a ghost, the lights
of Washington glowing in the distance. He was uncomfortable at first,
like the dean of a New England prep school visiting an anemic student scholar at the campus infirmary. He was tall and gray haired,
with an ascetic face, light blue eyes, and the weathered complexion
of a blue-water yachtsman. He carried an alligator coat over one arm.
He wore a frayed flannel suit, but wore it carelessly, as always. It was
expensive, like the soft patrician voice and the dark pebbled brogans
whose leather was cracked and tattered like old porcelain beneath the
Metropolitan Club sheen. He had brought Plummer two books.

He apologized for coming at so late an hour and then for not coming sooner. There was a stoicism to him that abhorred sick rooms or
illness, a reserve that grappled awkwardly with grief, spontaneity, or
compassion. Plummer understood. Roger's first wife had been a Bos-
ton woman of great beauty and fragility who had ended her years in
a mental institution. His son had committed suicide. He was in some
ways a brilliant man, and Plummer respected him, not for his mental
gifts which he thought brittle and abstract—his Cold War orthodoxy,
his improvisatory cunning, his historical and cultural memory—but
for the gentler and wiser man he sometimes sensed in Roger, ambushed by his reputation. He had hunted with him one winter in Bavaria and they'd fished together in Scotland.

Roger brought a chair from the corner and they talked for a while
without mentioning the accident. He had remarried again and had
two small children. He talked about them—how he missed them
during his travels. He had recently returned from Europe and had
stayed with Phil and Eva Chambers in Vienna. "Vienna's a remarkable
city," he remembered, the recollection settling a smile on his face, and
Plummer knew he was finally at ease. Reminiscences made him comfortable; like most men with a strong historical sense, he felt more at
home with the past than the future. "Not like London or Paris these

days. You can still get the sense of it there. The feeling's been drawn off in Paris. You don't find the same intensity. Metternich once said that Asia begins in Vienna—at the Lanstrasse. It does, you know. It begins in Vienna. You can feel it—Warsaw, Budapest, Kiev, Moscow. It begins there. The same wind blowing, the same intensity, the same feeling. You remember, don't you?"

Plummer said he remembered. Roger put the two books on the bedside table: "I thought you might enjoy these." Immobile in his neck and hip brace, Plummer couldn't read the titles. Roger finally mentioned the accident. "Something is always retrievable," he reassured him, trying to find the right words. "Somewhere, sometime. The task is to find it—to find out what it is, and then begin from there. The losses are never absolute. They mustn't be."

"Is that what Washington thinks?" Plummer wondered.

"Washington does little thinking. What we do is a substitute for action: special studies, intelligence estimates, political profiles. Some think them essential. Perhaps they are." He lifted himself to find an ashtray and sat down again. "Most of us are in the dark here. In Moscow too, I suppose. Don't they have the same problems? The same bureaucratic battles, the same competition for resources or authority, the same paralysis. Perhaps they're as chilly in Moscow as we are tonight. I wonder what our fuel analysts would say?" He smiled, but it was a brief smile and passed quickly from his face like a child's breath on a cold window pane. "But something is always retrievable, however badly it's smashed," he began again. "Nothing is ever lost—not absolutely. We'll find something."

"You read my letter then," Plummer asked.

"I read it, yes. Your resignation." He got to his feet. "Last week someone suggested that you come back to Washington, maybe work in plans. One of the Eastern European desks. Surveys, statistical abstracts, political analysis. The analysts say they deal in reality. Every week there's a call for a new appraisal. You can't imagine how much time we spend on them. So when another operation breaks down, we can always go back to the archivists, economic surveys, population charts, GNP. What can they tell us except what we already know. That's the death of the imagination, isn't it—capability equals intent. So they cling to reality, political and statistical reality, as an absolute. Others find ways to manipulate it. If you can manipulate the political reality without surrendering its social foundations, you've found the answer. Politicians do it every day, don't they—manipulate reality to their advantage? Why not diplomacy? Why should we be any less orthodox in protecting our interests abroad than in promoting our own domestic ambitions? Morality has nothing to do with it. Who these days pretends politics is a just art? No one. Just the politicians." He turned from the window and came back to the chair. "No, you wouldn't like Washington these days. Not after what you've done. You belong in operations, overseas. I was reminded of that driving out here. I remembered something someone once wrote about Louis the Fourteenth's court at Versailles. He said that court life was so artificial, so contrived, that when he left the palace he sometimes stood in the street just to watch real dogs chewing real bones. That's Washington these days."

He left soon afterward, as unobtrusively as he'd come, leaving behind the two books, the aroma of mild tobacco, and the puzzling ambiguity of a personal world not completely known, a world of the past, of tragedy and of ruins where one man still kept vigil for reasons his contemporaries had forgotten.

The psychiatrist from the Agency began his visits the following week. Plummer wasn't interested in talking to him, but immobilized in his hospital bed in a cocoon of plaster of Paris, gauze, and adhesive plaster couldn't escape his pseudologia. He talked about trauma, destructive energies, psychic confusion, and psychotic transfers. He discussed the burden of the struggle with guilt and absurdity, the logical and moral dislocations of our age, and the dilemma of suicidal sufferers like Plummer. Plummer's silence and the angry clarity of the brown eyes watching from behind the head dressing gave the psychiatrist pause, but in the end simplified his task. He brought with him on the final visit the bloodstained letter of resignation, stiff with dried blood and worn with handling. He told Plummer that he was suicidal, yes, but so were a great many people. He could still live a happy and productive life, could continue to serve the Agency. He didn't ask about Elizabeth Davidson and Plummer said nothing. Two letters lay on the bedside table, both addressed to her. He didn't notice.

It was late October when Plummer returned to Vienna. She hadn't answered his letters. He drove south to Pullendorf in the same blue Porsche. Ragged clouds drifted over the tree tops, already burned with autumn color. He stood in the deserted camp at Pullendorf, listening to a door squeak somewhere in the distance. Wild grasses overgrew the abandoned walks; the doorways had been boarded over. A forgotten dog skulked near the old generator room. He broke into a lope at Plummer's approach, tail between his legs, and disappeared across the field. Behind the boiler house Plummer heard the scrape of a shovel. He found an old, white-haired custodian filling a burlap bag with the last scrapings from the coal pile.

Plummer's letters had been returned to Washington—first from the UN office at Pullendorf, then Vienna, and finally Geneva. An official in Vienna wasn't certain of her whereabouts. Someone else said she was in Beirut. A few days after his return Plummer stopped by the Gwenhogg apartment. Peggy was there, just returned from shopping. She still had her coat on and they talked at the door. She didn't ask him in. She said that she'd heard from a friend in London that Elizabeth had left the UN and was engaged to be married. The announcement had come suddenly. She promised to find her address and send it to him. Plummer never heard from her.

In 1959 Plummer left Vienna for the last time. Some said that he'd resigned, others thought he'd been dismissed, while a few were convinced that he hadn't left the Agency at all, but was doing other things in other places—a British engineering firm in Antwerp, an American oil company in the Persian Gulf or South America. There was malice in some of the speculation, conjecture in others. No one knew the whole story except Phil Chambers and Roger Cornelius. Both kept their silence.

SIX

The Berlin weather was churlish and foul. The temperature hovered several degrees above freezing. It drizzled every day and the feculence followed indoors, licking its sour breath across rugs and tile floors, into offices, wet bars, and elevators. Fires smoked without heat, the mornings dawned without sunlight, and the afternoons dissolved sullenly into evening, vanishing in the thick yellow gloom of lamplight. Karlshorst was hidden beneath the mist; fog buried the airports, obscured the canals and the narrow streets near Strekov's flat. When he opened the door in the evening the debauch of fog and mist had crept there too, smelling of coal tar and sulphur, the black mornings of the Ruhr.

There were shootings along the Wall, where Soviet tanks and armored personnel-carriers loomed suddenly out of the bogs of yellow mist at unfamiliar street corners near the Soviet Embassy—sluggish sauropods on whose iron flanks the mist ran like quicksilver and iced into silver scales—their clumsy treads hobbling across cobblestone and brick, dragging sparks from the flint of the streets. In the evenings shots sounded along the motionless pond water of the Spree, and Strekov sometimes heard them from his desk at the Soviet mission. All of the identifiable landmarks seemed obliterated. Only the checkpoints into West Berlin seemed fixed, their lights a mustard yellow in the fog, like gas blisters on the gray shroud of the city.

On a wet November afternoon Strekov left the Soviet mission alone, walked for a few blocks towards the center of the city, and caught a tram. Fifteen minutes later he changed directions, caught a second tram, and descended at a street corner on the fringes of Kopenick. A block beyond was a small park with asphalt paths intersecting at the center where a small cast-iron fountain lay. In the summer the fountain blew a cushion of cool water into the green shadows under the trees, but the trees were bare now, black skeletons under the wet gray sky. At the center the walks were lined with wooden benches in iron frames anchored to concrete piers sunk into the earth. The anchor bolts had been replaced over the years, the asphalt freshly patched where it had eroded at the base of the concrete pier. Strekov crossed through the park, a newspaper under his arm, turned aside near the fountain, and sat down at one of the benches and tied his shoe. A few Berliners hurried by on the asphalt paths. With his right hand Strekov withdrew a small asphalt divot from the base of the concrete pier, retrieved a lump of plumber's putty, pressed a small aluminum cannister of film into the putty, returned it to the cache, and replaced the divot.

Twenty minutes later he bought a ticket at a small cinema in Kopenick and went up the foyer, past the ticket taker, and into the darkness beyond. The warm air smelled of sulphur from the state-owned tannery nearby whose smokestacks blistered the window paint and peeled the varnish from the neighborhood shop windows. The film was Polish with dubbed German dialogue. It described the problems of a rural youth who found a factory job in Warsaw and ran afoul of alcohol and absenteeism. Strekov wasn't sure what the factory produced; it could have been bricks or it could have been cottage cheese. The film broke halfway through the feature and the crowd could hear the complaints of the operator in the small booth. When the feature finally ended and the lights came on, Strekov looked at his watch.

Two seats away a young girl sat deep in her seat next to the wall, her knees propped against the back of the empty seat in front of her. As Strekov reached for his coat which he'd thrown aside in the seat that separated them, she held out a sack of bakery cookies. "You'll miss the short features," she said.

"They're all the same," Strekov said, looking at the German girl. She was in her mid-twenties, with dark, curly hair and bold green eyes. Her arms were slender but strong, like her shoulders, developed in the *aufbausschichten*, rousting cobblestones and carrying hod in the women's work gangs.

"They're better than the film. Have one." She held out the sack again and Strekov took one. She put the sack between her knees and dusted her hands. "You don't come here often," she said.

"Not often, no," Strekov said.

"I didn't think so," the girl said. "I work in the bakery around the corner."

"What do you do?"

"On the dough tables. What about you?"

"A trade paper," Strekov said.

"A journalist. That must be interesting. I'd like that. Never dull— like the bakery or this place."

"Why do you come?"

She shrugged. "It's close to the bakery. Solitude. I watch my sister's children during the day. Her husband is in Halle. In the army. Everyone's in the army."

"So you don't watch the films," Strekov said.

"I've seen them too many times," she laughed. Strekov smiled too, watching the remarkable green eyes. "What are you doing?" she asked. "Killing time?"

"I suppose so."

"What else is there? I work until eleven. Ten if I'm in a hurry. There's not much else."

"Are you usually in a hurry?"

"When I have someplace to go," she said. "But that's never. Everyone is in the army." The lights went down. Strekov looked at his watch in the twilight. "Do you know the bakery?" she asked. Strekov said he wasn't sure. "Two shops from the corner," she said. "My name's Maria."

"I'll remember," he said. He picked up his coat. "I must go. *Auf Wiedersehen.*"

"*Auf Wiedersehen.*" She watched him leave, still smiling, her eyes bolder in the twilight, glowing like those of a fisherman's cat.

Fifteen minutes later Strekov found the same park where he had sat at one of the benches and tied his shoe. Darkness had fallen. He stopped under the streetlamp to light a cigarette, striking his match across the iron post. Shoulder-high on the post was a small chalk mark. He identified it even before his match had flared in the gathering dusk. It hadn't been there when he had left the film tin in the lump of putty. The dead-drop under the nearby bench had been emptied.

"Everything interests me," Zhilenkov mumbled, staring out through the car window at the dark Berlin streets. Strekov sat beside him in the rear seat of the official sedan that was taking them to a reception near Soviet military headquarters at Zossen. Zhilenkov's heavy jowls smelled of spice, his graying hair was damply combed, he wore a fresh white shirt, and in the lapel of his heavy worsted suit was the Order of Lenin. Zhilenkov hadn't wanted to go to the reception alone. He would be ignored by the younger military and diplomatic cadres who knew nothing of his former prominence, and forgotten by those men his own age who knew more and who no longer feared him. He was in exile in East Berlin, a large man, barrelchested, with a heavy face, thick lips, and thin brown hair which was beginning to turn gray. In his mid-sixties, he was still vain about his appearance. He had a wife in Moscow, four children, and a dozen or so grandchildren, but he had a mistress in East Berlin, a small, dark-haired woman twenty years his junior who performed menial chores for the KGB housekeeping section at Karlshorst. He abused her miserably when he was drunk in his quarters, but she continued to wait on him hand and foot. She was Ukrainian, like Zhilenkov.

"What else is there?" Zhilenkov continued. "In your case, you can travel—get away. But what's in Berlin for a man like me? Everything's going to hell these days. There's no discipline. Changes are in the wind and here we sit in this graveyard. The man who comes last gets a picked bone. By the time we get to Moscow, all the bones will be sucked dry. It's every man for himself these days—*Vse boyatsa za svoyu shkury.* Save your own ass. If you're not in Moscow, you might as well be shut away in a *kolkhoz* for all anyone cares. Shut away with muzhiks, sour milk, and sheep turds. You might as well sputnik yourself to the moon for all anyone cares, anyone in Moscow. So what else can a Party member do—an old Bolshevik. I make everything interest me."

Zhilenkov despised East Berlin. He stared out the window at a group of East German workers standing at a street corner, waiting for a tram. "Like to get their hands on our throats, wouldn't they. Smash us in a minute if they got the chance."

Strekov wasn't fooled by Zhilenkov's protestations. He knew that the old man was looking forward to the reception at Zossen—the drinks, the conviviality, and the women, anything to escape the lonely cycle of his own exile at Karlshorst. He was an old Chekist who'd first come to prominence in the thirties when he'd helped decimate the Ukraine of its Yezhovites and counterrevolutionaries. He'd barely escaped hanging in 1954 when Beria was purged. At one time he had had powerful friends on the Central Committee and in the Administrative Organs Department, but when the destalinization campaign had begun, his friends had deserted him. He'd found refuge abroad, first in Bulgaria and later Hungary, helped by a few old colleagues in the KGB in finding a post in the East European backwaters where he could wait out the bureaucratic purges of old *apparatchiki* under the new liberalization policy. Prior to his assignment to Sofia his only contacts with foreigners dated from his NKVD days in the thirties when he'd worked in the Comintern offices in Moscow—with Poles, Germans, and Jews, an experience which had only reinforced his contempt for non-Russians and his pride in the absolutism of the revolution, a historical beginning only a Russian could share or understand. He was contemptuous of the Soviet diplomatic cadres who spent their lives abroad. He was suspicious of youth, of anyone born after 1917, in whose presence he was even more vulgar and coarse. The younger KGB cadres at Karlshorst mocked his thick Ukrainian accent, thought him cunning but uneducated, a prisoner of his peasant origins, his treachery born of violence and sustained by his fear of change and his dread of the future. He had suffered a heart attack six months earlier in East Berlin. The seizure had strengthened his fear that he would die abroad in some hated German hospital, alone and forgotten in his final convulsions.

He had no operational responsibilities at the KGB mission at Karlshorst. He was listed as a senior adviser to the *rezidentura*. He spent most of his time in internal intrigues, spying on those he mistrusted, and drafting lengthy, fatuous reports to his old cronies in Moscow, especially Orlov. Few were read. His talent for treachery was all that was left to him. Murder, terror, and assassination were no longer the crafts of advancement in his old trade. He had been shunted aside, a sly, semiliterate old Chekist left alone with his memories. In his drunken solitude at his second-floor flat near Karlshorst, he knew his obsolescence. He despised being left alone, even with his mistress, Mrs. Zlobin, whose simpleminded devotion only reinforced his self-hatred. He sometimes beat her. When he did, he would summon Strekov to help him compose his thoughts and prepare a note of apology. Ashamed and remorseful, he would insist that Strekov sit with him until his paroxysms had passed and his head had cleared sufficiently to find words of expiation. They sometimes talked until dawn.

Despite Zhilenkov's crudeness and treachery, Strekov felt a certain sympathy for the old man. He saw Zhilenkov as his link with the past; but even more, he had identified something else—innocence, perhaps. He could no better define it than that.

The reception was held in an old Hohenzollern residence near Soviet military headquarters at Zossen. The lights from the tall windows shone through the frosty darkness; official cars and limousines circled past the wide steps. The reception line began inside the door and followed a strip of crimson carpet along the white-paneled wall to a second doorway. A few steps beyond stood a senior Soviet general, flanked by the two ranking members of a delegation from the Defense Ministry in Moscow, who received the arriving guests. In the room beyond, a pair of enormous crystal chandeliers shed their light over the hundred or so guests who stood talking and drinking. At the end of the room hung an enormous portrait of Lenin against a crimson drape.

Zhilenkov disappeared soon after they passed through the reception line. Strekov wandered off through the crowd. The banquet tables were lined three-deep with guests. He went instead to a table at the rear of the long room where two perspiring Russian youths were filling cups from a punch bowl. Strekov asked for a whiskey but one of the youths shook his head and nodded off towards another bar in the far corner, crowded with people. Strekov looked without enthusiasm at the punchbowl as the Russian youth ladled a cup for him. A few spirit-soaked strawberries drifted across its languid surface, but most lay wholly sodden at the bottom. He moved away from the table and joined two of his colleagures from the Soviet Embassy who were talking to an East German colonel. As he listened he saw Zhilenkov moving alone through the crowd, searching for familiar faces among the members of the Moscow delegation.

When he saw him an hour later, he was still alone. He was slightly drunk by that time, wobbling on his bow legs, the alcohol exaggerating his slight limp. Strekov looked at his watch and turned aside to leave his empty glass on the nearby table. When he looked around again, Zhilenkov had disappeared. He found him a few minutes later, holding his empty glass and following a waitress who was carrying a tray of glasses of vodka. Zhilenkov exchanged his empty glass for a full one and turned back to the banquet tables. "Look at them," he said as he stuffed his mouth with a small sandwich, glancing towards a group of East German bureaucrats huddled together along the back wall, exchanging whispers as they looked out over the room. The senior Soviet general and his East German counterpart were exchanging toasts near the central banquet table. "Sweating with embarrassment, sick with humiliation," Zhilenkov said, moving back to the table. "Where's the herring, comrade?" he demanded of the Russian youth who was carrying away empty dishes.

Strekov and Zhilenkov were among the last to leave. Strekov found him in the corner behind the bar, collapsed in a brocaded chair, talking drunkenly to a middle-aged Russian woman who was gathering up cups and glasses from the nearby tables to take to the kitchen. "What's your husband do, eh?" he mumbled. "He's not in the kitchen, is he? Fetch us a bottle of champagne, that's a good woman. Bring us two, one for my young friend here."

With the help of the chauffeur Strekov managed to settle Zhilenkov in the rear seat of the sedan, amidst his complaints about the hollow extravagance of the reception and the perfidy of the East Germans. The stairs to Zhilenkov's second-floor flat in the old Prussian officers' barracks near Karlshorst were narrow and dark. Zhilenkov bumped his way to the second-floor landing, still complaining drunkenly, and reeled into the small flat. Mrs. Zlobin was waiting. She was small and dark haired, a bony woman who wore neither rouge nor lipstick; there were tiny dark lines, like cobwebs, around her eyes and mouth. She wore a clean white apron over her black servant's dress. She tried to help Zhilenkov with his coat but he slung it on a chair. The flat was chilly but a small table was set with plates and glasses, as if Mrs. Zlobin had expected Zhilenkov to bring back a few Russian visitors or colleagues from the reception. There were breads and cheese, hor d'oeuvres, smoked fish, bits of ham and beef, yogurt, spiced cucumber, bottles of vodka and brandy, a few liters of Georgian wine.

"They will come," Zhilenkov told her, sending her to the kitchen to fetch a bottle of whiskey. "But only for Andrei Ivanovich," he added, "not the others." No one came. Zhilenkov played records on his small victrola and talked about the Party Congress in Moscow. The moon shone on the cold quadrangle of courtyard beyond the gabled windows. From time to time a few cars crossed the cobblestones and left their Russian passengers at the flats across the way. Lights came on in the windows. More cars came. They heard doors slam, sometimes laughter. None of the footsteps came their way. Zhilenkov and Strekov ate from the plates Mrs. Zlobin brought them and listened to the Soviet radio station at Potsdam, broadcasting a speech delivered two days earlier at the Moscow Party Congress. Mrs. Zlobin cleared away the dishes. Zhilenkov fell asleep. Mrs. Zlobin emerged from the kitchen, a dark coat pulled over her shoulders, saw Zhilenkov's head lying back against the cushions, and drew Strekov back to the small lavatory at the front of the hall. She opened the medicine cabinet and brought out a small medicine bottle. In a whisper, she told him that Zhilenkov was to take two teaspoons before retiring. In the small enamel cabinet were other bottles, vials, pill tins, powder envelopes, and barbiturate capsules. Strekov stood looking at them silently. He had never thought of fear or courage in a clinical way, the will to endure reproducing its strength in some exact pharmaceutical likeness—stone crystal or silica, the sterile mimesis of a deadly coral blossom. The small lavatory smelled like an embalmer's bag and Strekov's blood ran cold.

He finished his drink and turned off the radio. The wind blew across the courtyard. When Zhilenkov roused himself and sat up, Strekov said, "It's late, Yuri Antonovich."

Zhilenkov pretended not to notice, as he searched the table in front of him for the brandy bottle. "What do you think, Andrei Ivanovich? Orlov respects your opinion. What do you see for us?" His eyelids were heavy. He was straining to keep himself awake, not wanting to be left alone.

"About what?"

"Where have our old colleagues gone? There was no one tonight. Where have they gone? What's happening?" Strekov thought that the Berlin crisis, the Party Congress, and Zhilenkov's recent heart seizure were inextricably mixed in the silage of his brain. His drunken eyes swept past Strekov's standing figure, took in the dark window, and returned to the table. He sat forward, resisting sleep. "What do you see?" he asked. "The younger men, like yourself—what do they see, what do they talk about?" He searched for his brandy glass, nearly knocked it over, and steadied it. He drank from it quickly and poured another, still fighting sleep. "What do you think? There must be some answers, eh? All of this talk—all of this confusion. What do your friends say? Will there be a war this time—in Berlin? The Germans again. Why not Berlin? Better Berlin, I suppose. Speak up. I can't hear you."

Strekov said, "I think not."

"Think not. Why not? Not a war? There always will be, isn't that the truth of it? Is that a car?" Strekov went to the window to look. There was nothing. The engines of a plane droned somewhere off to the northeast. "If the war came, it would be ugly, wouldn't it?" Zhilenkov asked. "Not just a battle. Everyone dead, is that what you see? We have missiles now. You know about missiles, don't you—with the Guards Directorate in Moscow." The old man was nodding toward incoherence. "Missiles—everyone dead—is that it? I'd hate to die before my time. In this barnyard most of all. My God, that would be the end of it—everything. Some will survive, they say. I'm not sure. How do you see it, Andrei Ivanovich?"

"A cruel war." Strekov still stood at the window.

Zhilenkov lifted his heavy eyes. "Cruel? How? Almost everyone dead. Is that what they believe in the Rocket Forces these days? Say a battle—a slaughter. Is that what they think? Is that what Malinkovsky warned the other day?" His eyelids fell. He was nodding towards sleep again. Strekov put his glass quietly on the table. Zhilenkov drifted into sleep and then roused himself, blinking his eyes. "Limbs smashed," he continued, "smoking weapons, everyone dead almost. What would happen then? Trees and cannons like broken match-sticks. Europe like Stalingrad, eh? Is that it? Rubble as far as you can see? What would happen? I can't hear you, Andrei. What did you say?" His head fell back.

Strekov had said nothing. "Like Stalingrad, I suppose," he said after a minute.

"A dirge?" Zhilenkov muttered, his eyes closed. "Even the cruelest of generals unable to look back?" He was half asleep. "What then?" he began again, like a sleepwalker.

"Silence," Strekov said, standing again near the window. "Just silence."

Zhilenkov's deep breathing filled the room. The wind worried the gable. He stood looking out into the darkness, thinking about Zhilenkov's vision of Stalingrad, of the dust thickening on the rubble of the city, of the wind blowing through the emptiness. Zhilenkov's empty glass slipped from his hand and fell to the carpet, rolling across the floor. Strekov turned to watch it and looked at Zhilenkov's sleeping figure. "Just silence," he said. "Cities far off in mourning. Crepe on every door."

Cities far off in mourning, he thought as he pulled on his coat, standing again at the window. He turned off the table lamp in the alcove. The wind raced across the open courtyard below. Crepe on every door, he thought. Widows weeping. That would be it, wouldn't it? But then among themselves the generals agree, somewhere in a stone chateau far from the slaughter, where flags are flying. The generals agree— Russian, German, American, and British. The war is over. The missiles will be retired, the bombs buried again. The night sky beyond the glass frame of Zhilenkov's dormer window was as transparent as crystal; there was nothing between Strekov and the winter night beyond. He touched the pane with his gloved fingers, Zhilenkov's drunken breathing forgotten. In the chateau where the generals are gathered are French doors, gardens in bloom, flowers, white-coated waiters fetching water carafes, diplomats bringing pen and parchment, anxious journalists milling in the reception rooms, television cameramen waiting in the courtyard. The generals agree and send for their presidents and prime ministers. No more wars. The treaties are signed, the announcements made. The sun splashes on the silver cornets. There is band music in the streets. The generals pose with their presidents and prime ministers. Purple plumes, sashes, and pectoral crosses. Mothers weep with gratitude. Wives think of their future again. Old men hold up their heads; young men finger their medals and lock their uniforms away. The ministers tickle their mistresses. The party plenums and parliaments resume. The brothels open. The Party Secretary's speech is drafted but color is lacking—an abverb here, an adjective there. The President's cabinet insists on a new draft for his own policy speech—stronger measures are called for in this paragraph, clarification is demanded in that—

And far off, among the gray corpses of battle, under a vile, decaying sky where no breath stirs, one head lifts. Just a simple, peasant head, straw thatched. With brown eyes, if you wish. Or blue, like yours, Yuri Antonovich. One head lifts and gazes about at the carnage, as if in a dream. One leg is gone. One hand is missing. The sound of the silver cornets hasn't reached him here. He has neither pen nor parchment.

"So this is what I see, Yuri Antonovich," Strekov said as he looked out across the dark courtyard toward the icy glitter of stars above the pantiled roofs. "This is what I know. Only what that solitary peasant knows as he lifts his head. That he must bind his own wounds. And then, having done that, he must learn to die again. That is what I know. Can you or I change that?"

Strekov picked up the glass from the carpet, wrapped his scarf about his neck, and stood in the doorway for a moment, looking at Zhilenkov's sleeping face. Then he left the flat, carefully closing the door behind him.

Dawn broke cold and gray. A few errant snowflakes drifted across Strekov's bedroom window under the eaves. The telephone awoke him and he drove to Karlshorst through the cold streets. He climbed to the *rezidentura* section where he found Orlov's telegram waiting for him.

Orlov wanted him to return to Moscow for consultations the week following. Strekov wasn't surprised. He had been expecting it.

There was fog in the streets that night in East Berlin. Plummer drove east from Alexanderplatz and crossed the Spree south of the Old City Parliament and turned southeast. Ten minutes later he twisted into a darkened side street and slowed to a stop thirty yards beyond, under a flickering arc light. He sat in his car, looked at the luminous dial of his watch, and got out. He lifted the hood and leaned forward to unclamp the distributor cap. Nothing moved in the street ahead of him. He waited a few minutes, looking at the cap in the dim light of the street. He removed the rotor, scraped at it with his penknife, replaced it, and snapped the distributor cap back in place. Still leaning forward over the engine block, he unsnapped a metal clamp from a grease-covered magnetic canister hidden near the base of the firewall. He rotated the canister 180 degrees, loosened the thumbscrew at the bottom of the canister, and a metal sleeve fell into his hand. He emptied the sleeve of the Minox camera and the five rolls of specially treated film, replaced it, and rotated the canister back against the firewall.

A gaunt German laborer carrying an empty plaster hod limped down the street and into the lamplight. His rubber boots were wrapped with rags and covered with a thin shell of plaster scobs. A filthy *Wehrmacht* campaign jacket hung in tatters from his shoulders. He looked at Plummer standing at the fender next to the raised hood and stopped, his Pierrot face gazing at the silent engine. Plummer slammed the hood closed, climbed back into the car, and started the engine. *"Alles gut,"* the German nodded, listening to the quiet glide of the Opel's four cylinders. *"Alles gut."* Plummer pulled away from the curb, watching the rearview mirror.

Thirty minutes later he was sitting in a small, brightly lit restaurant in East Berlin. Sausages, frankfurters, and knockwurst floated in the stainless-steel basins of the serving counter facing the small bar at the front, but Plummer was sitting beyond, where the white tile floor ended in a warren of booths. A toll telephone hung from the post in front of him. Through the dirty windows of the old doors along one wall he looked into a small courtyard where the wind blew and a sheeting of ice lay over concrete. In the summer there were white-clothed tables there under the trees. A few old couples sat in the booths farther to the front. Behind Plummer an old man was whispering to himself drunkenly. Twice he had raised his voice harshly, as if speaking to someone nearby. Plummer, the only person in the vicinity, ignored him.

When the telephone rang suddenly in the silence, he stood up and lifted the receiver before it rang a second time. "Is this Karl?" the voice asked.

"Karl here," Plummer said. "I waited for thirty minutes. What happened?"

"*Nein*. Not tonight."

"I have a few things for you," Plummer said. "I think we'd better talk. It's important."

"*Nein,* not tonight—"

"I think we'd better talk tonight."

"We'll talk later," the voice said. The connection was broken. Plummer stood with the dead telephone in his hand.

"All right," he said finally into the dead phone. "All right, then." He hung up.

When Plummer left the restaurant ten minutes later, the waitress followed him to the door and locked it. The bells in a nearby church tower struck the hour. Traffic was light. He crossed to the other side of the street, looked back at the restaurant where the waitress had drawn the shade, and got into his car.

The Minox and film were still in his pocket. He would have to find a quiet street nearby and return them to the canister. For almost four weeks he had prowled the East Berlin fog like a stray cat, loading and unloading deaddrops and film caches. He knew no more about the identity of the man who was providing them than he had that first night when he had found the films in the hollow buttons of his raglan. He had spoken to him on the telephone on two previous occasions. That night marked the third. Each time a meeting had been promised; each time a telephone call had postponed it.

The voice was familiar to him by now. But that first night in East

Berlin, Plummer had found something in it he recognized. He knew he had heard it before. Sitting in the front seat of the Opel, he tried to remember where he had met him, what they had talked about.

They were belting down the motorway in the pouring rain, the four of them, lost momentarily between Horsham and East Grinstead in Sussex—or at least Templeman was—rain sluicing down in buckets, sodden winter fields on both sides of the gray Jaguar as it raced back to London, Compton-Bofers at the wheel.

"And how, pray, amid such spiritual squalor and materialistic greed—how could anyone expect anything different?" Compton-Bofers moralized, hunched forward over the steering wheel. Like everyone else, he had drunk too much wine at lunch and was feeling its effects.

"Sorry?" Dunstan asked from the rear seat, an unlit cigarette in his mouth. "You mean the old general?"

"The Cold War," Beresford Perse answered with a Jacobin smile, the ice-blue eyes turning towards Dunstan from the front seat. "The Cold War, yes, but consider. If you'll excuse a comparison of unparalleled banality"—he paused to hold the wheel briefly as Compton-Bofers lit his own cigarette—"the clash of conscience on such matters puts me in mind of Gilbert Murray's comment about the conflict between obstinate mules and rampant griffins. The old general is simply an obstinate mule and there's nothing more to be said. Watch the lorry, old boy."

But Compton-Bofers was watching and barely managed to miss it, skidding sideways on the greasy roadbed and sending a sheet of water cascading over the windshield, charitably screening the Jaguar's occupants from the awareness of disaster a fender's breadth away. Compton-Bofers accelerated forward again. After a decent interval Templeman opened his eyes and lifted himself from the depths of the rear seat to peer out into the murk, only to discover in terror that Compton-Bofers still hadn't returned to the right lane, but was accelerating murderously down the wrong side of the road, oblivious to the rain, the tight little English curves, and the oncoming traffic; but then he saw in amazement a small Volkswagen float quietly past, also on the wrong side, and remembered gratefully the madness of English manners—that all of Sussex must know that this drunken Englishman is on the road: old ladies keeping mercifully to the left; vicars in Vauxhalls too; everything put neatly backwards, like a clergyman's collar, to accommodate this drunken peer of the Establishment during his heedless journey through the Sussex countryside. In Germany, Compton would have been demolished within fifty yards of the old general's front gate—but this isn't Germany, either. *Oh, Christ—it's England,* Templeman remembered, *right side, left side. His world gone mad.*

Compton-Bofers was talking again. Templeman no longer knew what he was talking about—being lost, the Cold War, or Kurdish rearmament, the subject the old general had discussed so loquaciously over the long lunch at his country house in Sussex. Was it a Chamberten Clos de Béze '48 with the cheese, as Compton-Bofers had insisted; or a Barsac Chateau Coutet '54 with the fresh fruit and cream puffs, as Beresford Perse had suggested. Templeman's head was swimming by that time. Barbarous, Dunstan had announced, but was he talking about the manor house with its awful Persian and Kurdish bric-a-brac, the errors with the wine, or the general's harebrained scheme for a massive British/American airlift to reequip Barzani's rebellious Kurds on the Soviet underbelly—Kurds first, and then Armenians—Dashnaks, of course.

"Bad taste?" Dunstan wondered aloud, the unlit cigarette still in his mouth. "Bad taste?" He groped still for his lighter, but unable to find it, leaned into the front seat, trying to reach the lighter on the dash.

"I'll agree with you," Beresford Perse continued, unable to focus his eyes, and leaning forward to wipe the fog from the windshield. "Both the Russians and the Americans were wretchedly ill-prepared at the time to share world power, and this explains in large part the latter's predilection to back the wrong horse."

"The old general?" Compton-Bofers asked.

"The Americans," Dunstan interrupted.

"Quite," Beresford Perse said. "I don't agree that containment was in any sense wrong, or that the Cold War could have been avoided. Now, of course—"

Now, of course, another shadow had loomed across the windshield, as dark as a prowling shark through a water glass, and Templeman slid deeper into his seat as the tires rolled savagely across gravel, bounced for a few rods across watery turf, brushed a privet hedge, and climbed back into the road again.

"Are you certain you can see where you're going?" Dunstan asked from the back seat. "I can't see a ruddy thing."

"Of course you can't see a ruddy thing. No one can—we're all flying blind these days!" Compton-Bofers shouted. Templeman remembered Mary Compton-Bofers telling her husband she would be back at the house by five. For reasons he didn't understand—marital ones, probably—Templeman knew that Compton-Bofers wanted to be home before his wife.

"Now, of course," Beresford Perse continued, "it may prove to be different. I'm not at all sure that the Cold War hasn't exhausted its capital. I don't see that it can include Asian peasants, as in Laos, or in Hanoi, as it once included European trade unionists. It seems to me that we've run our limit, or at least Washington has, since it's from there that our strategies are being managed. President Kennedy may move things about for a time, but I'm not encouraged by the Berlin crisis."

"Berlin was threatened," Dunstan observed placidly.

"Quite," Templeman chimed in, as shrill as a soprano, white faced too. *Fuck Berlin, fuck Kennedy too!* His life was hanging on the speed of Compton-Bofers's drunken reflexes, and they were talking politics. *Politics!*

"I agree," Beresford Perse said. "But the Russians have withdrawn their demands for a peace treaty, haven't they? I remember what Truman did in nineteen forty-eight when he faced a similar crisis—the Berlin blockade. He didn't try to boast his way through it, as young Kennedy is doing. He avoided a military solution, as his Pentagon war councils were urging. He simply flew over it. It was a technical triumph, wasn't it? An engineering solution. Not politics or diplomacy at all. I think you chaps do best when you leave the diplomacy to others," Beresford Perse said to Templeman.

They were in London then, driving through the wet gray streets toward Compton-Bofers's house on Campden Hill Square. They left the Jaguar and trooped inside. The fire was lit; whiskey and soda were on the sideboard. Compton-Bofers stood in his wet coat, unpeeling a bottle of whiskey.

"Mercer," he roared. "Mercer! Come here this instant!" But Mercer was already there, standing inside the door, as faint as a ghost.

"I'm here, sir. Yes, sir."

"It's five forty. Where is she?"

Mercer turned to look at the clock on the mantelpiece. "Out, sir."

"Out, eh. Friends of the Tate, is it?"

"Yes, sir."

"That's cock," Compton-Bofers said, a wistful, boyish smile on his rugged face, perspiration beading his forehead, his blue eyes looking at them. "An unemployed actor, I believe. Some such vagabond." His face was still young, the curly brown hair as tight as wool on his head, showing no gray. "Certainly it's cock—certainly—but it's believable too, you see, and that's what counts these days." He'd lined up the glasses by now and was pouring great, whacking double whiskies in each.

"A pity," Dunstan sighed when he left the house with Beresford Perse and Templeman an hour later. Mary Compton-Bofers still hadn't returned.

"'Tis," Beresford Perse agreed. He drove Templeman back to his hotel. The rain had stopped. "You chaps have a new source, I understand," he said as they waited at a stoplight. "In Berlin?"

Templeman's head was reeling. He thought Beresford Perse was talking to Dunstan until he saw Beresford Perse turn towards him.

"Who?" Templeman muttered. "Us?"

"So they say. Very hush hush, I understand. All kinds of remarkable lore. In Berlin, is it? Or more to the east?"

Templeman was puzzled. "Dunno," he said. "Who told you?"

"They were talking about it last night," Dunstan volunteered from the back seat. "One of your lads here. The Joint Intelligence Committee met last week, we understand. No minutes. Who was there?"

Beresford Perse said he didn't know. "All very odd," he said, moving forward in traffic again. "Very big, I understand. Only we're not getting a whiff. No one is. Your chaps in Washington have become very selfish, it seems."

Templeman said he'd look into it.

SEVEN

Plummer waited in the terminal near the international arrivals entrance, watching the passengers move through the glass doors from the customs counters. When they announced the arrival of the flight from Brussels, he went outside and watched it descend to the tarmac.

The baggage was delayed and by the time the passengers began to exit from the doors, the crowd waiting in the lobby had increased. Plummer watched Elizabeth come through the doors carrying a bright red poinsettia, followed by a porter carrying two suitcases. He slipped through the crowd and crossed to her, gave the porter a bank note, and relieved him of the two bags. "You'll never get a taxi in this mob," he said.

She turned, looking up at him. "You take long holidays," he said. "Welcome back."

"It was rather long, wasn't it?" Her face was as slim as ever but her blond hair was swept back from her face more severely now. There were shadows under her eyes.

"Three weeks," he said, taking her arm.

"But it wasn't three weeks," she protested. "It was only two."

They crossed through the parking lot to the Opel and Plummer put the bags in the backseat. She got in next to him and they left the airport, she holding the poinsettia in her lap. "I thought you were just going to Geneva," he said as they drove away. "You didn't tell me about Brussels."

"It came up rather suddenly."

Plummer looked at her hands but she was wearing gloves. He couldn't tell whether she was still wearing the engagement ring or was now wearing a wedding ring as well.

"That's a poinsettia, isn't it?" he asked. An armored car whistled across the intersection ahead of them. Plummer slammed the brake pedal, but she didn't appear to notice. Not knowing whether she was still wearing the engagement ring and excluded from whatever had happened in Brussels, he was suddenly depressed.

She lifted the flower slightly, studying its leaves. "Do you like it? It's lovely, isn't it? The children gave it to me."

"What children?"

She didn't turn. "His children. They gave it to me at the airport."

"He was married before?"

"I think I told you that."

"Maybe you did. How old is he?"

"We talked about that, too."

"Do you love him?"

The question surprised her. She didn't answer for a minute, looking away out the window, and he didn't repeat it. In the silence between them Plummer recognized the change in her and knew there was nothing he could do about it.

"That's very personal, isn't it?" she said finally.

"Maybe so. That's why I asked."

"It's difficult to talk about it."

"I understand." But he was irritated. He didn't want to understand, and he wanted her to know that. He said, "If you don't want to talk about it, that's okay. If you're not sure how you feel about him, maybe it's better you didn't."

"I didn't say that."

"I know you didn't. I did," he continued recklessly.

"I like him very much."

"That's all right, then. That's better than not loving him at all."

"Love is a more complex set of words," she interrupted, not wanting to hear any more. "Much more. The more time passes, the more impossible it becomes to define their meaning. I think women understand this much better than men. There are too many meanings. Some are painful; some aren't. Please don't ask me any more."

"You mean love takes courage."

She turned to look at him. "Yes."

"And you don't have courage?"

She turned away. "Not the way I once did, no."

"You're too hard on yourself," he said. "It takes courage to marry someone you don't love."

"That's most unfair."

He knew she was angry. "Is he Catholic?"

"What on earth gave you that idea?"

"The way you're going at it—trying to invent the logic for a faith you don't feel. Peeling the onion the way you are. Is that what being with him does to you?"

"He's not Catholic and it certainly wouldn't matter if he were."

"Okay, let's drop it," Plummer conceded. "Why did you go to Brussels? To set a date?"

"No." Her anger was gone. "We wanted to be together with the children for a few days. I thought I'd see them over Christmas, but they'll be with their mother instead. So we had a small holiday together in Brussels. A sort of premature Christmas."

"You had Christmas last week?"

He saw the look in her eyes. "Not a regular Christmas, no, but we exchanged gifts. We had a tree—"

"You had a Christmas tree?"

She looked away again. "It was a bit unusual, I admit."

"Whose idea was it?" He knew it wasn't hers. When she didn't answer, Plummer said, "What's this guy Buxton look like, anyway."

She didn't answer. He waited.

"Is he short, tall, thin, what?"

"That's really unfair," she said.

"I suppose Christmas at someone else's convenience isn't unfair. I think it's a little screwy if you ask me."

"It's understandable under the circumstances."

"If you think I'm butting in where I don't belong, I'll shut up. But it gets me that—"

"I think it's difficult to discuss love, or affection, or anything else in terms of appearances."

"Okay, let's forget appearances. What's he call you?"

"What do you mean?"

"Your name. What's he call you? When he telephones you from Brussels to say hello."

"He's far too busy to ring me from Brussels," she said firmly.

"When he writes you then, what's he say—'Dear Miss Elizabeth Davidson'?"

She flushed. "He calls me Elizabeth."

"I saw that," he said.

"Saw what?" The smile was gone. She turned innocently.

"That sneaky look on your face."

"You're terribly sly today, David, but the light has changed."

Plummer moved the car ahead quickly. "What's he call you, then?"

"I told you."

"No, you didn't. Is it a family name?"

"Elizabeth."

"Not Elizabeth, either."

"This is absurd."

"Sure, it's absurd. That's what I'm saying."

"Do slow down."

He was driving too fast, sliding through the corridors of traffic, gliding from one lane to the next with barely a backward look. "It's not Liz, is it? Libby? No—"

"I told you."

"I know what you told me, but the penny didn't drop." He turned to look at her, and then at the poinsettia she was holding. "Why don't we prove it. Are you ready to prove it?"

"I'm willing to do anything to stop this ridiculous nonsense."

"Good," Plummer said. "Then ask Aunty Poinsettia there—see what she says. Read the name on her little lace collar there."

Elizabeth looked at the poinsettia and the small white envelope tied to the bright red ribbon. She removed the card and held it for a moment. Suddenly she pushed it out the ventilator window and it was gone. Plummer eased the Opel to the curb and was out the door. "You're not," she protested, "you wouldn't," but he was already gone, moving through the late afternoon traffic—Opels newer than his; Mercedes trucks plowing fields of diesel fumes; snappy Fiats; lumbering Citroens like bottom-feeding sharks; angry Volkswagens horneting home. From the front seat she watched him bend over and retrieve something from the roadbed, dodge back through the traffic, and return to the car. He dropped the white envelope on the seat beside her without opening it and moved the car forward into the boulevard. "It's hopeless," she said, her face flushed. "It's simply hopeless."

Plummer disagreed. "It's never hopeless. Just screwy, sometimes. Give yourself half a chance and things may work out."

"I think you've been terribly unfair."

"Okay, I won't say anything else. No tricks. No more Keystone Kops. But listen for a minute. This whole thing's wrong. That's all I'm saying. It's wrong. It's got to be wrong. How could it be right when you've just got to pull on a loose string and the whole shebang comes smashing down?"

They drove in silence. After a moment, she said quietly: "Now who's giving instruction?"

It was dark. The boulevard lights had flickered on below. A light rain was falling. Plummer stood at the window of Elizabeth's apartment, looking out across the rooftops. In the drive far below, cars were circling under the overhang and discharging their passengers. A cocktail party was going in a nearby flat. He had put aside his teacup and helped himself to a whiskey while she changed her clothes.

She joined him at the window, her hair freshly combed, wearing a wool skirt and cardigan. Both smelled of cedar chips. She looked down into the street. After a minute she said, "I'm sorry I was abrupt. I didn't mean to be. You were quite right."

He didn't want to think about Brussels and Buxton. The mildness of her voice surprised him. "About what?"

"The name," she said simply. He followed her to the sideboard, took the glass from her hands, fixed the drink himself, and joined her on the couch.

Years ago her brother had given her a name—one she herself was responsible for. It was the confused little sound a small child makes of its own name early in life. As she grew older, her brother remembered it when he wanted to tease. She blushed easily, had a quick temper, and disliked the name. Her brother's friends knew the name too, misunderstood its origins, and thought it was a family name, affectionately given, affectionately acknowledged. It wasn't true, but how did one change that? Jim Buxton had been her brother's classmate. Her brother was dead now, killed on Crete, but Buxton and his two small children had brought the name to life again. That was the name on the card: *Leeby*. It no longer reminded her of her childhood, but of her dead brother. In time she would grow accustomed to it, to acknowledging a name to which she didn't belong, to becoming what the name asked her to become.

Plummer said nothing. She watched him after she had finished, brows raised, the corners of her mouth beginning to lift in a sympathetic smile as she recognized his stubborn silence.

"Why don't we just forget about all that," he said finally. "Why don't we get the hell out of here. We could go someplace."

She sat back. "You've said that before."

"How many times do I have to say it?"

She shook her head. "I'm afraid it doesn't make much sense, does it?"

"I thought it did. I still think so."

"I've never pretended it was simple—a simple thing," she admitted softly. "I thought sometimes it would go away. But now I know that it will never go away, that such feelings never do, even if I don't understand them and probably never shall." She sat awkwardly on the couch beside him, her head down, studying her fingers on the glass. "You've known other women," she said painfully. "I know you have. I think that bothered me at first. I suppose it was the security most of all. I'd never known anything like it. I rather expect I never shall again. I suppose that sounds terribly conclusive to you." She raised her eyes. "Naive as well. I'd never had an affair. I never expect to have one again—"

"Look," Plummer said, putting his glass aside. "Look, Elizabeth."

But she wouldn't look, her head was turned again, and she was examining the glass in her hand. "'Look—' It's what you always say when you mean something else. When you don't want to listen. 'Look' or 'Okay' or 'Something like that.' I know every one now," she said with a smile. "Every protest, every ellipsis, every preface and prologue, every evasion. I know what you mean now, I know what you're trying to say, as maddening as it is. It's your way of trying to reassure someone, I suppose. But I can't be reassured when there are so many things I don't know. Little things. Things I haven't even the courage to ask. I do care for you. You don't need to be told that. But if I can't ask, who will?" She raised her head and looked at him.

"What things?" He wasn't sure what she was talking about. She didn't answer. Then she lifted her hand and her fingers touched his temple and the irregular scar as white as wax in the lamplight, the cicatrix along the left eyebrow she'd noticed that first afternoon in Berlin when they'd met again after five years.

"This," she said. "If I can remember so much, why is it that I can't remember this?" She took her hand away. "Why is it that I can't even ask? It wasn't there in Austria."

Plummer had forgotten. He found the scar with his finger. "Maybe it was afterwards."

"How long afterwards?"

Only then did he remember. "How long?" How long was it from Pullendorf to Brussels that cold winter morning, how long from Brussels to Vienna a week later, snow falling over the Alps and along the southern Swiss plain, snowplows out along the Nufenen and Gotthard passes, fog in Brussels that morning when he left the hotel.

When he didn't answer, she laughed. "You see? That's the long and the short of it, isn't it?"

"I had an accident."

"I shouldn't be surprised the way you race about. Where?"

"Vienna." He shifted uncomfortably on the couch. "Someone stopped short in front of me and I hit my head on the mirror."

He was still sitting there, finishing his drink, when the phone rang. Elizabeth answered it. It was Peggy Gwenhogg. She and Peter had been to a reception and were going to stop by. Plummer left before they arrived.

Plummer picked up Chambers outside his small residential hotel in Charlottenburg. He'd arrived that afternoon from London. They drove back to Kreuzberg. Chambers wanted to know if he'd gotten the camera and film to his source in East Berlin. Plummer said he hadn't. He knew Chambers was irritated, but he didn't care. They had had two meetings at the airport in Frankfurt where they had exchanged film. Now Chambers had come to Berlin unexpectedly. Plummer didn't know why, but he didn't like it. He was in a foul temper anyway. He'd tried to reach Elizabeth a few times the past several days and she hadn't returned his call. At the flat in Kreuzberg Plummer gave him a whiskey and put a few lumps of coal in the iron grate. Chambers prowled about restlessly, examining the ugly paintings on the gallery wall, the paint spatters on the floor, and the books abandoned on the old overstuffed couch. Finally he sank down on the cushions.

"Who is he, David? We've got to know."

Plummer lifted his head from the hearth, his coat still on, his tie pulled loose as he puttered with the fire. "Who's got to know?"

"Washington. London. All of us."

"A good fairy that sits on the landing outside. I give her peppermints and she gives me Khruschev's morning mail."

"That's funny but you're closer to the truth than you realize."

"Sure, and you're standing right next to it. Don't give me any crap, Phil. I'm fed up with this goddamned place. I don't want to have to listen to you too."

"We've got to know. We've got to bring him under control."

"You mean Dahlem? Templeman? Screw Dahlem."

"We've got to control him. That's essential now—"

"So is his neck. What did you come here for today anyway?" There was a short wave radio on the mantel. Plummer stood up, turned it on, and adjusted the bandspreader to *Radio Deutschlandfunk* in West Berlin. "Okay, what's it worth? You've read the films now. What do they say?"

"Too much."

"How much? You said it was a paper mill in London."

"London was weeks ago. This is a new ball game."

"How new? What was in the films?"

"Enough to fly me here today. I can't say anymore. We've got to bring him in, get him under control."

"I didn't come here to run your assets for you. What was in the films?"

Chambers sipped his drink and sat forward, still wearing his overcoat: "Listen, David, we're sitting here in Berlin with maybe ten million dollars worth of commo equipment, cryptosystems, high speed transmission gadgetry, radios and cameras you can wire through a tonsil—all that and you're bringing us material passed over an open line, film slipped into a parked car. You're not controlling him. He's controlling you. You've got to turn him over to us."

"That doesn't tell me a thing. What was in the films? In Frankfurt last time you mentioned Lvov, but you still thought it might be a paper mill."

"It's not."

"Then what is it? What the hell's Lvov? You can overfly Lvov with a box kite and a piece of string. With Tiros or anything else. So what?"

"We don't think they're of Lvov."

"What then?"

"Beyond Lvov. Deeper than that."

"How deep?"

"Very deep. Listen."

"Don't yo-yo with me. How deep? Where? Kapustin Yar, where the Germans were?" Plummer waited, still squatting on the hearth, looking back at Chambers angrily.

"Beyond Kapustin Yar," Chambers capitulated finally, slumped back against the couch. "Beyond the ICBM range at Tyura Tarn. Eleven hundred miles east. Near Lake Balkash. That's all I can say."

Plummer didn't move. "A missile range?"

"I can't say. Don't ask."

"The hell you can't. It's my neck too. ICBMs? ABMs? What?"

"I can't talk about it. Let's talk about your asset in East Berlin. Who is he? We've got to bring him out for a few days."

But Plummer didn't seem to hear, still staring at Chambers. "You're crazy," he said finally. He got up, pulled off his coat, threw it against the chair, and poured a drink from the bottle on the table. "They're out of their minds. So are you. I could swallow the Lvov bit, sure. I could even believe something a few German scientists might have brought back from Kapustin Yar five years ago. But not this shit."

"I know how it sounds. I'm sorry."

"You're sorry! You mean you believe it too. You believe those bastards back in Washington? How desperate are you, anyway? You know what Washington is like. They want a few cheap successes while the budget's being drafted, something they can peddle over on the Hill to a few Senators before the liberals get the meat cleaver out. Don't talk to me about analysts."

"Sure I know. But that's not it. Not this time. You're wrong. The first generation Soviet missiles are almost obsolete. Now they're testing for a lighter warhead. That's what this is all about—most of the films. That's all I can say."

"Listen to me, Phil. Just listen. I've known you a long time, too long maybe, but that's the most half-assed job I've ever heard you try to peddle. It's a crock. It's horseshit. Use your eyes. Look at this dump. Look at that couch there. Look out the window at the neighbors. Do you think I've got friends in Moscow? It's bullshit—"

"I know how it sounds—"

"It sounds stupid, that's how it sounds. Are you stupid? You mean to sit there and tell me they've convinced you?"

Chambers lifted himself from the couch, crossed the room and turned up the radio. "All right, I'm stupid." He sank back wearily on the couch. "What the hell am I anyway? I'm too old-fashioned to think I'm an expert anymore. Who is? My generation is on its way out. What are the old OSS types good for now? It's the technology that has made us obsolete; the scientists that have made us bureaucrats. So I do what all bureaucrats do. I believe them when they tell me I've picked up something that might make a difference. Committees, special task forces, scientific watch committees. They're the ones that have been reading the films, not me. I never got beyond high school physics. If you told me the Soviet tank strength in Magdeburg, I could find out in two hours whether you were lying or not. Radio frequencies, order of battle, sure—that's DIA's stuff. The cowpies from the barn. They know where the Soviets are stockpiling their steel bridges, how many anti-tank guns they brought down from the Baltic last week. I know the difference between a soybean granary and a nuclear silo from the outside, maybe even from a Pullman window. But not this other. Igniter malfunction patterns or disintegration speeds for cyrogenic rocket fuels based upon humidity and altitude variables. Christ, no. Acceleration spring speeds for ABMs; integrational accelerator performances; circuitry loads for electronic switching radar. What the hell's that? I can't even wire a toaster. Maybe I could still count the ICBMs on the pad near Lvov at fifty thousand feet, like geese in a cornfield, but what could I do on the ground with a micrometer and a circuit schematic? Nothing. Nothing at all. So if you're trying to tell me I'm obsolete, you're not telling me anything new. But I believe them in Washington. If they've been taken in, then all of us have."

"And you're saying that this guy can do all that?"

"That's why I'm here," Chambers said.

"With what? What's he use? We're in Berlin, not Siberia. What's he do it with, a ouija board? His wife's tea leaves?"

"That's what we want to find out. That's why we want to bring him out, talk to him. Right now, no one is controlling him. He's controlling you and it isn't good enough. Who is he?"

"I don't know."

"Washington thinks you're holding out on us." Chambers opened the fire screen and threw his cigar against the coals, watched it take the flame, and sat down again. "Has he asked for money?"

"You've read the films. What do they say?"

"There's no operational stuff at all. We don't know how he meets you, how he gets the film to you, or anything else. Is he German?"

"Probably."

"The narrative detail is in German. Did you know him someplace else? Vienna maybe?"

Plummer stood at the window. Chambers waited, watching his silhouette. His glass was empty. The coals had died down again. After a minute Chambers said, "If we handled him out of Dahlem, it wouldn't be Templeman. We'd activate someone on the other side of the Wall. Maybe an East German." Still Plummer didn't move from the window. When he finally turned and came back to the hearth, Chambers knew that he hadn't been listening to him at all. He got to his feet with a sigh and buttoned his coat. "That's all you know then?"

Plummer nodded. "That's all I know."

"That doesn't change things. We've got to get a leash on this paranoid, whoever he is. We've got to get him out of the dark, set up some kind of operational structure, some kind of safeguards. How soon can you get the camera and film to him?"

"I don't know."

"You'd better start thinking about it then. Do you know anyone at the station at Dahlem, anyone you'd be willing to work with—to help us out?"

"No."

"You'd better make some friends then. You're going to need them. That's Pankow over there—East Berlin—not the Vienna woods. You're not going to be able to just walk out when you get tired of it."

Plummer was replacing the fire screen, his coat already on. "Screw you, Chambers," he said without turning and led the way out of the flat.

They drove through the empty streets of Kreuzberg. Chambers stared morosely through the windshield, huddled in his overcoat. A few idle snowflakes corkscrewed through the beams of the Opel. As they moved into the brighter boulevard lights of Charlottenburg, he roused himself.

"What's on your mind these days?" he asked Plummer sleepily, his voice cracked with fatigue. "The Davidson woman? I understand she's in Berlin now. Has she gotten to you, Miss Ban-the-Bomber or whatever it is?"

"That's not your problem. Butt out."

"You're my problem. You ought to get out of Berlin. Let someone else take the risks. You don't belong here anymore. It's not your game."

Plummer didn't answer.

A few dim lights showed in the windows of the East Berlin rowhouses. The sky was black, without stars. Plummer crossed the street to the tram stop and stood waiting with three East German workmen. It was too cold to smoke. His car was parked three blocks away. A few minutes later the tram moved towards them, swaying slowly on the rails like an inchworm on an autumn leaf. As the three workmen boarded the tram, he moved away into the shadows; by the time the tram had pulled away he was twenty yards down the intersecting street. At the next corner was a streetlamp suspended by cables from the electric pole. It moved in the wind as he approached. A dark sedan was parked twenty yards away from the corner. A man was sitting in the car, but Plummer didn't turn. On the corner the blue tiles of the old restaurant were as gray as dishwater. The yellow muslin curtains had been pulled closed and soft puddles of beige light leaked out onto the broken pavement. As he reached the corner he heard the sound of a car door opening behind him. He turned and watched the man approach him. There was nothing in his hands, nothing on the street beyond where the wind blew. As he saw the face lift from the shadows in the light of the street lamp, he knew he'd been right about the voice. It was Rostock. "Wulf, isn't it?" Plummer remembered.

"Wulf, yes," Strekov replied, the lips tighter now, the face colder. "You have a good memory."

"Too good," Plummer said, still studying the face, "it keeps me awake nights." Strekov moved past him towards the restaurant.

"I don't have much time. You said you wanted to talk. We can go in—"

"It's not necessary."

"You said you wanted to talk."

"I can talk here: two minutes, that's all. You've dragged me into something I don't want any part of. Some people I know are interested in what you're giving them: the films. I'm not. They want to talk to you in the West, probably West Berlin or Frankfurt. I don't care. I've got other reasons for being in East Berlin. They don't have anything to do with you or the people that want to talk to you. If you want to continue this, to go into the West and make a deal for yourself, I'll tell them that. If not, I'll tell them that too. Only deal me out of it."

"I'd prefer if you spoke German. Other business you said?"

"The oil business. I told you before. That's what I'm here for. Nothing else."

"They sent you here to tell me that?"

"They want me to turn you over to a team working out of Dahlem in West Berlin—the US station there. They'd handle you—"

"Why?"

"Because they don't like the way things are happening. Because they can't reach you except through me. Because they think I'm a poor risk these days. Because they think someone else can do it better—"

"I know what they want," Strekov said. "It was in the last films you passed. They want a new schedule of deaddrops, some in West Berlin. I told them no—the arrangements aren't to change."

"Maybe you'd better think about it awhile."

"There's nothing to think. It's cold out here. You don't stand on street corners in this neighborhood. Come inside."

A half-dozen tables stood in the center of the low-ceilinged room. A bed of coals guttered in an iron stove at the far end of the room where a handful of men in workclothes were sitting on stools and benches. At the opposite end of the room was a row of unvarnished wooden benches where a few middle-aged couples sat. Strekov took a booth nearby, facing the door. Plummer sat opposite. An old man with white hair took their order and crossed the room towards the kitchen.

"What is it that you're telling me?" Strekov asked. "That you're a businessman selling oil and nothing else?" A younger woman returned with two glasses of beer.

"That's what I told you in Rostock."

"I know what you told me in Rostock. I didn't believe you then and I don't believe you now. You're a man with a guide book and a timetable, with an itinerary always well-prepared in advance. Every minute, every hour. You go only where told to go. Rostock, Berlin, Bonn, Zurich. Back to London at precisely such-and-such an hour. Don't talk to strangers; don't get overdrawn; don't miss your plane; don't get lost."

Plummer picked up his glass. "I go where I bloody well please."

"You go where you're sent. It's not your schedule at all. It belongs to your travel office in London or Washington where some anonymous little man files your reports and drafts your checks, goes home at a fixed hour, has his sherry or whiskey, his book, his wife. Not anonymously. Not in a restaurant like this, either."

"I've got better things to do than listen to this. I've said what I came to say."

"Don't misunderstand. I'm not trying to frighten you."

Plummer put his glass down. "Frighten me?" He leaned across the table angrily. "Who the hell do you think you are?"

"It doesn't matter. What's important is that you're not whom you claim to be. The oil operation is a clumsy attempt at espionage, nothing more. You do it well, but that much is obvious."

"Obvious to who? To you? To the Ministry of State Security? It's as real as anything else in this phony little country of yours. That's the problem with paranoids like the SSD. Your country needs what I've got to sell—that's the sickness in all this. They need it." The door opened and two laborers in quilted welding jackets came into the restaurant.

"Your firm is using the oil transaction to obtain information on the machine tool industry and the maritime fleet," Strekov continued, lowering his voice.

Plummer said, "Who told you that—your Soviet friends? I'm talking about technology and you're talking about espionage. Who's going to help East Germany with the technology—your Russian friends? Christ."

"They're learning. The Soviet Union now has the technology. It's improving. Soviet scientists are learning."

"Learning from what?" Plummer demanded. "How are they going to learn? They can't learn, that's the point. What paranoid can? That's their sickness, isn't it? Your Russian friends are cripples, they're technological spastics. So they lie, thieve, and plunder to make up the difference—to give their own filthy system the semblance of normalcy. Look at this barnyard. They've picked this carcass clean."

"You said that once," Strekov said coolly. "You don't know what you're talking about."

"Forget it then. What's your game anyway? What are you looking for—a way out?"

"No. If you dispise East Germany so, why are you here?" Strekov asked. "If you're so contemptuous of it, why do you stay?" He emptied his glass. "But we know the answer to that, don't we? What about motive?"

"Money," Plummer said contemptuously, draining his glass and standing up. "If you believe everything else, why wouldn't you have figured that out?"

"Probably because it's not that simple," Strekov muttered.

In the dark street outside, Strekov said he had no intention of going into the West or changing the present arrangement. He told Plummer that the SSD had periodic contacts with Kohler and a few of the warehousemen at the Treptow warehouse: "You've known informers, haven't you? Widows, old men, bored secretaries, neurotic malcontents—the thousands of people being bought and sold, like lottery tickets, and then torn up or discarded when they're not the right ones."

Plummer was still annoyed. "What makes you so different?"

"The fact that I understand that," he said. "The fact that you do too."

The cocktail party was ending but winter coats were still piled high on the chairs in the foyer and in the pine-scented study. "And what keeps you in Berlin?" the Englishwoman asked Plummer, who was looking in the other direction toward Elizabeth Davidson. She was talking with a group of guests near the front window.

"We'd anticipated a vacancy in mathematics," the woman's husband was saying, putting his glass on a nearby table and searching through his flannel pockets for a match. Elizabeth had introduced Plummer to the couple by saying that he'd once been interested in teaching in Africa or in the Middle East. The Englishman and his wife were both teachers in East Africa.

"The snow and cold comes on like a shock," his wife said, wiping her bony finger along her brow. "It's summer in Kenya."

"I have a few American colleagues in Nairobi," the Englishman said, still eyeing Plummer over his match flame, "but I don't know much about technical schools—trade schools. I suppose that would be more in your line." His eyes moved from Plummer's gray shirt and the dark worsted tie towards the couples moving near the door.

"Elizabeth said you were an engineer," his wife droned on, "and I suppose there's hardly an adequacy of those these days, even in America." She smiled suddenly at Plummer's silence, quite baffled by what Elizabeth had expected of them.

"You're not an agricultural engineer, are you?" her husband inquired politely. "An agronome, I mean. I suppose there's a demand for that sort of thing these days." Again his eyes wandered towards the couples at the door who were pulling on their coats.

"I've suddenly come over terribly sleepy," his wife said.

"I suppose it's time," replied her husband.

Plummer's glass was empty and he wandered over to the bar and replenished it from the whiskey decanter. The lamplight fell across the white woodwork, the white scallops of the bookcases, the crimson silk of the Bokhara carpet on the floor, polished cherry and walnut, silver salvers and urns. Only an hour away from the blue-tiled restaurant in East Berlin, he felt as though he'd come in the wrong door. He'd forgotten about Elizabeth's cocktail.

"Did you talk to the Woodward couple?" Elizabeth whispered, standing at his shoulder, a coat over her arm. "They teach in Kenya."

"Do I look like the public school type?" He followed her across the floor.

"I don't suppose you do," she muttered, "but that isn't quite the point." She went into the foyer, leaving Plummer behind.

"There you are," Peggy Gwenhogg called with a cold smile. "Fancy seeing you here." She moved away from the couple she had been talking with and directly into Plummer's path. "I had the idea you've been avoiding me," she said. She was wearing a dark green dress which clung like wet silk to her angular figure. Her hazel eyes were as bright as Sheffield steel and her voice had an edge to it, as sharp as the Royalist blade that had razored Monmouth. "We seldom seem to meet these days. Elizabeth tells me you've been quite busy."

"A little."

"So you haven't been avoiding us."

"Not recently," Plummer said. He saw Elizabeth cross the room and disappear through the door into the rear hall and kitchen. He followed her and caught up with her in the kitchen. An old German woman was collecting glasses at the sink.

"You're not leaving?" Elizabeth said.

"I thought I'd come back later."

"When?"

"After the dishes were put away and you had a little time to yourself."

"That's awfully sweet of you but I told the Ramseys I'd join them for a bite. They've already made reservations. You could join us too. I think Janet and Peter will be there."

"Maybe tomorrow then."

She nodded. "Maybe tomorrow. I'm sorry you won't join us."

"It wouldn't be the same."

"Will it ever?" she asked, her eyebrows lifting for a moment.

"One of these days," he said.

EIGHT

The Antonov-12 landed at Vnukovo II in Moscow on a winter afternoon. A light mist was in the air, hanging on the limp windsocks and the racheting windcocks of the airfield, on the distant spires of the city, on bronze roof and onion tower, on stone battlements and the intervening skettle of birch and pine. Closer by it silvered the rain-sheathed foil of the Illyu-shin-18s that would fly south at dusk to Cairo, Khartoum, and the Congo. Standing on the unslung carborundum tread of the rear ramp, Strekov saw the II-18's being loaded, immobile as giant geese among the tendering tank trucks, identified the stacked pine crates standing nearby, as fragrant as myrrh from the forests of the Caucasus—oiled Tokarevs, Simonovs, and Kalashnikovs. He felt on his face the warm breath of Africa on a mild autumn evening in 1957, Cairo's swarming streets as the light fades from the west on the great brown colon of the Nile, jasmine dancing like popcorn on necklace-threads of silk looped over the taxi mirrors, taxis bolting under the blue-white arc lights of the boulevard, henna-eyed girls flocking through the streets, Persian and Nubian gold at their throats.

But it was Moscow he'd come home to now, where sunset would bring frost, fracturing this autumn ease from the air, and pinching its rictus of ice around the pods of ice along the boulevards. A Volga ZIS-10 hissed across the wet tarmac and came slowly to a stop at the foot of the loading ramp. So Strekov had come home for a few days. He tasted cinnamon for a moment, steaming molasses, and baking bread. He heard the ruffle of faraway cornets and flutes, a Christmas canzone of strings, brass, and woodwinds. But no. It was only the wind of the West coming home with him, soaring with a rush through the anodized bay, and lost immediately in the immense spaces beyond, leaving a faint ammoniac mist that stung his eyes. Zhilenkov had awakened from sleep and stood behind him on the ramp, drawing great breaths of air into his chest. The Volga spirited Strekov away.

At the apartment house on Kutuzovsky Prospekt, Strekov carried his suitcase to the lift and ascended to the third floor. Orlov's apartment was overwarm, a place of silences, heat-dried flowers on the hall table, a silver vacancy of mirrors along the walls of the corridor, and the sunless smell of a museum, even in the small salon, where the gray eye of a Temp-9 television set sat facing stiff-backed damasked chairs, a hard-cushioned couch, and a glass-fronted cabinet. Orlov's houseman told him that the colonel would be late. His name was Merkurovich—a gray-eyed Siberian, like Strekov, the skin drawn over his bony skull like silk over a darning egg, the silver of the snow fields in his light-flecked eyes. Down the passageway to the rear bedroom, carpeted with claret and plum-colored Turkoman rugs. A smoking stand stood near the bed; on the other wall, a bookcase, and an American armchair under a reading light. Merkurovich turned down the bed, and drew water for the tub in the adjacent bathroom, fetching a scalding kettle from the kitchen to heat the tepid water drawn up through the imperfect pipes. He stood in the blowing steam afterwards, enjoying its therapeutics while he brought Strekov up to date on his family life in Moscow where he bathed once weekly in an icy bathroom shared with four other families in a ramshackle barracks behind Smolensk Boulevard. If the life there was harsh, there were children, sons, daughters, cousins, bread shared in common; there was no life left here in Orlov's rooms: wife dead now, sons and daughters gone—

The hot bath had made Strekov drowsy. Distances still soared by; his bones still throbbed with the sting of airfoil; the chattering of the metal plate at his feet; the scut of wind against his ears—woods, mountains, and rivers still lay beneath him like buried veins hidden under the great albino egg of the Baltic storm front. He slept, waking first in the darkness to the sound of the telephone at his bedside, and afterwards to Merkurovich's gentle knock at the door. He lifted the receiver from its cradle, uncertain for an instant whether he was at Highgate in London, at Karlshorst, or somewhere in between.

"Andrei?" It was a woman's voice, tentative, far away.

"Who is it?"

"Maryna. Andrei?"

"Yes. Yes, I'm here."

"It's Maryna. Do you remember?"

He couldn't remember. He was staring out the window at the dark sky beyond and the lights of Moscow, as soft as starlight. Was there another woman he remembered now through this gauze of winter light, through the screen of distance that separated him from his Moscow past like evening snow falling through winter birches, someone he remembered more than life itself, someone still able to speak his name out of the past; or was this only one of the uglier tricks of sleep, something his empty heart had now conceived in desperation, something his broken mind would accept eagerly?

"Andrei?"

"Yes." He sat up in bed. "Yes, Maryna." Was her voice her own, this warmth touching his ear; or instead an empty succubus of carbon filaments, rheostats, and diode tissue, ministered over by white-coated technicians structuring with capacitators and intensity meters the voice imprint itself?

"You remember now?"

Strekov remembered and apologized. Maryna was Orlov's youngest daughter. He told her he'd been sleeping.

"Papa said I might call. I'd like to see you." He heard music playing in the background.

"Of course."

"Tonight?"

"Tomorrow. How can I reach you?"

She gave him her telephone number. Strekov said he would call her.

He sat on the edge of the bed, the room still in darkness, holiday horns still in his head, a spinet playing somewhere, perhaps in the flat above. No, not with the smell of anise, a canzone that begins with the sound of flutes. Something forgotten in his skull, some forgotten asphyxia, dead ferns rooted in old fissures, beyond the toxologist's art.

Fever still? No, his forehead was cool. The night was frosty beyond the window-panes. Moscow was waiting.

He hadn't yet learned why Orlov had sent for him. He dressed and left the bedroom to wait for Orlov's car. They would talk at the da-cha at Gorky this evening, a late dinner. While he waited he smoked a cigarette, studying the old photographs in one of the glass-fronted cabinets. He found a picture of Maryna in pigtails, a gap between her front teeth, her face just recovering from a boisterous schoolgirl laugh. Nearby was a photograph of Orlov's dead wife, standing between two pieces of old porcelain. He wondered if Maryna had put them there. On the shelf above were a few polished medals lying on swatches of watered silk—the Order of Lenin, the Order of the Red Star, the Hero of Socialist Labor, a medal from Czechoslovakia, awarded by the Czech Ministry of Defense at the completion of Orlov's tour as senior intelligence adviser.

When Orlov's Chaika arrived at the street entrance below, Stre-kov was disappointed to see Zhilenkov in the rear seat. Orlov wasn't there. Chernyak sat next to Zhilenkov. An old Chekist, like Zhilenkov, he had formerly been Orlov's lieutenant and was now a department chief with the Central Committee. Zhilenkov's eyes shone with mois-ture in the yellow reading light. Strekov was surprised at Zhilenkov's transformation in the few hours since their return to Moscow. He was bundled in a heavy overcoat and smelled of tobacco. The excitement of his return had given a promiscuous wheeze to his basso profundo. He greeted Strekov with an affectionate bear hug and moved aside, giving up his seat at the window. Chernyak also wore an overcoat. A black felt hat was pulled over his bald head to keep out the frost, the sharp metallic cold. His steel-rimmed spectacles stared out from beneath the hat-brim like the eyes of a carp. There was something fishlike in the wreckage of the face beneath—the cartilaginous jaws, the cadaver's wax nose, the hollow cheeks scarred by frostbite.

The Chaika turned across Arbat Square and down Frunze Street towards the Kremlin, where they were to meet Orlov. They entered through the Borovitsky Tower entrance above the river. The great courtyards were as bright as day under the arc lights. A group of workers with brooms were moving across the open expanse in front of the new Palace of Congresses where the Twenty-second Party Congress was still in session. The Chaika drew to a stop near a side entrance to the Presidium. Militia regulars and Guards officers patrolled the building. A flotilla of Zils and Chaikas waited nearby. A Guards officer directed the Chaika to a corner of the building, and led the three passengers back across the courtyard to a side entrance. They went in via a storm entrance carpeted with coarse sisal rugs, dodged through a nearby door and down a long corridor into a brilliantly lit reception room. A score of military officers, bureaucrats, and party *apparatchiki* were waiting for the completion of a meeting taking place on the floor above. Their figures were multiplied in waxen gray, green, and flesh-tinted pools from the polished floor, and redoubled by the loggia of gilded mirrors at their backs. Cigarette and cigar smoke obscured the scrolled ceiling. A Guards officer and a trio of KGB officers sat at the pair of desks at the foot of the staircase, faces locked in concentration as they studied the waiting crowd.

Strekov scanned the faces around him, eyes narrowed against the gilt. His pulse had quickened and he was a schoolboy again, stepping back into the pages of the history books at the school at Strelka. These were still the days of empire, the Kremlin its heartbeat, with the coachmen waiting outside in the cold. Who has not been here? In the wainscoted rooms upstairs the murmured breaths of policy stir below gilded ceilings whose highest tracery was still dusted with the pollen from French snuff boxes; smoke from Romanov braziers still blackened the tiles where logs crackle and burn; and on a forgotten centimeter of diamond-hard pane somewhere down a dusty corridor, Stalin's breath still clouded the view into the courtyard on a cold, frosty morning. Hussar's boot leather creaked around him like dry snow; whispered conversations he could not hear, but could only imagine—like a Siberian schoolboy again.

A few *apparatchiki* bustled down the steps, giving quick hand signals to the officers below. The KGB troika at the desk stood up. Strekov could see nothing. A polite scattered applause lifted spontaneously from those nearest the staircase, who were looking up the carpeted stairs. Strekov recognized Marshal Malinkovsky's leonine head as the group descended. Shelapin and his KGB staff aide were close behind, followed by Colonel Orlov. The group passed within five feet of Strekov, but then the crowd closed in behind it, and Strekov was swept forward through the door and out into the winter night.

The wind blew through the pine trees beyond the dacha forty kilometers from Moscow. The coals from the open hearth were reflected in the dark panes within, but outside the moonlight cast the shadows of the blowing trees across the roof, and across the frosty path, illuminating the silver meadows and the distant copses. Villages only eighty kilometers to the north were already blanketed with snow, which would fall in Moscow within a day.

It was late. Strekov knew that he would have no chance to talk to Orlov alone that night. "I'm not a scientist," Zhilenkov was saying drunkenly, emptying his wine glass for the last time and now picking up the bottle of vodka from in front of Chernyak. "Maybe I'm not an intellectual, either. Maybe to the *kolkhoz* peasantry I'm an intellectual—a scientist too, but a scientist of the Party. Let's be honest about it. We've only one specialty—the Party. The Party's history. Both. What did I need to know except the Party? What did any of us need to know except the Party?"

"Statistics," Chernyak suggested with a laugh. "How many of us were there." They had been talking about the past.

"One hundred megatons is a statistic," Zhilenkov said. "Our statistics. One hundred megatons and the Party makes a policy anyone can understand. Even the Germans."

The younger men said nothing. Orlov waited. They had said little, letting Orlov's old colleagues dominate the conversation. "Everyone has his hands full with the Party," he said finally. He slouched in a wooden chair at the end of the table, a pipe in his mouth, his short legs thrust forward, a wine glass balanced on his belt buckle. Tight iron-gray hair covered his square *muzhik* head like the nap on a saddle blanket. His face was ageless. His eyes were small, blue-green, without depth or expression, like bits of broken glass. His strength was his face; it gave away nothing. In the presence of his two old colleagues from his Chekist days, Zhilenkov and Chernyak, he belonged even more to the present while their own faces, in their corruption, their fears, and their self-indulgence, made them even more the prisoners of the past. Younger men found in him an ally; older men, a fellow conspirator. Both were right; both wrong. His career had flourished on the memories or the hopes of others.

On his feet he wore a pair of black felt Siberian boots with which Merkurovich had provisioned him over the years. He'd shed his Western suit coat and wore instead a shaggy gray cardigan. Iovenko and Surkov, his young staff aides, had also joined them around the crude wooden table. The dishes had been pushed aside. His tongueless, bat-faced Ukrainian cook stood just outside the door to the smoky kitchen, watching Orlov like a hawk, waiting for a signal. They were sitting in the cook's scullery and wash room, not the dining room where the table had been laid. Orlov preferred the rustic crudeness of the scullery, with its smell of wood and picket fires, the bivouaclike improvisation of a field kitchen, an open brazier, the blackened kettles and washtubs, the occasional drafts of winter air, the stuffed gray fox on the pantry top. Besides, if the guests came as promised, they'd want a late buffet, a clean table cloth, no crumbs on the floor; and the old cook was terribly slow.

Zhilenkov and Chernyak resumed their argument about the Twenty-second Party Congress, still debating the decisions which were made about China, Albania, and Berlin, still speculating about what would happen if the young intellectuals continued to put the screws to Khruschev, pushing him towards a new legality, a new justice, the fulfillment of destalinization, the truth about their bloody patrimony. Zhilenkov and Chernyak competed in the righteousness of their denunciations, like a pair of old lechers, each trying to read in the other's face the terrible corruptions of his own. Even if their faces weren't sly enough about keeping their secrets, it didn't matter: Few of their generation still active weren't knee-deep in crime, in blood, and broken teeth, whatever their pretenses of respectability—pottering around in their new dotage, spade in hand, bringing new flowers to old graves; while a younger and more cynical generation rioted outside the gates, broke through the fences, and scampered along the parapets of the old prisons—Lubyanka, Lefortova, Butryka, and Sukhanovka, to say nothing of the Gulag—ripping off the roofs with crowbars, disinterring the dead with poems, plays, broadsheets, legalisms; flooding the Moscow skies with the stench of carbolic. "What do they know about justice, about criticism?" Chernyak asked scornfully.

"We should remember that criticism, self-criticism in particular, has always been a fundamental principle of Leninist party-building," Surkov told them finally, interrupting their dialogue. Surkov was the youngest at the table—horse-faced and blond-haired—with a sterile precision to his sermonizing that annoyed both men. He'd interrupted twice previously.

"Whose criticism?" Zhilenkov asked. "We've all practiced self-criticism. Let them howl."

"We've been introspective to a fault—all of us!" Chernyak joined in, cracking a nutshell on the table before he lifted his head to let Surkov have the full malice of those glittering gray eyes. "Where did Lenin say that?" he asked coldly. He knew very well where Lenin said it. But he'd soared beyond his ken, this weak-eyed old bird, and a moment later was frantically searching the tabletop for his lost nutmeats, leaning forward myopically, fingers sorting through herring bones, cheese crumbs, olive pits, pistachio shells: a blind old usurer who'd lost a sou—

"Volume forty-one, page one eighty-four," Surkov said.

"Volume forty-one? You are sure?"

"He said that our duty was to openly criticize our weaknesses so that they could be eradicated more radically."

"Radically?" Zhilenkov smiled. "Radically?" His eyes found Orlov's at the head of the table, then Strekov's. Neither spoke. "Radically—did he truly say that?" Zhilenkov asked Surkov with mock seriousness. "But what weakness? Whose weakness?"

"I'm not so sure it was page one forty-eight," Chernyak muttered, still searching for his lost nutmeats.

"Open criticism isn't at all radical," Surkov continued. "Neither radical nor subversive."

"Not when your whistling the tune," Chernyak volunteered. "Not when you're hiring the coffinmaker."

Zhilenkov banged the table with his fist, rattling the crockery. "I'm fed up with this talk about corpses," he shouted. The talk had unnerved him; so had the liquor. "Digging up corpses! Corpses stink! But the fish stinks first from the head—Stalin was the head! Stalin stinks now—in everyone's nostrils. So Khruschev will tell them again! Let him, all right? But until then, shut up about it, for God's sake." He lifted the package of Bulgarian Solnse cigarettes from the table, took one, lit it quickly, and blew the smoke towards the ceiling.

"Nikita Sergeivich is unreliable on his feet," Chernyak reminded them slyly, referring to Khruschev. "Like the village braggart—telling fibs, half-truths. The Twenty-second Congress has too much loosened his tongue, like the wine has loosened mine. Like the buffoon in the village, he'll only know what he wants to say after he has said it. And then, it will be the academicians who will identify its importance for him. If you talk endlessly enough, it's inevitable that you will say profound things. The important thing is not to kill off too soon those who will remember them for you. But Nikita Sergeivich is cunning. He will only give them crumbs, not the whole loaf."

"Give them crumbs!" Zhilenkov shouted. "If they want crumbs, let them have Molotov. If youth wants a new justice, let them begin there." But Zhilenkov was too reckless. His reputation in Moscow had been earned in the old NKVD foreign department. He'd known Molotov well. They all remembered, except Surkov, who was too young to remember anything, even how much wine he had drunk. The room fell silent. Orlov calmly smoked his pipe, his eyes half closed, looking at the shadows from the trees waving against the window.

"I don't believe we should be afraid to admit that many things in the revolution haven't turned out brilliantly," Surkov reassured them in his thin, literary voice.

"Oh, God," Zhilenkov groaned, his face in his hands.

"Lenin said as much," Surkov continued. "Revolutionaries who have perished in the past have fallen victim to their blindness in understanding their strength, their cowardice in admitting their weaknesses—"

"That isn't Lenin, goddamnit," Zhilenkov shouted. He'd had enough of this intellectual upstart with his filthy insinuations.

"Volume forty-five, page one eighteen," Surkov replied.

"A revisionist's edition—a white-collar Lenin—the assholes,

the *sluzhashiye!* Andrei?" Zhilenkov turned wildly to appeal to Strekov. Orlov sat forward and put his pipe on the table.

"Nikita Sergeivich's position is weaker than many understand," Orlov said calmly, trying to nudge his young aide out of Zhilenkov's drunken path. Zhilenkov no longer mattered; Chernyak did. He was a powerful man, chief of the Central Committee's Administrative Organs Department.

"That isn't Lenin," Zhilenkov insisted.

"It's Lenin, old colleague," Chernyak advised sadly. "Volume forty-five, as he says. Popular with the intelligentsia these days. The poets and crackpots. The literary hacks, the novelists, every new painter with two kopecks worth of dog shit on his canvas, eh Surkov? Tell me, are you a scribbler?"

Surkov was embarrassed. "No."

"A Jew?"

"Not a scribbler, not a Jew," Chernyak continued mercilessly. "What then? What school do you come from?"

"The Leningrad—"

"What school? What was that? Speak up, for Christ's sake! We're all comrades here. Our school was the Party. We know nothing but the Party. Nothing else. What do you know?"

The cook's tin clock ticked away on the pine boards above the dying coals in the brazier, where the meat and fowl juices had burned as black as tar. Vats of wash water were slowly warming. The wind could be heard. On the top of the old cupboard the eyes of the stuffed fox, although made of glass, seemed to take on sentience as Strekov listened to the wind.

"I know that for a time there was nothing else to know," Surkov said in confusion, "nothing but the Party."

"What's different now?" Chernyak asked him dangerously, leaning forward over the littered tablecloth. They were after Surkov's ass now—these two sly old killers who had first come together in Moscow in 1938—Chernyak and Zhilenkov, working together by instinct, like a pair of wolves, trying to separate this young calf from the barn.

"The Party matters, of course," Surkov said. "Because it matters, it must take fuller account of what is now happening—the acceleration of scientific and technical progress; the reduction of the rural population; and the passing of the*kolkhoz* peasantry. The ratio of rural to urban populations is rapidly being reduced. In twenty years the need for unskilled labor will have vanished. In the process the worker will disappear. The worker will be replaced by cadres of scientists and technicians."

Zhilenkov mopped his face. Statistics were like marsh flies to his unlettered mind, and he was trying to think. Chernyak was thoughtful, his wasted face pushed towards Surkov. "What are the implications?" he asked coolly, hearing an echo of seditious prophecy in the young man's words.

Surkov sipped from his wine glass and returned it to the table. The others watched him curiously. "The changes in the *kolkhoz* peasantry and the *sovkhoz* workers will eliminate social differences—differences between the industrial nucleus, the working class, and the intelligentsia. We will see an end to the century-old difference between physical labor and mental labor, between the worker and the intellectual." Surkov's face was as cool as ever.

Strekov was curiously touched by the words, by the young man's confidence, his hope, his idealism. It didn't matter that he himself believed in nothing, that he had nothing but contempt for the two old buffoons facing Surkov; for the moment he was moved by Surkov's courage, by his belief in the future.

"What about the Party?" Chernyak interrupted crudely.

"Criticism within the Party?" Zhilenkov demanded. "What does it mean?"

Surkov's voice had gained confidence. He said, "The purpose of criticism is to strengthen the ties of the party—the Soviet, the trade union, and Komsomol organizations, to strengthen the ties with the masses. To end poor economic management, bureaucratism, and extravagance. To expose speculation wherever it is found. At the same time, care must be exercised to insure that the publicity we create by self-criticism, whether in the mass media, in the newspapers, the radio, and the scholarly journals—to ensure that it doesn't merely entertain the Philistines, the petite bourgeoisie, or reactionary gossip. No. Our purpose is clear. The end of criticism is to increase the awareness of the labor collectives and the working masses. The end of criticism is the exposure of parasites in a businesslike manner . . . by the *Oblast* Party organizations, by Party committee plenums, bureau sessions, Party *aktiv* meetings . . . by conferences of primary Party organizations . . . by the secretariats . . . whose purpose should be . . . to generate organization and discipline."

Strekov sat in sorrowful silence. Even Orlov was stunned, his face cleansed of the expectation of hideous crimes and boundless punishment by this prophylaxis of modernity parroting the cliches of a mindless bureaucracy. Iovenko continued smoking, his face inscrutable. Zhilenkov and Chernyak looked suspiciously at this scoundrel Surkov, not believing their ears, cheated of a lifetime of emotions. But it was true—every word. They saw it in his face. They were prepared for any unnatural eruption of nature—tidal floods, rain pouring down, graveyards vomiting forth their dead, raising the specter of long vanished comrades—anything but this. Crusted and barnacled with crime, what sentencing could they imagine that they hadn't already suffered, as they dragged its guilt daily towards their graves? They stared blankly at this new instrument of justice, this prosaic Leningrad economist who, punishing them for a lifetime of crimes they could no longer remember, would serve them with the writ of poor economic management, the stigma of bureaucratic buggery.

"Oblasts?" Zhilenkov wheezed after Surkov had left the room, sent by Orlov to learn what was detaining their guests. *"Oblasts?* Did he say that?"

Chernyak was still shaking his head in disbelief, smiling too, despite the severed muscles in his withered jaw, the white potato-rot of frostbite along the bone—really a grotesque sight, not so funny either—something in his face reminding Strekov of other mutations privately discovered these days: bats that bark like dogs; rats along the canal practicing toothpaste grins by moonlight along its black waters, where the milky refractions from a germ-laden moon lift from the septic mud the mirror of our debris below—rubber tires, bomb-fins, a broken doll's head, old dentures, newspaper headlines, condoms, and chewing gum foil.

He remembered a cool autumn day walking along the Embankment in London. He felt the prickle of sweat along his brow, under his collar.

It was late. The guests had arrived; the buffet had been served. A phonograph was playing in the room beyond. A few army officers were there: a handful of KGB functionaries from Orlov's staff. A few young girls had been brought in—trollops in flounces and ribbons, smelling of cheap perfume that on the first breath recalled wild flowers, lonely days in frontier posts along the Siberian frontier. They were robust young girls, as frisky as colts, newly fetched from the countryside, with firm bottoms and bouncing breasts which their new dresses couldn't disguise. They hadn't yet learned the guile of cosmetics, but there was no need for them. Their skin was as creamy as milk fresh from the udder. They were on their way to Prague and East Berlin to ease the loneliness of Soviet garrison life along the Western front.

Strekov and Iovenko were talking in the darkened study. The door was closed against the intrusions of the music from the room beyond. Zhilenkov stood suddenly in the doorway, looking at them suspiciously. "Where is Finkelstein?" he demanded, swaying on his feet.

Strekov said, "He's not here."

"Who?" Iovenko asked.

"Surkov."

Why, Zhilenkov wanted to know, why weren't they dancing. It was unnatural, wasn't it? Talking, eh? What about? Surkov? That young dolt—that foundling sired by the bureaucracy. No patrimony, no past, no village—nothing! Who fathered him? A rubber finger from a Jew's surgical glove at Serbsky! Zhilenkov tottered across the room to the old lounge chair and sank into it gratefully. He picked up a half-full brandy glass someone had left behind on the table, sniffed it carefully, and emptied it. His face was wet. His thinning gray hair was plastered in spit curls across his forehead. "You've drunk too much," Strekov said, still watching him.

"Let us come home, Andrei," Zhilenkov pleaded, short of breath. He waited for the wind to fill his lungs again. "Come home," he sighed. "Put the rest behind you—Europe, Asia, the Near East. Changes are in the wind and you know what they say. The man who comes last gets a picked bone. It's every man for himself, Andrei Ivanovich. Save your own skin. If you're not in Moscow these days, you might as well be shut away in the Gulag for all anyone cares. Out of sight, out of mind. Eh, Comrade Iovenko? Am I right? Tell Andrei. What do you think? Would you go to Berlin in times like these—shut yourself away in a pigsty with cowshit and rotten spuds? Might as well rocket your ass off to the moon."

"I would go where I was needed," Iovenko said. "I would serve where the Party needed me."

"You would, would you?" Zhilenkov gasped, still short of breath. He pulled a handkerchief from his pocket to hide his contempt, wiping his face indignantly. *Oh that's horseshit, pure bunk, and everyone knows it! What a liar! What deceit, what perfidy! What a toady!*

Two ministry officials entered the study, looking for Orlov, who would soon have to leave if he was to keep his late-evening appointment in Moscow. A young girl followed them, her milky skin lathered from her exertions on the dance floor. Her jersey dress clung to her arms and back. Tufts of dark hair showed under her arms as she lifted her damp hair from her neck. Zhilenkov watched her without rising from his lounge chair. He looked at Iovenko and then Strekov, wondering who would take the girl home, who would end up straddling her in the backseat. It was Andrei's face that absorbed him—the smooth blond hair, the bony abstract face, the lynx eyes, as lidless as a snake's. He never sleeps, this man—and clever too, as sharp as a shithouse rat. Iovenko and the others pretend they've forgotten the past; but not Andrei, whose hands are as bloody as anyone's. He doesn't give a damn for anyone and will carry his load like the rest of them when the time comes. But this Iovenko is a slippery customer too. Look how he sips his brandy—like a caged bird. The same at the table in the kitchen: less than a toothful of vodka with each sausage. Watch how he nourishes the conversation with his quiet nods, his philosophical silences—never giving himself away, never pulling his prick out in public—why? Because he has no past—no mother, no father. Raised in the rotting slum villages of Belorussia. Maybe he's really a Pole, this Iovenko. Whose name did he use when he finally chose one? Perhaps Zhilenkov will waken one cold morning after an obscene night like this—waken in the frozen darkness of Kolyma, an icy basin on the floor, lice in his beard, shit in his nose, and be summoned to a colder cell down the corridor where Iovenko's antiseptic face will be waiting for him, maybe Andrei's too, reading his writ. But not for economic mismanagement, no—not for angina pectoris either. So be it. *The dead are dead.*

Zhilenkov emptied his brandy glass, exhilaration suddenly filling his weary body, his eyes swimming towards Iovenko's cold face, Strekov's brooding silhouette, the young girl standing nearby. *So be it.* He had six grandchildren now, two mistresses. *Fuck you, Iovenko.* He was suddenly an old man, very drunk.

Strekov drove back to Moscow with Orlov and the two ministry officials. He sat in the front seat, listening to the three men talk of the Party Congress. Strekov had first met Orlov in Poland in 1945 during the final months of the war. Strekov had been an infantry lieutenant with the Fifth Shock Army; Orlov was an NKVD officer attached to corps headquarters.

The second week of January 'they'd broken out of the Pulawy and Magnuscew bridgeheads east of Warsaw and begun the final push on Berlin. The weather was cold the morning they started out, the roads icy, the clouds low over the treetops. The German high command believed that the Russians would wait for more favorable weather before resuming their offensive and had grounded their planes. Three hours after the Russian infantry had stormed out of the fog, it was too late. The Forty-eighth German Panzer Corps was destroyed, the Twenty-eighth Panzers slaughtered in their reserve area. On January seventeenth Warsaw was taken; within a few weeks Upper Silesia and East Prussia were lost. The first Russian soldiers had reached the banks of the Oder on the German frontier, only a day's march from Berlin.

A January thaw had brought out the purple crocuses, a few daffodils, and clumps of snowdrops along the fencerows. The ice had melted on the Oder. The thaw was general—on the land, the rivers and streams, along the roads, and in the hearts of the Russian soldiers, like Strekov, advancing towards the Oder. They were no longer animals, but men once again, the liberators of their homeland who were asking of Providence only what was theirs—justice. Justice for Stalingrad and Smolensk, for dead families and smoking villages where the wind blew drifting snow over corpses scattered like cordwood in the ditches and lanes, for the years of starvation, desolation, and hopelessness. So spring was already there, in January, and they sped on, knowing in their hearts that victory was theirs. Mile after mile across the abandoned Polish countryside—fifteen, eighteen, twenty miles a day, passing in the ditches and roads the abandoned equipment of the German army in headlong flight to the west. Where would it end?

Then suddenly, on the evening of January twenty-sixth the skies darkened. A cold wind swept down from the north. The first few snowflakes floated down, as dry as parchment, as large as apple blossoms. They clung to caps and shoulders, to eyelashes and cheeks, and drifted down across a suddenly estranged countryside. Still they moved on, the thaw over, dim shadows in the falling snow. The lights were gone from the villages ahead of them. The villagers had fled. They lost a few trucks in the deep snow. Strekov was billeted that night in an empty blacksmith shop at the far end of a deserted Polish village. The wind howled all night. Snow sifted through the cracks in the planking, scratched at the boarded windows, and burrowed under the crude doors. When dawn came, it was still snowing, slashing across roads and fields, raging through the empty streets, wiping out the sky. Strekov fought his way towards battalion headquarters, but lost his bearings twenty yards outside the blacksmith shop, was knocked from his feet by the wind, and when he finally lifted himself again was blown like a leaf back into the drifts against the old building. More than sixty soldiers had found refuge in the blacksmith shop. Huddled in their overcoats, in blankets, burying themselves in the straw of the floor and loft, they waited for the storm to blow itself out, unable to muster, to draw rations, or to find their officers.

For two days the blizzard swept across Central and Western Europe, burying roads, highways, and towns. For two days they waited. Some of the men in the blacksmith shop thought it a premonition. *Why?* they wanted to know. Victory was almost theirs—*why now?* They were simple men, illiterate many of them, some of them superstitious; but they were also Russians, the primitive sons of a primitive past, men who had fought against extinction and had survived, men who had abandoned God, but who were also fathers and husbands. They had come swarming against the gates of the West, pursuing their enemies, seeking justice. But Nature had put her icy finger in the balance. Why? To protect her own children, the progeny of reason and order?

On the second night Orlov appeared suddenly in the blacksmith shop. Strekov had never seen him before. He had come from headquarters. Snow covered his hooded head and clung to his whiskered face. His feet were trunks of ice and snow. The same questions were put to him. He was angry, looking through the lantern light at the soldiers who huddled near the old forge in rags and blankets.

"Because you're rabble," Orlov told them angrily. "Mindless rabble—all of you—filthy, verminous rabble! Stinking dogs! Curs! Godless orphans! The sons of whores, murderers, cut-purses! Russia was your grave. Who leaves the grave? Maggots and feeding rats! Are you satisfied? Do you want more? You're rabble—the scum of the earth! What do you expect? What do you want? Crocuses? Lilacs? To sit in their parlors and drink tea with their sisters and mothers in Berlin? They thought you were dead, gone to your graves. To your graves, rabble! Do you lie back down in your grave because God is spitting in your face? And now you ask me why? Why? *Because you're rabble, scum, stinking dogs—*"

A few minutes later Orlov disappeared into the falling snow, taking with him the two ranking officers he had found in the blacksmith shop. The impression he had made on the soldiers was electric. A few thought the officers would be shot. But they weren't. They returned within the hour to report that the storm was easing. In the days that followed they dug themselves out of the buried village. The pale winter sun began to thaw the anvils of ice which imprisoned the trucks, troop carriers, and tanks. They hammered them free of their crystal shells; the roads were opened again, and they took up the pursuit. But when they reached the Oder to join the advance Russian units that were waiting there, the Germans had already regrouped to the west. They waited on the Oder until April.

Strekov saw Orlov again late one night in the battalion headquarters mess tent. He was alone in the tent except for a Mongolian orderly who was preparing soup and hot tea. Orlov was slumped in a camp chair, his muddy boots stretched out towards the stove. They were bivouacked in the marshy bottomlands of the Oder and Alte Oder on the German frontier, preparing for the assault against the Seelow Heights to the west. For weeks the trucks had come from the east, bringing new artillery pieces, new troops, more tanks. A corps commander had told Strekov's company that twenty-five thousand artillery pieces would be in place the night of the assault, guns lighting the sky like an Arctic dawn, thunder shaking the earth from Berlin to Warsaw in the west. It would be the last great assault of the war. Strekov believed it. The war would be over.

That night in the mess tent Strekov told Orlov that he had been in the blacksmith shop the night he had come in out of the snow. Orlov nodded but said nothing. A wet mist had gathered along the Oder. Fog crept up from the riverbanks. Strekov talked about the coming assault against the Seelow Heights. Orlov listened, waiting for the Mongolian orderly to bring him soup. A small metal cup of vodka was balanced on his belt. His face was tired; he had been traveling for two days; and his tunic, like his boots, were splashed with mud. When Strekov said that the war would soon be over, Orlov made no response. Strekov thought he didn't want to talk and arose to go. The orderly left his stove and slipped out the rear of the tent to the supply wagon. Orlov turned to watch him go. "There will be other wars," he said, looking at the swaying tent flap. He turned back to Strekov. "And then, when the socialist wars are over, the final wars will begin. The basic war."

Strekov was surprised. He didn't know what Orlov was talking about. The older man saw his confusion and smiled, nodding his head towards the sound coming from the supply wagon. "The final war," he muttered. "Between us and people like that. Or even people like you and me. But first the others."

At the time, Strekov hadn't known what he was talking about. It worried him for days. Then he forgot about it.

Orlov's car sailed along the highway towards Moscow, its headlights searching the road ahead of them. In the backseat they were talking about Khruschev's latest speech. *Time passes and we shall all die,* he had said. *But we're all mortal and so long as we have the strength to do so, we must tell the truth to the Party and the people. Even if we can't bring dead men to life, we can honestly tell their story and record it in the annals of the Party.* From the front seat Strekov heard their words, but saw only fields of white on the Polish countryside. The years dropped away and he was a young officer again, barely twenty-one, racing west with the others from the Pulawy bridgehead. He saw the white road ahead of him, mantled with falling snow, saw the fields, the shadows of soldiers, the sky open overhead, a great bowl; and the universe itself beginning to stir again, to awaken him to its mysteries once more after those long years of suffering and of silence.

Strekov went alone through the early morning mist in Moscow, up the steep incline on Kuznetski Most towards the eight-story building at 11 Dzerzhinskay Street where he had been working for two days now, waiting to talk to Orlov. The Twenty-second Party Congress was still in progress. Changes were still in the wind, but Orlov wouldn't talk about them. He was irritable and depressed, like an old dog with boils, uncertain of their consequences for him. The chief of the KGB was to be replaced.

Beads of moisture stippled the black marble base of the old building. The stone passageway and chilly courtyard were crowded with cars—with Volgas, Zils, and Zim limousines. A muddy Volga, returning from some nightlong assignation, blocked the departure of a sleek Zil limousine leaving urgently for the Kremlin. The back curtains of the Zil remained closed while the two drivers exchanged insults. Strekov entered a side doorway with a single number etched in copper plate on the door panel. The pale-green walls were bleached even lighter by the milky ceiling lights.

On a floor above, a guard was waiting to take him to Orlov's suite where he'd been working on Orlov's draft recommendations for reorganizing the Western European Illegals Directorate. Orlov had already left for the Palace of Congresses. Surkov greeted him in the outer office. But he led Strekov past the small desk where he had been working, through Orlov's large office, and into a small committee room adjacent to it. The room contained a large table covered with green felt, a few wooden chairs, and a strip of old carpeting the color of seaweed on the parquet floor. Three large safes stood against one wall; two barred windows looked down into the courtyard. Five large boxes of files stood on the felt green table.

Sitting at the table was a small, heavyset clerk in a worsted suit. He got to his feet, took a pen from his pocket, and asked Strekov to sign the document he pushed across the table. Surkov was confused by Strekov's reaction. "Didn't you talk to him last night?" he asked. Strekov shook his head as he studied the paper. At last he signed it, and returned it to the clerk, who put it in a briefcase and left without a word. "He said you were to work here," Surkov continued, still perplexed. "The documents are not to leave the room. He said you would understand."

Strekov searched through the nearest box, looking at the captions and the date lines. He moved from box to box until he had found the most recent cables and dispatches. They were in the last folder. Among them he found his telegram to Orlov from Rostock, recommending Bryce's evacuation to Moscow. Scrawled in the margin of the cable was a single word: *Impossible.* He recognized the handwriting. It was Orlov's.

"I understand," Strekov muttered. Surkov went out; Strekov locked the door behind him.

The files and dossiers had been assembled from Orlov's own working files, from other repositories on the floors below, from the Third Department, from the Eighth Communications Section elsewhere in Moscow, from the musty old Comintern archives kept in a building near the river, from technical services, from the illegals wing of the intelligence directorate, from the records of the Central Committee itself. Only a few officials had had access to the documents assembled there, many of which hadn't seen the light of day since their arrival in Moscow years earlier, gathering dust behind steel doors, in forgotten closets, steel cabinets, or ribbon-bound Tsarist folios. The system had always been appalling, the KGB institutional memory as antiquated as the bureaucracies it inherited—GPU, OGPU, NKVD,

MVD—as primitive as the Russian bureaucracy itself, as any of those thumb-worn ledgers in a rural railroad station or customs post. Files had been misplaced, purged, or forgotten; dossiers had disappeared with the times—like the people they accused—plundered to gratify ambition, revenge or fear . . . subpoenaed by the Prosecutor General, by the NKVD board of inquiry, or by the military collegium of the Supreme Court. Names had been deleted, inked over, or scissored out, signature lines ripped off in the convulsions of Stalinist mutilation. Dates, names, essential facts, even years, were missing.

The earliest document in the file was dated 1934 or 1935—Strekov couldn't be sure—and was mottled with age, as brittle as nineteenth-century parchment, handwritten in a pale, coppery-green script that was a model of old German calligraphy, as ornate on the line as the gothic spires of Lubeck against a pale Baltic sunset. Only a man proud of his education could have written it, but who was he? The name had been inked out. Unknown and nameless, he was probably German, Strekov guessed, recruited by the NKVD at a time when the foreign sections were heavily populated with foreigners, with Germans, Jews, and Poles, many of them recruited out of the Comintern. Most would perish in the purges of 1938 and 1939. The document described the recruitment in Berlin of a young Oxford graduate who was studying German on a nine-month traveling fellowship from Balliol, preparing for his Foreign Office examinations for the Diplomatic Service. He'd come to Berlin well recommended. A Balliol don who'd joined the Communist Party in 1926 following the general strike had written a letter to an NKVD agent in Amsterdam suggesting that the *apparat* in Berlin contact him:

> He was one of our failures. He seldom came to my rooms, never joined the reading parties, professed no interest in the Party itself, but in the depth of his social conscience and his contempt for the life at Oxford, he was the most interesting undergraduate of recent years. He is a man of parts. The Diplomatic Service cannot hold his talent. He is a man of action rather than words. The Nazi destruction of the socialists now taking place will rouse him to action. British policy is anathema to him.

In Berlin the young Oxford graduate met a German girl from the Baltic, studying to be an actress. There was Danish in her bloodline; she was from Tallinn, her ancestry reached in a long, misty line to the Teutonic knights and German barons who'd once made serfs of Tallinn's Estonians. She'd joined the Communist Party in 1933 as a seventeen-year-old student. Blond, blue-eyed, and long-limbed, as promiscuous as Berlin itself, she introduced him to the NKVD agent one spring afternoon. They recruited him under the chestnut and linden trees of the sidewalk coffee houses near the old Karl Liebknecht house. During his remaining months in Berlin, he served as a courier delivering documents smuggled out of the IV Cypher Section of the Foreign Ministry by a code clerk to NKVD drops in Bern, Paris, and Amsterdam.

The same year he passed his Foreign Office examinations, entered the Diplomatic Service, and dropped from sight. When he reappeared again he was in Paris as Third Secretary of Embassy, responsible for the classified registry, ciphering, and the diplomatic bag, in addition to his other duties. A Soviet NKVD agent in Paris had contacted him soon after his arrival in Paris, but the relationship wasn't a satisfactory one. The NKVD agent was dilatory in his duties, spoke no English, and was more interested in the number of documents the young Third Secretary could obtain than the information they contained. The Englishman resented it. He addressed his complaint to the NKVD Directorate in Moscow through his old contacts in Berlin:

> It is true that my apprenticeship was not learned at a South Wales coal face, nor in the humiliation of a genteel, mercantile bankruptcy. I've never been inspired by nonconformist eccentricity, or the woodnotes wild of *"Cwm Rhondda"* brought to the family hearthside by the wretched winds of the colliery. But this doesn't make me a dilettante, as your man in Paris seems to assume. My commitment is genuine and fit for more enlightened responsibilities than the pilfering of the Ambassador's most recent minute, or the dispatch which sets out his recent conversation with a drunken French minister at the Italian residence.

Who is this man? someone had scrawled in purplish-black ink in the margin. *Is he English?* Yes, he was English, English to the core they would learn in time. It was Dimitar Menzhinsky who taught them. It wasn't until Menzhinsky took over the Western Sections of the NKVD Illegals Directorate in Moscow a year later that the letter received a sympathetic reading. Menzhinsky's origins were obscure; some said he was a Pole; others, a German Jew. He'd become a Bolshevik, and taken a new name after the war, abandoning both God and nationalism. During the Civil War he'd joined the Cheka and later transferred to the NKVD. He'd served in Vienna and Berlin during the twenties as an illegal resident, was later in Bern, and returned to Moscow to be assigned to the Ukraine. A short, diffident man, a pipe-smoker with iron-gray hair and cool, blue-green eyes, he had no sentimental attachment to the past. He'd been six months in his new post and was preparing for a clandestine trip to Vienna, Paris, and Bern when he discovered the Englishman's letter, ignored for almost a year. It was 1937. The first Moscow trials were over; the first old Bolsheviks had been purged; his former NKVD and Comintern colleagues in Western Europe were being lured back to Moscow to be shot or imprisoned; those preparing to make public their break with Stalin over the trials, Soviet policy in Spain, or Stalinism itself, were quietly being tracked down and liquidated abroad. The revolutionary ferment which had moved a generation of NKVD and Comintern networks abroad had given way to the self-destructive impulses of the times. NKVD staffs at Soviet embassies were staffed by gray mediocrities, spawned by the Moscow *apparat,* foreigners to the West, their languages as well as their cultures, while the NKVD residents were suspicious of one another and of their staffs, transferring abroad the poisonous suspicions of Stalin's Moscow. Menzhinsky's faith was unshakable. Stubborn, ruthless, yet gifted in ways which made him superior to his times, he sensed in the young Englishman's letter the prospects of a new beginning, an affirmation of faith from a new generation which wasn't merely German, Jewish, or Russian, which had no identification with the past, no deep intellectual identification with the Party or it's past, and no need for the tormented subjectivism, Trotskyite or otherwise, that was dividing the Party and moving it further from its past.

They met in Paris in a small cafe on a cool, rainswept evening. Menzhinsky was alone. He knew little about England or the English. He'd come to learn of the future, to escape from the present. He saw before him a cool young British diplomat, coldly handsome, arrogant, who spoke both German and French with equal fluency. His mind, Menzhinsky wrote afterward, was as cold as a machine. As he listened Menzhinsky was conscious of his own age, his halting German, his ill-fitting worsted suit, his broken history. Perhaps it was the spring evening, the unfamiliar cafe, perhaps the look of strange bottles on a strange tabletop or Menzhinsky's own remoteness from Moscow and the Europe he had known ten years earlier. It was a different world. Strekov squinted, trying to read the notes.

> What we struggle for, he possesses. What we dream of, he enjoys. We spoke little of politics. It's difficult to judge what moves him. In that sense, he is nothing that we know at all. Yet he will be useful to us. There is no doubt about that. For a time, he will be useful. But he must be wisely used. The diplomatic service will not long hold his interest. He must be groomed for other responsibilities. I have instructed Serofin, the resident in Paris . . .

The Englishman left the diplomatic service eighteen months later and joined British intelligence. The dossier was incomplete. It wasn't clear to Strekov whether he'd done so at Menzhinsky's urging, at the request of Serofin, or on his own initiative. In the summer of 1939 he was seconded to the British special forces. In London on leave he received a brief note from the Oxford don who had recommended him to the NKVD. Still a Fellow at Balliol, he had broken with the Party over a year earlier. The signing of the Nazi-Soviet pact had been announced three days earlier; few in Britain didn't believe that war was imminent. Rejected by the British forces as medically unfit, the Oxford don had turned his patriotism to the past, carefully sorting through his correspondence for every letter, note, or scrap of paper describing in any way his old affiliation with the Party and its agents, whether in England or abroad. On a warm August afternoon at Oxford he presented his former student with a small packet of letters, four in all, which included the letter sent to the NKVD agent in Amsterdam. He let him read them and, when they were again locked in his cabinet with a dozen similar sets of correspondence, told him that he intended to present the complete correspondence to British intelligence within the week. A vain, foolish man, there was an odor of orthodoxy to his confessional: he'd joined the Roman Catholic Church six months earlier. He'd discussed his intentions with a Jesuit friend who'd helped him decide to notify in advance those who might be innocent of any wrongdoing. If so, they could hardly object to his plan. His former student was mildly amused. He raised no objections: he hadn't known of the letter at the time, and it meant nothing to him now. The don was relieved. He spent the remainder of the afternoon gossiping about old friends and they parted amicably, with a vague promise to keep in touch.

The packet of letters never reached British intelligence. The following weekend the professor joined some friends on a holiday outing a few days before Britain and France declared war on Germany. He didn't rejoin them for dinner. He was found dead at the foot of Beachy Head where he had gone walking alone, his neck broken. The same night his rooms at Oxford were ransacked. His correspondence turned up in Moscow almost six months later, brought in by diplomatic bag from the Soviet embassy in Paris.

Menzhinsky's intuition had been correct. He was a remarkable man. The war confirmed it. He joined British Special Services and fought in Libya, the Near East, and the Balkans. Parachuted into Crete, he led guerrillas against the Germans in the White Mountains, served in Yugoslavia and Greece, was with the Special Service units that recaptured the Aegean Islands, and was mentioned in dispatches after Patmos was taken. Following the war, he returned to civilian life, but later rejoined British intelligence. To Moscow, he hardly seemed the same man. A Soviet intelligence officer met with him in Berlin in 1947 and found him sluggish and bored. He wrote:

> He seems to care nothing about Marxism-Leninism, the Party, or the dangers of a resurgent Germany. Any Moscow schoolboy knows more. He was unwilling to talk about the

German threat, except to deride it. He recognizes British im-
potence, which he seems to share. The only subject that seems
to interest him is the Americans. He seems obsessed by them,
for reasons which he didn't make clear.

Others concluded that the Englishman was no longer important, that
Menzhinsky had been a poor prophet. But they were wrong. In late
1947 and early 1948, his work showed an improvement. As the American intelligence effort was reorganized, his sluggishness disappeared.
When the Americans airdropped Belorussian exiles into the Soviet
Union to their slaughter in the forests of Naliboki, he betrayed them.
When Moldavian and Lett nationalists recruited out of the displaced
persons camps were dropped along the Baltic coast by American
aircraft flying out of Frankfurt, he had already advised the Moscow
Directorate of their names, the dates, and the map coordinates. He
betrayed other American operations mounted through the Black Sea,
through Turkey and Greece, gave details regarding the infiltrators being trained by the CIA at Bad Wiessee, Bad Tolz, and Kaufbeuren in
the Bavarian Algau. When the Americans desperately tried to resup-
ply the last Ukrainian rebel outposts about to be overrun by Soviet
forces in the Carpathians in 1951, he provided Moscow with the details of the CIA effort—dates, hours, equipment, even the flight paths.

He had an operational name by then: Solo. Few in Moscow knew
more. Those who did, like Orlov, were even less sure who or what he
was. Menzhinsky had tried: *He is nothing that we know at all,* he had
written in Paris twenty years earlier, *but for a time he will be useful for
us.* What more was there to know? He was English to the core, Menzhinsky had said, but only because he knew no more. None of them
could explain; he had eluded them all.

Khartoum was where he was born, in the vastness of the Sudan, which
he never forgot. His father was an English officer in the Sudan political service; his mother, the daughter of a peer. As a schoolboy in England separated from both, he was lonely, miserable, and out of place.
On cold winter nights in bed at his first boarding school he dreamed
of the acacias of Kordofan, naked in the noonday sun, Baggara Ar-

abs on horseback churning the dry earth to feathers of wind-blown dust as fine as silk, the frenzied Dinka dancers bringing to his father's campfire the smell of smoke, ashes, and kaolin mixed with mud, the blooding of his youth among the Nuer after he'd shot his first gazelle. At chapel there arose with the anthem the recollection of the Galla horsemen trooping the Regent's colors on the fields of Entoto in Abyssinia, royal purples and blood reds far brighter than the empty ritual of the Anglican communion. On winter or spring holidays with older cousins and shrewish aunts in cold country houses he relived again the long, indolent steamer ride up the Nile from Wadi Haifa to Cairo at the end of the summer, the final bath at the Semiramis Hotel in the late afternoon, washing away the dust of Africa for another year while beyond the door the tutor waited—the clothes on the bed, the books already on the table, the pages marked for the daily lessons that would accompany him back to London.

There were few pictures left from those years: from Africa, from Charterhouse and Harrow afterward, from the undergraduate years at Oxford. On the walls of the small cottage behind his grandfather's seventeenth-century house in Devonshire were the views of the Nuba mountains, Kordofan, the Nile, the plains of Althi in Kenya, the white-washed mud-and-wattle banda at the Governor's compound in Uganda where he had spent the first Christmas he could remember. On the walls of the Devonshire cottage were his great-uncle's and his father's guns—the DB .500 cordite, the single barrel .400, the Holland .303, the Purdey 12 bore x 24. A few dim photographs hung there too, growing paler as he grew in size until at last they seemed to belong to a Lilliputian world that had long ceased to exist except in his own imagination. His father was dead then. Invalided home from the Sudan service two years after the divorce on a meager 500 pounds a year, he found a position as senior clerk in the Sudan government offices. He lived in a two-room flat near the Strand those last years. Following his dismissal from the senior clerkship, he translated Arabic erotica for a millionaire's private library in Mayfair to supplement his pension and to enable him to finish his own translation of Ibn Khaldoun. The translation was never completed. Already weakened by tuberculosis, he contracted influenza. Feverish and bedridden, unable to purge his mind of the obscene doggerel of his most recent translations and return to the classical purity of his life's work, he left the gas on one frozen December night and died on the floor nearby, trying vainly to reach it.

A few pictures of the father were at Devonshire, taken with an ancient box camera in Darfur and Kordofan. They hung beneath the Masai pig spears brought from Kenya and the *chicotte* that he'd given to his son after a visit to the Congo: a whip of steel-hard hippo hide as sharp as an awl used among the rubber plantations of King Leopold's empire where the twenty-lash law ruled the local villages. There were photographs of his grandfather taken in his office at Whitehall and at the Cairo conference, standing near Winston Churchill and only a few feet from T.E. Lawrence. There were pictures of his stepfather, mother, and stepsisters taken after the divorce, standing in the apricot sunshine of the Carleton terrace at Cannes at the hour of the aperitif, or gathered along the rail of the P&O steamer that would take them to Greece, Rhodes, or Cyprus. But Solo was never there. In his teens by then, he had become a solitary, like his father.

In Northumberland with his stepfather he roamed the moor with his .22 rook rifle. At Devonshire he still kept the old desk, the bookcase, and writing table where were piled the dog-eared copies of the *Geographical Journal,* the Ibn Khaldoun manuscript, the Sudan reports, and his father's ledger books retrieved from the flat near the Strand. In his younger days he sat at the desk while he planned his return to the Sudan, to Abyssinia and Uganda where he would climb Ruwenzori as his great uncle had, shoot with the Nuer and Dinka, ride with the Baggera Arabs, or explore the Danakil; but he no longer talked of these things. There were no pictures from these years, none at all. At school he was an enigma. He was remembered from the playing fields and the classrooms, but his face was never found in the photographs of the assembled prefects, forms, or teams. If there was evidence of his presence, it showed only in the vacuum of his absence. There were summers at Harlech in North Wales, the Alpine assaults later in Bavaria, but no photographs. He was there, of course—the name on the class rolls, the honors list, among the team captains, and in the memories of the teachers and headmasters, but their recollection was always punctuated by a curious pause, by a bafflement which, like Menzhinsky's years later, never wholly discovered itself: *O yes, a marvelously deep chap. A splendid midfield player, one of the best ever. But solitary, you know, headstrong and ill-managed, I daresay. But then, you can't make bricks without straw, can you?*

It was as if his solitude had already discovered the path his future would take, if not in Africa then someplace else; and that the curious searching among the sepia photographs hanging in the commons room or discovered on their bookshelves would find nothing, while his contemporaries were locked in timeless innocence, imprisoned forever in this dusty mezzotint their past had become. Not Solo. In his own way he'd put his boot beyond them, as if he recognized that one day the great silver curvature of time's mirror would bend backwards, and with its imperfect gray light seek him out in the fifth form, on the rugby field, or the library steps; and, in the name of whatever apostasy he'd committed, attempt to locate its roots in the more banal treason of upper middle class English family life—the betrayal of youths taken from guns, from cricket bats, hearthsides, and Christmas puddings; the sniveling faces seen in a Victorian coach window on their way back to school after the holidays and whose misery would bring flooding back to gray-haired men the terrible treacheries of their own youth— the G-forces gathering in rattan canes whistling through the winter cold; the smell of chapel; the despair that cowers in knickerbockers in the twilight along the edges of winter playing fields, petrified that the leather ball will find them out; the icy clasp of the swimming bath, as cold and malevolent as the universe itself.

Solo denied it. In his meeting with Menzhinsky in Paris he said that all that was wrong with England and the cabinet office was the mindless tyranny of the public school. It was something he had escaped, he explained, but no other Englishman he had ever known had. It was a tyranny, a subjugation of sorts, an odor almost which lingered on long after Cambridge or Oxford: something in the clay not completely fired; something damp around the buttocks; something of an abiding adolescence that made grown men turn suspiciously, even in middle age, on the floor of Commons, in the corridors of the City, doomed by the misery and nastiness of public school life to think constantly of their own shit.

At Oxford he earned a blue at football and cricket, a first class honors degree in history. He thought of the Sudan political service, preceded by a few years at Magdelene to study Arabic. A blue to punish the blacks, his stepfather said disapprovingly: a bog baron. Why waste such talent? The diplomatic service interested him, but only until he could make up his mind. He won a traveling fellowship at Balliol and went to Berlin to brush up on his German. He met a young German girl studying to be an actress. She had a small flat on Savigny Platz. She was blond, blue-eyed, had never met an Englishman before. Tired of lovemaking and searching for adventure, they sat in the late afternoon sunshine, talking conspiratorial politics under the chestnut trees.

The sky had grown dark outside. Strekov's head ached. There were too many names, too many memories. He locked the dossiers away in the two safes, closed the door behind him, and went through Orlov's empty office into the secretarial suite. A radio on the cabinet in the reception room was playing broadcasting from the Palace of Congresses at the Kremlin. An address had just been concluded, and the party hacks were applauding. "A merry liveliness pervades the hall," the announcer intoned solemnly. "Everyone is standing . . ."

Outside in the darkness a few stars hung on the horizon. The night air cooled his face. He walked back toward Orlov's flat, head sunk in his collar. Menzhinsky? Where was Menzhinsky now? The young German girl from Berlin, where had she gone? Had she escaped Berlin? He knew the fate of some of the others, but what about her? Serofin, the NKVD resident at Paris during Menzhinsky's 1937 visit, was dead—garroted by the NKVD at Nalchik in the Caucausus in 1940. The NKVD illegal in Berlin when Solo was recruited had been shot in Moscow the year following his return. What about the others? He stopped, looking up at the sky. The stillness of the Moscow night astonished him . . . even now, after all those years.

Strekov stood in the doorway of the tiny third-floor flat near Borisoglebsky Alley, north of Arbat, the smell of anise, warm bread, and bubbling molasses in his nose. The two small children hid behind the flour-dusted skirts of their grandmother, looking up at him shyly. They were blond, like Strekov, but their eyes were as dark as their mother's. Colonel Aronovich stood beyond, tall and dignified in his worsted coat and trousers, tieless, a pair of pebble-lensed spectacles on his beaked nose, a copy of the *Artilleryman's Journal* in his rough hands. He had been reading in the peevish gray light of the front windows. He was smiling at his grandchildren, like his wife, a short, plump woman with a round, wrinkled face, small brown eyes, and a tooth missing deep in her jaw. She embraced her son-in-law, tears shining on her cheeks, and brought each of the children forward from beneath her skirts to send them towards their father. Strekov kneeled and embraced them, a son against each shoulder, breathing the smell of their sticky faces, their milky breaths, and the clean, dry warmth of their hair and shirts, as fresh as wind-dried laundry. But they were still shy, a little secretive, their necks rigid. They held their faces away from their father's cold cheeks to look curiously into the distant gray eyes, so unlike their own, their grandparents', or others in this dark-eyed neighborhood. Colonel Aronovich's niece was also there, the daughter of a rabbi in Minsk. She had been studying for her examinations at the university. She came forward to embrace Strekov lightly. In the hard, clear light of the small flat, Strekov found it difficult to hear their voices: lips were moving around him, but he heard no words. The apartment was as silent to his intruding presence as the small graveyard, less than a kilometer away, where he had stood that morning in the winter cold, bringing flowers to his wife's grave in the corner of the lot under a row of old poplars. He had wanted to take the two boys with him, but it was too early. Standing at the graveside, he had known too that their presence would have been too much for him. An old *muzhik,* is face cruelly scarred from smallpox, squatted on his knees at a nearby grave, tearing away leaf mold and broken twigs from an older grave, muttering incoherently to himself. His cap fell from his head. His hair was short, closely cropped, as if he'd just returned from a prison camp. He began to weep.

For each of the boys Strekov had brought a shirt, a sweater, a pair of dark blue mittens, and finally, the music box. It stood on the oil-clothed table in the center of the room where they drank hot tea and shared the fresh cakes just brought from the oven. The wooden drum rotated slowly, like a carousel, turning to the small wooden figures standing atop the drum—the flutist, the cornet and tuba players, the plump violist: a small group of baroque musicians from Berlin's Kurfürstendamm, a holiday canzone of strings and woodwinds. The two boys watched it wind down, brown eyes level with the tabletop, drawn closer as the music faded, the musicians grew weary. But the key was wound again, the arms moved once more, the heart fluttered and recovered its metronome.

Tomorrow he would take them to the park, perhaps to the circus. They were intrigued. Should they accept? They turned to their grandmother, who stood near the kerosene cooker, wiping her eyes; to their grandfather, with his crusted pipe, the wrinkled gray coat that they knew so well. When it was time to leave, they came forward as shyly as at their first greeting, urged on by their grandparents. They touched their cheeks briefly to Strekov's face, then retreated backwards again, still holding their cakes, eyes turned towards the gift, which hadn't moved since the adults began to talk of other things. Would he leave it behind?

Out into the cold streets, across the alley, and down the uneven cobbled street to the small park with its gravel paths and the few small trees shivering in the wind. Maryna was waiting, sitting on a small bench nearby, reading a book. She looked very intellectual, very distant, bored. She lifted her head and stared at him, her face stung by the cold, her dark hair lifting in the wind. They were strangers for a moment. But she was younger than the roles she assumed. She smiled and got to her feet impulsively, pocketing the book without marking her place.

"I doubt that they look much like you . . . your children," she told him that night, lying next to him in the darkness of her flat. Her small head was propped on one hand, the other touching his face, drawing circles along his temples and forehead where the hair was still damp. His body smelled of her body, his skin of her skin. They were covered by a light cotton sheet and the phonograph was still playing from the table near the window. She made love by music, this young girl whom Strekov had known since she was twelve and he far older. Once excited by circuses, story-book ballets, the first winter snowfall, she was now moved by fantasies far beyond the life of Moscow, which she found so stultifying. Strekov was their symbol, mysteriously disappearing from her life every two or three years, fetching back with him upon his return the romance denied her—the travel, the excitement of remote cities, the smells of the continent, a cosmopolitan world she had never felt so fiercely except through him. It was a world she didn't know. She imagined she loved him. She was still only a child, but her English was almost as good as his; her French, better.

That evening, after they'd returned to her flat from the concert, she had played American jazz music for him, taped from a VOA broadcast by one of her friends, and had been disappointed when he'd been unable to identify them. But it was Shostakovich she'd returned to in the end, the second movement from the Second Piano Concerto.

She sat on the bed, naked, cross-legged, like a yogi, smoking a cigarette, her curiosity still moving her on. What had he done, what had he seen? Strekov lifted his head sleepily from the pillow and finally rolled to his side, facing her. Her nakedness startled him; the boldness of her position as well. Was it a position fashionable among her peers, the young poets and intellectuals, the painters and editors who squatted on the floor and talked all night over the music, the wine, and cigarette smoke; nothing denied, nothing implicit, everything there for its gratification—the young breasts, the slope of the stomach, the arch of the pudendum? But she had dieted too since Strekov last saw her. Her body had matured but she had grown as thin as a wasp; her lank hair fell against her bony shoulders; her hipbones were prominent under her bony elbows. She seemed eternally awake, not merely alive, but poised for something else, some access to deeper thoughts and emotions. What could Strekov offer her? He knew that he was as old fashioned as everything she'd grown to despise. Only his absence had nourished her infatuation all these years.

"Don't say that," she reprimanded him. "It's not infatuation. You feel as I do—you despise it as much. You're as much ashamed of its vulgarity as I am."

"How do you know that?"

"How does a child know such things? I always knew, from the very first day. Now I know even more. Others know it too." It had been almost a year since Strekov had last seen her, standing alone in her father's living room the night he had left, angry at him and proud, refusing to say good-bye.

"Others?" he asked

"Yes," she said stubbornly. She saw the skepticism in his face. "They do," she insisted. Strekov laughed and she picked up a pillow and flung it across his head, pouncing on him, holding it against his head. But he didn't resist. At last she lifted the pillow, looking down at him. He took her face and brought her down against him. She lay against him silently, like a child, her eyes closed. "When will you believe me?" she asked gently. "When will you believe anyone again?"

That night he dreamed. He had come in from hunting and hadn't undressed because of his exhaustion, only removing his muddy boots to lie on the bed while he heated the kettle for a glass of tea. His wife was already in bed and asked him to come under the covers with her because she was cold. But he'd fallen asleep instead, and when he arose he was wearing a stiff dark suit with a sprig of lilac in the button-hole. The room was in darkness, but he could smell the sweet, heavy bloom of the lilies. Through the half-open door he saw her lying in the wooden casket, her hands in the same position as when she lay under the covers, the body lying cold and silent under the same cold sheets no intimacy would ever warm again.

He stirred and sat up. Maryna was still asleep at his side. He stared at the dark frame of window, the black sky beyond, the night suddenly an agony for him. But then he remembered: I'm going to die, he thought. And when I do, I will have forgotten that I ever existed.

He and Maryna took the metro together to the outskirts and walked together through the woods along the deserted ski trails. He had brought her here as a child and taught her to ski in the deep winter snow. A sudden rain had washed the woods that morning, the air was mild, and the sun appeared briefly, conjuring a thin, broken mist from the raw earth. An old man approached them on the path and stood aside to let them pass, his whiskered face smiling towards Maryna and then Strekov. He nodded and spoke to Strekov, who replied familiarly.

Maryna had been talking and hadn't noticed. "Who was that?" she asked after the old man had gone.

"Who?"

"The old man. You spoke his name."

"Menzhinsky," he said. "Wasn't it Menzhinsky?" He turned and looked back along the path, but it was deserted, only a few wisps of mist lingering in the fading shafts of sunlight.

"I don't believe I know him," she said. "Who is Menzhinsky?" For a moment Strekov stood rooted to the spot. At last he took her arm and turned back along the path.

"It was nothing," he muttered. "I made a mistake."

Near mid-afternoon, Strekov returned alone to the building on Dzerzhinskay Street. He sat for a long time at the table in the committee room adjacent to Orlov's office, his coat still on, the boxes of documents piled on the table and floor nearby. At last he sat forward and on the blank pad in front of him wrote the words:

Today I saw Dimitar Menzhinsky walking in the woods outside Moscow.

He sat unmoving, his mind a blank. He had been suspended in time this past week, like Menzhinsky, the girl in Berlin under the linden trees, and those others of an earlier decade, not belonging to Moscow's new world at all. Their history had been his history—deaths, disappearances, purges, betrayal. Menzhinsky had been one of them. And suddenly he knew: Menzhinsky was dead too, executed at Dubrolag in Moldavia in 1946. His mind had been playing tricks again. For a week he had forgotten, the present suspended, as he had struggled with the past in the hope that justice might bring a different conclusion and absolve them of the history they must otherwise accept. So he had been one of them, sharing their world these past five days. But nothing would change the present, not even the pathetic delusions of his own mind as it struggled to cleanse itself of the past. Nothing could change the present; not for Menzhinsky, or for Bryce, not for himself.

The pad was still on the table when Zhilenkov entered the room an hour later. Strekov had gone. The safes were closed and locked.

Nothing Zhilenkov saw there gave him a clue as to Strekov's solitary research this past week. But Zhilenkov was still curious. He found the note pad and the single sentence scrawled across the top of the page. Was it a joke? He stood over the table, looking down at the name of a man who had been dead for fifteen years. At last he leaned forward, tore the page from the pad, and put it in his pocket.

"After the war there was a falling off," said Orlov, speaking of Solo. Strekov sat opposite him at the dining-room table in Orlov's apartment. They were alone. "He was inactive for three, almost four years. From 1945 until 1948. What do you suppose happened? Was it that Marxism-Leninism had become less interesting for him?" Orlov leaned over his salad, his fork lifted, his jaws still in motion from his chop.

Strekov knew he was being coy. Irritated, he said, "The Party never interested him." Merkurovich brought another dish. Orlov removed the cover, peered into it, and pushed it aside.

"After 1949 he became more active than ever. He was useful in a way he'd never been before. Do you understand why?" Orlov had left the television set on in the salon. Strekov wondered if it was customary when he dined alone in the apartment.

"I believe so. He was an imperial orphan, your Solo."

Orlov looked up. "Orphan?"

"The Empire's orphan."

"What made him change after 1949?"

"Probably the Americans," said Strekov. Orlov knew very well who was responsible. Of course it was the Americans. After the war, nothing was left: not his undergraduate romanticism, not German fascism, not even the Empire. The Americans had saved him. They'd given him something more positive than belief. They'd given him a thing to despise, as he had once despised the Empire—something big, grandiose, vulgar, powerful, philistine, and middle class.

"The Americans gave him something to betray," said Orlov. He waited for Strekov's reaction.

Strekov nodded. "That too."

"He loathed his own class," Orlov added. Again he waited. "The English bourgeoisie. You saw that?"

"I think so," Strekov replied, less interested in his own thoughts than Orlov's. He knew why it was so easy for Orlov to understand Solo. Was it the Party which had created his own faith or his hatred of those who would have condemned him to servitude, like his father? Was that what Menzhinsky had seen in Solo—that he could never commit himself to creating the future, only to betraying the present, and hating the past?

"Now, of course, it's the Americans," Orlov continued. "He sees the nature of the enemy now, as he did in 1937. American fascism."

Orthodoxy again. Was Orlov talking of the future or the present? If the future, it couldn't be proven; if the present, what was the evidence? In Moscow each new sign of American power only strengthened the neurotic conviction that it was evolving towards fascism. It had become an article of faith among the sentimental Left abroad, mathematicians as well as physicists, who in passing nuclear secrets to Moscow had justified their treason by the conviction that without a parity of nuclear weapons the Americans would have blown the world to smithereens by 1951. Faith or fact? But Solo didn't deal in future worlds, only present ones. No, the rationale was Orlov's, not Solo's.

"You disagree?"

"The Americans were his deliverance," Strekov said. "I think there's little doubt about that." The dreadful Americans, of course—that was enough. The dreadful Americans with their vulgarity, their provincialism, their materialism, their triviality, their greed, their messianic pretenses. Not fascism at all. He would have despised Moscow no less. He would have treated the Party parvenus with the same contempt. Didn't Orlov understand that?

"You believe he's a hypocrite?" Orlov asked.

"I believe that's an element. Hypocrisy for its own sake. Games. Expensive, clever, and malicious games."

"Now he's become a nuisance as well. A neurotic nuisance," Orlov said, throwing down his napkin. He pushed his chair away from the table. "He refuses to see anyone in London since the Bryce disappearance. He suspects something and has asked for a meeting in Europe. Barcelona. Is he worth it? There's no one I can send."

"How soon?" They had killed Bryce to protect him. Now Orlov was asking him whether he was worth it. The bureaucracy was prodigal in everything—its architecture, its paperwork, its monuments, its waste.

"Soon. Very soon." Orlov was expecting guests. He looked at his watch and arose from the table. Strekov followed him into the salon.

"Do you know Barcelona?" Orlov asked. He turned off the television set and put a record on the gramophone. A moment later Merkurovich summoned him to the telephone. Strekov leaned back, listening to the music of the Caucasus. A woman sang of the wind moving through the forests of olive and beech. In the distance at the foot of the mountains, the Black Sea was visible through the passes.

Probably Orlov would ask him to go to Barcelona. And if the Barcelona meeting went well, he would ask him to go to London as an illegal. He would be asked to handle Solo and monitor his movements. Solo's demands had come at an inopportune time—policy in flux, a new leadership in the KGB, personnel changes imminent, a few key officials already dismissed but their successors not yet identified. In the meantime some of the old guard, like Orlov, kept the *apparat* going, but they were as vulnerable to the past as anyone else. They had to trust to their instincts, to the loyalty of a few trusted friends.

That was why Orlov had brought Strekov back from East Berlin. He knew that now.

"You know Barcelona, don't you?" Orlov asked when he returned to the room.

Strekov said that he did.

Maryna lived in a second-floor flat on a back street near Vtoraya Frunzenskaya, down an alley, through a doorway. The flat was old, the furniture broken and down-at-the-heel. Her job at the Ministry was deadening, her friends suddenly tiresome, like her own life. What moved her these days except the romance of a new beginning? She shared the flat with two girls her own age. One was in Leningrad, visiting her parents; the other she had persuaded to move in with her sister and brother-in-law for a few weeks.

Strekov had promised to meet her that afternoon. She had left the Ministry early, pleading a doctor's appointment, and had walked to the small park and waited for an hour. A light sleet had begun to fall, mixed with rain. She'd waited another thirty minutes and when Strekov didn't appear, had returned to her chilly flat. Her shoes were wet, her dark hair fell in wet strands across her cheeks. Her blue beret was a coarse, wet sponge. She was sitting in the chair under the lamp, shivering in her wet clothes when she heard his footfall on the stairs, then his knock at the door.

They had dinner at a small restaurant. A few of her friends were there but she ignored them. They talked of travel. She was thinking of Vienna, yes, Paris, the Dalmatian coast of Yugoslavia; Spain, Copenhagen, London. Was it so impossible? No, he told her—not impossible. Why then didn't he transfer to the diplomatic cadres? Strekov listened to her without answering, watching the animation in her eyes. The English girls were no more lovely than she that night, whatever their freedom—moving through the crowds along Piccadilly, or lounging in the grass near Marble Arch; she could be among them, in Copenhagen or along the paths near the Seine, on the Aegean at Mikanos or Patmos, hair blowing in the wind, in blue jeans and leather sandals, the laughing green eyes lifted to all who pass, all who dare, young and old alike.

In her flat she showed him the pictures she'd clipped from magazines—the pictures of Paris, Vienna, England, Scandinavia. She sat on a pillow on the floor, her portable radio nearby. She turned the dial carefully, watching him slyly as she found the station she was searching for and the sound of American jazz. She put her finger to her lips. She had to be careful, she told him, lifting her eyes towards the flat above. An old soldier lives overhead, alone, with a few medals for his wounds. He reports the complaints from the food lines, who is listening to foreign radio or whispering sedition in the streets. He reports the latest gossip to the *Beshniki* and then comes home to feed liver to his cat while a few blocks away a neighbor is being brought in for questioning. The old Polish widow who lives across the hall sometimes does the same. Her dead husband was once prominent in the Polish Communist Party; but now she lives alone with her blind sister, shipwrecked among dusty trunks and yellowing cargoes of old Polish newsprint, rusting birdcages, faded monochromes of Paderewski on the walls, acres of cracked crystal on the tables and shelves, ivy in milk bottles, fishbones on the kitchen floor.

The trickle of water sucked at the drains and eroded the edge from their voices, the music from the VOA on the radio, like surf over sand, and cushioned the sounds of the few cars moving across the square a block away. A small atlas lay on the floor between them, a bottle of brandy and two glasses, too. She lay with her head in his lap, eyes and face shining, her existence recovered from the nullity around her. The wind cried overhead. Didn't he understand how she felt? Wasn't it possible to begin again—for him to begin again, a new life for both of them? Yes, he understood. He watched the mystery that glowed in her eyes, in her face and skin. Her breath and mouth were as warm as summer. She would teach him that nature still had the primordial strength to rekindle, recreate, provide again some visible sign of our creator's affection, and who was more his creature that night than she, despite everything else.

Strekov couldn't sleep with the coming of dawn. The barometer was falling, and the cold penetrated his sleep, bringing winter under the covers. He moved the covers aside and slipped away from her sleeping figure. There was much to do that day. His watch read six fifteen. A curtain of gray had begun to leak from the small cold kitchen. The talk with Maryna had simplified his own problem for the moment, like all talk, but now morning had come again. He must prepare for his late-afternoon flight back to East Berlin, the return to the West, his own problem as insoluble as ever. So you had to be careful about midnight conversations these days, like everything else—not to be betrayed by them in little ways, not to believe for even an hour that words and reality were in any sense identical.

She discovered his absence almost immediately, sat upright suddenly, her nakedness forgotten, breasts whiter than snow save for the crescent of glacial shadow that curved from her hips. "What is it? What time is it?"

"It's early. Go back to sleep."

"Tonight? I'll see you tonight?"

"Tonight," he said.

It was dark, close to midnight. Maryna hadn't seen Strekov for three days. She had spoken to Merkurovich at her father's apartment, but he had been unable to tell her anything. She hurried through the cold streets. She had spent the evening with friends and suddenly had a premonition. Tonight would be the night. She'd excused herself and found a taxi. She ran the last block, her beret in her hand, her dark hair flying as she turned into the dark street, up the steps, and into the hall. She unlocked the door and moved into the flat, calling his name. He would be here tonight. He'd returned, she knew he had. She called his name again.

But there was nothing there, only silence. She moved like a ghost through the dark rooms, her heart beating quietly. The wind blew; the stairway creaked on the second-floor landing. Across the hall the old Polish woman wakened to see her blind sister sitting upright in bed, pawing the air like a blind kitten. Nearby the old soldier whined in his sleep, buried again among the corpses at Kiev.

Maryna stood in the cold bedroom, looking at the empty bed and the cold walls where nothing had changed since Strekov had left three days ago. *Come,* the wind seemed to call. *Come. We're waiting. Come join us—you too.*

NINE

The wind swept through the street far below and rattled the sky-light panes of the old top-floor studio in West Berlin's Kreuzberg. "Good God," Plummer complained, his breath a white vapor on the raw winter air. Chivied from the bed where Elizabeth had left him alone, he found colder air leaking from every window crack and sash joint. Wearing a bed blanket over his shoulders, he knocked at the bathroom door, but water was thundering in the tub, and she didn't hear him. He moved between the bare rooms, lighting hearth fires in a myriad of gas-fired and paper-choked grates, pulling aside curtains, drapes, and old window shades to let in the morning light. Except for the living room and bedroom, the rooms were bare of furniture. Berlin lay beneath a skin of fresh snow that had fallen during the night— earth, sky, and horizon annealed in the same seamless hemisphere of medieval gray, winter breathing in the windows from a forest of blackened chimneys on the roofs beyond; wires, scarves, and quills of smoke trickling from a geometric grid of sloping gables, dovecotes, mansards, and gothic spires.

It was colder in the kitchen. A side window had been left open during the night. A rope of fresh snow cushioned the window sill. Plummer turned on the oven and lit the gas rings, filled the coffeepot, and brought bacon and a saucepan of eggs from the refrigerator. He put a jar of sluggish jam in the oven to thaw, removing at the same time the biscuit tin where it had been hidden overnight from the roaches. He took the loaf of bread from the tin and began to slice. The knife was dull. Of his first five efforts, only two were salvageable. The first three were empty frames of crust, flattened like coat hangers, to which a few wads of dough clung. He threw the crusts on the snowy shed roof of the fire escape a few feet below the window where the pigeons gathered, balls of powdered soot, their feathers raked to silk by the wind. A tug thumped slowly up the canal through the screen of snow, nosing through the gray porridge like a Baffin Island mail boat. A tram moved through Mehringdown, its clabber dulled to brass by the falling flakes.

Elizabeth joined him, already dressed for her office in a wool skirt and cardigan. She had slept with a pair of ski socks on her feet, insulation against the chilly sheets. Now they were gone. She finished making breakfast while he shaved, teeth chattering, the blanket dropped from his naked shoulders as he braced for the cold like a swimmer, filling the small bathroom with steam from the boiling basin, wintergreen from his shaving soap, his hand chasing the reclusive face through the fogs on the mirror, but getting the job done. The electric fire at his feet had warmed his toes and ankles by the time he finished; steam was tapping in the radiators; coffee was bubbling on the gas ring in the kitchen; and the streets below were quilted with December's first snow, fields of white between gray battlements, a few flakes still drifting down.

In the courtyard at Charlottenburg, Elizabeth pulled up her collar and opened the car door, pulling the plaid scarf over her head. "What time?" she asked, turning.

"Ten," he said. "Maybe ten thirty."

She hesitated. "You'll be in Treptow?" He nodded. She searched his face, but said nothing. Then she retrieved her small overnight case from the floor and slipped from the front seat. "Ten thirty, then," she said.

The checkpoint was white and deserted, as clean as a New England meadow. He drove slowly into East Berlin. A Russian Mosca picked him up two blocks beyond and followed him all the way to the warehouse. There was more Soviet armor on the streets; the barricades were manned by East German soldiers who had replaced the police. As Plummer entered the snow-filled alley behind the warehouse, the Mosca disappeared to the east.

The snow had eased by ten o'clock and they sat in the chilly warehouse, waiting for a shipment of oil drums to be delivered from the canal. The trucks were late. As they waited, sitting on the wooden steps that led to the gallery office, Plummer was telling the warehousemen that Russian rats weren't anything, nothing at all. He had nothing personally against Russian rats—Uzbek, Georgian, Azerbaijanian, or Armenian either—only that he didn't think any of them could hold a candle to a little red-eyed Roman mountain rat. Try sleeping in the Alban hills below Rome if they had any doubts. Just as you were beginning to drift off to sleep, a battalion of gopher-sized panzer rats would blitzkrieg out of the catacombs behind you trying to drag you back into their second-century bone-yard. You knew that shit had to stop and sometimes with a little scrounging around you could manage it—wire yourself up like a ten-string banjo with a little brass and percussion on the side—tin cans and metal lids the Italians used, to shingle the accordion wire at the front of the caves; wire up knee and elbow, ankles too; so when you rolled in your sleep the tin cans would explode like a battery of .88s, like a Mississippi minstrel jamboree band on New Year's Eve, and the SS or panzer rats that were sneaking towards your nose would go roaring back into their holes, stampeding the foot soldiers along with them. You woke up too, of course. That was the problem. He'd never solved it.

The six German warehousemen sat looking silently at Plummer. The youngest was suspicious. He looked cynically at his colleagues, but said nothing. Finally one of the older men asked if there were rats in America. "Of course they have rats," Munch volunteered. "But not so many as Treptow."

"Why is that?" asked the youngest German dubiously.

Munch shook his head. "I don't know," he said finally, taking the pipe from his mouth. "Ask him."

"Why is that?" the young German repeated, watching Plummer.

Plummer shrugged. This wasn't the argument he wanted to make. He looked out the open door toward the old building opposite, where an ancient wooden sign still hung, the German script barely visible now: *Troller's Machine Works.* "Maybe it's because of the trolls," he improvised.

No one spoke for a few minutes. "Trolls?" an old man asked. "What did he say? Trolls?"

"There are no trolls left in Treptow," an old man said slyly.

"Of course not," Munch said instantly. "The communists killed them."

"So that's Marxism for you," Plummer interrupted easily, trying to get Munch off the hook. "Trolls are the natural solution, but if they're free traders, what can you do?" He was conscious of the young German's angry look. "No politics intended," he continued, wishing to hell the trucks would come. "But if you're looking for final solutions, the only answer to a red-eyed Roman rat is a little red-eyed mountain troll, as mean as a rat can make him, since who is it that goes roaring through his trap lines, his mine shafts and tunnels; who is it that keeps dragging all this rat crud through his factories and gold-sluices, fouling up his tackle, frightening his women, bankrupting his economy. The rats, that's who. So the troll is the rat's natural enemy down underground and the only one who can get rid of him."

"They say there are still some trolls in Rumania," a middle-aged warehouseman volunteered.

"There are no trolls in Rumania, in Italy, in America, or anyplace else," the young German said in disgust, getting to his feet on the gallery stairs. "There never were. It is folklore. But he isn't talking about rats or trolls. He is talking about something else. And it is dangerous for you to listen—for all of you."

"He is talking about rats as far as we're concerned," Munch said. "And as far as I'm concerned, Ukrainian rats are the worst of a bad lot." Someone had flushed a rat from the rear bay of the warehouse that morning before Plummer arrived. Munch, the ex-*Panzerschütze*, had begun describing the rats he'd found in the Ukraine. Plump country rats, at first, fed on soy and sunflower seed, on wheat and corn. But after the first winter the quality of Russian rat life had changed. By the end of the third year it had grown unspeakable: rats fed on corpses, on charnel slime; armies of rats rose out of mass graves where bone and flesh had been plowed under like fodder, rats far larger and more malevolent than the poor, confused Berlin rat flushed from the rear bay that morning. Munch's bitter tirade had grown so graphic that no one doubted that it carried a political message as well. The young German understood it immediately. He was a paid informer, sent from the SSD offices on Normannenstrasse to spy on the warehouse work and on Plummer. When the American interrupted his warehouse foreman and began his own rambling, improvisatory journey on the character of Roman rats and finally trolls, the informer was momentarily confused, but grew convinced that Plummer was embellishing Munch's own seditious talk. He would have to file a report, but Plummer's commentary had thrown him off the track. Now he was more than ever convinced that Plummer was slandering the GDR and the Russians, too, but how? How? He'd seen political satire cleverly done, poisonously effective, but this made no fucking sense at all.

"Listen," he called to Plummer. "Herr Plummer . . ." But Plummer, summoned by the bookkeeper, had already climbed the steps to the office above.

The oil shipment had been turned back by East German customs. The documents weren't in order. Plummer telephoned customs himself but the senior official refused to discuss the matter over the phone. Plummer drove through the snowy streets to the customs offices. He was kept waiting for thirty minutes. The official refused to see him.

Darkness came early. Plummer was still in East Berlin. He left his car on a side street near an old theater where a Brecht play was being revived. A number of West German diplomatic cars were parked along the side street. He walked past the theater and in the next block caught a tram. Fifteen minutes later he descended at a crowded square. He sat in a smoky coffeehouse for thirty minutes. The interior was dimly lit. Someone was playing a guitar in a far corner. At eight thirty he picked up his coat and moved towards the door. On the wooden screen separating the interior from the front door messages had been tacked up— announcements of student meetings, items for sale, amateur recitals, concert dates, lyrics from the songs the musicians would play, a fragment of doggerel entitled "Frontsoldat" under a newspaper showing an American battle unit entering West Berlin:

> I never learned his name;
> We never knew his corps;
> Dead in the Neisse that day;
> The Man Who Lost the War.

He pulled up his coat collar and went out into the square. At the corner he stood with the crowd, waiting for a few armored cars to go rattling past. As he stepped from the curb, Strekov joined him. "We don't have much time," he said. "You wanted to talk to me?"

"They're worried," Plummer said. "Worried about you, worried about Berlin. They want to know what's happening. An update."

"I don't like meetings."

"Deaddrops are too slow," Plummer said.

"It's obvious what's happening," Strekov replied, looking out over the square. "The Berlin garrisons are being reinforced. More troops and more weapons."

"What's it mean? Will your Soviet friends back down?"

"Is that what you came here to ask me?" Strekov was annoyed. "Are your military experts so blind they don't see it? What do they expect me to tell them? You're here as well as I. Look around you. They're wasting our time, my time and yours."

"Not if we know what's happening."

"What's happening is that the military on both sides is increasing the pressure. The Americans bring in another military unit, then send you scurrying into East Berlin to ask me if the Russians are frightened. If the answer is no, they'll bring in two more units and send you back over to ask if they're frightened yet. And when I tell you no, you'll go back and more guns will be brought in. It's idiocy. That's the way wars start." Strekov walked in silence, head down. "The only way to prevent it is to know the future. Precise weapons information. Precise capability—what a missile will or won't do. That's the only way to find stability. Exact information. Equilibrium. When both sides have that, they'll have stability. They won't have to gamble with lives while asking you and me to speculate about intentions. No tactical or strategic advantage will be possible."

"That's what they want to know now. What do the Soviet garrisons have in mind?"

"What they always have in mind—bigger and better weapons. The military advantage. Isn't that what the military always wants?" He glanced at Plummer. "Isn't it?"

"Maybe."

Strekov laughed. "The military likes crises," he said. "They always have. It lets them know their importance, their value. It gives back to them the meaning of their lives, something most of us have learned to live without. It lets them leave the boredom of the barracks or the brothel. It lets them swagger through the streets with their guns. It quickens their appetites when they lie down with their whores. Then the next day they feel better when they put their feet back on their desks." He stood at the curb, searching the street. A small dark Mosca was parked on the far side of the street, just beyond the street lamp. Its motor was running. Two men were sitting in the front seat.

"One was behind me when I crossed over this morning," Plummer said. "You get used to it in time."

They crossed the street. As they reached the curb, Strekov said, "I think we'd better take the tram. We'll go to your car, wherever you've left it. I'll drive with you as far as the Wall."

Plummer looked towards him. He knew then that he couldn't trust this man, not because of his treachery, but because he didn't care. That was what he had seen in his face during their meeting in Rostock; now he saw it again. "You think I can't handle it?" Plummer asked.

"I think it's dangerous to try. It's not like Prague. In Prague they were novices, learning their trade, trained at Praha Pohoreclec or U Vorliku. These men are different."

"So it was Prague," Plummer said. "You were in Prague?"

"Yes, it was Prague." They walked in silence towards the tram stop. After a few minutes Strekov said, "You did it very well in Prague. We expected you to run. You didn't run. It's interesting to watch someone stand his ground. After a certain time whether he is right or wrong is beside the point. It takes on a certain logic of its own. But then you broke Kuimov's jaw that afternoon in front of the hotel. I was disappointed. You told us the game was over. Those men in the Mosca aren't playing games."

The tram was crowded. Standing at the rear, they swayed over the narrow track. Strekov watched the snowy street behind. At a signal from Plummer he moved towards the door and they left the tram. "I think we'd better postpone further contacts for the time being," Strekov said as they passed the theater. "There's nothing to be gained by it."

They reached the car. Plummer said, "You've run out of things to say, is that it?"

"I suppose that's true, when you think about it. Why involve other lives, other people? I'd never intended to do that. That's why I didn't see any point in meeting here in East Berlin."

They drove back towards the Wall. Plummer lit a cigarette and watched the rearview mirror, still thinking about what had been said. He drove carefully. The car that was behind him turned into a side street. Now the street was empty.

"What did you think I was doing in Prague?" he asked.

"You were running a few Czechs," Strekov replied. "A small network."

"So you thought."

"Yes, so I thought. Not everyone did. Coincidence, they explained. But I was more suspicious in what I saw, more conservative in expressing it. I kept my mouth shut. I didn't talk about my doubts." They crossed a darkened intersection. Along the block beyond, stumps of broken chimneys showed against the snow-filled rubble. The car springs were as hard as a farm wagon as the Opel thumped through the potholed street. "I was right, wasn't I?" Strekov asked.

"No," Plummer said. "Who were those people back there in the Mosca?"

"Curious men. Interested in you, in what you are doing in Berlin." Strekov sat forward, peering through the windshield. "There's a roadblock ahead."

"Were they East German?" He slowed down.

"Here things are never black or white," Strekov said. A group of East German militia was deployed along the street ahead of them. A Soviet truck with its fog lights on blocked the center lane. A German lieutenant came to the window and looked in. Plummer passed him his documents. Strekov spoke to him in German, then Russian, and gave him an identity card. The German saluted them and motioned them on. "So you came here to sell oil and nothing else, just like Prague," Strekov said after a few minutes. He laughed quietly. "Just oil."

"It's true," Plummer said. Strekov laughed again. "For Christ's sake," Plummer muttered. They drove in silence, Strekov staring out the window ahead of them, still amused.

"Piously," he resumed at last, rousing himself, "book in hand, bringing order to the barbarous German frontier." After a minute he said, "Like St. Boniface."

Plummer glanced at him. "St. Who?"

"St. Boniface. Sent out from Catholic Britain. Bringing a Latin faith to the savage Saxons beyond the Vistula. A Catholic imperialist. Don't you know your own history? Turn at the next corner."

"Screw history," Plummer said in English. "Screw East Berlin too."

Strekov said, "The same trade-union mentality, the same provincial pride. The same shallow anger. At Rostock they thought you were a trade unionist. In Prague, the same. Something of a bully. Anger is cheap, isn't it? Cheap and automatic. Nothing you have to think about very much. But it's not a creed to live by. Maybe it's the price you've paid for survival all these years. Is it? Doesn't it get tiresome after a while?"

"As tiresome as all this talk."

"Yes, that's tiresome, too." He took a card from his pocket and wrote something on it and handed it to Plummer. "If you have to get in touch with me, call that number. But only emergencies. Don't call from Treptow. Someplace else in East Berlin. Don't use the old number."

"They want to talk to you. Someplace in the West. West Berlin, Geneva, Paris, Copenhagen. You name it." Strekov didn't answer. They moved into the yellow-gray lights of Unter den Linden. "We can give you the documents," Plummer resumed. "It's important that they talk to you."

"Impossible," Strekov muttered. "I have nothing to say. I can get out here."

Plummer moved the car to the curb. Strekov got out, backed away into the shadows, and was still standing there when Plummer drove on. Thirty minutes later Plummer was in West Berlin.

The following day was even colder. Crusts of snow still lay on the streets and sidewalks. The American tanks on the western perimeter at Friedrichstrasse had again been reinforced; so had the Soviet and East German mechanized forces along Unter den Linden. Militiamen in dark-blue overcoats stirred behind them on the frozen streets. Gun-metal gray bristled in the biting December cold. The breaths of the waiting troops smoked like skirmish fires along the streets near the Wall. No sightseers were there, no crowds, no spectators. Assembly was forbidden. Casual transit was suspended. Overhead, Soviet fighters droned through the dirty skies, like wasps shaken from their winter sleep.

Plummer was detained at the checkpoint. When he arrived at the ministry building on Leipzigerstrasse, he was an hour late. It was his first meeting at the Planning Commission since his shipment had been stopped.

Kohler told him he was late. "I said ten o'clock," he said coldly. "The deputy minister couldn't wait. He won't see you now."

Plummer told him he had been delayed. They could talk instead.

"All decisions in your case are being made at the ministerial level," Kohler said.

"I told you I was delayed at the checkpoint."

"That is unacceptable."

"Then I'll explain to his secretary."

"You cannot see his secretary."

"What are you trying to do?" Plummer asked. "Do you want oil or not? Customs has stopped all shipments. What the hell's going on?"

"It's out of my hands now. You've humiliated the deputy minister."

"Then I'll talk to someone else."

"Stop shouting," Kohler said. "Conduct yourself with decorum, even if you can't do so with dignity."

"Stop stalling! Where's the vice minister's office? I'll go myself."

Kohler was livid, rising from behind his desk. "Stalling?" he shouted. "It is you who are stalling. Delaying the shipments, compromising the agreements! Stalling on behalf of the revanchist leadership in Bonn that pursues aggressive aims, that puts a half million men under arms, that incites hatred among the masses, that glorifies the barbaric history of German invasions! Did you see the tanks on the streets? Did you?"

"What are you talking about?"

"You have had meetings with criminalistic elements!" Kohler yelled. "You have been in secret contact with enemies of the GDR!"

"You're not making any sense."

"You've slandered my government! I heard you myself—on the train from Rostock!"

"I want to see the deputy minister."

"That's impossible. You have no pass! I'll call the security guard!"

"Call them then! Go ahead—call them! If you're going to throw me out, do it right—the way the Russians taught you. Fifty truncheons and a floorful of teeth, isn't that it? Come on, Kohler! Don't screw around like this, Kohler! Do it!" He went out. On the floor below he found a staff aide to the deputy who told him that the meeting would be re-scheduled for the following week. When Plummer left the ministry, he thought the lubricant agreement's obituary was already being drafted, and that a few frightened bureaucrats, like Kohler, were temporarily protecting the vacuum which policy had already abandoned.

T-54 tanks rattled across the Potzdammerplatz. Trucks with armed infantry under canvas rattled across the intersections. Plummer thought that he would drive to Treptow but changed his mind and drove back into West Berlin. Late in the afternoon he had a drink in a bar on the Kurfürstendamm to celebrate the season, killing time before he picked up Elizabeth after her Christmas party at the refugee barracks at Marienfelde. The barman who gave him his drink said that the streets outside reminded him of Berlin in 1939.

Later that Christmas Eve the Soviets and East Germans closed the autobahns into West Berlin. Soviet MiGs buzzed the air corridors and threatened to intercept all commercial air traffic into Tegel and Tempelhof. Soviet tactical units across the Wall were reinforced. In Paris the ambassadors to the NATO Council were summoned from receptions and formal dinners, from family firesides, wassail bowls, wives, and mistresses to an emergency meeting at NATO headquarters in the Bois de Boulogne at the lower end of Avenue Foch.

Phil Chambers was there, standing on the fringes of the groups gathered in the corridors as the envoys began to arrive and assemble in the NATO crisis room near the secretary-general's office. A few of the ambassadors were in evening clothes; the Belgian and Portuguese wore white ties, the British a Norfolk jacket over a gray turtleneck. Chambers had arrived that afternoon from London. He wore an unfashionable Ulster and clutched a worn calfskin briefcase. There were pouches under his eyes. "Is this a wake or a wedding?" an American quipped. In the background the teleprinter to SHAFE headquarters at Vaucresson outside Paris chattered out the details of the most recent Soviet tactical maneuvers.

The aides and staff assistants waited outside as the NATO council began to meet in secret session. Couriers, military and political advisors, and notetakers shuttled in and out of the crisis room, bringing the latest cables, instructions, ELINT intercepts, position papers, and sitreps, trying to illuminate every vagrant mote that stirred on the continent that night, however distant from the Berlin storm center. Through the opening door to the crisis room Chambers saw the unworldly translucent moonlight from the lucite situation board limning the seated figures as they received their first military situation report. A Soviet armored force in Thüringen had been reinforced by the Twenty-fourth Soviet Tactical Army and had begun to wheel towards the border, its radio frequencies monitored by NATO listening posts across the frontier. The First Soviet Guards Army was also on the move. All westbound railroad traffic at the Brest-Terespol interchange point on the Soviet-Polish frontier had been stopped. Soviet telecommunications traffic in East Berlin, at Karlshorst, Zossen, and Rontguntal had increased tenfold in the past six hours. A Soviet delegation from the State Committee for Defense Technology had abruptly departed from a Prague reception and was returning to Moscow, canceling its East European tour. A US SAC B-47 out of Goose Bay in Labrador was overdue from a Norwegian patrol. In crisis rooms along the five-thousand-mile NATO front the lights had flickered on—along snowswept runways, in the warm underground moleholes where the fighter-interceptor pilots, the B-47 and tanker crews played pinochle, poker, grab-assed, and watched television; under frozen tarps and beneath ice-bearded hatchcovers dipping in the North Atlantic swell, the muscles were being readied, the responses prepared. It was all there—wherever one looked that night—the wheat, the chaff, the fucked-up electronic scud, the gremlin dwarfs hotdogging in the ionosphere, the real nuclear menace—

"We think it may be slowing down a bit," a young officer told Chambers at two o'clock on Christmas morning. The face was young and eager—too young to know, Chambers thought. He waited for the crisis-room door to open. No one had entered for thirty minutes. A military analyst from the US NATO staff told him that the order had gone out to the US military commander in Berlin: He could respond to pressure, but he wasn't to provoke it. They thought the Soviet commander had been given the same message. Chambers wasn't convinced. He took a steaming cup of black coffee from the service table and sipped it slowly, his eyes fastened to a sprig of sea-green mistletoe one of the secretaries had stapled to the molding above the door to the NATO crisis room. The coffee stung his throat. A moment later he felt a stinging blow in his chest. He reeled with the pain, the bright corridor swimming around him for a moment. Nausea swept him back up the corridor towards the anteroom. He slumped into a chair near the door where a trickle of cold night air could be felt, sucking grotesquely for breath, trying to bring the air into his chest. His head swam; his right hand still clutched the briefcase, his other the coffee cup. His fingers were scalded, but the pain against his sick heart was sharper. He summoned the will to move the briefcase to his knees, to dig the vial of glycerine tablets from his coat pocket.

He was still sitting there when the meeting concluded, slumped in the chair, still in anguish, face numb, arms and hands as lifeless as wood, not belonging to him at all. Terrible fires still burned in his chest; a furnace of white hot coals raged with each small breath he drew. Finally the first cooling draught came, then a second. The corridor was empty. An hour had passed. His car was waiting outside and drove him back to his hotel. The lift had closed down, and he climbed the stairs to his room like a somnambulist. A bottle of whiskey and mineral water at his elbow, he sat at the elegant writing desk in front of the towering windows and watched the first flush of dawn creep up from the skyline. Because it was Christmas Day and his wife would be sleeping on the second floor of the house in Kensington—because he was still awake, like the *nachtwächter* he had always been, watching the evening fires, the battlements, and the premonitory skies, he wrote her a letter, putting to paper the terror of his thoughts those few hours earlier when the first seizure had come outside the crisis room, terror which had dogged his footsteps ever since, even in the car that had swept him away—followed him under the iron limbs along the Avenue Marshall Foch, like a blind man, tapping its white cane through the darkness behind him.

Strekov was at Karlshorst that night. He had just returned from the Soviet mission. He stood in the chilly courtyard crowded with cars, their gray exhausts coughing like poisoned sheep out over the cold cobblestones. Voices called drunkenly through the darkness. The watch was changing. He saw Zhilenkov's repellent face in the headlights of a small Mosca as he stood talking to an East German SSD official. Strekov had been awake since dawn; and it was now nearly four o'clock in the morning. He stood looking at the sky, trying to retrieve something from memory, something he had written at the dacha near Kiev. He saw the antennae and the microwave masts against the dark sky, watching and waiting. Then he remembered:

> The meteoric dark
> Is monitored to hear
> The news we're waiting for:
> A star born far away—
> The parabolic arc—
> The wings against the shore;
> A bat or madman bark;
> A wounded planet roar.

On Christmas morning Plummer awoke and found frost on the gallery of windows. He thought it was snow. He'd heard the knock at the door, but arose too late, still half-asleep, shambling down the hall to the front door, the bed blanket across his shoulders, to find the landing empty, the telegram on his doormat. He carried it to the window and watched the messenger climb onto his motorbike and drive off.

An old man smoking a pipe pushed an iron skeleton of a bicycle along the street in the opposite direction, a few loaves of bread stacked like cordwood in the wicker basket tied to the back fender. A few pigeons flapped around the smoking chimneys along the line of roofs to the east. The telegram was a one-liner from Phil Chambers in Paris. He would be arriving at Tegel at eight that night.

It was a little after ten when he left his office and drove to Elizabeth's apartment house in Charlottenburg. She was surprised to see him and thought he might have returned to London for the holidays. They hadn't seen each other for three weeks. She was on her way to the eleven o'clock services at the Anglican church. He drove her himself, but didn't go in. He found a quiet little coffee shop in a downtown hotel and read the papers. He picked her up after the church services and they drove to the *Lietzensee,* left the car, and walked along the path near the lake under the willow trees. The wind blew across the corrugated surface of the water. Ducks and swans drifted there in summer, but the lake was deserted now. Patches of ice as fine as Flemish lace had formed along the shoreline. A few elderly couples moved along the path; a nurse pushed an old man in a rubber-tired wheelchair. Plummer stopped to watch a plane drop quickly out of the sky towards Templehof.

"Does that bother you so much?" Elizabeth asked, stopping too, and following his eyes. "They closed the Helmstedt checkpoint again this morning. I heard it on the wireless."

"No, it doesn't bother me." A jet screamed suddenly overhead, plunging like a hawk out of the gray clouds to the east. Below it a silver Fokker transport lumbered like a goose in broken flight towards the airfield. "They're buzzing the corridors," he said. The jet peeled off in a half roll and climbed into the dark skies above Pankow.

They walked in silence. She was hatless. A long tartan scarf was wound around her neck, its flared ends nearly reaching the hem of the twill coat she wore. The wind bothered her hair. He stopped again: "Are you cold?"

"No."

"We can go in if you are."

"I'm not. Do I look cold?"

"The wind's a little brisk. Airish, they say."

"Say where? 'Airish'?" She stopped too, her hand to her head, catching at the long strands of hair.

"Airish. That's rural Virginia! 'Mite airish out.' Why do you make me think of that?"

"Of what?"

"Rural Virginia. The high-shoe country."

"Like 'chink a joint,' you mean?" They walked on. "Maybe it's because you think we English invented the language," she said.

"Maybe it is. I suppose you've been pretty busy."

"A bit."

"You don't much get away from it anymore?"

"Not as much as I'd like."

"In the evenings?"

"Occasionally." They walked on along the path. As they passed the patches of ice again, he realized they'd done a full turn.

"The mission people, I suppose," Plummer said. The last time he'd seen her she'd been with a roomful of people, all of them British.

"Pardon?" She turned.

"The people from the British mission—the ones you go out with. Most of them are with the mission?"

"A few, yes."

They walked around the lake again and back through the woods to the car. They had a late lunch at a small French restaurant near the edge of the Grunewald. Families of smartly dressed Germans sat nearby. She said little during lunch. They heard a siren on the street outside. A half-dozen military vehicles flashed by, led by an olive-drab British Ferret with a red flasher on its hood and a whip aerial bending like a fly rod from its rear bumper. Some of the Germans got to their feet; a few clapped their hands approvingly; others shouted encouragement; but the demonstration died away quickly. She turned her head without rising, and Plummer saw again the silver of her eyes, the long silhouette. As she moved her head again, her eyes met his, and she looked away self-consciously. When she did, he knew that she was as aware as he of how much ground they had lost since the Dunstan party months earlier.

"Maybe we'll have an English Christmas after all," he said, looking at the dark clouds that had rolled in over the Grunewald.

"Perhaps we will." She watched the clouds for a moment. "How much longer will you be here in Berlin?" she asked.

"I don't know."

"A few months more?"

"Something like that."

"And where will you go then? Would you teach?"

"No," he said, tired of that old canard.

She didn't seem surprised: "I never really thought you were that keen on it."

A German baroque ensemble and choral group were giving a charity concert in a small church near the refugee headquarters. She had bought tickets. At four o'clock they were there, sitting on the hard wooden benches in the last row, listening to Praetorius. The church was less than half-filled; they were alone in their aisle; Plummer's mind was elsewhere. He hadn't been in a church in over twenty years.

"How nice," she said later in the frozen twilight outside. "How very nice." Plummer knew nothing had changed in the Berlin streets. He remembered coming out of theaters in Canada, England, and on ship during the war, returning to a grimmer, harsher world than he had left a few hours earlier. They drove back to her apartment. In the car she asked him if he'd been to Rostock again since they last met. She'd recently met an East German refugee at the refugee offices who'd worked on a fishing vessel out of Rostock; a factory ship, he had called it. *Factory ship* was such an ugly expression. She remembered her history classes as a child, how terribly the price of herring had dropped at Yarmouth when Tamerlane was at the gates of Vienna. It had sent shivers up her spine. At night during the war, she remembered it each time the German bombers came over. At the time she'd associated the bomber crews with the German infantry troops she'd seen in the newsreels, goosestepping through the boulevards of Warsaw and Vienna. Not at all the knees-up Molly-Brown style her brother had admired so.

"Do I make any sense to you?" she asked. They were in her apartment. There was snow on her collar, in her hair. The long, carpeted room beyond still held the spice of the small pine tree near the draped window. She turned on the Christmas tree lights and stood up in their glow, waiting for his reaction. Plummer stood looking at the tree, his damp raglan over his arm, snow on his shoes. He touched the green needles. There were Christmas cards on the silver salver, burying the table beneath it, on the mantel, on the cherry desk. She was in the kitchen, quietly rattling crockery, trays, glasses, bottles, her ice jug. Looking at the cards, his coat still over his arm, he heard the planes flying through the snow-filled darkness outside, descending towards Tegel. It wasn't until he had turned to the window that he remembered Phil Chambers, waiting for him outside the international arrivals gate at Tegel.

She turned from the kitchen table, the glasses already on the tray, ready to lift it, when she saw his face, the raglan he was pulling on.

"I have to see someone at Tegel," he said. "Just thirty minutes, that's all."

"I didn't know—" He saw the confusion in her face.

"I forgot. He's flying in from London."

"Probably we did lose track of time, didn't we?" She tried to smile. She put the tray down. "An hour you say? I'll make some sandwiches." She turned away.

"Just an hour," he said.

Plummer was late arriving at the terminal. Chambers was waiting in the falling snow outside, wearing an old Ulster. His face was stiff with the cold, his voice heavy with rheum. Plummer drove him to a small residential hotel near Dahlem, carried his bag to the small suite on the fifth floor, and tried to beg off until the following morning. Chambers swallowed a few pills, mixed a drink in the small bathroom, turned on the radio, and sank down in the armchair near the bed. He was still wearing his old Ulster. "Tomorrow won't do; it won't do at all. We've got to find out who he is."

"Christ."

"Who is he?"

"I don't know, for God's sake. I told you that before."

"I know what you told us. The fact is that you got the film in East

Berlin and the narrative detail is in German. So the logical conclusion is that he's German—posing as a German anyway."

"What are you talking about?"

"Posing—playing out a role. But they don't think he's German at all." He watched Plummer's face; it showed nothing except suspicion. "They think he's Russian."

They had drawn the conclusion on the basis of the films and the filmed typescript, the camera technique, the documents themselves, and the consistency of the lapses from German prose practice, particularly the use of the Russian adjectival form, common in translations by Russian speakers. Plummer listened, still watching Chambers suspiciously. "What do you think?" Chambers asked. "You've met him."

"I don't know."

"But you've got an impression."

"Maybe. Maybe not."

"He's never identified himself."

"I didn't say that."

"You didn't have to. It's obvious. He's never identified himself. That's interesting, isn't it? Someone who hides in the dark, who doesn't want money, avoids recognition."

"Maybe he's got a harelip."

"It's not funny. They'll kill you, goddammit!"

"What are you trying to do?" Plummer snapped. "What the hell's on your mind? Run him until he's no good anymore, bring him over, debrief him, find out whether the urge is suicidal or just manic-depressive because he hasn't been promoted in ten years? What are you going to do, wind him up, send him back in and let the crows take the rest? Like the Russians you and Roger recruited out of the displaced camps who thought you were going to back them up with an army after thirty days, the ones they cut down in the trees, still in harness? You'll kill him in your own way and you know it."

"So what? What makes him so special?"

"Nothing." Plummer mashed out his cigarette in the ashtray on the desk. He still wore his raincoat. "I just admire his instinct, that's all. He doesn't want you bastards to identify him. He knows how you work."

"He wants his own terms, is that it? You say he knows how we work. That's interesting too. So he stays in the dark. No money, no identification, nothing given up. Why?"

"I just told you—instinct."

"Instinct won't do it. This man's a professional. Why all this concealment? Not instinct at all. Habit."

"Whose habits?"

"The habits of someone who's handled agents himself. Our habits—yours and mine. His habits too."

"Who psyched that one out?"

"Think about it. You say you don't know who he is. You weren't looking for him, but he's found you. He ran you to ground because he read the signs, because somehow he knew what you were up to. He knows who you are. Who'd know that—Vienna, Prague, and the rest of it? A KGB or GRU type, that's who."

"What else does he do? You've already told me he's a weapons expert, a physicist, a student of ballistic missiles! What the hell else does he do? He knows cybernetics, microcircuitry, and organic rocket fuels. What else? Come on. Does he read Sanskrit and play the nose flute? For Christ's sake, Chambers, get your act together."

"He doesn't have to be an expert. If he'd served in the Guards or First Directorate in Moscow, he wouldn't have to know any more than the briefcases he was responsible for, the scientists they belonged to, what the code word designations were—delta, omicron, whatever they were. Only a KGB officer would have access of that kind. There were photographs of technical detail. Some showed evidence of damage—damage by fire. Anyway if we're wrong, we're talking about an operation that includes a dozen people and reaches into laboratories and testing facilities all over the Soviet Union, from the Urals eastward. We don't think that's an intelligent assumption. We think we're talking about one man who had access at the very top. But just one man."

"How many of your shoe clerks did it take to work that one out?"

"More than one. Why did he choose you?"

"Because I was available. Because I was an American. Because I had connections in London. Because I had access through the Wall. Christ—"

"But he doesn't trust you, does he?"

"Maybe he's just smarter than I am. Maybe he just wants to be left alone."

"Maybe he doesn't give a damn about you."

"Maybe he wants his privacy."

"People who want privacy want it for a reason."

"And it has to be a dirty one, is that it?"

"He's KGB!" Chambers shouted, his patience exhausted.

"So what? So he's KGB. What does that make him? Any different from me or you?"

"You're goddamned right it does!" Chambers's voice was louder still.

Plummer watched him coldly: "What's your problem? What the hell's on your mind?"

"Nothing. I'm drawing you a picture. What are you defending him for?"

"I'm not defending him. I'm giving you a few reasons for letting him do it his way, the way he knows best—out there in the dark."

"Why? Do you think he's worth saving?"

"That's not the point. That's not for me to say anyway. Anything's better than a cage in Dahlem's zoo."

"Does he matter? Is he any better than the ones we couldn't get out. In Ostrava? In Prague? In Vienna? The Soviet code clerk? The Czech that hung himself? Does he matter anymore than they did? They're dead. You remember now, don't you. Dead. And bastards like this killed them."

"That's a filthy excuse."

"It's a filthy game, isn't it?" In the dim light of the room Chambers's face was a damp, spectral smear. He struggled to control his temper; but the short, violent breaths gave up his decay; and Plummer knew how desperately sick he was. "Who set up the operational rules?" Chambers asked hotly, his composure gone. "You? Me? No. He did. Have you ever controlled him? Never. He's running you—right now. You know what he is, don't you? He's a fucking killer, that's what he is, and when you get close enough to him to find that out, he's going to kill you. He's going to blow your brains out or have it done for him, and when he does you'll be so far back in the back alleys and cesspools of that filthy world over there, no one's going to hear you go down—no one! No one's going to find a body over there: not the bones, not the teeth, not even a belt buckle! You have yourself convinced that he's some quiet little bureaucrat, don't you—some God-fearing little dissident that's going to stabilize the balance of terror and promote a *pax ballistica* so that the left-wing poets and the Western intelligentsia will be able to put flowers on his grave a hundred years from now. Well, I'm telling you that's bullshit. He's not a schoolteacher, not a scientist, not a civil servant either. He's a murderer, a KGB killer who's stalked you against the light and one day is going to put a bullet in your brain. I've seen the films. I know—it's insane, giving you the film the way he has. It's madness, and one day he's going to realize that—"

"And you're going to cut his throat, is that it? Blow him in place?"

"Why not? We've thought about it. If he won't come out, what good is he to us? Sure we've thought about it. You use everything you can, don't you? Everything. And when there's nothing left, you use that too! Desperation. Desperation is a weapon too . . . even futility. When there's nothing left, we'll use that."

"You bastards."

"Give him to us then. If you don't have the stomach for it, turn him over to us. Dahlem will handle him—you can't. Give us the drops, the timetable. He'll kill you alone. You've got to turn him over."

Plummer got to his feet and found the bottle: "You need another drink."

"We've got to bring him under control, into the light, into regular channels. You're finished, don't you know that? You were finished in Vienna. They wiped you out. We know that now."

"You don't know anything."

"We're thinking of you. All of us are."

"Go to hell. You didn't come here to save my ass, so forget it. Do you want a drink or not?"

Chambers filled his glass and collapsed back into his chair again, his breath slow in coming, his face damp and pale. They wanted an updating on Soviet activities in the Zone as soon as possible. He gave Plummer two small canisters of film. Plummer pocketed them without a word. As he was leaving, Chambers said, "When they dig up your carcass in East Berlin a hundred years from now, I'll have the satisfaction of knowing I warned you, that I told you what kind of killer you were protecting." Plummer didn't answer, listening to someone pass along the corridor outside. Chambers said, "Did you hear what I said?"

Plummer still waited, buttoning his coat, his head turned. A door slammed. The corridor was silent again. He looked back at Chambers. "Sure I heard. That's the same old bullshit too," he said. "All the dead ones were the ones you and Roger were protecting."

Elizabeth saw it in his face when he came into the foyer. "What is it?" she asked.

"Nothing. Sorry you had to wait." He tried to shrug it off but he wasn't convincing.

"It didn't go well," she guessed. "Something happened." She was still searching his face.

"A business problem. It's okay."

He knew she didn't believe him. She brought the plate of sandwiches from the kitchen and put them on the coffee table in front of the couch. Sitting there together both discovered they'd lost their appetites. Unwilling to lie to her, Plummer said nothing. Not sharing his thoughts, she was silent as well.

"I feel rather helpless," she admitted finally.

"I'm sorry." He didn't know what to say.

"Perhaps some tea would help."

Nothing's going to help, he wanted to say. "Why don't we just get the hell out of here," he said instead.

"It's been a lovely day," she said. "Let's not spoil it."

"Who's spoiling it? We could go to London. Spain for a while while I sold the house."

"For how long?"

"Long enough to forget all of this."

"The way we forgot Austria? Pullendorf?" She got to her feet and Plummer followed her into the kitchen.

"Maybe it's not my day," he said, "and if that's an excuse, okay. I'm sorry about Pullendorf. I tried to get back, but it didn't work out, so that's tough. A lot of things don't work out. Pullendorf was five years ago. A lot of things happen in five years. Some things don't change. How I feel about you hasn't changed. Sometimes I get fed up with Berlin. I got fed up tonight. But that doesn't change how I feel about you. Nothing ever will."

Her back was to him. She put waxed paper over the sandwiches and put them in the refrigerator. She took a tin from the breadbox and Plummer watched her slice a small loaf of fruitcake, then open the cupboard and take out a few plates. The steam from the enamelware kettle hung in small clouds over the stove. She burned herself on the hot metal and nearly dropped the teakettle while he stood in the door watching her keep busy, moving between the table and the sink, between the sink and the stove, the stove and the table.

"Why don't you sit down too?" he asked her as he sat at the table. She sat down finally at the place she'd set opposite him, her head turned towards the dark rectangle of window above the kitchen sink. It was still snowing out. She put a piece of fruitcake in her mouth. When she found she had difficulty chewing, she lifted the cup of tea to her lips, but it was far too hot, so she sat instead with the moist fruitcake against the roof of her mouth, her head still turned away, her light brown brows lifted slightly, as if trying to flush a cinder from her eye. But the tears crept under her lashes despite herself, and she lowered her head, eyes closed, trying to free the convulsive breath that was struggling deep in her throat. Plummer saw the tears, arose noisily, poured another cup of tea, found a tin of evaporated milk, and sat down again.

"What is it?" he asked her finally. Her eyes were still wet, still lifted towards the window. She shook her head without looking at him. He waited for her to say something, but she didn't speak. When he couldn't sit there any longer, he stubbed his cigarette out in his saucer, put his cup in the sink, and went into the front hall and got his raglan. He stood in the foyer for a long time. He went back into the kitchen. She was standing at the sink. "Are you all right?" he said. She didn't turn.

"It's nothing," she said.

"It's something. I know it is."

"I'm tired. It's been a long day." She still hadn't turned. He took her shoulders and turned her towards him. He kissed her on the forehead, on the cheeks, and brought her head up. Her mouth was cold at first, as stubborn as her will. He spoke her name, spoke it again, and she responded at last.

"It's madness," she whispered. "It is. Why. Why?"

"Don't think about it."

The wind moved in the streets far below; tires whispered by; her telephone had rung too, but from someplace far away; and they hadn't stirred to answer. It was as far away as the distant planes droning towards Tegel, burrowing into silence as the wind sheered, settling them again in the darkness and the smell of cedar and the chest from which she'd brought an extra blanket.

A chilly wind blew up the Ramblas from the harbor in Barcelona, the December light fading after an afternoon of rain. The two men sat together in the twilight that gathered as thick as a Thames fog among the worn green benches below the Canaletas fountain. Black clouds obscured the Montjuich peak and lidded the oyster eye of the horizon. The milky sea bobbed like ditch water under the rain, its tongue thick with resins and bilge tar, with rafts of dead squid, wine corks, and yellow foam. Its salty breath lifted beyond the sea wall and breathed up the narrow streets and passageways, up the Ramblas itself and towards its Jurassic progeny beyond, the vault-ribbed basilicas, chapels, and crypts; the towering spires where squadrons of gargoyles crawled like pterodactyls over battlements black with rain.

The Englishman wore a dark raincoat and a gray hat, dripping rain. His thin, colorless hair crept like dry moss from beneath the hatbrim. The face was elusive—now narrow and angular, with a wedge of jaw like gray pumice; now thicker and undulate, like that of a robust Yorkshireman. The eyes behind the thick glasses were curious, glistening like garden slugs through apertures of skin that were dark at their edges, as if colored with burnt cork. Solo wore a moustache as well. His voice had a false, metallic ring—neurotic, Strekov thought—and he seemed unable to control his facial muscles. For the first few minutes Strekov thought that Solo had had a terrible accident recently and that the face had been reconstructed in some grotesque parody of its former self. The light was dim. Strekov looked away, down the Ramblas, as Solo stuttered in his indignation, trying to describe his contempt for the *apparat* in Moscow that would have recruited George Bryce. "A man of no conceivable skill, of no imaginable enterprise; a man with nothing to offer, without a fiber of decency in his body, an obscene little maggot—" The voice seemed to lose its resonance, to flutter and cycle away with an odd susurration, like a radio with a ruptured speaker. Strekov turned. He caught the movement of the hand away from the dead patches of skin on the face, as if the fingers had moved to ease the pain in the cruelly scarred, reptilian jaw. It was only a moment; the gesture was slight. But the hanging skin moved more naturally again; the ugly, metallic rasp of the voice returned. Strekov continued to study him. He wore a beige scarf high on his throat which covered the lower reach of the chin; the drooping rain hat was pulled low over the eyes. The lifeless hair clung in curious clumps to the waxen skull, like lichen on a dead tree. Only at that moment did it occur to him what he was seeing; and he was astonished, not at his own dullness in recognizing it, but at the evil audacity of this man sitting next to him for whom nothing seemed beyond his capability. Solo must have sensed Strekov's discovery. He turned, the wet eyes fixed in his direction, staring at him unnaturally through their burntcork holes, and when they did Strekov knew he was right. This wasn't Solo's face at all. He was wearing a sheer rubber mask, the shining eyes darting like newts in the darkness beneath.

"He would belly down to any hearthside that promised him warmth," Solo said, the eyes even more predatory under the hatbrim. Strekov only nodded, convinced that there was nothing he would learn from their conversation more important than this. "They know every movement he made from the time he first took to his heels. They found the radio, the keying device. They found the crystal. They knew he was terrified when he left London—"

Strekov listened in silence, his head turned away. The lights along the Ramblas bloomed through the dusk. The fog blew thicker from the narrow side streets and drifted up from the Paseo de Colón, licked into crypts and passageways, and beaded the trunks of the plane trees nearby, chilled by its passage over stones colder than the Armada, as old as Christendom itself. Office workers moved by, carrying newspapers, flowers under wet tissue. There were raven-haired Spanish shopgirls, old men and old women under spiked umbrellas.

"We've been honest with you," Strekov explained at last, wearied by Solo's querulous voice. At that moment there was nothing more he wanted to know. "We've told you what happened."

"Admission of error never creates confidence."

"Then we must rebuild confidence. How do we begin?"

"It is difficult to rebuild a faith once it has been destroyed," Solo said. Strekov turned to look at him. A few small volumes in octavo lay in a plastic wrapper under his gloved hand, fetched from a series of antiquarian book arcades near the Plaza del Rey. Nearby a florist was closing down his stand. A slurry of water mixed with flower petals trickled past Strekov's shoes.

"What do you propose?"

Solo had refused further contact with the illegal *rezidentura* in London. He had always disdained the use of a cutout or a *dybok*, a deaddrop where documents or film could be concealed until picked up by his handler—an idiosyncrasy dating from his prewar days in Berlin and Paris where his NKVD handlers had maintained personal contact. He still insisted on maintaining the anachronism in violation of one of the basic precepts of Soviet espionage, demanding that whatever documents or films he had obtained he be allowed to pass directly to his Soviet contact. It was one of the privileges of his class, rooted in a disdain for modern conveniences or the vulgarity they bred. He had neither a telephone nor a radio in his old Elizabethan cottage in Northumberland; his suits, like his shoes, were made by hand in Old Burlington Street in London. Strekov listened to Solo's demands. He insisted that Moscow continue as they had begun that night—to send a senior Soviet intelligence official from Dzerzhinskay Street headquarters to meet with him periodically in London or on the continent. Only in that way could Moscow demonstrate to him that its trust was equal to his own. He had taken great risks, extraordinary risks, and Moscow had treated him shabbily. Dzerzhinskay Street must now assume a risk of its own. Men like Boris were expendable, as Bryce had been expendable. But if Moscow expected him to resume the old relationship, some demonstration of equal faith on its part was essential.

Strekov argued with him. He knew it was impossible. He knew that Orlov would never agree to such an arrangement and he pitied Solo for thinking it possible. Solo was unremitting. In the end Strekov agreed to pass his request to Moscow. Solo said he was satisfied with that, he hadn't expected more. They moved away from the Ramblas through the blowing fog. The mist smoked up from the drains; taxis slashed down the driving lane along the broad promenade. "London would be more convenient for me during the next several months," Solo said. Strekov didn't reply. They walked together down the narrow passageway. Solo told him that he would meet his wife at the great doors of the Basilica de Santa María del Mar where she would light a commemorative candle in one of the crypts in memory of her dead brother, lost at sea off the Spanish coast during the war. Some of his shipmates had come ashore on a nearby beach in 1941 after the destroyer had been sunk by German U-boats. His body had never been recovered. She was Catholic, Solo said, descended from that recusant Popish gentry of East Anglia. She came every year for the ceremony. Solo laughed. An odd family, he continued. Brother a priest; uncle, a bishop. Curious connections with fascist Spain. The family library in East Anglia remembered them—that recusant Popish gentry who aided Jesuits to priestholes, lit their escape from Elizabethan martyrdom with candles, tallow-soaked rags, bonfires on the meadows beneath parapet and loophole, guided them to the beaches of the Norfolk coast from which they'd come. Wasn't there a parallel after Burgess and McLean had fled? Someone had pointed it out to him over port and cigars in the common room at Balliol one night. His wife knew the history. English priests had found exile here, on the same Iberian peninsula, where, at the court of Philip of Spain, they wrote their heartbroken histories, declaring their innocence in ecclesiastical Latin, swore their loyalty to a Catholic Philip who was also Philip of England. Would the history of his time remember his name so well as those of his wife's bishops, recorded in the family annals in East Anglia; remember his own terrible submission to a Holy See farther from Rome than London? Surrender now

. . . surrender . . . before the pitiless winter night of All Souls takes you, nights as damp as this, soot spilling from damp fires and grates, breathing across the misty windows and through the fog whispering in the alleyways, milk-and-water smiles lifting from their breviaries in East Anglia: *Who were you, Solo? What was your name?*

Solo laughed again. He'd never joined the Church, he said. Could never stomach it. The voice had changed—resonance, pitch, timbre. Even his step had changed. "Belief, that's what it comes down to, doesn't it? A matter of belief? Those who have it. Those who don't. Those who steal it from you, lock it away in their own parched souls."

The burnt-cork eyes turned towards Strekov. It was the same face. But for a moment Strekov had heard another voice, more distant than the few meters which separated them, the puzzled voice of a young English boy sent back from the Sudan each summer at the end of the holidays, the African dust scrubbed away, another face greeting him in the mirror as he stepped from the old iron tub in the rooms at the Semiramis at Cairo after the long, lonely journey up the Nile by steamer. Not his face at all.

They parted in the fog. Strekov turned in the other direction, the voice still ringing in his ears. He wasn't at all sure what Solo's words had meant. He had his own impressions to contend with now, and Menzhinsky's report seemed to him less important, a relic of the past. He didn't remember reading that Solo's wife was a Catholic. If this fact had been mentioned in the dossiers assembled in the committee room on Dzerzhinskay Street, he had forgotten. Even so, what difference would it make? That her faith was genuine, ancient, and durable—a survivor of the martyrdom of the past—while his was not? Solo a schoolboy again, returned from Africa to England, punished for crimes of which he had no recollection?

Twenty minutes later Strekov found the Basilica de Santa Maria del Mar, where Solo had said he was to meet his wife. He moved into the recesses of the great church. It stank of mold. He stood uncertainly in the cold interior. Shopkeepers, fishermen's wives, and old widows in black veils were lighting candles in the crypts, kneeling on the same stones where Catalan sailors had received absolution before the tides carried them out across Barcelona's fourteenth-century maritime empire, where the wives, mothers, and children waited for the first news when the great storms battered the coast, crusted the old walls with its salts, and blackened its copper. The air was dark, thick with wax, old tallow, incense, the dust of old bones. A choir was chanting somewhere in the loft. He searched among the altars and crypts for almost an hour. Solo and his wife were not there.

He flew from Barcelona the same night. The flight was crowded. The plane ascended through fog, turning towards the French coast far at sea. Strekov drank a whiskey and looked out at the star-filled sky. The cabin lights had been turned down. When they landed at Cannes it was raining and a blond American woman took the seat next to Strekov. She took him for British. In her purse she was carrying a tiny gray poodle with a rhinestone collar. The takeoff was delayed and Strekov watched the anxiety in her face as the plane waited at the end of the runway. Their eyes met and Strekov told her that they were waiting for a plane that was making its approach. She seemed relieved and followed his turning head towards the descending plane. When its landing lights came on, she told him above the roar of the engines that she was afraid of flying, and sitting alone only increased her fears. She lit a cigarette after the plane was aloft. She preferred to have someone to talk to, she said. She wasn't accustomed to traveling alone. As the plane flew north, she talked about her house in the south of France.

Strekov listened and thought about his own dacha on the Dneipr. He had left his fishing rods in the larch cabinet and wondered if they were still there. He thought about the strawberry beds, the way the west wall sloped, how the snow lay against the crooked stone chimney on winter mornings, the spirals of smoke that curled up from the chimney, like pine curls from a knife blade. There was a shadow of moss on the stone foundation on the north side of the dacha. What about his saw rack? Had he left it there? It was in the small cabinet to the left of the door, together with the seine, the mattock, and the kerosene lamp.

Then he wasn't at the dacha at all, but standing alone outside the basilica of an old city. Was it Kiev, Tallinn, or Barcelona? Fog moved through the streets; the cobblestones were wet. The basilica loomed ahead over him; a faint curtain of candlelight crept forward from the interior. Strekov was standing next to a bench where an old man was sitting, head down, his hands in his lap, as if ashamed of his unspeakable condition. His clothes were loose and damp; they smelled of mold. Clay clung to his fingers.

"Why did you bring me here?" Strekov asked him. "Why have you tricked me and brought me here? Moscow is waiting!"

"Listen," the old man pleaded, his face bent forward, still hidden from Strekov. They waited. Then Strekov heard the voices coming from deep within the basilica. The curtain of light grew stronger, spilling forward into the dark street. The anthem increased in volume as the choir moved forward. Strekov stood motionless as the choir came towards him, faces and figures hidden by the radiance of candlelight. He heard the magnificence of the music and knew then that it would be all right, that he had nothing to fear. He was transfixed by the music. He could distinguish individual tapers, the small flames balanced atop each candle. Then he heard the words of the anthem and he stood alone again, rooted to his own terror:

> Here in this darkness, soft with rain,
> We breathe our natures, cannot name
> The smoke, the tallow, or the flame—

They were his words, his refrain, written years earlier, and hidden among the end pages of his books at the dacha. There was nothing there in the street, in the basilica. The voices would come no closer; already the candlelight was dispersing, as gray as fog. "You've tricked me," he cried, turning to the small figure seated on the bench. "You've tricked me!"

The old man had lifted his face toward Strekov. It seemed to swim in the murky light, oddly fluid, as loose as old rags, or wrinkles of loose skin, flapping in the dim light, hair leaking down like dry moss—a rubber mask of the sheerest skin, eyes staring up at Strekov through the burnt-cork eyeholes, as lewd as death itself.

"Who are you? Don't pretend! Menzhinsky? Is it you?" Strekov seized the hat and attempted to pull the rubber mask from the vulgar, lifted face.

"No," the voice warned, "no, no"—deeper than Menzhinsky's voice, the mouth beginning to dissolve through the rubber lips, the wet eyes shrinking away from the small apertures, glistening for a moment as they contracted in the darkness, like a slug's body burrowing deeper into the decay where it feeds. "No. No." The voice came again, beginning to disintegrate and crumble into no voice at all as the rubber mask seethed and contracted: no voice, no shape, nothing within at all—a bladder full of corruption, like a dog's corpse found in the winter woods, part of the earth now. Whatever was there fled under Strekov's hands. The mask seethed, eyes gone; the smell spilled out; the blackness came, driving Strekov back.

Sleep failed him and he awoke violently, straining in his seat, his hands tearing at the armrests. In the next seat the American woman was cradling her poodle, watching anxiously. She continued to watch as he sat back and shut his eyes again. She leaned forward finally and poured some whiskey from her miniature bottle into a plastic glass. "I never fly unless my astrologer tells me it's all right," she told him, holding out the glass. "Drink this. It will be good for you." She watched him drink from the glass. "You see, it's all right," she smiled. "I told you."

TEN

Plummer was summoned to the East German Planning Commission but neither the vice-minister nor Kohler would see him. He met briefly with a protocol officer who gave him an official envelope, asked him to sign for it, and told him the lubricant agreement had been terminated. The announcement would be made at noon the following day. Plummer had twenty-four hours to close down the warehouse at Treptow and get out of East Berlin. On his way to the warehouse he was stopped three times by East German security patrols. At Treptow an East German customs official was waiting for him. By the time he had sorted through the files and identified the documents he wanted returned to London, it was mid-afternoon. The customs official sealed the boxes, put them in a van, and drove away. The warehouse was empty; the warehousemen had been informed the previous day. Plummer locked the door for the last time, and left his car in the alley behind the warehouse. He walked east, towards the tramline four blocks away. At an old hotel near Dimitroffstrasse he made a telephone call and waited for an hour in an old smoking room off the lobby, reading the East German papers. It was an old hotel, dimly lighted, but the snow which glazed the streets outside gave a glacial coldness to the high-ceilinged room. There were Persian carpets on the floor, their medallions trampled into dust; and an arboretum of tropical plants in the far corner. At the writing desks nearby, two young Russian officers were writing letters. Dusk was beginning to fall when he left the hotel by a side door. He walked for forty minutes and entered a small tavern whose windows were hung with moisture. He drank a lager at a table in the rear, looking towards the mirror above the bar which reflected the gray, discordant shapes of the room. The talk was of Russian and East

German troop movements. He left the tavern and passed within two blocks of Soviet military headquarters. The streets had been cordoned off; only official vehicles were permitted to enter. Fifteen minutes later he entered an open square and crossed the cobblestones past an ancient gothic church and a large auditorium where a crowd of workmen were leaving an early-evening meeting. They moved stiffly, legs cramped by the cold of the old guildhall. Across the snowy square, in the shop windows, the lights were stronger; the evening crowds had begun to move along the square. Plummer was crossing the far side of the square when a motorized Soviet rifle battalion rumbled into view. He stood at the curb watching the Russian soldiers as they passed. Strekov stood on the opposite corner, also watching the troop carriers.

"For show," Strekov told him, "nothing more." They sat among the rear tables of an old-fashioned restaurant across the square from the church and guildhall. A few meters away was a bus station serving the provinces; next door were a cinema and a state department-store. At the wooden tables groups of Germans sat in overcoats drinking coffee, tea, or lager, watching the streets through the steaming windows, waiting for trams and buses, waiting for friends or relatives, for the next film to begin. The floor was wet, the door seldom closed. Vendors with baskets of nuts, knitted gloves and scarves from the provinces, herbs and roots from the countryside, and plastic combs and toys passed among the tables. The table where Strekov and Plummer sat was in the shadows; those nearby, occupied by the sedentary trade—old men and women who spent their summer days in the parks and their winters in chilly, one-room flats, waiting for the cold to leave the streets. A few generations earlier the restaurant had included a dance floor and bandstand at the rear where middle-class Germans once passed their Sunday afternoons, dancing and listening to the music, watching the chestnut trees through the wide window as they ate their sherbets. Now a thin matchwood partition closed off the rear. In front of the partition a few old men sat, playing chess.

"What happens out there isn't too important," Strekov continued, looking at the windows. "Tanks or troops moving in public never are. You wake from a bad dream willing to accept what you were before sleep—the *status quo ante*. That's what this crisis is all about. Khruschev is only walking his leashed dog along the NATO frontier, that's all."

Plummer, saying nothing, watched two East German policemen enter. They moved through the tables to the serving counter. The GDR evening newscast was playing from the radio behind the counter. "They want to talk to you," he said finally. "They're insisting. They don't care much where it is. They just want to talk."

"What did you tell them?"

"What I told them before. That it wasn't in the cards."

"So why did you come?"

"To ask one last time. They don't think I've handled it very well. They think someone else might be better." He picked up his coffee cup. The coffee was cold and he put the cup down.

Strekov said, "Do you agree with them?"

"Not much." He looked towards the two policemen again.

Strekov laughed. "The same neutrality, the same indifference—at whatever cost. Doesn't it get tiresome?"

"You asked me that before. I'm tired of this goddamned place."

"Where you came to sell oil and nothing else." Plummer didn't answer. An old man stood in front of them, selling newspapers. His eyes shone with water; his face was red with the cold. Strekov bought a paper and put it on the table without looking at it. "I thought you were lying."

"That's your problem."

"It didn't occur to me that it might be true. Your contempt seemed to make it true. You didn't care whether I believed you or not."

"It's true," Plummer said. "I came here to sell oil, nothing else."

"What about Prague?"

"Prague was different."

"Then I picked the wrong man. Is that what you're saying?"

"I told you that from the first."

"But it doesn't matter, does it? What you're doing now is what you did in Prague all those months. Keeping yourself intact, not falling to one side or the other, continuing to do what you know."

Plummer said, "Look. Let's get it straight once and for all. What I did or didn't do in Prague doesn't matter anymore. If you want to get out, I can help you. If you don't, that's your business."

"I appreciate your lack of sympathy. It's complete and total. No misunderstanding. What about the others you've helped. Where are they now?"

"I don't know."

"You don't see them after they're out? It's just a business, like everything else."

"It's their life. Some make out all right. Others don't."

"But it doesn't concern you—"

"It's up to you. If you want your privacy, you can manage it. If you're an agitator, an activist, they'll use you—get you a hearing on Capitol Hill before a few congressional committees, screw a microphone in your wooden head, then get you a consultant's job someplace—a windbag or a horn-tooter for some captive nations league, some ethnic society lobbying for a bigger share of the immigration quota. It's a zoo," he said. "It always has been." He picked up the cold coffee cup, remembered its metallic taste, and put it down again. Strekov sat watching him.

"Why do you do it, then?" he asked suddenly, sitting forward. "Why do you do it? What is it? Perhaps you know enough of the dogma to despise it; not because you understand it, but because of what it does to people. An excuse for tyranny. Is that it?"

Plummer said, "What dogma?"

"Marxism-Leninism."

"I don't know much about that," Plummer muttered.

"Why do you do it then?"

"It's finished—I told you. I came here to sell lubricants to the East Germans."

"You mean politics doesn't interest you anymore?"

"It never did," Plummer said.

"Because abstractions don't interest you? What about ideas?"

"What ideas?"

"Nothing seems to interest you," Strekov said, "but you're always busy. Never bored." He sat back, still watching Plummer's face. "Except now, perhaps, because words interest you least of all. Isn't that true?"

"Probably." He didn't know what Strekov was driving at.

"Words and ideas, then," Strekov said. "Work interests you more, doesn't it? Keeping busy. Selling drill presses or lathes in Prague; selling oil to the East Germans. That's tangible—concrete." Plummer thought he was wool-gathering. "But that's an advantage, isn't it? The greatest advantage. To be able to keep busy," Strekov continued. "To master the technology and then let it demand of you all that it will; performance, not words. To know in that way what few men in public life know, what politicians and bureaucrats don't know at all—that men who live so exclusively among words can't help telling lies?"

Plummer didn't understand what Strekov was talking about. "What are you saying?" he asked.

"It's the illness of our generation, isn't it—of our century?" Strekov asked without answering the question. "Why is it you believe you can escape from it?"

"I haven't escaped from anything."

"But you say you were finished, that you left. Now what? Are you leaving Berlin?"

"That's something else."

"It's personal, is it?"

"Something like that," Plummer said.

"So it makes no sense to you, either," Strekov smiled, seeing the stubbornness in Plummer's face. "That's the price you pay for isolation, isn't it? For being cut off from everything else—family, friends, even your own country. The moral price. Knowing that your lies are treasonable, whatever they are. You've been cut off, too, haven't you— like those years in Prague? We all learn to live alone in our own way— with words, with ideas, with cowardice. Or with activity. But the test is whether you can continue to live alone and survive. Not physical survival; moral survival too. To know at the end that what you felt was real. That's the test."

Plummer said, "They'll hang you. You know that."

"There are worse penalties."

"Like what?"

"Corruption. Moral extinction. Madness, insanity. Far worse. There's no reprieve."

"What do you want me to tell them?" Plummer said. "Make it simple."

Strekov didn't answer for a moment, staring across the room, still thinking of what he had said. At last he shook his head. "It's finished," he said. "It's over. There's nothing more to do."

"You won't talk to them."

"No," Strekov said. "It's over."

Plummer nodded. He wasn't surprised. "What about the Berlin crisis? Is that over, too?"

"For the time being. But there will be other crises. That's hard for Americans to accept, isn't it? The lack of final solutions. It's an advantage the Europeans have over you. They understand. So do we. An older Bolshevik once told me that when the war was over, there would be other wars, the wars of national liberation, and that when those wars were over and socialism finally triumphant, the final war would begin. War, he said, would then acquire its ultimate character. That was in nineteen forty-five. I was young at the time. The man who said it was an old Chekist, assigned to our corps. I didn't know what he meant. I thought it was treasonable and that he was testing me. Marxism makes such wars unthinkable; yet he was a Marxist. At the time he said it, a Mongolian mess orderly was outside the tent, rummaging in the commissary stores. I didn't know what he was talking about for a long time. Years later I finally understood. Race against race; man against man. When political and social distinctions disappear, the racial ones will be all that's left. So that night I was thinking about the end of the Great Fatherland War and there he was, down at the bottom of things, telling me there would be no end to it. He's still there," Strekov continued "—down at the bottom of things, an obscene old relativist willing to kill others in the name of an absolute, a man who knows that even when the socialist victory is complete, wars will continue as long as men die. It's not our blindness or stupidity that makes war necessary, but our mortality. Wars will last as long as men continue to die. Does the Party teach that? No."

Plummer said, "If you get there before I do, send me a postcard." He picked up his gloves from the table. Strekov laughed. "You're leaving Berlin?" Plummer asked.

Strekov nodded. Two Russian soldiers sat down at a nearby table with two young German girls. One of the girls carried a transistor radio tuned to Radio Volga in Potsdam, broadcasting in Russian for the Soviet forces in Germany. "Where are you going when you leave?" Strekov said. He picked up his scarf and the newspaper.

"Away from here. Away from Europe. The US. My time is up." He got to his feet. "I'm overdue."

"That's typically American, isn't it," Strekov replied, still slumped in his chair. "Always someplace else to go. If not this world, then the next. If not this age, then another. Maybe the moon. Where else does that kind of freedom exist—physical freedom, physical space. Or is it freedom? Or is it restlessness instead." He frowned, studying the door.

"What about you?" Plummer said. "Why'd you begin all this? Why'd you do it?"

Strekov shrugged and sat up with a smile. "I don't know," he muttered. "To show that it could be done. To ask the question. To force others to ask the question. *Why*. When all answers are known, it's the unanswered question that forces us to begin all over again. I don't know. Will the others?" He got up. "They'll pretend to. But they won't."

They parted in the darkness outside. "Good-bye," Strekov said calmly. "I know it's been tiresome, but no matter. Don't miss your planes, your schedules, your debriefings. Don't get overdrawn. Don't get lost."

"Good-bye," Plummer said.

The streets near the warehouse at Treptow were cold and empty. A few lights burned in the windows of the second- and third-floor flats. Snow lay frozen on the sidewalks; ice sheeted the alley behind the warehouse. He stood in the darkness by the door of his car, key in hand, looking towards the rear door of the old warehouse. The light was out. He was still standing there when he heard the sound of tires crunching over old snow. Turning his head, he saw a car roll forward from the shadows at the end of the alley and stop under the streetlamp. The engine was off; the cold headlights gleamed through the shadows like the eyes of a nightmoth. He heard the creak of a door opening and saw a man's silhouette standing behind the door. The dry snow crunched under his feet. In the light of the alley the face was incomplete, like the face a child might make on the nub of a clothespin.

"Herr Plummer," his voice called. "Herr Plummer." Plummer moved away from the car towards the center of the alley, studying the figure. His right foot ground fragments of glass under his sole. He remembered the light over the door of the warehouse, knew that it had been broken from outside, and turned, but it was too late. A foot scraped the darkness behind him and he spun, arm raised, but the lead sap stunned the bone of his skull below the ear, and dug like a hammer into the muscles of his neck and shoulder. He fell forward. The car's headlights glowed on in the distance, like freezing fog. Far away an ignition clicked, a cold engine turned over. Plummer was lifted by his shoulders and dragged away from the center of the alley. He lay inert on his face, still stunned; but when his right knee dropped into a tire rut in the roadbed, he dug his leg forward and drove blindly upwards, like a tackle at a blocking sled, smothering the smaller figure back across the alley and into the warehouse wall. Plummer slammed his forearm across the man's neck, smashed him against the wall a second time, saw the hand holding the revolver, and ripped him across the jaw with his left hand. He heard the sob from the strangled face, and smashed the head back against the wall a final time. The revolver fell to the snow. Plummer snapped the collapsing body upright, holding it upright as, shoulders braced against the wall, he shielded himself from the brightening beams of the moving car. As the headlights flooded the snow and ice at his feet, he heaved the figure into the roadbed and dropped sideways along the wall, searching the darkness for the revolver. The figure collapsed forward, head and shoulders impaled by the headlights, but then his head and shoulders jerked sideways convulsively as the moving car struck him. Prone in the alley behind the car, Plummer heard the fender grind along the opposite side of the alley, dragging sparks from the old brickwork. He found the cold revolver with his frozen fingers, snapped the butt upright against the snow, and fired twice from the darkness. The first bullet shattered the doorpost behind the driver; the second exploded the rear window.

The car spun wildly, slipped sideways out of control, and smashed into the iron corner-shield of the old building down the alley.

The driver staggered from the door, face bleeding, glasses splintered from the impact. Plummer didn't know him. He hauled him up, bounced him back against the door, and hit him twice. He found a wallet in his coat pocket, lifted him a final time, and threw him into the back seat. He heard the static from the radio in the front seat and listened for a moment. A voice was calling from radio control someplace to the east. Down the alley Plummer's assailant lay twisted in a small broken mound, eyes half open, almost yellow in the dim lamplight, full of pain and fear, like the eyes of a poisoned cat. He didn't recognize the face. In his pockets he found the lead sap, a small notebook, and a leather wallet. Plummer opened the hood of the Opel and retrieved a set of papers and an accommodation passport from the magnetic canister. The distributor had been ripped out and lay in broken wires and severed leads over the block. He couldn't repair it. He left the alley on foot.

Templeman arrived in London the second week in January on leave from Berlin. He wanted to take a few weeks to sort out his problems and to talk to Phil Chambers. Things were going badly for him in Berlin and he thought Chambers might be able to help—perhaps recommend his transfer to London.

He stayed at a small hotel in Mayfair where he usually stayed and the second night had dinner with Chambers at Wiltons in Chelsea. Over oysters and grouse Templeman talked about his problems in Berlin. Most of the groups he'd been responsible for during his initial assignment to Berlin a decade earlier had been penetrated, discredited, or had simply passed out of existence. He wasn't on very good terms with the station chief, who was German born, and everyone knew what that meant. The reports officer was a younger man who was inclined to ruthlessly edit his drafts, and Templeman thought this kind of fastidiousness more symptomatic of the general climate of uncertainty at the station than of the character of his reporting. His second wife was ill in Washington and hadn't been able to accompany him. In addition he'd replaced a CIA man who'd retired and, with a terminal assignment, had let his strings go slack. His assets weren't very good, some he couldn't find, and two he doubted had ever existed. It was all rather untidy.

So Templeman had cast a fly over Chambers, but he hadn't seen him rise, and he watched uncomfortably while Chambers fiddled with his coffee cup, smoked another cigarette, and finally accepted a small brandy, his porcine face steadfastly refusing to offer Templeman any hope. He remained silent. It was Templeman who finally proposed a few alternatives—perhaps Paris, maybe Brussels or Rome. Templeman studied Chambers and waited, hot and guilty in his embarrassment, perspiration on his brow and upper lip. He tried to remember whether his wife's alcoholism was a clinical fact when they had served together in Paris, or just in-house gossip. Chambers was silent, mouth pursed, the heavy jowls sucked in, as if he were having difficulty getting his breath. "Do you think you might do something, Phil?" Templeman asked him finally, abandoning pretense and pride, his whole career naked on the platter in front of them, as pitiful as the grouse carcasses had seemed to him a few minutes earlier. Chambers had nodded noncommittally, his eyes aimlessly searching the room. It was only then that Templeman noticed how ghastly his face looked, as if he'd just come from his deathbed. In the car he promised to look into it and to give Templeman a call at the hotel the following week.

In the days that followed, Templeman moped about London disconsolately and finally went to his tailor on Old Burlington Street to cheer himself up. He had lunch with a crusty old British diplomat at his club, but the old man was fifteen years retired, forgotten by the FO, by everyone else it seemed—except Templeman. The first hour he spent identifying those in the dark paneled room with whom he'd once served—at Riga, in Cairo, in Berlin before the war. None of them gave more than a contemptuous glance towards the corner where they sat. By the end of the week Templeman's engagement book had run out of entries, and Phil Chambers still hadn't called. He drank alone those nights. Sitting alone in the Savoy Bar one evening, fortified by a few whiskeys, he contemplated his face in the dusky mirror behind the bar, hidden behind the pyramids of crystal. His career was disintegrating before his very eyes, and he was losing the will to resurrect it. In the weak light his hair seemed thinner than usual. He had found balls of blond hair in his brush that morning. Now he was losing his hair as well. He climbed off the stool unsteadily, and went out to the lobby, where he put a call through to Chambers's house in Kensington. No one answered. He went back to the bar and picked up his coat and the few newspapers and magazines he had bought that afternoon, emptied his glass, and left the bar, determined to find a woman in the streets nearby—an older woman. Fifty or fifty-five would do famously; she'd have extravagant pretenses of gentility, would wear sheer purple undergarments, but once in bed would be as ruttish as an old sow.

On the steps outside, Templeman heard a booming voice: *"By God—Temp! Temp, you old soak! You've come back!"* Compton-Bofers stood next to his gray Jaguar, arguing with the doorman about parking; someone else was leaving the car too to join the argument, both of them just returning from an official reception at Lancaster House, and both three sheets to the wind, like Templeman himself. The chap with Compton-Bofers was a middle-aged diplomat from the FO.

They ended up the evening at a small flat near the University of London where the diplomat's young secretary lived; sharing plates of spaghetti and tumblers of red wine with her two roommates. They paired off—Templeman with a short, raven-haired girl from Scotland with plump legs, plump arms, and milk-white skin. He wondered if her breasts were as white. Her thighs were. They were struggling together in the corner of the couch, her skirt slipped back over her thighs, her hand in Templeman's pants, his hand between her legs, his fingers slipping within the labia minora, when more visitors arrived. The evening had come to nought, and nothing was exchanged between them afterwards except Templeman's desperate looks, quiet talk, music, a few ill-conceived attempts at dancing in the tiny sitting room, more wine, and too many cigarettes. When finally they staggered down the stairs, it was three o'clock in the morning. Templeman had asked the raven-haired girl if he might take her to lunch the following day and she'd given him her phone number. He awoke the following morning with a godawful hangover and a painful hard-on. Sitting on the chair next to the phone, he couldn't remember her name. Mary or Martha;

Alice or Felicia? No, Felicia was the secretary's name. Or was it? He sat in his shorts, his head spinning. Why lunch? That had been the ghastliest of his errors. It was two o'clock in the afternoon. Compton-Bofers couldn't remember her name either when he saw him the same night. His friend from the FO had gone to Sussex. They spent the evening at Compton's club, drinking and playing billiards, then off to a late dinner somewhere in Soho where they were joined by Beresford Perse, who'd come straight from the Foreign Office. By the end of the week Templeman's hangovers had multiplied; he was rarely out of bed before two in the afternoon; but each night, as he dragged himself between the sheets, his thoughts still returned to the young Scottish girl.

He confronted her late Friday evening on the steps of her flat, where he had been sitting for an hour, half drunk, watching the rain sweep through the streets beyond. He stood up when she entered, moving aside on the carpeted stairs to let her pass. A young man was with her. "It's me," he said fondly. "Remember?"

"No," she said as she went by him. "Who are you?" She didn't turn. Her young man followed her up the steps. Templeman watched her go, picked up his crushed Irish hat, and stumbled down the stairs. Standing in the street outside, he found he could no longer remember the name of his hotel. He walked through the rainy streets until he could remember the name of the hotel. When he did, he stopped on a street corner and waited for a taxi. The driver left him at Piccadilly and he picked up a woman outside a penny arcade. "Had a bit too much, have you, luv?" she whispered as she lay against him in the backseat of the taxi. She lived in Paddington in a fifth-floor flat under the eaves.

On the following Sunday, Templeman rented a car and drove to Cornwall. He spent four days at a remote inn to dry himself out, walking along the gray shingle by day, sitting alone with a cup of tea or cocoa in front of his coal fire by night. He took a few books with him but he didn't read them. He listened to the BBC on the radio. When he returned to London he hadn't had a drink in five days. He was mentally and physically prepared for the talk Chambers had promised him that night in the car leaving Wiltons. He called Chambers the night he returned. There was no answer. He called three times that night and listened to the phone ringing through the darkened house in Kensington. Chambers wasn't there. The following night he called again. There was no answer. He opened the bottle of whiskey and had his first drink in seven days. He had dinner at a solitary restaurant on Lower Regent Street, thinking about his return to Berlin and what he might do. He had no answers. He drank a bottle of wine. It was almost nine o'clock and he was alone again in his Mayfair hotel room, pouring his second whiskey, when the telephone rang. Although he hoped it might be Phil Chambers, it wasn't. The caller made a brief attempt to disguise his voice, but Templeman recognized it. It was Compton-Bofers. He was calling from a residential hotel in Bayswater. He was in room 403 and someone had stolen his pants. A frightful mess, and where could one find a pair of trousers this late in the evening if not from one's friends? Did he think he might sneak down a pair of extra trousers, never mind the fit; maybe a belt too, a set of braces?

It was a grim, leprous residential hotel of smoky brownstone, derelict in the shadows between a spaghetti parlor and a West Indian dry cleaning shop. A creaky lift carried Templeman and an odd pair of flannel trousers to the fourth floor; his own uncertain footsteps moved him down the faded runner to 403 where Compton-Bofers was waiting, standing behind the door which was slightly ajar, his eye glued to the crack. He was wearing a striped blue shirt, tie, dark-blue socks to his knees, polished black oxfords, white undershorts, but no pants.

"Temp, you're absolutely splendid—absolutely miraculous. Just splendid. What else can I say?" Standing in the middle of the room, Compton-Bofers pulled on the trousers. "A bit snug in the middle, but first rate. By the way, who is your tailor these days?"

A bottle of whiskey stood on the table; a glass nearby. The bottle was almost empty. Templeman thought Compton-Bofers had been drinking alone for most of the afternoon, and had taken a shower to sober himself up. His boyish face was pink; his dark hair still damp; his eyes were rimmed with red. It was a plain vulgar room with flock wallpaper, dark furniture, a broken grate in the fireplace, a few glass vases holding plastic flowers on the mantel. Templeman had no idea whom the room belonged to. To the left of the front window a bedroom door was drawn closed. A thin crack of light showed beneath the door. A woman's coat was thrown over a chair—an expensive coat with a mink collar, Templeman noticed—and beneath the smell of Compton-Bofers's bay rum and whiskey, a woman's scent hovered mysteriously in the air.

"What happened to your pants?" Templeman asked.

"Damned if I know. Someone nicked them. Odd, isn't it? Packies probably. Down the hall, ten to a flat. Smell that?" Compton sniffed the air. "Curry, isn't it? Believe so. Silent as thieves, all of them." Templeman could smell only the whiskey, the bay rum, and the woman's fragrance. Compton moved to the window, standing to one side and brushing the dusty curtains aside. "Something queer going on, Temp. Something vicious." He stared down into the darkness. "I've been at it too long not to recognize the signs. I don't care a damn about myself, but there are others."

"You mean because of the pants?"

"The trousers! Good Lord, no," Compton laughed. "Not that at all. No, no. This other business. It's a filthy game they're playing. Who's doing it, your people or the Joint Intelligence Committee? Special Branch?" He stood peering through the curtain into the dark street. "Is that your car there, the Ford? There, near the corner."

"I came in a taxi," Templeman said blankly.

"They've been following me for weeks now—months. Ask your chaps in London about it. What's his name, Chambers? What are they up to? Perse noticed it, too. So did Dunny a fortnight ago when he was in. We'd all be dead keen to hunt this chap too if we knew what you were looking for. Who is it, Temp? Who are your lads after now?"

Templeman didn't know what Compton was talking about.

"Drunk again, is that what you think? Needless to say, it complicates the private life. Look here, have they brought you in on it?"

"In on what? What are you talking about?"

"I wish I knew. Parallel personalities, would that interest Chambers? Psychic suicides? We all are, in our own way. Read a devastating book on the subject just recently. But not mine, you understand— that's a game, too." He stood looking at Templeman, amused for a moment, the same sly boyish smile on his face, the same peculiar distant light in his blue eyes.

A key rattled angrily in the bedroom door and an instant later the door was flung open. A slim young woman stood in the doorway, her lovely face framed against the lamplight. Her beauty was so striking, her features so perfectly balanced, her face so flawlessly made up, that Templeman knew at once she was either a model or an actress. She was dressed like a model, with a flared woolen skirt and a cape of the same material. "Who are you talking to?" she demanded.

"A friend," Compton answered with a broken smile.

"Where did you get those trousers?"

"I thought you were sleeping, Rachael. I didn't want to bother you."

"Who are you?" she asked Templeman. She had been crying.

"An old friend," Compton said lamely. The young woman turned and a moment later flung Compton's wadded trousers at him, then his wallet. The wallet bounced from his arm and fell to the floor.

"It's empty—as empty as your wicked head," she told him. "With everything else finished, you'd steal someone's decency too, wouldn't you, you thieving braggart. What did he tell you?" she asked Templeman sharply. "What did he say?"

"Please, Rachael," Compton urged.

She turned angrily. "You beast! Give me my ten pounds. That's all I want from you."

"Could you?" Compton pleaded, turning to Templeman. "She's off for a holiday. I mean, would you mind?" Templeman fumbled dazedly for his wallet.

"It's not what you think!" the girl said, her face flushed as she read the look on Templeman's face. Templeman was looking at the astonishingly lovely face and remembering what he'd paid the woman in the fifth-floor flat in Paddington.

"Of course it's not what he thinks," Compton said soothingly. "It's not what anyone thinks. How could it be. Nothing is these days." She took Templeman's ten pounds and moved to the door.

"Don't come back," she told Compton bitterly. "Don't come back—ever." Tears filled her eyes and she bit her lip. Compton moved towards her impulsively, but she shoved him out the door and slammed it in his face. A moment later the bolt slid forward.

They found a taxi in the street below and drove to Compton's club, where he had left his car. "The beauty of the female sex is its mystery,"

Compton said sadly, sitting in a deep leather chair and looking beyond the brass fender into the fire, a whiskey in his hand. It was the first word he had uttered in almost an hour. "Its capacity for taking us into the unknown," he continued mawkishly. He was very drunk. So was Templeman. "It's not a matter of lust, you see," he added, carefully articulating his words. "I'd like to say that I'd never seen that young tart before in my life before this evening, but it's not true, is it?" He turned to Templeman for confirmation.

"No," Templeman advised, trying to keep his eyes focused on the swimming firelight. "No, it's not," he mumbled haplessly.

"She's lovely, don't you think?"

"Damned attractive."

Compton agreed. "A Catholic cousin from East Anglia," he muttered. "Lived with us three years. An *au pair* orphan from the provinces. Wife's cousin, that is. Puts a different wrinkle on it, doesn't it? Living with us those years while she was a schoolgirl. Now an actress. My God, what would the cousins think?"

They'd had five whiskeys and it was after midnight when they left the club. Compton was too drunk to drive so Templeman slipped behind the wheel, not too steady himself, and within ten minutes they were hopelessly lost. Compton wanted to return to room 403 in Bayswater to pick up Rachael and give her the week in the country he'd promised so they could talk about their future. A bit dodgy, though. He knew he'd never come back. By the time Templeman got his compass straightened out, they were along the Thames near Chelsea, and Compton-Bofers was describing his wedding in 1940, how his wife had looked, how she had changed. "Stop—stop here," he cried, seizing the wheel, and Templeman had no choice. He moved the Jaguar to the side of the road and followed Compton across the tarmac to the bank of the Thames, listening to the drunken Englishman describe the wedding, his wife's bridal veil, the silk-sheathed virgin underneath. He'd volunteered to serve in her uncle's fire watch the week before the wedding. He had come back on leave. It was during the height of the *Adlertag*—the Thames a lagoon of light—Lambeth, Vauxhall, and the Surrey docks burning; Woolwich and Lime House in flames; the East End leveled; and the Thames pool below the Tower a crater of crimson lava, cinders drifting across the river, flaming barges and water lights, the sky illuminated by a million candlewatts, drowning the searchlights that probed overhead for the Junkers 87's, the Heinkels and Dorniers. Stepney leveled, Shoreditch and West Ham; cinders flung like comets through the darkness; burning boats like pyres; barges moving to the bourrée and hornpipe of the Water Music, a Royal Fireworks; and he had a seat in the Royal Box.

Compton stood on the lower step, level with the Thames, arms directing the dark flood of the river past them. He was still very drunk, but not too drunk to hear the ugly drizzle of water from nearby. A figure stood ten feet away, back turned.

"What are you doing?" Compton demanded.

The head turned; a mop of oily hair bobbed in the weak light; a cigarette dangled from the lips. "Pissin'," came the reply. "Pissin' me guts out."

"What!"

"Pissin' in the Thames like yur mates over there." The youth in the black leather jacket jerked his head towards the shadow of Parliament. The cinder of his cigarette was sucked skyward suddenly as Compton jolted him viciously into the water, boots and arms thrashing; but Compton slipped forward on the greasy stones and into the water himself with a great tidal splash, surfacing a few yards offshore.

"You whoreson maggot! You bloody—"

Templeman stood in drunken silence. The youth slithered out of the stinking water, and a moment later Compton-Bofers was after him, pounding into the darkness in his wet shoes, chasing him on foot all the way to Sloan Court, Chelsea, where he caught up with him near a taxi stand and gave him a savage beating. The police were there when Templeman slipped unsteadily from the Jaguar. Compton-Bofers was locked up overnight, awakening in a cold sweat at dawn, not knowing where he was, listening to the barnyard sound around him. Down the corridor his wife, Templeman, Beresford Perse, his solicitor, and two priests waited. Beresford Perse had brought the lawyer; the priests accompanied Mary Compton-Bofers. In the same cell with her husband was a small dockworker named Jamie, his scurfy head half covered with adhesive plaster from a bar brawl the night before.

"Oo's the bugger with ye, Jamie?"

"Fuck off with yer yellin.'"

"Oo is 'ee, Jamie. Wot's yer name, matey?"

"Otto the nark, ain't it?"

"Give us a smoke, Otto."

"Where am I?" Compton croaked.

"Dartmoor, matey."

"Yer in the Scrubs. That or a twopence kip."

"Where do you do yer drinking, Otto?"

"Where 'ee does 'is wenching. Up between the legs where 'is ole lady wears 'er moustache."

"Where am I?" Compton groaned.

"We tole you," Jamie said, helping himself to one of Compton's cigarettes from the packet that had fallen on the floor. "Yer in Kartoom, matey, an' I'm Gunga Din."

A savage beating followed. Jamie was lying semiconscious and bloody on the filthy floor when the turnkeys dragged Compton away.

He was fined two hundred pounds in magistrate's court the following day. "A trifle, a mere trifle," Beresford Perse said as the car took them away. "It's too piddling, too piddling for words." Templeman wasn't so sure. The same afternoon Compton-Bofers called him and asked him to come to the house. It was after eight when Templeman arrived on Campden Hill Square. He waited down the corridor in the library. He could hear voices from the rear living room—Compton's, Mary's, and the voice of the middle-aged priest Templeman had met in jail. She took instruction from him three times a week. From the conversation Templeman guessed that Compton-Bofers had written a letter of resignation and that his wife was opposed to it.

When Compton finally joined him, he closed the door behind him, and crossed to the coal grate. He threw a letter in the fire, watched it burn for a moment. "They've taken it from me, carried it off. It's in their bloody iron grip and I can't do a thing. My life's not my own anymore." He sat down helplessly. "They can have my conscience, Temp. It's the life I want back."

That night in London, Compton-Bofers told Templeman that he wanted to meet privately with Phil Chambers. He wanted to talk to him about a subject of the greatest sensitivity. He asked if Templeman could arrange it. He'd prefer to meet with him someplace outside London. He didn't explain himself further and Templeman didn't ask.

But Templeman couldn't arrange it. He called the embassy the next day and learned that Phil Chambers had had a massive coronary two days earlier and had been evacuated to Washington in a coma. He wasn't expected to live.

From her window in Charlottenburg, Elizabeth watched the winter dawn dissolve the Berlin darkness and in the first bitter light discovered that it was snowing, a cruel, meager snow that harried the casement and reappeared like hoarfrost against the dark streets below. Only when it was fully light did she call the refugee watch officer and ask if there had been any messages during the night. It was the reflex of her own solitude the past several weeks since Plummer's disappearance—never to telephone someone until he was decently awake, never to plead the causes of the day against the agonies of the night.

No one had called. She no longer knew what to do. She had thought of talking to Peter Gwenhogg or to Dunstan but had decided against it. She'd called the London telephone number Plummer had left her, but had been unable to reach Phil Chambers. She'd refused to leave her own number. Two days earlier, however, she'd left her name and telephone number with the American secretary who had answered, and asked that Philip Chambers call her. He hadn't returned the call.

She had a solitary breakfast listening to the BBC, and afterwards carried her teacup to the window. The snow fell more heavily now and she watched the flurries uncurl as the wind increased, sweeping the cluttered air in deep strokes against the roof of the church beyond. On the steps far below a few figures as small as street sparrows made their way towards the door of the church, leaving their tiny footprints on the sidewalk. She took her heavy winter coat from the closet and let herself out of the apartment. Berlin was silent under the gathering snow—roofs, turrets, and spires, the medieval armories, the smoky chapels and the equestrian iron. She took a taxi to the refugee headquarters. The snow clung to the stone balcony on the second floor, and beaded the stone griffins. Her office was chilly. The staff was beginning to arrive, bringing into the silence the smell of wet wool and galoshes. The building custodian brought a basket of coal for her grate. He had just finished nursing the fire to life when her secretary entered and told her she had a visitor. He was English, short, with a ruddy face, quick brown eyes, and graying reddish hair.

"Ivor Simpson," he told her as he took off his coat. She studied his face. He had been in the sun recently; his skin was fair. He wore a tweed coat and flannel trousers. There were traces of snow on his shoes, which were British; heavy-soled brogans, meant for inclement weather, country roads, Rhinish cobblestones, Antwerp quays, steep Istanbul streets near the Golden Horn. She recognized his name and knew why he had come. "We have a mutual friend," he said, smiling for a minute. "David Plummer."

Snow and ice swept Saxony and the regions to the south the next week. Traffic on the Munich-Berlin autobahn was slowed by snowdrifts; construction on the Saale River bridge near Hof was suspended. Fog drifted along the Saale and obscured the frontier fortifications separating Bavaria from East Germany. On a damp, misty morning in February a motorized patrol from the East German *Grenzpolizei* found a breach in the inner wire fence flanking the mine field along the north bank of the Saale not far from the East German village of Hirschberg. East German laborers had been working within the wire fences for several weeks, replacing wooden-box mines with more reliable plastic ones. The rain and snow forced them to suspend work. The earth where the new plastic mines had been buried hadn't compacted properly, and their locations could be identified by the slight depressions left in the tamped topsoil. Two hundred meters from the breach in the inner wire fence, the Gropos found the path made by the escapee through the new minefield. The outer wire fence had been cut. Beyond the outer fence lay the swift, wide current of the Saale and Bavaria beyond. The Gropos thought at first that one of the Germans in the laboring force had escaped. They were wrong. A day later the escapee turned himself in to the Bavarian border police at Tiefgengrun. He had no papers. The border police notified the West German liaison office in Berlin, which informed Dahlem. Two days later a CIA officer arrived in Tiefgengrun. But the escapee wasn't the American they were searching for. He was a German railroad worker from Dresden.

A week later two automobiles were stolen one cold, bitter evening in East Berlin, both by the same man. The first car was recovered before its owner knew it was stolen; the second car wasn't recovered at all. The second and more important car was a small, bottle-green Alfa Romeo sports coupe. It had been parked near a restaurant that evening in a reserved parking area. A press card was stuck in the front window; the Alfa carried West German diplomatic plates. Its owner was an Italian journalist from the Roman communist paper *L'Unita* who had been stationed in Berlin for several months. At ten o'clock in the evening the owner of the Alfa drove away from the curb in front of the restaurant. From the shadows fifty meters away another car pulled away from the curb and followed the Alfa. It was an East German sedan of no identifiable color. It belonged to an East German professor at Humboldt University and had been stolen from the street outside his flat only thirty minutes before. The window had been forced, the ignition jimmied, and the car started by crossing the two starter wires. The car had been stolen with a single purpose in mind—to overtake the Alfa on the streets of Berlin and to hijack it. Had the Italian journalist left the Alfa in a less ostentatious place that evening—outside a crowded restaurant with an East German police post only a few steps away—the thief would have stolen the car from the street. As it was, he had no choice.

The East German sedan caught up with the Alfa two blocks away from the restaurant and trailed along after it. Twice during the next ten minutes the Alfa driver drifted to the left at busy intersections, slowing for a left turn, but each time a traffic policeman had waved him on. The driver of the sedan trailing him recognized the Italian's impatience. He was afraid the Alfa would maneuver into a U-turn or bound like a hare into some narrow alleyway which the clumsier sedan couldn't negotiate. He decided that the next opportunity might be his last, and determined to make the most of it. The two cars were in the center of the block at the time, the lights brilliant about them, headlights streaming by in both directions from the conclusion of a diplomatic reception at one of the large hotels nearby. The Alfa slowed again near the steps of the largest East Berlin hotel. With a sudden surge of speed, the sedan smashed into the Alfa from the rear, the high front bumper chopping a jagged shelf in the polished beetle body before the sedan reversed quickly. The driver of the sedan was out the door the same instant, racing towards the front seat of the Alfa, from which the Italian journalist was just emerging.

In an informal hearing held at the SSD offices on the following day, the East German officials decided that the Alfa driver had made two mistakes: leaving the engine on, and not waiting for a policeman to arrive. *Three mistakes*, a senior investigator wrote silently on his notepad as he listened to the testimony: *getting out of the car*. The journalist's nose was broken, both eyes were black, his lip was swollen, and when he put in his appearance at the special inquiry, his right arm was in a cast. But he was an Italian, after all, and the East German inspectors studied with some suspicion the plaster-of-Paris cast, and the dramatic facial shadow, which might or might not have been the result of the altercation in the street the night before. He was hysterical at the loss of his car, and even more hysterical at the suggestion that he had been a co-conspirator in its theft.

The testimony of the half-dozen eyewitnesses suggested that the Italian was anything but a co-conspirator. Observers on the sidewalk in front of the hotel heard the angry collision and saw the two cars stopped in the middle of the busy boulevard. All agreed that the driver of the old sedan had left his car first. One witness thought that he was rushing to the Alfa to warn the driver of the possibility of fire. Some believed that the Alfa had struck a pedestrian and had slammed on its brakes only to be unavoidably smashed from the rear by the lumbering sedan. The Italian driver said that he'd struck no one. He'd been deliberately assaulted by the car behind him and had left his car to inspect the damage. From that point on, he seemed to recall very little; even for a journalist he was remarkably unobservant. He couldn't recall his assailant, whether he was large or small, whether he was wearing a beard, or a beret. He didn't remember even seeing him. He only knew that he'd been ferociously attacked and beaten while dozens of onlookers watched. The other witnesses agreed. The assault was swift, brief, and savage. The journalist was thrown backwards over the trunk of the Alfa and into the grillwork of the old sedan. A few policemen had almost reached his assailant but the Alfa sprinted away even before the door was fully closed.

An East German security team returning from a surveillance operation at the Hotel Sofia saw the green Alfa race past and immediately pursued it. So did a Russian jeep with two East German militia officers. Few who had seen the car speed by doubted the hijacker's destination. He was headed for the Wall. An East German policeman outside the hotel had given chase for a few feet, fumbling with the flap of his pistol case, but by that time the crowd had doubled, and the Alfa had already sprinted through the intersection at the end of the block. The policeman ran to a phone in a nearby restaurant and called his headquarters. An official on the third floor of the hotel also made a telephone call. He had leaped to the window as soon as he heard the sirens, looked down at the large crowd gathered in the headlight beams, among the confused howling of horns, and thought to himself, *Ulbricht is dead. The old man is gone. The streets are going berserk.* Three other reports were also relayed almost simultaneously to the command headquarters. Some confusion resulted, since the headquarters was also receiving radio reports from the SSD officers in the pursuing car as well as the radio-equipped jeep. For a few minutes the watch officers thought that they were faced with three separate incidents. It took some time to realize that they were faced with only one.

The young officer at the Friedrichstrasse control point received the warning a few minutes late. He wrote the preliminary details on his pad, his mind not fully engaged. The evening had been monotonous beyond belief after the crisis-filled days a few weeks earlier. Now settled in his torpor, he wanted only to be left alone this night. His wife had prepared a sandwich for him, but the bread was stale. As he took the message over the telephone, he lifted the corner of the crust mistrustfully to inspect the meat and dressing within. A copy of *Neues Deutschland* was lying under the sandwich, and his eyes moved to the article he'd been reading as he waited for the voice to return to the other end of the line to give more details. Still he waited. But after a minute he realized that the man on the other end was still there. He heard his breathing, then his voice as he spoke to one of his staff in the message center.

"What time?" he asked. "What time did you say?"

"*Time! Time!*" the voice cried back. "*Are you still there, you idiot! Now. He's on his way now!*"

Outside a siren began to wail. He jumped to his feet, dropping the telephone, searching for his coat but not finding it, and running instead into the passport-control office. The room was empty. The siren came on again, louder this time. "Close it," he cried. "Close it down!" He stumbled out the front door and down the steps. The icy air drove the heat from his face. Three diplomatic cars returning to West Berlin were drawn along the right side of the roadbed while their occupants stood nearby, waiting for the completion of the document check. "*Close it down!*" he cried again. Across the road the three Vopos swung the heavy iron barrier back across the roadbed and locked it in place. At the same moment they heard the thin, angry whine of a car's engine, far in the distance. The Vopos at the searchlight heard it too. The lights flooded on.

Two hundred yards away the small green Alfa was caught in its glare but Plummer was low over the wheel, sighting along the arc of the green hood, looking between the two inert T-54 tanks twenty yards inside the barrier and ignoring everything except what he could see dead ahead—the open shaft of the checkpoint roadbed as bright and polished as a shotgun bore. They had all seen the car by then, had turned with the whine of the 1900 cc engine that sent the tiny car smoking like a tracer through the beams of the searchlights towards the massive iron of the barrier. The Soviet tank crews watched in anticipation and lifted themselves in reflex out of their turrets. The Vopos with automatic rifles moved back a step, then two. All watched the green apparition that was less than a hundred yards away and still accelerating insanely, watched with that sudden enervation or lethargy that mixes the same facial muscles in the presence of catastrophe, that rictus of fright, terror, or lewd comedy that wrenches its grotesque laughter when death stalks comic ambition—cliff walkers with rockets at their ankles and feathers on their wings, pratfalls on the great wire above Niagara, holiday planes full of ski pilgrims growing apart like mold spores in the great bull's-eye of winter sky—

None of them saw what Plummer saw that night or had seen repeatedly during his crossings at the same barrier on countless other winter nights. The East German engineers, like their Russian mentors, had always been the prisoners of their primitive roads and potholed highways, producing a rigid, high-clearance suspension design that was as archaic in the West as the Conestoga wagon. They might as well have designed a 707 with a beaver hat in mind. The barrier was the product of the same mental rigidity; it took no account of a decadent *laissez faire* pluralism. On the East German frontier, these sins were never noticed. At Sebring or Watkins Glen, they would have been as obvious as a Model T Ford.

Halt! Stehen bkiben! Halt! But no answer. Only the shriek of the rpm's.

"Halt!" Another voice tried but the car's fate was fixed now—beyond recovery.

"He can't do it," an Englishman's voice came. "He can't."

They moved back away from the roadbed and into the sheltering shadows of the control barracks, away from the incinerating explosion that would follow. The Vopos held their automatic rifles. The youngest among them dropped to one knee, raising his weapon and sighting along the forward edge of the T-54 tank tread where the Alfa would emerge, but there was no time. The screaming green projectile was just a blur as it shot past them. Those who looked away at the last minute heard nothing. Those who watched saw the horneting green shape drill the barrier like a bullet, passing beneath the barrier and vanishing beyond, streaking like a green laser, mysteriously into another world, seeming to shed in its passage that ugly mass and weight which had promised catastrophe only an instant earlier. They looked on in disbelief at its vanishing apparition, and then back at the unmoving iron barrier beneath which the car had escaped by a full eight inches.

Plummer was gone, flashing through the West German checkpoint by then, the hot smoke curling up from the compressed frame, a blizzard of black rubber particles spitting out from the rear wheels. He eased up on the brake and floated free on the cushion of rising suspension, coasting forward into the empty streets of West Berlin.

The car turned into a dark drive in Wilmandorf, head-lights sweeping a screen of evergreens first, and then the heavy iron gates. When the gates opened, the car crunched forward and stopped thirty yards beyond under an old carriage roof at the side of a three-story limestone residence. It had been a foreign chancellory during the days of the Weimar Republic. Now the Agency owned it. In the formal garden to one side lay a shallow pool, carved stone benches under an arbor, and light Doric columns flanking a pair of stone steps. A black Chrysler and Chevrolet with Berlin plates were parked in the drive. It was almost midnight.

Plummer was unshaven, dirty, and tired. He had left his overcoat in the old sedan in East Berlin, and was wearing an old woolen jacket that belonged to Munch in East Berlin. For three weeks Plummer had lived in the attic of the Munch pension in Lichtenberg, waiting for the weather to clear so that he could make his way south and cross into West Germany between Ostheim and Coberg. But Munch had been arrested four days earlier. His wife and daughter brought food for him for two days, and then told him he must leave. The same afternoon Munch's wife was taken in for questioning. He knew the daughter wouldn't be able to stand up to it alone. He had left the attic the same day. For two nights he had slept in a half-demolished apartment building. The following afternoon he had seen the Alfa.

Plummer followed the two Americans out of the car to the side entrance. The American at the iron-grilled door seemed to know Plummer. He singled him out and led him up the wide staircase to the second floor, opened a door within a larger set of french doors, and said, "Go on in. He's been waiting for you." The door shut behind him. It was a huge old room, probably a ballroom at one time. Now it was almost entirely in shadow. At the far end of the room a man sat in ducal solitude in front of a large stone fireplace where a coal fire was burning in the grate beyond the polished brass fender. Plummer's footsteps echoed across the bare parquet floor as he crossed towards the fireplace and onto the old Persian carpet. Two American armchairs were drawn near the chair where the man sat and for a moment he thought they were occupied. But they were empty. He heard the music then—delicate, strongly figured; a baroque terpsichore resonantly at home there in the seventeenth-century ballroom, designed to be tonelessly functional, a thick auditory fog intended to smother conversational details.

The man in the chair was Roger Cornelius. "You're right on time," he said, getting to his feet. "Still cold out, still snowing?"

"Still cold," Plummer said, looking around. There was no one else.

"You don't seem much the worse for wear. Have something." A small bar cart was drawn up. To the right of it was an easel holding a large polychrome map of East Berlin. "I imagine you could use it. Scotch and bourbon. Gin too, but no vermouth. Sorry. Shall I ring?"

"When did you get here?"

"Not too long ago. Just after you disappeared. Will whiskey do?" He filled a glass with ice, added the whiskey, and gave it to Plummer. "Times change, don't they? I once used this room in forty-nine and fifty. I understand it's not used much at present. I wonder how many men we have in Berlin now?"

"Too many," Plummer said. He tasted the liquor, shivering suddenly.

Cornelius smiled. "That's right—too many. Sorry, are you chilly? He lifted the fire tool from the hearth and pulled aside the wire mesh curtain, his face bent over the coals. "There's safety in numbers they say. It takes bodies, certainly. But they never replace the one good man in place, do they?" On the floor near Roger's chair was a leather attaché case with a blue KLM tag at the handle. Plummer looked at it woodenly. "We didn't think you'd make it," Roger said, following his eyes and replacing the fire tool. "The odds were against it."

"Whose odds?"

"Our odds. Their odds too. The Soviets are looking for you," he said quietly. "In the deadliest way. They're looking right now."

"Who told you that? Phil Chambers? Listen—"

"No, not Phil. No one has talked to Phil. No one at all. He's in a coma. He had a coronary, almost fatal. He's in Washington, paralyzed. A blood clot."

"When did it happen?"

"Over two weeks ago. Who helped you get out?"

Plummer lifted his head from the fire: "No one. Why?"

"You came out alone? Whose car was it?"

"I don't know. I picked it up on the street. What the hell's this all about?"

"The Russians are looking for you," Roger said. "The intercepts tell us that, the code word traffic, both from Karlshorst and Moscow. Quietly and secretly. No howling in the kennels; no watchlists. They want you for themselves. They haven't even told the East Germans. The KGB goes after the quick, not the dead. That's why we've been waiting. We knew they hadn't found you yet, that you were still loose in East Germany." He waited, watching Plummer's face. "They don't go after people they don't care about. Even their assets who decide to opt out or who are no longer of use. They simply leave them in a civilized way, the way a Frenchman leaves his mistress, and it's mutually understood. It doesn't end up in the streets or the papers. But this is different. They want you and they want you badly. It's reasonable to assume that, given enough time, they'll find you. Can you tell us why?"

Plummer didn't answer. He looked around the room. Roger waited. "I'll have to think about it. Is there a telephone here?"

"Telephone?"

"I want to call someone," Plummer said.

Roger seemed to understand. "The Davidson woman," he said. "She's in England. She left over a week ago. I talked to her myself. It seemed the best thing under the circumstances."

"What'd you tell her?" Plummer asked angrily.

"We told her nothing. There was nothing we could tell her. You'll be able to see her in London once this matter is cleared up. We'll be flying to Frankfurt in a few hours. The plane is already standing by. In the meantime we have a room for you here. Your room is just down the hall. We brought your clothes from Kreuzberg. You can probably get a few hours' sleep. I imagine you're tired. Take the bottle with you if you like."

ELEVEN

Plummer sat on the back seat of the Chevrolet, watching the dun-colored countryside roll by. Beyond the deep meadows the pine woods stood under a gray sky. He saw the flash of a frozen stream in the woods; a dappled pony stood motionless in his traces nearby as a woodcutter loaded his sleigh with cordwood. The driver slowed as he passed through a small village fifty kilometers south of Frankfurt. Some ten kilometers beyond he turned into a narrow, tree-lined lane. At the first bend in the lane he moved the car into a side road. Hidden behind the screen of conifers was a low stone gatehouse with a mansard roof. A plume of smoke uncurled from the chimney and hung motionless in the windless air. An American MP with a carbine over his shoulder stood at the gatehouse. He looked at the driver's pass, then at Plummer in the backseat, unlocked the gate, and waved the car through.

They drove for half a mile through dense woods thatched with old snow. The lodge stood on an open expanse of meadow, a weathered stone-and-stucco building with heavy wooden crossbeams under its gabled windows, a half-dozen chimneys, and a forest of radio and microwave masts on its roof. Plummer remembered it from a long time ago. Two enlisted men carried his two bags into the dark foyer where another American was waiting. "Howdy," the man said. The foyer smelled of wood ashes and freshly cured hams.

"Howdy," Plummer replied. The American looked him over carefully, inspecting his rough, uncut hair, the shapeless German jacket, and the worker's shoes, readjusted his white golf cap on his head, and led Plummer into the small office off the foyer. He was a small man with a creased neck and face. He wore a loose-sleeved golf sweater, a sport shirt, and a pair of officer's suntans. His hair was closely cropped beneath the golf cap and he smelled of after-shave lotion and the PX economy.

"Warrant Officer Franklin," he introduced himself as he gave Plummer his room key, then readjusted his cap and lowered his voice a decibel: "Seventy-second CIC." He led Plummer up the wide wooden stairs to the second floor. His two bags were waiting outside a room halfway down the hall. Inside, Warrant Officer Franklin opened the closet doors and the drapes with a practiced hand, as accomplished in his craft as a bellboy captain. "Well, you got yur skeet range an' duck pin alley," he said. "Some bird shootin' too, if you like. You got yur bar an' grill on the first floor, a set-down restaurant on the second for a nice candlelight meal if you want; got yur library and a sauna bath just out back. Got some rib-eyes just in, sirloins too. Beaucoup rosay wine. Drinks and mixers in yur closet there; icebox fulla beer. We got everything except a nine-hole golf course and a ten-hole cat house, and if them Russian bastards in Berlin give the generals a hard-on long enough like their doing, we'll have that, too. How's the pussy in Berlin?"

"Expensive," Plummer said.

"That's what that li'l old nurse over at the hospital in Frankfurt keeps a-telling me. Maybe that's why she gives it away fur free. Anything you need, just give a holler."

The door shut. The suite was large. On a small table in the alcove were a dozen glasses in individual wrappers; behind them were new quarts of Scotch, bourbon, rye, gin, and vodka. The mixers were in the refrigerator; cold bottles of beer were stacked on the bottom shelves. Plummer inspected the suite and afterwards stood at the bay window looking over the rear meadow and a line of rugged, pine-clad hills to the east. Everything he needed, the warrant officer had said: whiskey, beer, cigarettes, food—all of the bromides that relieved the depression of easy consumption. He was still depressed. He mixed a drink and discovered dinner music leaking into the room, like the patter from a dripping faucet. The sound system was wired into bedside speakers from a console on the floor below. He found the control switch and turned it off. Afterward he stood again at the window. Wouldn't it have been better in the long run to put bars on the windows, he thought—Simonov carbines at the door, .82 mm recoilless rifles at the checkpoints, the way the Russians and East Germans had; so that weak men might know what it was they had to escape from?

They questioned Plummer for two days, sitting in a large conference room on the ground floor of the east wing. It was a cool refectorylike room with whitewashed stone walls, a ceiling of acoustical tile, and a pair of deep windows looking out over the hillside. An MP with a carbine sat outside the door, but this wasn't necessary. Only Plummer and Roger Cornelius and his four-man team were in the lodge that week. Plummer didn't know any of them; he remembered a few names, but he had forgotten their faces. He had grown tired of his own voice.

"Among other things, we still don't know what he looked like or what he spoke," Roger said. "Apart from the German, I mean. What we do know is that he wouldn't come into the West, as you requested. He didn't want to be debriefed in West Berlin, Copenhagen, or anyplace else."

"It's over, Roger," Plummer said. "It's finished now. He's quit. He wants out."

"The way you wanted out in Vienna?" Cornelius asked, lifting his eyes from his notepad.

"I don't know what his reasons were."

"But having left yourself, you could sympathize with his feelings?"

"It wasn't a matter of sympathy."

"I'm sure you realized how dangerous this operation was—that it violated the most basic operational rules. Didn't it occur to you that with a minimum of routine surveillance—which you must have had in East Berlin—the East German services could have rolled up this operation in an afternoon's work? Didn't you think about that?"

"Every time I went through the Wall."

"Did you ever ask yourself how you survived?" Plummer didn't answer. "Did you ever think you weren't intended to survive?" Roger continued.

"No," Plummer said.

"Not even after the kidnapping attempt in the alley the last night?"

"No."

"Did you think this man was possibly psychotic, unbalanced?"

"Maybe a little," Plummer replied carefully.

"What about Phil?"

"Phil thought he was a killer. He didn't know what he was talking about."

"The fact that they tried to kill you the last night didn't change your mind?"

"No," Plummer said wearily. "You're track sore, Roger. You're wobbling all over the place. Maybe he was a bastard, okay. So what? How many crimps and psychotics have you hauled in through the years?"

"He wasn't a defector," Roger reminded him. "He didn't come out. He refused. It's something we must keep in mind."

"I have kept it in mind, all this bloody time. We've lost him. That's tough, but there's nothing anyone can do about it. It's finished. So why don't we wind it up and get the hell out of this icebox."

"That's an oversimplification," Roger sighed, "but probably it's as good as any at this point." He took off his glasses, wiped his eyes, and stood up. He stood at the window, looking out across the darkening hillside. The others waited. "Lost him," he said after a minute. "Lost him?" He turned back to Plummer. "That assumes too much, doesn't it?"

"If you're still looking for him, you've lost him," Plummer said.

"I don't deny we're looking for him. But 'lost him'? That assumes we controlled him at one time. That we owned him, that he worked for us. Who controlled him? You? You didn't control him; he controlled you. Chambers? You said Phil thought he was neurotic, dangerous, probably KGB. So Phil didn't control him either. Who did? No one. No one at all. That's the inconsistency we're faced with. Can you solve it?"

Plummer didn't answer. He was watching Roger's face. Roger turned back to the table, swinging his glasses. "If we had controlled him, the assumption would have been that he was producing for us, that he was a genuine asset. But we didn't control him. Was he an asset?" He slumped down again in his chair and pulled an old briar pipe from his pocket. "Tell me, what codename did Phil give this operation?"

"I don't know."

"But he thought it a valuable one."

"I told you that yesterday."

"That's right. He told you why he thought it was valuable; he told you what was in the first films." Cornelius lit the pipe and put the matches back in his pocket. "That was a little dangerous, wasn't it? You were acting as a courier, as a cutout. There was no sensible reason for you to know the contents of the films, and practical reasons for you not to know. Yet he told you. Why?"

"To keep me on the point. To show me the operation was important and that I had to help, whether I wanted to or not."

"But it was unusual."

"Sure it was unusual. He talked about ICBM's and ABM ranges. He gave me some garbage about performance data on second-generation rockets, and over-the-horizon radar. It was hard to swallow; and he didn't know what he was talking about. It didn't matter. He wanted to impress me, to keep me on the point."

"Were you impressed?"

"No."

"But he didn't tell you about the later films, the ones you gave him in Frankfurt at the terminal. He didn't tell you about those?"

"No. I didn't see any of the analytical work on those. It was all done in Washington."

"So except for the initial films, you weren't really in a position to say what the importance of this operation was or to deny Phil's claims. What you knew about it was hearsay, nothing more."

"I'm not an analyst. Neither was Phil. Sure it was hearsay."

"Let's talk about funding," Roger said quietly. "Did Phil ever tell you how he was funding this operation? Phil was a liaison officer to SIS in London. He had no operational responsibilities on the continent. How did he fund an operation in Berlin?" Plummer said he didn't know. "And as long as you were getting paid, it didn't matter?"

"Getting paid?" Plummer laughed. "BIL paid my salary, not Phil. I went to Berlin for an oil company, not for you guys."

"But Chambers topped off your salary, didn't he? Hadn't he helped you get the job with BIL and recommended you to Ivor Simpson?"

"No. I got the BIL job through an employment counselor on New Bond Street. After I got it, Ivor called me and asked if I'd do some work for the Brits on the continent. I turned him down."

"And it wasn't Phil that gave your name to BIL originally?"

"What are you talking about?" Plummer complained. "Who told you that? Phil didn't have anything to do with my getting the job."

"Let's come back to that," Roger replied. "Yesterday you told us you felt Phil was somehow getting out ahead of Washington with this operation—that there was a time-lag between his talks with you in Frankfurt and Berlin and his instructions."

Plummer said, "It was a bootstrap operation. He was running it out of his hat. That's the way it sounded sometimes."

"So he was handling it alone?"

"I think so. He was overworked, too."

"Did he tell you what the urgency was—where the pressures were coming from?"

"From Washington. He was overworked. Christmas night in the car, he smelled like an embalmer's bag. He'd been taking pills all day. You could tell."

"Did you ask him about it?"

"No. Maybe I should have but I didn't. He never talked about how he felt, even when he didn't have enough muscle left in his chest to pull his blood out of his socks. That's the way Phil was."

"When was that?"

"Christmas night in Berlin."

"Is that when he told you that he thought this man was KGB?"

"I think so. You can check it out. Maybe he made a memo of our talk. Probably it's in your briefing book there."

"It isn't," Cornelius said quietly. "None of this is. But that's not surprising, is it? He was terribly busy that last week in December. We know that. But Phil's files are deficient in other respects too. There's a puzzling lack of information about the operation you were involved in. An enormous quantity of hard fact is missing. You said Phil was out ahead of us in Washington. You're right. If you looked at his official correspondence, you'd see that this operation occupied little of his time. Yet during a week when he was occupied with an extremely sensitive matter in London, he flew to Frankfurt to meet with you. Then on Christmas Day he left the NATO ministerial meeting in Paris to fly to Berlin to talk to you. It's puzzling. Even bizarre. But it shows one thing—that for Phil, Berlin had an extraordinary significance—more that anything else he was doing. He was scheduled to give an intelligence briefing to the NATO special intelligence committee on Christmas Day but he went to Berlin instead. Why? No one knows. When he returned to London, he had a medical checkup at Eva's insistence, and the doctor was concerned enough to recommend hospitalization. But he refused. Why? We don't know. Who was he seeing? Who was he talking to all of this time? We don't know that either." Roger paused for a minute, lifting himself from his chair to put his cold pipe in the ashtray. Plummer watched him with growing perplexity.

Cornelius said, "For the past two weeks we've been trying to get a handle on this operation you were involved with. It's been difficult. Phil can tell us nothing. What we've learned to date isn't very much. What we do know is that from the time Phil first visited you in Berlin until the afternoon of his heart attack on the floor of the taxi taking him to Liverpool station, everything he did was done in a state of total exhaustion."

"What is this?" Plummer interrupted suddenly, conscious of the silence that had gathered around him in the whitewashed room, as hard as winter frost. "What is all this goddamned guesswork?"

"Guesswork? Yes," Roger nodded, "it is guesswork. It must be. That's all we have. All that you have, too. Because there's nothing in the records about this operation that amounts to anything. The account is empty, blank—it's bankrupt. Nothing about missile performance, ICBM's, or over-the-horizon radar. In fact, nothing at all. That amounts to a defalcation, doesn't it? We think it does. Embezzlement. You see, David," Roger continued calmly, "all that we have is what you've told us here in this room. And what you've told us is that an unidentified agent, presumably a Russian, was receiving an inordinate amount of filmed material for which there's no explanation, no explanation at all."

"What are you driving at?" Plummer was on his feet.

Roger looked up at him calmly, without surprise. "The most plausible explanation possible under the circumstances," he explained. "The likelihood that this wasn't our operation at all, but the Soviets', and that you were its courier."

Plummer looked at him blankly. The room was silent. Roger didn't move. No one else moved. *"Their operation?"* Plummer heard himself say. *"A Soviet operation?* Are you crazy! Are you out of your goddamned minds?" He looked from one face to another, but the room was no longer there in the same dimension, and the white walls had collapsed softly about him like an enormous bank of wet snow. His voice was far away, his chest ached, and he wondered insanely what a coronary must feel like, whether Phil Chambers's body had weighed as much when they'd lifted it from the floor of the taxi outside Liverpool station.

"Are you all right?" she asked. "You didn't smash into a lorry, did you?" Her voice was very far away. She was in London. "Are you all right? They said you are, but I must hear it from you. Are you?"

"I'm fine," he said. He was standing in the communications section, two Air Force communications NCO's sitting at the table in front of him. "Are you okay? I missed you. Everything all right?"

"I didn't worry. I tried not to. Does my voice sound odd?"

"It's the phone," he said.

"There are all these strange people about. I'm not quite sure where I am. How long will it be?"

"Just a few days. Where will you be?"

She said she was going to Kent and would wait for him there. They talked for fifteen minutes, and after Plummer had put the phone down he went back to his room. He stretched out on the bed without turning on the lights. He was still lying there when Roger knocked at the door and told him they were gathering for dinner.

After dinner they sat in the library, the doors closed. Roger had his briefing book with him. The others were still drinking their coffee. Plummer told them that it didn't make any sense. Roger disagreed. They were still arguing when the door opened and Ivor Simpson joined them, just arrived from London and still carrying his briefcase.

Plummer was puzzled; Ivor, a little embarrassed. They were still arguing when one of the mess stewards pushed a portable bar through the door. Plummer looked at his watch and realized that it was almost eleven o'clock. He had eaten little at dinner. He took a drink without enthusiasm but it was soon gone.

"How do you explain it?" Roger asked him patiently. "The void we've been talking about. How do you account for it?"

"I don't," Plummer said. "I'm talked out. You've bled me dry. How many times do I have to crawl over the finish line? I said it doesn't make sense and it doesn't." He picked up his glass and filled it from the ice bucket.

"You said earlier that Phil ran this operation out of his hat," Roger commented. "No gimmicks, just wild cards. Was that the way it was in Prague?"

Plummer thought for a minute. "Pretty much. We were just learning and didn't have the technology."

"This Berlin operation had the same ring?"

"Maybe. But it wasn't our improvisation. Too amateurish, I suppose. In Prague we improvised a lot, but we had to. We didn't have what you have. No Samos, no satellites, no miniaturized keyholes."

"So Phil knew that an operation like this one would have appealed to you," Roger suggested.

"He knew no operation would appeal to me," Plummer said. "I say it doesn't make any sense. Why would he have done it? What was behind it?"

"The Berlin crisis, I'd guess," Ivor Simpson observed. "The NATO conference. A few odd networks here and there."

"That's garbage," Plummer said.

"The networks?" Roger said. "Don't be foolish. The extent of the NATO alert? The mobilization plan? Order of battle? I can give you a hundred reasons why it isn't. Where the nuclear tripwire was; what the Soviet command at Zossen could expect. If that's not important, then perhaps we should all pack our bags and go home."

"NATO is a bloody bridge tournament," Plummer said. "Everyone reads the hands right off the wall. It leaks like a sieve. Do you think

Phil would have thrown in the towel for that? Never. He thought he was getting something else—something he couldn't get anyplace else, not from Samos, not from the monitoring stations at Diyarbakir, or anyplace else. Soviet missile capability. That's what he thought."

"I don't blame him," Roger said easily. "It would have been a neat trick—a *coup de théatre*. But we don't have one shred of evidence that this was what he got."

Ivor Simpson said, "And you're trying to tell me Phil was trafficking in NATO secrets? Christ, Roger. With the French, Greeks, and Italians all sleeping in the same bed, who needs Phil? He was going to compromise that?" Ivor Simpson sat back with a sigh and looked at Cornelius. "If NATO is a nunnery, so is a Hamburg whorehouse. Give it up, Roger. It won't wash."

Cornelius didn't answer for a minute, still looking at the fire on the hearth. "It never does, you see," he answered finally. "It never makes sense at the time, and yet that's the very reason it does succeed. It happens all the time. People come apart. They just die inside and walk out the door and never come back. The way you did in Vienna in 1958. Some take a briefcase with them and catch a train or go up the gangway of a Polish freighter, or just jump out the window. Sometimes they take a toothbrush; sometimes they take a file or two; sometimes they take twenty years' service in Soviet Affairs in the FO or the State Department. Or the Company." He was still looking into the fire. "Something happened to Phil Chambers. I don't know what it was, but something happened, and he couldn't cope with it. He was worried about a nuclear confrontation—we all know that. Maybe he thought he could do something about it, I don't know. So it does happen. It happens, and when it does people like you and me, David, sit here and shake our heads and say that it didn't—that it couldn't. All I'm saying is that it can and does."

"I still don't believe it," Plummer said.

"I suppose not," Roger muttered. "But you think it might have worked. I suppose that's all we were really after."

"Okay, it might have worked. It's clever, devious, and a little morbid. That's what counts when you do the autopsy, isn't it? It wasn't the heart attack that carried him off but syphilis of the brain. Well, it's bunk, and you know it, Roger. It's credible and damn ingenious, but it's bunk."

"I think it's rather persuasive," Ivor said quietly.

"Except that Roger left one thing out."

Ivor's face went blank. Roger turned: "Left what out?"

"The man we've been talking about," Plummer said. "The man on the other side, the Russian you say was running Phil. Maybe Phil could have faked a few things but he couldn't fake him. No one could—not you, not Ivor, not the PhD's back in the Agency. Your taproot just doesn't draw from that far down. Whoever this man was, whatever was bothering him, whatever he believed, he was more real than anything else in this whole rotten operation, and no one could have faked that."

Roger nodded in agreement. "That's right," he said, "but then he didn't have to, did he?"

Plummer was confused for a minute. "Didn't have to? They had to take me in—to make me believe in what they were doing."

"That's the whole point," Roger said evenly. His voice was tired. He was exhausted, but neither his civility nor his intellectual gifts failed him, even then. "Because as it happens, Phil didn't have to invent this man, nor did the man himself. They knew you'd do it for them. They gave you a few bones and you put the flesh on them, the way an old dog would. They counted on it. So Phil told you about the ICBM's and ABM's to embellish the lie. You'd left us once. Phil knew your exhaustion as well as he knew his own. That's why he picked you." Roger paused, looking at Plummer sympathetically. "You don't understand, do you? Even now."

Plummer didn't answer. In the room behind the study someone dropped a glass. Ivor Simpson hadn't taken his eyes from Plummer's face, but Plummer didn't turn. Roger said, "Phil gave your name to BIL before the Bond Street employment office called you. Ivor gave you a recommendation. Phil asked him for it. He knew that when you got to Berlin, you'd protect the man on the other side. They were counting on it, both Phil and the Russian. It was essential. We think the Russian was already operating in London and had been for some time. We think he was in contact with someone in the FO and that Phil knew about it. We don't know how but we believe he did. So they chose you. They knew your own alienation, your own search for solitude, and in the end they trapped you in it, confident that whatever happened, your own neurosis would protect them. It gave the whole filthy operation its final dimension." Roger paused wearily. No one moved. "You never gave us much credit, did you? You thought from the beginning that we wanted to write you off. The fact is you were already written off. You were finished a long time ago, the day you walked out of the door in Vienna. The only one who didn't know then and doesn't know now is you, David." Roger turned to Ivor Simpson. "Ivor."

Simpson sat forward. "I'm sorry, David. I am sorry. I suppose my own role in this effort isn't very clear to you. It's hardly clear to me, but I'll try to explain. What Roger said is true. Phil gave your name to BIL and then asked me for references. That's why I was somewhat surprised when you turned down my offer. I rather imagined that was the *quid pro quo*. In any case, I was moved to other responsibilities in the meantime and didn't give it much thought."

"Solo," Roger joined in from the fireside. Plummer hardly seemed to have heard him.

"Solo," Ivor repeated with a wan smile. "Quite. In any case, it was in connection with this other work that I happened upon something that rather puzzled me." He fumbled with his briefcase and withdrew a manila folder. He slipped a photograph from the folder and handed it to Plummer. "This is quite recent," he explained. "Just a few weeks ago, as a matter of fact."

Plummer moved the photograph under the table lamp. Ivor stood up and leaned forward, pencil in hand. He pointed to a man standing near a newspaper kiosk at Liverpool station. The man was wearing a dark macintosh and was hatless. The face was partially turned, and the angle wasn't a very good one. The photo was an enlargement, extremely rough grained, and lacked detail. But Plummer thought he recognized the man. He lifted his eyes towards Ivor Simpson, who was taking a second photograph from the same folder. "This one is somewhat older," he said. "Probably you'll recognize it. It was collected by our naval attaché in Copenhagen several months back. There must have been a dozen photographs in the acquisition, brought back from East Germany from an officer on the *Seebad-Warnemünde*. This one certainly wasn't of much interest. It's a GDR Ministry of Information photograph, as a matter of fact. The cachet is on the back."

At first glance the photograph wasn't familiar. It might have been taken at a military reunion at a neighborhood pub. A dozen figures were lifting the glasses in the direction of the photographer. But as Plummer stared at it, the scene acquired focus. He found his own face, heard the distant voices, the sound of the sea breaking beyond and the strains of the "March of the Black Sea Fleets" fading in the background. The photograph had been taken at Rostock on a cold autumn afternoon in November while the rain drenched the windows and the gray sea marshes beyond. Plummer was holding a glass of beer. His Russian companion was drinking a light whiskey. Ivor's pencil pointed to Strekov's face. "The two faces are vaguely similar," he explained, "but they're rather long odds. Yet if I had to hazard a guess, I'd say that they were the same man."

"Who's the man at Liverpool?" Plummer asked.

Ivor shook his head. "We don't know. We have our suspicions but at this time, we simply don't know."

"How did you get the photograph?"

Ivor sat down in his chair. "A surveillance," he said quietly. "One that's engaged us for rather a long time. One of our own, I have to confess—someone from our own services who we suspect has been in touch with the Russians. It's only a suspicion, mind you."

"Solo," Roger said quietly.

Ivor didn't answer. "This chap you see here—at Liverpool—had met with our lad the same evening at a pub in Chelsea. We got the photograph after he'd left a taxi at Liverpool. One of Chatwood's fellows took it. Rather good, I think."

Plummer studied the photographs. They waited. At last he handed them back to Ivor, who took them without returning them to the folder, his eyes still fixed upon Plummer, waiting for his response.

Still they waited. Roger Cornelius finally got to his feet and went to the ice bucket and filled his glass. "What do you think, David?" Roger asked. He didn't turn. Plummer could see neither his face nor his hands. But then, looking at the way Roger was standing, the way he held his shoulders, he knew he wasn't going to turn.

"I think they're the same man," he said.

London was cold and wet. In the car speeding from Heathrow, Ivor Simpson's face had an unaccustomed grimness to it. Plummer watched him silently from the backseat, Roger Cornelius sitting alongside, staring out through the windshield at the wet roadbed ahead of them. It was early evening.

"I think it rather improbable that Chatwood would turn up something tonight," Ivor muttered. "It's much too soon, but then you're never sure in this wretched work."

"How long have you had a surveillance on your FO man?" Plummer asked.

"Two years or so, isn't it, Roger?" Ivor replied. "Special Branch took over last summer."

Roger winced as the bright red lights of a lorry flashed near their rain-streaked fenders. "Good Lord, he takes chances," he muttered. The Special Branch driver didn't turn. "Two years," he said. "That's right."

After the sedan jerked to a stop in the dark underground garage in a large building in a familiar London borough, Simpson flung open the door and was across the darkness before Plummer and Roger Cornelius were out of the rear seat. They followed his bounding steps up three flights of stairs, past a handful of building guards, and down a brightly lit corridor into a large crisis room at the end of the hall. Against the far wall were a few long tables where a half-dozen men sat or stood, some in raincoats still wet from the streets below, some in shirtsleeves or tweed jackets. Two pairs of loudspeakers were mounted on tables at opposite ends of the room; two enormous polychrome maps of London faced each other from opposite walls. Seated at odd tables around the room were men wearing headphones and monitoring individual radio receivers. In the center of the room was the command radio receiver and transmitter. A man sat at the console, his face locked in concentration. With one hand he cupped one earphone close to his head, with the other scribbled a few words across a large pad on the table in front of him. The writing grew erratic, like that of a telegrapher reading a dying signal. The men at the polychrome maps left their platforms and moved towards the center of the room, where a few of the other radio operators had gathered, too. In the far corner a woman sat at a small PBX switchboard. A dozen telephones sat on the tables.

Simpson peeled off his coat and went towards the man at the console, Roger Cornelius at his heels. Plummer stood inside the door, looking around him. Roger and Ivor stood behind the operator as he scrawled a few words on the pad and handed it back over his shoulder. Plummer joined them. The men in the room were monitoring a surveillance operation being directed by a joint Special Branch/MI5 operations team from a stationary van somewhere on Regent Street. Plummer knew then what he should have guessed earlier in Frankfurt. Ivor Simpson wasn't with MI6 any longer. He was MI5's counterintelligence liaison officer with Scotland Yard. The men in the room were an odd lot. Some were MI5; some were from the Yard's Special Branch spy catchers. The voices which crackled from the loudspeakers came from a dozen different locations—on the street, in cars, trucks, and taxis, in the control van itself. They stood in the center of the room and listened. As the other voices died away or signed off, one voice emerged, dominating all others—a curt, strident, Midlands' voice.

"Chief Inspector Chatwood," Simpson grimaced, lifting his eyes to Plummer's. "Special Branch. His blood is up now." He turned towards the map of London behind him, looking at the small red triangle marking the location of the stationary van. Plummer, still looking at Ivor Simpson, didn't turn. He wondered if Ivor had been with MI5 when he'd approached him the previous summer before he went to Berlin with BIL.

"Unless I miss my guess, it's over," the radio operator said.

"They picked someone up?" Roger asked.

"No one. If there was someone, he slipped off—clean as a whistle. Chatwood thinks it was a false alarm. Chap you're looking for didn't show. The other is homeward bound now—home for a suburban supper. Anyone got a fag?" Ivor gave him a cigarette, still studying the map. "Listen to Chatwood," the radio man said. "Calling in his hounds. Mad as a hornet, he is. Flogging through the muck and nothing to show for it but a pair of wet boots. He's got his copper's reputation to think of. Won't miss next time."

"The next time it won't be hounds-and-hares through Piccadilly," Ivor muttered.

"You think he might have been warned off?" Roger asked him.

The radioman answered for him. "Not bloody likely," he said. "Smooth as silk, Chatwood is. Steal your ears off your nob and you wouldn't know a ruddy thing until your topper dropped over your chin. No, not Chatwood." He looked at Ivor's worried face, still smiling. "Chuck him in the strongbox, would you?"

"In time," Ivor muttered, "in due time."

In the car taking Roger and Plummer to an accommodation residence in Kensington, Ivor told them that the Home Secretary's office would talk to Special Branch the following day. MI5 would take over what Special Branch had begun. That was the policy he'd brought back with him from Frankfurt.

Ivor and Roger met with Chief Inspector Chatwood the following afternoon at Scotland Yard. Chatwood had just returned from a meeting with the Special Branch commander and his Detective Superintendent. The joint operation would continue, but MI5 would make the decisions. The goal was to pick up Solo's Soviet contact without Solo's knowledge. Chat-wood was a tall, stoop-shouldered man in his early sixties with iron-gray hair. He had huge hands, a lined, troubled face, and blue eyes as cold as a Norwegian fjord. He was still angry. "You chaps come crashing back from Germany and I get a new set of orders, not to squash this man when I pick him up, but to lift him off the pavement like a ruddy butterfly. It's impossible. Don't you chaps know that? It's impossible."

"I know it's difficult, George, but it isn't impossible," Ivor said weakly. "It isn't at all—"

"I've been searching for this man Solo for a decade now, and when I finally believe I've identified him, you tell me I can't touch him! That I can't do a thing."

"We'll explain in time, but it must be this way for now," Ivor pleaded gently. "It must be. There's no other way."

"I'll follow instructions, but I don't like it. I want you to know that, Ivor. You have your job, and I have mine. You're interested in recruiting spies and I'm interested in catching them. You want to use them and I want to hang them. But when I catch this Russian chap or whoever he is and put him where he belongs, people like you will come along in a month or two and arrange to have him released in exchange for someone you've lost on the other side. And when it happens, he'll walk out of the Scrubs with the same insolence on his face that was there when we picked him up. He'll get on a boat or a train and that will be it. And your man will get on a plane in Moscow and come back to London and get an OBE and that will be it. It's not enough in my opinion."

The secretary moved into the room from the outer office and pulled the door closed. Roger and Ivor sat in front of Chatwood's desk, as silent as schoolboys. Chatwood was still standing. "A man gets what he deserves in this life," he shouted, "and you chaps have upset the whole bloody balance. I know a hundred decent chaps still rotting behind bars that deserve better than what they got from me than these filthy diplomats and spies! I know a million God-fearing Englishmen that have spent more time doing their bird for smash-and-grab than some of these filthy bastards have for trying to bring down the whole empire! And for what! For what! Spies should be caught. It's the dirtiest business I know. They're scum—liars, cheats, murderers, fags. Psychotic scum and rubbish! And you want to let them go. What about the poor sod that puts his wife's head in an oven because that's where his brain has gone—to his barmy fingers and thumbs? What about him? What's the Crown or the FO going to trade for his life? What's anyone willing to give up for him except his length of turf on a pauper's green somewhere. Answer me that, Ivor!" After a few minutes Chatwood sat down wearily.

"I know how you feel, and it's true," Ivor answered at last. "It's true. I know it's true, and it's sickening. But this case is different. It is. You'll see in time."

Chatwood didn't answer. The secretary brought coffee. They stirred their cups, and Chatwood said, "What do you want me to do?"

"We'll wait," Ivor replied. "We'll wait. It may take a month, maybe more. But we'll get them. Both of them."

Chatwood lifted his eyes. "You have a plan?"

"I believe so. I think we've got a plan. The tactics are up to you."

The sky was cloudless after the night rains. Spring was in the air, the Sussex countryside touched with green. On the flagstone terrace behind the remote eighteenth-century house whose roofs were spired with the later addition of ugly Victorian iron, Elizabeth sat in a cushioned lounge chair, a white canvas tennis hat on her knee. Her slim face was burned from the winds of the Sussex downs where she had spent much of her time walking these recent weeks. Now she was dressed for traveling, wearing a cardigan and a woolen skirt.

"Perhaps you could join us," she suggested to Plummer. "Majorca is so lovely this time of year. Have you been?" He shook his head without speaking, slumped deep in his chair, his back to the french doors. "I'm sure it would be good for you," she continued, his silence moving them apart again. "You have time, don't you? Then you could return later."

He didn't answer, looking across the fields towards the distant Sussex downs. Tired, discouraged, isolated even now, his reflexes slow, he felt like an old fighter, shadowboxing in a deserted gym. When he'd driven down from London two hours earlier, he'd expected to find her alone. She wasn't. A half-dozen cars were parked beyond the screen of laurel and hemlock in the courtyard. Her aunt's house was crowded with last minute well-wishers, neighbors and friends. "A 'Cocktail d'Adieu'," Peggy Gwenhogg had explained in her small, clever voice. Her aunt was closing the house that afternoon, on her way to her Mediterranean cottage on Majorca. Elizabeth would accompany her, so would the Gwenhoggs, whose luggage was in the front hall.

The sun was warm. Plummer had left his raglan in the car, but his woolen scarf was still around his neck. He wore an old corduroy coat and flannel trousers. His shirt was open at the collar. He pulled the scarf from his neck, looking out towards the green fields beyond the old stone wall and the laurel hedge. He didn't know this country, but he mistrusted it. It was peaceful and remote enough to make her forget everything else; its quaintness made him suspicious. In time it would reclaim her. Already they were strangers again.

"You don't know Sussex, do you?" Elizabeth asked.

He shook his head. A copse of young oaks lay beyond the corner of the terrace; primroses climbed along the stone wall.

"Not Sussex, not Yorkshire, not Kent."

"Kent's your home, isn't it?" he remembered.

"Yes, but Sussex too. I spent many summers here as a child."

Plummer didn't want to hear about it: what she had done, how she had lived, who her friends were in the village, the names of the people inside whose voices he could hear through the french doors. He looked at the afternoon sky, conscious again of the time. At five she would drive with her aunt to Dover, where they would catch the boat train for Boulogne. Plummer had to be back in London at seven. Ivor Simpson's team of spy catchers had followed him from London and were in the village, waiting for him. Everyone else had taken the weekend off—Cornelius, Ivor Simpson, even Solo, who had gone off to Northumberland. The warm spring day, the cloudless sky, and the lime-green English countryside seemed to him part of the same conspiracy, freeing everyone to his own indulgences. Had Roger Cornelius managed that too?

"You're thinking about something else," she said.

"Maybe a little." He looked at her face, but she had turned her head towards the french doors.

Peter Gwenhogg came out onto the terrace followed by a stout, red-faced Englishman wearing a tweed hacking coat. Both were carrying drinks. "Peggy told me you were here," Gwenhogg said. "Bit of luck, isn't it, this weather? On holiday now too?"

"For a few days," Plummer said.

"Fothingill," said the man in the hacking coat. "What is your function?" He held out his hand.

"This is Mr. Plummer," Elizabeth explained before Plummer could. "An old friend."

"I suppose we'd better take a look," Fothingill said to Gwenhogg. He wore an ugly toothbrush moustache and a military rosette in his buttonhole. "I'll be knocking the side garden into shape while Isobel is gone," he told Elizabeth. Plummer thought he smelled whiskey.

"Look us up when you get back to Berlin," Gwenhogg said to

Plummer. "A pity we're losing her, wouldn't you say?" The two men went down the steps and disappeared around the corner of the house.

"I should think that's the last thing you want to do—return to Berlin," Elizabeth said.

"I suppose you were pretty busy there the last weeks," Plummer said.

"Reasonably busy, I suppose. But not like last autumn. And you?" They still hadn't talked about East Berlin.

"A little."

"I'm sure it will be better for you now. Going back to Washington or Virginia. They're very close, aren't they? I looked them up. They seem close in the atlas. I'm not surprised you're keen on that."

"Do I look keen?"

"Not now, but you will, I'm sure." She looked away suddenly, across the terrace. A car had come into the drive in front. A door slammed and a few minutes later the voices beyond the french doors lifted in unison. She sat back finally, tired herself of their impasses, their silences and mutual evasions. She turned the glass in her fingers.

"How long will you be in Majorca?" he asked.

"It will be different, won't it?" she struggled again. "Washington I mean. Not like Vienna or Berlin. It won't be like that, will it?" She met his eyes finally.

"You didn't answer my question."

"I'm not sure. A few months probably. Perhaps less. Tell me about your plans."

"There's nothing much to tell."

"It won't be the same as before, will it? Your work?"

"What's the question?"

"You're really not helping much. I suppose I must seem terribly naive to you in many ways. I've always thought that—from the beginning, from the very first day. I don't pretend to understand what you were doing all of that time. You were always rather vague about it. But surely it must be over now. Your work in Vienna and Berlin, it must be finished, mustn't it?"

"What work?"

"I try not to ask questions. Not at Pullendorf or Vienna, not in

Berlin either. But in my own way I suppose I've always known that you were involved in something difficult, something horribly complicated. It was the only excuse I could give myself—your not returning after Pullendorf. Loyalty to something. One's country, one's ideals. I'm not sure. Are they identical? I don't know. I've tried so not to think about it. I suppose that now I'm searching for some kind of reassurance. Washington is such a long way, such a terrible distance. Now there are other places too."

"You never asked."

"I talked of everything else, didn't I? It didn't seem to matter to you. But it does matter. I'll worry about you. I always have. A habit, I suppose. I've had it for years now."

"You're right about the work," he said. "It was complicated. It always is. I never wanted to bother you with it. You were a way of forgetting about it—another world. What could I tell you worth saying—it's finished."

"When you left Berlin this last time and disappeared, I didn't know what to think. It was like Pullendorf again." She stopped and took a deep breath, turning to look down through the trees towards the open fields. She began again: "A few days after you disappeared in Berlin someone from London came to see me. He wasn't interested in talking about refugees. He wanted to talk about you. An American was with him. I don't remember his name. But I knew who the other chap was. His name was Simpson. He's with the intelligence services." She looked back towards Plummer, who hadn't moved, still slumped in his chair.

"What did they say?"

"Very little, as a matter of fact. Questions most of all. They knew far more than they admitted, I'm afraid. They suggested I leave Berlin. Since I'd already submitted my resignation, that wasn't difficult. They said I could best help you by leaving Berlin as quickly as possible, so I did. But it was the atmosphere that frightened me most; not for my own safety, not in a personal way, but something else. Another world. Utterly chilling—"

"They thought you knew something, that I had told you more than I'd told anyone else."

She nodded. "So I gathered. When I reached London, Mr. Simpson came to see me again. He asked that I not talk about you or Berlin, that I not mention it to anyone." She shook her head sadly. "Whom would I have mentioned it to? Couldn't he understand that? Couldn't anyone understand? It's quite hopeless—demoralizing, even talking about it. How do such people think? I don't know. Now you're about to disappear again."

Plummer sat in his chair, looking at her face. "It's a long story," he said finally. "It doesn't make any sense, so don't try. They told me they looked you up in Berlin and got you out. But forget about them. What they think doesn't matter. What you think does."

"Their work is your work," she said. "That's what you've been involved with—the intelligence services? Why? That's what I don't understand."

"It was a way to get things done."

"But there must be other ways."

"The other ways don't work. Their ways do."

"But at what cost? That's what I don't understand: how one becomes involved knowing the costs."

"As easily as anything else these days."

"That's not an answer."

"What is? It's as easy as stupidity, as ambition. As cheap as indifference. Some do it for principle, some for excitement, some like the money. Don't ask me. I don't know anymore. For some of them it's just a job. For others it's a way of controlling behavior—political behavior more than anything else. Everyone tries, don't they? The UN, Moral Rearmament, the knee-jerk behaviorists, the lobbyists, the influence peddlers, the pope, the KGB, the House of Commons, you name it. Some are still trying to put moral splints on mother nature. Others know she's just a whore and are trying to buy her into their bed. For some that's the answer. Others just enjoy the hypocrisy. That's an advantage, isn't it, a cynic's advantage in a world where piousness or piety is the people and mediocrity its king. I don't know. Don't ask me anymore. What's more corrupt than talking about it? What keeps anyone honest these days?"

"Conscience. What else? Ourselves," she insisted. "Of course, it's not easy—"

"Conscience? Whose conscience? Who thinks about conscience these days? How many jug-eared tourists rambling around Europe these days think about it? How many villas in Majorca think about it? How many of the people you know or I know think about it? What was I supposed to do—die in place ten or twenty years ago like they did when they put their uniforms away and went back to the suburbs? Take a plane to Europe every summer to worry about the tap water, the tourist traps, and the rate of exchange? That's the US these days. How do you beat idiocy like that—just stop thinking about it? What's any better, sitting here or in Mayfair or Richmond mewling about it?"

"It's a terrible way to live. It is!"

"So it's a terrible way to live. So what? The fringes always are, aren't they? Whether you're talking about Majorca, Berlin, or Kensington. Pullendorf too. A rotten way to live, but you get used to that, too. It'll always be that way for most of us. What's going to change that? Nothing. Not as long as they push your life to the limit. So you go there too—to show them—to beat them in limbo at their own filthy game. To cut their throat the way they'd cut yours. That's how it works." He was looking across the terrace towards a tall young Englishman in a Shetland sweater who'd just come around the corner of the house. He was carrying a small gray poodle and a wire traveling cage. He disappeared into the house.

"And you?" she asked after a minute. "What about you? What were your reasons?"

"You just heard my reasons," he said. "They don't matter now. It's finished. They beat me at it. I lost the game. It's over."

"Does it matter that they did?" she asked. He was looking down through the trees towards the rear meadow, his jaw locked, his eyes narrowed now, but not from the sun.

"No," he replied finally.

"And Berlin? No more Berlins? None of that? That's finished too, all of it?"

"That's finished too."

"Then it's all finished. That's what I want to know. That it's all finished and done with."

The wind blew across the terrace. Behind them the conversation from inside the house lifted and fell. The door at the far end of the terrace opened and the guests came out onto the flagstones, carrying their glasses out into the bright spring sunshine.

"Let's go somewhere," Plummer said. "I can't sit here, not like this."

They drove down through the tree-lined lanes away from the village. He parked the Rover on the verges near a small stone bridge and they climbed down the bank to a small clamshell of turf. The lake lay beyond, fringed with trees. The waters of the lake brimmed over a small stone spillway and under the bridge. She sank down on the grass among the trees.

"There's nothing to what I have to do," Plummer said. "It may take a few weeks, that's all."

"You said you're going back to America."

"Something like that." She turned abruptly and looked up at him.

"And that's all?"

"All I know of now." He walked down to the water's edge and stood looking out across the lake. Finally he turned. "Look—"

"I'm not any good at games. I'm not. I'm sorry but I'm not. I won't ask anymore."

"I haven't finished yet. Berlin's not over."

"I said I wouldn't ask."

"I want you to understand."

"Why haven't you finished? Why isn't it done?" When he didn't answer, she said, "You'll be doing the same thing, won't you—here, in London. The same thing, all over again. They want you to do something else." Her eyes were as dark as his in the afternoon sunlight. "I'm trying to understand," she cried.

"I'm trying to understand too. In two hours it'll be over for you. Finished. You're going to Majorca. Buxton'll be there too. What then? In two hours I've got to be back in London."

"Stop taking so much for granted. I'm trying to understand your own plans and I can't. I simply can't."

"I can't leave London because it's not finished. Does that simplify it? It isn't finished yet. There's still a piece left. A loose end. Okay, so I'll be used. They want to use me. They've figured out a way to get me to help them, to make me believe what they want me to believe. That's okay. I'm used to that. When you do something well, you keep at it. Something small and trivial, like Pullendorf, something no one cares about. But I'll beat the bastards this time."

She gazed up at him, searching his face. "Beat them? Whom? I don't understand. Beat them? Do you mean that's all there is to it? All that it's ever meant to you? To beat them? Just that and nothing else?"

"This is different."

"You're not serious. You can't be." She searched his face, hearing words which no longer had any meaning for her, hearing again after all those years the savagery behind them, like faraway thunder, bringing on the storm. She remembered Pullendorf, the Hungarian lying in the rain, the man in the upstairs hall outside her room. She remembered the rear garden in Kent when she was a child, the cold wind turning dark leaves to light as storm clouds blew in from the sea. She sat in the blank sunshine, her mind a vacuum, holding only the ugly words, the mindless complacent insanity of it all. She looked away, turning for the reassurance of the quiet Sussex lake and the bordering trees, the gambrel roofs that showed in the distance.

Her shoulders were as slim as ever and the long curve of her neck as graceful as Plummer had always remembered. She didn't move for a long time, her head held away from him. The sun had dropped into the tops of the trees; the shadows were deep on the grass. She wiped her eyes with the limp crown of the tennis hat and got to her feet. They moved down the bank towards the small wooden jetty. "We've had the entire afternoon and what have we done with it?" she said disconsolately.

"An afternoon isn't enough. I'm not ready to go, not until we work it out."

"I'll never understand. People push their lives so, you said—to the limit. Isn't that what you've done? Isn't that what you're about to do? It's terrifying and ugly. You hate it so—I know you do—as if there were nothing left. That's what's so terrible and hateful, that you could feel that and nothing more. Malice. Drawing your life through the eye of its needle."

"It's not that way." She didn't answer. "In a few weeks we could leave."

She was looking out over the lake. "Why not Majorca? You could come there. You could forget about everything else for a while."

"What do I do while I'm thinking about it—carry the bags, tip the bellboys, keep the cats off the back fence on your wedding night?"

"The trip would do you good."

"Those people aren't my mob."

"I know that. I wasn't thinking of it that way."

"We could go someplace else."

"And the rest of it—beating them, all of that?"

"It was finished once. Years ago. Now it's something else. Don't ask. Let's just get the hell out."

She lifted her eyes. "It's not simply a matter of going away for a few weeks or months together."

"I wouldn't have asked you if it were."

"It's so easy to say now, isn't it? So easy to say and then to pretend that it's true for a few days or a few weeks. But that's not what I want. That's not what I want at all."

She was silent during the drive back to the house. Both had forgotten the time. Plummer turned back on the long lane. Loose pebbles and fine gravel rattled like birdshot against the undercarriage. Janet Gwenhogg was waiting anxiously in the courtyard, standing with two other couples near the lifted trunk of a gray Humber. Some of the other automobiles had gone.

"We've been out of our minds," she exclaimed. "We've searched all over for the two of you. Where on earth have you been? We're ready to leave." Plummer leaned across the seat and opened the door for Elizabeth.

"You've loaded my luggage?" she asked Peggy.

"Peter's gone to fetch it. Don't worry, pet. He'll manage it."

Elizabeth turned to Plummer. "I can't. I simply can't leave like this."

"I'll be back. Wait for me. Thirty minutes, that's all."

"But there's simply no time, no time at all," Janet protested.

"Caravan taking shape, is it?" Fothingill said, standing unsteadily near the car window. He smelled of malt whiskey and was slightly drunk. Elizabeth slipped from the car and ran across the courtyard, carrying her hat.

"It's too much," Janet complained. "Such a hectic day. And now you're leaving. It's a matter of *sauve qui peut* now, isn't it?" she smiled. "We'll survive, I'm sure. Do look us up in Berlin."

"Good-bye, Janet," Plummer said.

He drove into the village and found the two Special Branch men in a pub, watching television. He told them that he wouldn't be driving back to London for another hour or more, and that he wanted to drive back alone. He suggested that they call Ivor Simpson in London, tell him to call off their eight o'clock meeting at Ivor's office, and reschedule it for the following day. He told them to go back to London without waiting for him. "Not bloody likely," said the shorter Special Branch man suspiciously. Neither wanted to call their control center at Scotland Yard for instructions, so Plummer crossed the road to the lobby of a small inn and called Ivor Simpson in London while the two detectives waited nearby. Ivor was skeptical at first, but Plummer was insistent.

"You can have your meeting tomorrow," he told him. "I need more time."

"Time for what?" Ivor's voice came back uneasily. He knew Ivor was still suspicious. He'd seen it in his face as they flew back from Frankfurt; he'd discovered it in his silence during the days that followed.

"I'm in Sussex, for God's sake! Nothing's happening in Sussex. I'll be back in London by ten." Ivor said he would talk to a few people and call him back.

Plummer waited for his call, standing in the bay window of the lobby and looking out into the narrow road. On an open green three small boys were trying to run a kite aloft; a few elderly couples had taken to the benches nearby in the fading afternoon sunlight. There was no wind. It was an unseasonable day and the weather wouldn't last. He supposed that Ivor was talking to Roger Cornelius now, trying to guess what was on his mind. Roger would reassure Ivor: it was his deception after all. Why should he believe it hadn't worked? But he knew Ivor wasn't sure. Until he finally ran Wulf to ground he'd never be sure that the Frankfurt deception had worked, and that Plummer wasn't deceiving them, biding his time until he could get to Wulf and warn him off. Ivor was right, of course. Plummer watched the kite lift into the sky, veer suddenly in a ground loop and spiral back to the turf. He knew what Roger and Ivor wanted. They wanted what Chambers had always wanted—to bring Wulf into the West, debrief him, give him a false sense of security, and send him back into East Germany again as their agent. Solo didn't matter anymore: he was expendable now, like everyone else. He wondered about Chambers, whether the heart attack was genuine or had been faked too, like everything else.

A blue sightseeing bus stopped near the hotel, and a group of foreign tourists disembarked. Some had cameras around their necks. They looked like Swedes or Danes on holiday, returning to their London hotel after a day in the salt air at Brighton or Eastbourne. The girls and women had straw-colored hair, and were thin-legged. A few came into the tearoom. He didn't move from the window, watching the fading sunlight stream across the roofs and ignite the windows of the old cottages. Somewhere a churchbell tolled the hour.

When you did something well, you kept at it, he had told Elizabeth. Was that truly what he meant? And if you couldn't, where could you hide these days? In a village like this one, with cobblestones outside your front door, and a tea shop down the lane? Was it any different in Stockholm, where the tourists were going? In Oslo, Cambridge, or Lake Forest? A terrible way to live but the fringes always were, he had told her. In Notting Hill or Newark, Georgetown, Pebble Beach, your fringes or mine, he should have said, poverty or indulgence; the desperation was the same. The same fringes. They always would be, in every place and every time; people, like nations, pushing their lives to the limit, and then standing in terror at the vacuum on the other side: in a frozen alley in Treptow, on an Italian hillside, at a Manhattan dressing table, finding in the mirror a dying face whose promise could never be reclaimed, listening in terror to the idle chic of the cocktail chatter waiting below. Standing numb and blind in a frozen East Berlin cul-de-sac or the snowy wastes of Novaya Zemlya, watching Khrushchev's megatons bloody the Arctic dawn. Take your choice: your fringes or mine. Watch that or watch your breath take shape on a Connecticut windowpane on a Sunday night as you stare into a winter swimming pool, full of old snow and winter leaves—the bottle finished, the television turned off, the weekend over. Scratch quietly enough and it was everywhere.

Beat them at their own game. Beat them all, even if winning meant only survival, nothing more.

The phone rang and Plummer went back to the desk. It was Ivor from London. He said that they had postponed the meeting until the following day; Plummer could take his time coming back. The Special Branch team would have to stay with him—Chatwood's orders.

Plummer knew Ivor was still uneasy. The two Special Branch men followed him in their car out of the village, but drew aside on the shoulder near the lane back to the house. They waited in the car, the engine off. He continued on alone and turned back along the driveway under the trees. The cars were gone from the courtyard. The old house was empty, its ugly Victorian iron black against the bright sky. The dying sun flamed a few small windows high on the eaves. A few pigeons and swallows soared near an old stone turret. The heavy front door was locked, and he made his way around the side of the house, between a few flower beds, and through a trellised colonnade to the stone steps leading up to the back terrace. Far in the distance the downs were still bathed in sunlight beyond the meadow, but the darkness had deepened in the back garden under the trees. It was chilly in the shadows.

She was sitting alone next to the stone wall where she had sat that afternoon, white hat on her lap.

"It's cold," he said. "You didn't get a coat."

"I didn't dare, I suppose," she replied looking down at the hat. His scarf lay under it. She sat looking at the scarf. "There was a terrible row. I can still hear it."

"I should have stayed."

"No, it was better this way. It was no use anymore, no use pretending. One grows utterly tired of the arrangements others make, utterly exhausted. There comes a time when one must do something." She studied the scarf in her hands, examining the frayed herringbone of weave, her fingers exploring the frayed ends. "You left your scarf here.

Was it deliberate?" She looked up with a brief smile. "I always knew it would be like this, the two of us this way—no plans made, nothing certain anymore." She smiled again and touched the scarf to her chin, raising her head. "I shan't pretend I'll grow accustomed to it quickly, but I shall."

Night was coming on. He took off his coat and put it over her shoulders. "What have you been thinking about?"

"Where we shall go. What we'll do."

"Where would you like to go?"

"After London? A long holiday someplace. Someplace simple."

"And after that?"

"Someplace simpler still."

"Maybe my castle at Ballygoran, my loch at Orkney." She didn't answer. "Maybe Virginia—the Rappahannock." He watched her face.

"Something like that. Would it suit you? I should like very much to see it."

"We could try it."

"Yes," she said. "We could try it."

Elizabeth stayed in London with a cousin. Plummer lived in a rented house in Kensington that belonged to one of Ivor Simpson's colleagues posted to Turkey. He saw Elizabeth almost every evening, sometimes at her cousin's flat, sometimes at the house in Kensington. She met Roger Cornelius and Ivor Simpson there one chilly evening, the first time she had seen them since they visited her office in Berlin. They had drinks together in the small sitting room. Roger was in a cordial mood, the business of the day forgotten; Ivor was as guarded as ever. Roger asked Elizabeth if she'd ever visited the US. She said she hadn't but was looking forward to it. They moved to the rear sunporch where Elizabeth and Plummer sat on a rattan couch, surrounded by towering green plants, listening to Roger reminisce for Elizabeth's benefit about his many journeys back and forth across the Atlantic. In the old DC-3 days you flew from London to Ireland and on to Iceland, to Gander or Goose Bay. "But Gander no longer matters now," Roger explained with a smile—the cold wastes and the frozen lakes below where he'd fished with his father for salmon and brown trout. "Now at thirty-six thousand feet you seldom see it, a faint cuticle of something, no longer than an ice sliver in the frozen daiquiri on the 707 tray in front of you. But the lake hasn't changed its dimensions—not the lake, not the salmon either."

Ivor said he preferred the old days.

"It isn't whether you prefer one to the other," Roger explained. Travel was simply proof of the other dimension to a world that was out-racing them all, a dimension that made diplomatic decisions more difficult, military decisions infinitely more complex. Intercept times must be computed, counter-strokes considered. The principle political challenge of the time was to find ways to make that new dimension inhabitable.

"Inhabitable?" Elizabeth asked.

"Inhabitable," Roger said quietly, "to buy back cubits of time in which men can breathe, can calculate their options and choose from the alternatives at hand, say farewell or good-bye, raise families if they were lucky," he smiled, "watch the olive trees grow."

It was all for Elizabeth's benefit, but Plummer knew why Roger was so expansive that evening. They had been working on it all day, and now it was in Roger's face—a sort of energy, a conviction, a dynamism, like the hum of an electrical field. They'd prepared for the CIA liaison officer at the embassy a summary of a debriefing of an East German defector who'd been shipped to Washington the previous autumn. He'd headed the Western European Division in the *Hauptverwaltung Aufklanung* and had collaborated with the KGB station at Karlshorst, running a few networks in West Germany. Among the list of possible Soviet agents he'd passed to Roger's division was the name of a British intelligence officer at the Olympic stadium in West Berlin. The evidence was circumstantial. The East Germans had tried to recruit an English secretary working in the same office, but had been warned off by the KGB. The defector had concluded that the Brit was already a Soviet agent and didn't want to risk compromising him. The East German's debriefing had been closely held for almost six months, but Roger had doctored it for passing to the British. He was tired of waiting for Solo and wanted to smoke him out. Ivor thought it was premature, but agreed to make certain that Solo was on the secret registry's reading list when the material was passed to British intelligence services the following day.

After Roger and Ivor left, Elizabeth was unusually quiet. Plummer had already told her about East Berlin and Frankfurt, and she knew what he intended to do in London. She accepted his determination to reach the Russian before Cornelius and Simpson could, but the deception at Frankfurt puzzled her. Seeing Roger Cornelius and Simpson again for the first time since they had visited her offices in Berlin, she was troubled.

They drove to a small restaurant in Chelsea for dinner. Elizabeth had borrowed her cousin's small cream-colored MG. For the first time since their return to London they weren't accompanied by a Special Branch car. She hardly seemed to notice.

They found a candlelit booth at the rear of the restaurant. After she put aside the menu, she said, "Is there no one else who can possibly help? Must it be you?"

Plummer said there wasn't anyone else. She wasn't satisfied with the answer. "You're sure then that they've misled you. You're utterly convinced that they deliberately deceived you at Frankfurt?"

"They rolled me at Frankfurt. Roger, Ivor, everyone else."

Rolled? She didn't know the word.

"Like a drunk in the gutter, the kind that are too far gone to know whether their pockets are being picked or not. The ones you can kick senseless and not care about. The ones that are finished, burned out, gone to seed—"

"And that's what you believe they did?" she asked.

"They tried."

She sat back against the wooden booth as if she understood. "That's what you meant then when you talked about beating them. That's what you meant in Sussex that afternoon."

"I was talking about getting to him before Cornelius and Simpson do."

"And you despise them for it, for what they've done, for what they're about to do. Or is it something else?"

"What else is there? He's worth saving. He wants to be left alone."

"I was thinking about you," she corrected, her eyes searching his face. He hadn't understood. She saw it immediately. "You said they were only using you," she explained. "You despise them for that. That's the ugly part of it, isn't it—knowing what they must have thought all those years. Isn't that the most destructive part of it, knowing that you can't forgive them for that—for what they must have thought of you all of that time, not as an individual, with rights and feelings, but as something else. It's wicked of them, it's beastly; but it's what it does to you that most frightens me."

"If I don't help him, no one will. Someone is after him right now, the way they were after me that last night in Treptow. I think it's someone from his own services. He doesn't know that. When Cornelius and Simpson run him down, they may not tell him."

"Then why don't you go to Roger Cornelius and Ivor Simpson and tell them precisely that. Tell them everything, the way you've told me." It seemed to her so simple; but seeing his face, she knew it wasn't at all.

"They wouldn't listen," Plummer said. "Then they'd lock me up, out of the way. They'll take any risk they have to take to get him back to East Germany."

"So you can't forgive them, can you? Not until you've shown them in your own fashion. But it's as brutal as their way, isn't it?" She lifted her eyes, waiting. He didn't answer. "Are you sure that it's this Russian that matters most to you, that it's his life you're trying to save, and not something else and not what they might think of you, not simply your own pride and self-respect?" His eyes met hers and for an instant he was puzzled. "I'm sorry, but I must ask you. You mustn't be cross with me. I'm trying to understand. Are you sure it's his life, and not your own, not your own sense of decency and self-respect? Is that what you think they've taken from you?"

"They tried," he said at last.

"But that's enough, isn't it? Yes." She answered her own question and sat back helplessly. "They tried." She looked away. "We could walk away tonight—out that door and down the street. We could simply leave and go away. What they thought wouldn't matter. Nothing else would matter." She turned back to him, but his expression hadn't changed. "You'll never surrender, will you?" she said sadly. "Never. All these years," she remembered painfully, "all the years we were apart. And when we go to Virginia or someplace else, what will it be then?" She smiled despite herself.

"It'll be all right then."

"You can't forgive the others for what they've done. Could you forgive yourself if you failed, too?"

"We'll have tried," he said. "That's all we can do."

"Pushing our lives so," she remembered. "Yes, we'll have tried too."

The CIA documents reached Solo's desk four days later. At eleven o'clock on the following day, he recalled them from the Top Secret Control registry, studied them alone in his office, and personally returned them to registry. At noon he phoned his wife and told her he wouldn't be returning too late that evening. He was going to Oxford to talk to a retired diplomat. He lunched alone at his club and stopped at a telephone booth and placed two calls. The Special Branch/MI5 surveillance team was unable to trace either of the calls.

Simpson thought Solo had taken the bait. So did Chatwood. It had rained heavily that morning, but by one o'clock had begun to clear. Standing at the window of Chatwood's office at Scotland Yard and looking at the broken cloud cover, Roger Cornelius thought there was a good possibility that they might have decent weather all the way. Chatwood said they hadn't seen the last of the rain and that it might muck things up good and proper. He was right. By six o'clock the rain had returned, as monotonous and dreary as ever.

It was raining when Solo left his office near Queen Anne's Gate, wearing a beige raincoat and carrying an umbrella and a small attaché case. He caught a taxi for Grosvenor Square, entered a hotel lobby, climbed the marble stairs, had a whiskey alone at the bar. He left the hotel and walked briskly through the rain to Oxford Street where he entered a department store, made a telephone call from a pay phone in the foyer, strolled through the basement for fifteen minutes or so, made a purchase in the household wares department, and left, carrying a small package. He walked west on Oxford Street, stood for a few minutes in a bus queue, looked at his watch, and changed his mind. He crossed the street and continued west to Park Lane, where he found a taxi. The taxi drove him to Sussex Gardens. Solo left the taxi on West-bourne Terrace and went into a small Italian restaurant.

"Do you know what day it is tomorrow, Ivor?" Chatwood asked suddenly from the front seat of the closed van where they sat, gazing through the rainstreaked windows towards the restaurant.

"Holiday?"

"Precisely," Chatwood breathed. He'd forgotten. "A pound for a penny it's Paddington." He was wearing a dark, belted raincoat, a blue beret, and gum-soled suede shoes, like a North Country schoolteacher on holiday. Roger Cornelius thought he looked suitably predatory; Ivor Simpson, a bit rum. Ivor leaned forward and stared through the tick of the windshield wipers. One of Chatwood's team, a woman in a yellow nylon rain slicker, splashed from a taxi and entered the restaurant a few minutes behind Solo. The rain was coming down in sheets by then, bringing a colder wind with it. They waited in the chilly florist truck, staring out through the windshield. The woman didn't return.

"He's alone, then," Simpson said.

"Can't be sure," Chatwood cautioned. "But I'd wager he is."

Ten minutes later Solo left the restaurant and moved off through the rain, headed for Paddington station.

Until that moment Plummer had waited. Now he was certain. He stood in the monitoring room at control center, listening to the babble of voices from the Special Branch/MI5 communications network. The dour Englishman at the console turned to him with a smile. "No mistake tonight. Paddington it is. That's where he's going. The old fox was right." Plummer nodded and looked at the polychrome map, where a monitor wearing a headset was moving a bright yellow cross to Paddington. A second monitor stood nearby, a telephone cradled against his ear, identifying with smaller red triangles the fleet of prowling trucks, vans, and police cars that were beginning to converge on Paddington station. Plummer turned to one of Chatwood's men standing near the door.

"Is there a head around here?"

"Sorry?"

"A head. A WC?"

"End of the hall," he said, "then to your right." He watched Plummer go out, a little amused.

"Who was that?" an MI5 man asked.

"The Yank," he said. "About to wet his ruddy britches."

Plummer ducked into a darkened office down the hall and made a phone call. He found the stairs, took the last flight of steps in four leaps, and bounded like a cat down the long carpeted corridor. A steel gate was pulled across the entrance where the marble foyer began and he slid to it just as the police custodian arose from the lighted desk in the guard office. He came into the corridor, buttoning his shiny serge jacket. "In a hurry, eh? Shouldn't be. Wet out—filthy night. Visitors out the front unless you have a pass. Sorry." It was a constable's voice, as warm as buttered rum, trained to soothe the ire of outraged housewives, angry shopkeepers victimized by smash-and-grab, dignified dowagers with rumpled fenders. "Back door this is, sorry. Have to ring upstairs."

Plummer had turned with a quick, ugly smile. The constable suddenly found himself too close, tried to back away, but the legs were slow, the reflexes stiff. He was standing as flat-footed as a barrel of nails when Plummer hit him. The blow struck him amidships. He never saw it coming. It suddenly crushed the strength from his body, stood him rigidly against the wall, and lifted him onto his toes, fluttering his swimming eyes back into the wet red silk of his skull. Plummer leaped up the wicket gate and kicked himself to the top seven feet above. He was lifting his heels carefully over the ugly lance tips when the heavy oak door was unlocked from outside, and a small man in a raincoat pushed into the vestibule, his gloved hand still clutching at the key in the lock. In one arm was a stack of mimeographed documents protected from the rain by a sheer plastic skin. Balanced atop the papers were four cardboard tea containers and two bags of chips. The key was stubborn this night and wouldn't withdraw. He settled his shoe against the base of the door and tugged. "Give it up, you bleeding—" He heard the creak of bowing iron, like the sound a child's iron swing makes with a heavy body flung out at its apogee, lifted his eyes, and saw a dark ceiling collapsing upon him from the shadows. "Jesus God, Mother of—" The words were drowned in the bubble of his voice as he was swept backwards out through the yawning door. He vanished into the shrubbery next to the rear stoop, a blizzard of white papers fluttering over the thrashing boughs like gulls over a dropped seine.

Plummer raced up the lamplit street towards the corner. He found traffic moving on the boulevard beyond, but Elizabeth's MG wasn't there. A taxi had drawn to a stop at the curb near the corner. Plummer moved to a sprint. An umbrella was being eased closed gingerly when its owner felt a sudden jolt, grunted involuntarily from the excruciating pain in his ribcage, and thrashed sideways as he lost his balance, dragging one polished oxford in the trickling gutter, and sat down heavily on the curb. "Damn! In the name of heaven!"

The young taxi driver heard the cry, raised himself curiously to look back, but the door slammed shut and a cold, heaving voice was at his neck. "Paddington station. Move!"

"This ain't no bleeding ambulance, mate."

"It is tonight. Move your ass. Kick it right through the floor."

Chatwood deployed six men to the front entrance of the station and left the panel truck in the blowing rain, Cornelius and Simpson splashing after him. They entered through the service passageway. It was poorly lit, heavy with carbon monoxide and the smell of oiled concrete. Two of Chatwood's men were moving an iron-wheeled baggage cart across the alleyway to interdict vehicle traffic. The huge old station beyond was crowded with holiday-bound commuters. At the far end of the station beyond the iron gates two trains shunted out slowly, steam boiling up from the undercarriages. Chatwood eased through the crowd, moving his head slowly as he walked, a pair of donnish spectacles on his nose. One hand was thrust into his pocket; the other carried a briefcase. Inside the briefcase was a small two-way radio; the tartan scarf about his neck held a small lapel microphone. Roger Cornelius trailed after him leisurely, and Ivor Simpson followed. Cornelius hadn't drawn a deep breath since they'd left the panel truck. He stopped and forced himself to exhale, like a diver blowing his ears. He took a deeper breath as Simpson passed him ten meters away, drawing into his lungs the smells of jetting steam, old iron and mortar, citrus, and coal smoke. Someone passed him with a jolt, running for a distant train gate, and Roger jerked his head. Chatwood and Ivor were ahead of him, still moving calmly through the crowd. He was moved a second time by a late passanger, and he realized that he was adrift, his own steps as random as the irregular Brownian motion of the late evening crowd across the wet floor. He concentrated carefully on Chatwood and Ivor. Both had stopped and moved forward again. Both were drifting towards the station bookstore and fruit stand. In front of the bookstore a man in a green Alpine hat stood looking at the evening papers in the vending rack. Like the woman in the yellow raincoat, he had been at the morning brief at the Yard.

Solo was in the bookstore. Ivor had found Chatwood's right flank and stood at the fruit stand. He bought an apple, crossed to a row of benches, and sat down with the evening paper. Roger took a magazine from his pocket and moved to a closer bench and found a seat.

"We won't make it, mate. Not in this bleeding traffic." The cabby turned, less than two blocks from where Plummer had climbed in. Cars were waiting a dozen deep in the lane ahead. Through the rain-streaked windshield, Plummer saw a flashing light interdicting traffic in the right lane where two cars had collided.

"Back out."

"Not unless you've got wings." Cars had blocked them from the rear. Plummer flung a bank note through the window and went out the door. He raced up the curb through the unmoving line of headlights and crossed the intersection. He waited on the opposite curb, searching for a taxi. As the light changed, he moved out into the boulevard. A dozen cars rumbled past, but no taxi. The light changed again. Looking down the intersecting street, he saw the small cream-colored MG. He sprinted across the roadbed against the light and into the headlights of the oncoming cars. The MG slid sideways on the wet street as Elizabeth slammed on the brakes. Plummer wrung the door open and was in the bucket seat alongside.

"Are you all right?" She turned.

"I'm fine," he said. "Paddington station. Do you know it from here?"

"I think so. I was completely turned around for a moment. You're drenched."

"I'm okay." She looked at his rain-soaked head and pulled the scarf from her neck.

"You'll catch pneumonia," she said. She heard the angry din of horns behind her. "Oh shut up," she said, slamming the car into gear again. The MG bolted forward. "Do we have much time?"

"Not much."

"Oh, dear." She careened around a corner and through an amber caution light twenty meters beyond. The tall frame of an old brewery truck lumbered across her bow, but she whipped the car behind it without braking and was gone. "This brutal rain. I absolutely couldn't find the right street corner after you called. Then there was an accident."

"I saw it."

"I think we've both taken leave of our senses," she said, hunched forward slightly, moving her skirt back from her knees. Plummer laughed. "What is it?" Her eyes didn't leave the road, but she smiled. "What is it? Do I look a fright? I'm sure I must."

"You look fine." He leaned forward and wiped the mist from the windshield in front of her.

"Who will be at Paddington? There won't be a dreadful row, will there?"

"Inspector Chatwood. Simpson. Roger. Phil Chambers too, probably."

"Mr. Chambers! But I thought he'd had a heart attack."

"There wasn't any heart attack," Plummer said. "He's here—someplace in London. I can smell him."

"There will be a row, then."

"Not if we get there first." She sprinted beyond a bus that straddled the center lane and whipped neatly back through the closing gap made by a pair of onrushing headlights, oblivious to the car's horn.

"I don't think I quite understand. I'm certain I won't, either, until you explain it to me. It's senseless, all of it. Racing through London like this. It's terrifying."

"You're doing fine."

She was pleased. "Do you really think so? That's lovely." She shifted down at the next corner, pulled her skirt away from her knees again, and shot forward into the dark tunnel of boulevard beyond. "But you shouldn't say so," she smiled. "I'll lose my concentration. It's really not my cup of tea, David."

Roger studied Chatwood above his magazine, barely conscious of the din around him. A young English girl sat next to him, listening to the tinny, perforated music from a small transistor radio which she occasionally held to her ear. He looked away, trying to forget the music, deciding whether he should move or not, when Chatwood turned. He looked directly at Roger, a cold, angry, penetrating look, and for an instant he was bewildered. *Had they missed him?*

Solo had left the bookstore and had collided with someone near the door. Something had fallen to the concrete—a book, a shopping bag, a folded newspaper. Apologies then; a mutter of dismay; a quick exchange of capsized possessions, and that was all. Ivor Simpson had watched it, had identified the man approaching the bookstore even before the exchange had taken place. Roger Cornelius saw only the retreating back, moving through the crowd towards the center of the station. In the other direction Solo was moving towards the Oxford train. He passed through the gate and disappeared into a rear coach. Roger Cornelius got to his feet, moving with Ivor in the direction of the retreating Russian. He moved without haste, mixing with the damp holiday crowd, his silhouette indistinguishable from the hundreds of others moving under the station dome, as if his work had been accomplished so perfectly that the evidence had perished with its execution, like a meteor burning itself out in the night sky, leaving only a momentary wink to puzzle the brain long after the ashes had burned themselves to dust.

He moved to the far corner of the station and stood in front of the windows of the meat-pie counter, looking at the hand-chalked sandwich board above the green window frame. He bought a hot beef-and-tomato sandwich from the fat woman behind the counter, took a mug of hot tea, and carried both to the aluminum trolley nearby, where he stood alone, looking out across the station floor. He put a corner of the sandwich in his mouth, still looking gravely across the crowds moving towards the train gate. He drank from the steaming tea cup. His face was still wet from the rain, his raincoat dark at the shoulders, his blond hair damp, his shoes as soggy as those of any other Londoner who had come to Paddington that night.

Roger approached him from the rear, carrying a tea mug from the sandwich counter. He faced him across the aluminum trolley, looking at the high cheekbones, the damp face, and the distant, unfathomable gray eyes. The facelessness of the photographs and the dossiers was gone; anonymity dissolved, and the man who was in part real and in part fictitious was in front of him now. Strekov felt Cornelius's gaze. The glance was brief, cool, and wholly detached. Then he raised the steaming tea cup and drank again.

"We'd like to have a word with you," Roger said quietly. "You don't know who I am, but I know who you are and why you're here."

Strekov looked at him without expression. "I'm sorry. Were you speaking to me?" The accent, like that of almost all Russians who spoke English, was American. Ivor Simpson had joined them, carrying a tea mug.

"Keep your hands on the trolley," Ivor said quietly. "We're as thick as terriers hereabouts and it wouldn't really do." Strekov turned to him. Ivor smiled, almost apologetically. "My name is Simpson from Special Branch. We'd like to have a chat. It's rather serious, I'm afraid. Violation of the Official Secrets Act." Ivor stirred his tea.

Strekov remained immobile, holding the mug of tea, his head turned away as he looked out over the station. The coat cuff was frayed. The hand was strong; the shirt wrinkled, the suit as gray and nondescript as that of any other Londoner who might be having his supper in this tawdry corner of Paddington on a wet evening. Strekov stared out across the gray distances as if listening for something, as if waiting for someone; but there was nothing—only the crowd, the coal smoke, and the rain-sluiced streets beyond. He put the cup down and his hand shrank away without leaving the table. Ivor took the small plastic briefcase from in front of Strekov and put it under his arm.

"Finish your tea if you like," he suggested. "Then we can go someplace and chat for a bit." He sipped from his own tea mug. "You managed it rather splendidly in Berlin, I must say. Quite remarkable. But London is different these days, you know. Despite the confusion. Off to your left you'll see a baggage corridor. We'll go that way, if you don't mind. There's a car waiting. A black sedan. You'll go first. We'll follow. But not too quickly, you understand. The Oxford train should be leaving shortly. We'll go when it does."

From the shadows nearby at the edge of the baggage tunnel, Phil Chambers watched the three men at the sandwich trolley. The sedan waited twenty yards behind him. In front of him were two iron-wheeled luggage carts piled with mail sacks. Five Special Branch and MI5 men stood nearby, some wearing coveralls. The rain was still coming down and a fine cold spray blew back the tunnel from the wet street. Chatwood had left the bench near the bookstore and was moving across the station towards the tunnel. A moment later Chambers heard footsteps behind him. He turned and saw, pushing past the sedan, a figure who thrust a Special Branch officer aside and bolted towards him. Momentarily confused, Chambers retreated a few steps towards the baggage carts before he recognized Plummer's face. A constable was at Plummer's heels.

"Grab him!" Chambers cried. "Don't let him through!"

"Just a minute there, lad!" a Special Branch officer called, moving in front of Plummer, arms raised. Plummer was still moving. He smothered the grappling fingers first and then slammed through his face like a mattress full of bricks.

"Catch him, quick!" another officer cried. An MI5 man in blue coveralls leaped on Plummer's back from the baggage cart, carrying him sideways into the masonry wall.

Plummer saw Chambers. "Phil, you goddamn lying bastard!" An arm was about his throat. "You can't do it! Listen!" The two officers carried him backwards. Another two joined them, trying to pull Plummer's raglan down across his shoulders. Plummer doubled forward, dropped his head and shoulders, and slammed sideways into the picket of grappling fingers, hands and arms, elbows high. He freed one arm and flung it out, still trying to turn back towards Chambers. The blow hit a thin, raincoated policeman like a hammer and crumpled him.

"Stop it!" Chambers cried out. "Goddamnit—"

"You bastards!" Plummer shouted, his arms pinned for a moment. A heavyset Special Branch officer pinned his forearm against Plummer's neck and hit him twice in the face. Chambers saw the blood along Plummer's cheek. A Special Branch officer in coveralls was riding Plummer's back; but a moment later Plummer straightened, threw him higher on his shoulders, and drove backwards viciously against the wall. Chambers heard ribs pop, a sickening grunt, and the limp hands slid from the shoulders as the man in overalls dropped to the floor.

"It's too late," Chambers called hopelessly. "It's over, goddamnit."

Across the station the Oxford train was leaving. Chatwood stood in the entrance to the tunnel. "They're coming." His voice died in his throat. There were eight men in the alleyway, moving against Plummer from both sides. The heavyset Special Branch officer, his square face swollen and cut, moved against Plummer like a light-heavyweight at a body bag, grunting with each short heavy blow. Plummer's arms and shoulders were held. "Finish it," Chatwood said. "Finish it, for God's sake!" Plummer was still swaying, trying to rise, and the man holding the heaving shoulders let go with one hand and smashed him with a leather-covered sap behind his right ear.

"Move the car forward," Chatwood called. "Quickly." The sedan came slowly up the tunnelway. Plummer lay along the wall, face down. He didn't move. Blood welled behind his ear, down his neck, and gathered along his collar. One of the Special Branch men flung his coat over his body as the car rolled by.

"Here they are."

"David? David!" A woman's voice came from the far end of the corridor. "David?"

The three men came into the alleyway from the station and got into the backseat of the sedan. Roger Cornelius saw Chambers's face in the weak light of the tunnel and hesitated. Beyond he saw a half-dozen figures standing silently against the wall. "What is it?" he asked. Chambers only shook his head. Chatwood got into the front seat and a moment later the car backed out.

She stood aside as the car moved past her, without looking in, and when it was gone, walked back down the passageway. "David," she called again. A man was standing in the corridor near the baggage cart, his hands in his pocket. A group of workers were standing beyond. "I'm looking for someone," she said.

"We'd better bring the ambulance," one of the men said to Chambers, who only nodded, still looking at the woman's face.

"He's over here," he said woodenly, and walked over to the wall where Plummer lay. Two Special Branch men were kneeling at his side. One pulled away the coat. She pushed between them and dropped beside him. Together they turned him over.

Chambers stood gazing down at the figure, but when they had turned Plummer over and she sat on the dirty pavement, cradling his head, he went back down the corridor to where the rain was falling, letting the mist blow across his face, letting the rain hide the emptiness of his mind. He was still standing there when the ambulance came.

TWELVE

It was after three o'clock in the morning when Chambers was summoned from the interrogation room. They had been with Strekov for over three hours by then and had nothing to show for it. The room was still in semidarkness, half-illuminated by the glow from the film projector near Strekov's chair. Roger Cornelius had reviewed for him every film Plummer had received in East Berlin—its technical detail, its significance for US analysts, where it had been received: date, time, deaddrop. Strekov had said nothing to suggest that the films held the slightest interest for him. In the room also were a Russian linguist from Washington, two Agency weapons specialists ready to assist Roger with a few of the more technical details from his briefing book, and Inspector Chatwood and his senior deputy. They sat in the shadows, watching Strekov's face as they listened to Roger's voice carry it alone.

In the room outside Chambers found Ivor Simpson waiting with a Special Branch officer. They'd traced the documents Strekov had had with him when he'd been picked up at Paddington. He'd arrived in London six weeks earlier as a landed immigrant from Hamburg. He had a flat in Ealing and a small office nearby where he traded in surgical and scientific instruments from the continent. His name was Herman Cook. Chambers looked at the report and gave it back to Ivor. "It can wait," he said. Ivor nodded and the Special Branchman turned and left. On the table between the drawn chairs were bottles of whiskey and vodka, a soda siphon, an ice bucket, and a few crystal tumblers. They were Roger's idea—a small celebration after they'd broken Strekov's story, and he'd agreed to cooperate—but now Roger's optimism seemed merely pathetic. Chambers stood looking at the bottles, his head throbbing, his mouth dry. Too much had happened. He felt suddenly isolated from the interrogation in the next room, from the strategies that had led them there—isolated, betrayed, and inconsequential—the triumph smashed. Outside the rain drummed lightly against the window and washed down the slate roof.

"No luck, eh?" Ivor asked.

"Cold as a fish," Chambers muttered, "not a word. I've never met anyone like him." He took a glass, filled it with ice, broke the seal on Roger's ceremonial bottle, and poured a drink. "Never."

Ivor took the bottle. "I don't suppose we ever will again," he added. "How long can Roger keep at it?"

"All night I suppose. It's the time factor that worries him. He may have a plane to catch, a handpass somewhere."

They stood in silence, nursing their drinks. "The man's an enigma," Ivor said after a time. "A complete enigma. I had my doubts that he'd come around. Those chaps never do—schooled the way they are. How's Plummer by the way?"

"A slight concussion. A few broken ribs."

"Sorry. I understand we've two constables at Paddington Hospital. One with a ruptured spleen. Too bad. The chap deserved better. Frightful scene, I gather. Incredible man, Plummer. Almost pulled it off, didn't he? I had my doubts that he ever bought Roger's story at Frankfurt. Saw right through it. Where is he, by the way?"

"US hospital at the air base." The door opened and Ivor turned to see Chatwood's deputy standing in the door.

"Cornelius wants you both," he said. "You two and the inspector. Everyone else out." They left their drinks on the table and went back into the interrogation room where Roger and Chatwood were talking quietly near the door. Strekov sat alone in the center of the room. Ivor gave Roger the Special Branch report on Herman Cook. Roger read it as he moved back to the brown leather armchair. He sat down, still reading, and when he had finished, put it in his briefing book. The Russian linguist and the two weapons specialists had left. Chambers, Ivor Simpson, and Inspector Chatwood took their seats next to Roger.

"As I said a few minutes ago," Roger began, "Solo no longer matters to us. He's unimportant. We could live with him another year, another two years, or another ten years if we had to. What he's done here isn't important to us; what he could do in the years ahead wouldn't change things either." Strekov watched him without moving. "There are dozens of Solos about—here in London, in Paris, at NATO headquarters, in Brussels or Bonn. We don't care about Solo. He's not so much a man as an attitude—a pathology, if you will. You probably know that. You recognize him for what he is, I'm sure." Roger waited for Strekov to reply, but Strekov said nothing.

"We don't care about Solo," Roger continued finally, "but we care about you. We care about you and what you've done for us. We tried to repay you when you were in East Berlin . . . to repay you by protecting you. From the very first, that was our principal concern—to protect you. Phil Chambers was the man principally responsible"—he turned briefly to Chambers—"but it was a matter of concern to everyone involved." Strekov looked curiously at Chambers. "Let's go back a few months," Roger began again, sinking back in his chair. "Let's go back to Berlin a few months after the Wall was built. Try to put yourself in our position. We're faced with an impossible task: trying to protect an agent on the other side of the Wall who refuses any sort of collaboration except on his own terms, whose motivation defies analysis in the traditional sense—an *acte gratuité*, if you will." Roger Cornelius saw the flicker of recognition in Strekov's eyes. "You understand what I'm saying?"

"I understand."

"So here is what we were faced with—a man who refused to identify himself, who refused to come out of the darkness and into the light, who was arrogant, contemptuous, or proud enough to ignore our pleas for prudence, for safeguards, for the simplest kind of intelligence security, and yet someone who continued in his own reckless way, as you did, to provide us with intelligence of that daring, that sophistication, that genius. For himself, he took nothing; he asked nothing. How can you cope with this rationally? You can't. Not really. Yet that was Phil Chambers's operational problem. It was our problem too, a problem we couldn't solve for some time. Phil Chambers finally cracked it for us. He isn't a ruthless man, not at all cruel, but he is efficient, and in the end he found a simple solution. He compromised himself. He gave you information. He passed to you documents which would enable you to claim that he was giving you intelligence information, not the other way around. It was NATO information for the most part, the sort of thing the East German services are interested in, but it was wholly insignificant in terms of what you were providing us. But at any given moment this NATO material would have enabled you to prove that Plummer and Phil were *your* agents, providing you with essential information on NATO activities at the time of the Berlin crisis last December and January. We don't know whether you passed it on or not. But it was an honest effort on our part to shield you."

"I know what it was designed to do," Strekov interrupted. "That was obvious to me. But you didn't tell your man Plummer that, did you?"

"No," Roger said. Strekov wasn't surprised by his admission. The others were; they sat in stunned silence. Phil Chambers was the last to accept its significance. It had been revealed so casually, so matter-of-factly. "It would only have worked had Plummer not known," Roger said quietly. "It would have been beyond him otherwise. He could never have pretended what he didn't believe."

"You expected him to be arrested?" Strekov asked.

"It seemed a possibility to us, yes, but then it always does."

"He would have despised you for it," he said coolly. "I'm very tired. What is it you want of me?" He looked distastefully at Chambers, at Ivor Simpson, and then back at Cornelius.

"What you want for yourself. It's up to you now."

"What are my choices?"

Roger held up three fingers. "You have three. You can refuse to acknowledge that you provided Plummer with the film and insist that you know nothing, in which case you'll be arrested along with Solo." He paused. "I take it you're now willing to concede that." Strekov didn't reply. "You can acknowledge that you were the source of Plummer's film, in which case you can either call it quits and retire in the West, here or the US, or you can continue to cooperate with us in an operational role. But there are risks."

"There are always risks," said Strekov.

"For you," Roger added. "We think it likely that someone from your services may suspect something. Following Plummer's last meeting with you in East Berlin, someone attempted to grab him in an alley in Treptow. Whether East German or your own service, we don't know."

Strekov nodded, as if he already knew about the incident and it no longer interested him. "If I were to remain here in the UK, what would you have me do?"

"Whatever you wished. An adviser. A consultant on intelligence matters."

"I'm not a weapons or a missile specialist. You should be under no illusion about that."

"There are other things. There are people you know, events you've witnessed, operational procedures you're acquainted with."

"A traitor in residence," Strekov said. Roger Cornelius didn't answer. "You also mentioned an operational role."

"Yes, I did," Roger replied. "Doing what you do best, in East Germany, in the Soviet Union."

"Returning, you mean?"

Roger nodded. "Returning. As you are now. Continuing in the same way."

"And what about Solo?"

"We'd handle that. We're ready to begin tonight. If things went well, you could be on your way back to East Berlin in a week or ten days. Perhaps less."

Strekov sat studying Roger Cornelius. "You're willing to assume that I'd cooperate once I returned to East Berlin?"

"After what you've given us—yes. It's unthinkable that we wouldn't under those circumstances. But as I said earlier, there are risks, far more for you than for us. Only you can measure the extent of the dangers." He studied Strekov's face. "If the advisory or consultant position appeals to you, then of course we'd manage that too. It's useful. It takes bodies as well. That's a bureaucratic principle in Moscow too, isn't it—safety in numbers? So when another operation breaks down, you can always go back to the staff work, to the ecological surveys, gold and fissionable ore production, population charts, GNP." Roger smiled tolerantly, a bleak, wintry smile. "Some do it very well; others don't do it well at all. I imagine your own instincts run the other way, don't they?

I would say you're operationally prone. Real questions; real answers. I remember an anecdote someone at the French court at Versailles once told—that everything at Versailles was so artificial that when one left the palace it was a pleasure to stand in the street watching real dogs chew real bones."

Phil Chambers sat in sudden discomfiture, suffering the awkward embarrassment of things already known. He had heard Roger tell the same story in the past, most recently to an East German defector. As he watched, the shame of its recollection grew. The room was in semi-darkness; perspiration sprang to his forehead and neck. He remembered now: the East German had been run to ground two weeks later. Didn't Roger remember? His agony grew as he watched Roger's face. In this historical anecdote, made trite by familiar usage, he sensed now the familiar horror of something already known, and suddenly it was as if they had been buried alive—Roger, himself, all of them; their words, like their minds, repeating the same sterile circuits, like flies in this dark, closed, empty room.

The interrogation ended inconclusively. Strekov was taken to a room on the floor below for a few hours sleep. The interrogation would resume at nine o'clock the following morning.

"He'll go," Roger said as he sat for a moment with Chambers and Ivor Simpson, sharing a nightcap in the room next door. "I'm sure of it. Back to Karlshorst, to Moscow . . . wherever. He'll cooperate."

Ivor Simpson agreed: "I rather imagine you're right. I wouldn't have thought so an hour ago. But now I do. I suppose that means that we'll have to begin on the Solo business right away."

"In the morning," Roger said. The rain still moved against the window. Far below, a solitary car splashed by on the wet street.

They were still sitting there when the telephone call came from the USAF hospital. It was the Agency officer who'd been assigned to Plummer. The arrangements had been completed for Plummer's evacuation to the US. He would be put aboard a C-141 MAC flight bound for Dover Air Force Base in Delaware, accompanied by an Air Force nurse. The plane would leave at six thirty the next morning, but the Englishwoman hadn't yet been cleared.

"Clear her then," Chambers said. "She's to accompany him. She's not to stay here. It's already been approved in Washington. They'll waive her passport requirement."

After Chambers hung up, Roger said, "Who was that?"

"The man at the air base. Plummer will be airborne at six thirty. The Davidson woman will go with him."

Roger nodded and got to his feet. "Good. Ready for your run at the Soviet rabbit?" he said to Ivor.

Ivor stood up and emptied his glass. "I daresay we're ready."

Three weeks later the Opposition spokesman in the House of Commons formally asked the Government if it was prepared to answer accusations that a member of the political staff of the Prime Minister's office had been supplying secrets to the Soviet Union for over two decades. The rumors had been circulating in London for ten days. The charge was heatedly denied. The following week a Tory back-bencher told the press that he'd received reports that an investigation was underway, but that the suspected agent wasn't in the PM's office. He was in MI6. The same day a London paper carried a report that it was the Americans who had informed the British of the Soviet agent. They had identified him following the defection of an East German official from the *Hauptverwaltung Aufklärung* the previous January. Two days later the Opposition spokesman repeated his accusations and cited the newspaper article. The Government promised a White Paper on the question by the end of the month.

The publicity in Commons and the London press was deliberately contrived. Roger Cornelius and Ivor Simpson had provoked it. It was the final embellishment to the strategy which had first begun with Phil Chambers's bogus heart attack in London. The first phase was designed to take in Plummer and to persuade him to acknowledge Strekov's identity. The second phase was designed to take in Solo. Strekov's willingness to cooperate with Roger and Ivor had made it possible.

After two days of interrogation following the Russian's apprehension at Paddington, he agreed to cooperate. He told them that he was a KGB officer who'd arrived from Karlshorst in East Berlin two months earlier as a Soviet illegal assigned to handle Solo. He had no other responsibilities. Both Moscow and Karlshorst were concerned about Solo's increasingly erratic behavior. They were prepared to write him off if necessary, but first they wanted to observe him more closely. The Russian had been given the assignment. He had a flat in Ealing and a small office nearby. He traded in surgical instruments and laboratory equipment imported from the Continent. His name was Strekov. Prior to his arrival in London he had been assigned to Karlshorst in East Berlin as a special operations officer. He traveled often to Western Europe and occasionally London. He knew it well. He had served in London in the early fifties under another name, as he'd also served in Prague, Cairo, and Istanbul. He was vague about other operations he'd been involved with, as he was also vague about his reasons for providing Plummer with Soviet weapons information in East Berlin. Roger concluded that he was disillusioned with the extent of Soviet liberalization under Khruschev. He also believed Strekov bore some professional resentment against his superiors in Moscow. About other Soviet operations or officials in the UK or on the continent, he told them little they didn't already know. He did tell them that Bryce had been murdered in Rostock, but that file had already been closed in London and Washington. He said that he wasn't interested in resettling in the West. He had a family in Moscow and exile held no attraction for him. In the end he accepted Roger's proposal that he return to the Soviet Union and at an opportune time resume the clandestine work he'd begun in East Berlin. Strekov could demonstrate, if need be, that he was running Plummer and handling a network which penetrated the American services.

So Strekov agreed to cooperate. The only problem remaining was how best to manage his return to the Soviet Union. Solo was the key. The vague accusations in Commons and the deliberate leaks in the press were the beginning. In due time Solo would be brought in for questioning. The MI5 chief interrogator and Special Branch's spy catchers were convinced that they could get a confession. Ultimately Solo would be sent to Wormwood Scrubs for violation of the Official Secrets Acts. But even before his arraignment at the Old Bailey, Strekov would be in flight. His prison would be larger—snow, birches, black streams, and sorrel meadows; sun-filled plains, white with dust, vast in a way only a Russian might understand; but a prison nevertheless, no larger than Hamlet's nutshell. Roger Cornelius would be his warden, as Ivor Simpson had been his turnkey. Strekov accepted this almost with indifference. Roger was troubled by his resignation, but he kept his misgivings to himself. In one of his final cables to Washington he wrote that Strekov's willingness to cooperate reflected his growing concern at the boldness of Soviet military ambitions. Strekov had never told him that.

It was Solo who almost wrecked their plans.

On a cool spring evening the week before Solo was to be summoned to Scotland Yard for preliminary questioning, the Reverend Bayard Brainwater and his young niece left a taxi at the international departure doors at Heathrow. Inside they checked their baggage through to Nairobi at the BOAC ticket counter and moved through the crowd to passport control. Reverend Brainwater carried a fly rod in an expensive case under one arm and a BOAC flight bag under the other. He wore a clergyman's collar, a salt-and-pepper Norfolk jacket, and a pair of shapeless serge trousers. His teeth were slightly maloccluded, his voice high pitched. A rain hat, from which hung a pair of wispy, muttonchop whiskers, was pulled down over his forehead. On his nose was a pair of iron-rimmed spectacles with tinted lenses. His niece was more conventionally dressed. She looked like a Catholic-school girl on her way to the village sweet shop. She wore a blue jumper, long blue stockings, and a floppy white tennis hat, but even the adolescent attire couldn't conceal the professional beauty of the small, cameo face scrubbed clean of rouge, lipstick, or eye shadow. At passport control the customs inspector studied Reverend Brainwater's passport, looked at the photograph again, and the address in Surrey, and excused himself. When he returned, he was accompanied by two Special Branch officers and Ivor Simpson. Ivor stood behind the counter, looking at the passport.

"Brainwater?" he asked finally, lifting his eyes to Solo's face.

"Really not responsible, old boy," came the exasperated, falsetto reply.

Ivor continued to look at him, the passport still in his hands. "It really won't do, Alan," he said sorrowfully. "It really won't do at all."

"Are you mad?" Solo laughed preposterously. The teeth slipped against the wet lip. Solo's fingers found them and pushed them back. One of the Special Branch officers moved forward.

"No need for a scene now—"

"Take your hands from me! Look here!" he protested. "Is there someone of authority about? Come, Rachael. This is truly inexcusable." He turned wildly. The girl hadn't moved. Ivor stood silently watching him. Solo saw her face and turned back. "Look here—"

He smashed the fishing case across Ivor's head, knocked the Special Branch officer sideways, and bolted back through the crowd. "Rachael! Come, child!" The girl hadn't moved. Ivor lifted himself from the floor and scrambled from behind the counter. Two incoming passengers carrying luggage were sent spinning aside as Solo leaped through the closing doors. He ran into the open roadway outside, stopped, and looked back.

"Rachael! Rachael!"

A policeman's whistle blew from the end of the roadbed. The moon was a luminous white bone overhead. A Bombay-bound jet was lifting off; nearby a dozen sets of turbines were shrieking as the incoming jets closed off their engines. Solo hesitated for an instant, then dodged in front of a taxi and raced down the roadway towards the domestic terminal. The noise was deafening. He was in full flight, and the truck speeding down the service road with late cargo for a departing flight struck him head-on as it rounded the corner. Solo never heard it. The bumper and grillwork sent him hurtling across the oiled tarmac like a bundle of limp rags. The body spun twice, smashed across a stone coping, and flopped over into the plot of green grass where it lay twisted and broken among the planted bulbs.

The hat lay on the tarmac, trailing the loose moss of whiskers. The glasses were on the sidewalk in front of the doors, the lenses unbroken. Ivor Simpson joined the two Special Branch men standing in the glare of the truck's headlights. He was carrying the hat and glasses; his head ached and there was a deep cut across his scalp where the edge of the fishing box had struck him. A small crowd had gathered across the roadbed. Cars passed by slowly, their occupants craning their necks for a glimpse of the body lying along the grass. Ivor moved between the two Special Branch officers. The legs were crossed. One shoe was gone, and the head hung limply to one side. Ivor Simpson stood looking at Alan Compton-Bofer's broken face, still boyish now, as it hung to one side, as if dangling by a single thread.

"Bloody awful," the Special Branch man said.

"It is," Ivor said after a minute. "Indeed it is."

"She wouldn't give him a divorce. Never," the girl told him as they drove back to London. "She wouldn't. It was the only way. She pushed him to the wall. He wanted to put an end to it." She began to cry again.

"An end to what?" Ivor asked gently.

"Everything. What he'd been mixed up in. His life with her. She was worse than the Pope. He wanted his freedom." On Ivor's lap was the BOAC bag. The two additional passports were inside, hidden under the bottom board. From Kenya they were to go to Rhodesia with new identities, man and wife, resettling on a tobacco farm in the highlands. "He knew Africa," she said. "Better than anyone. He told me once he should never have left it. It was the only thing he had and they took it away from him."

"Is that what he told you?" Ivor asked her gently.

"It's true," she said stubbornly.

"Yes, I suppose it is," he replied, looking out the window.

In his office in the old Georgian house at Queen Anne's Gate, he gave her a cup of tea. They sat on a horsehide sofa. Books and old newspapers were stacked to the ceiling on the old bookshelf in the corner. There were three telephones on the desk. A dog-eared map of *Mitteleuropa* hung between the windows, left over from Ivor's days on the Continent. On the wall behind them hung a series of dusty wartime pictures taken in Holland and France.

"You said he wanted to put an end to everything," Ivor began again. "I understand that his wife wouldn't give him a divorce, but what else do you think he might have been talking about?"

"He was mixed up with something once," she said. "Something he'd done. The Americans were after him. He wanted to make a clean breast of it."

Ivor was puzzled. "Something with the Soviets?"

She nodded. "He'd been trying to arrange it."

"Arrange what?" The telephone rang and Ivor waited a minute, still looking at the girl. When it rang again he answered it. Roger Cornelius was calling. "Tell him I'll ring him in a few minutes." He sat back down and when the phone rang again, he ignored it. "Trying to arrange what?"

She said she didn't know. He wanted to meet with an American who worked in London and had asked another American friend to arrange it. He hadn't done it. Alan believed that the Americans didn't want to talk to him at all. "Do you remember the name of this American friend?" Ivor asked.

His name was Templeman. She'd met him once at a friend's flat where she and Alan sometimes met. They'd had an argument that night. She'd wanted to leave England the next weekend for Rhodesia. He insisted that he had to straighten up this other matter first. He told her that they would have no peace until he could settle his accounts with the Americans. She wasn't sure what he had meant.

Ivor sat for a long time studying the girl's face. His tea had grown cold. At last he shook his head, and got up. He called Roger Cornelius and asked that he come over. "Good Lord," he said as he put the phone down. "Good Lord."

Compton-Bofers had been prepared to deliver Strekov to the Americans for the asking. Only they'd funked it. They hadn't asked.

In Compton-Bofers's cottage in Northumberland they found a crypt under the bedroom floor. It had been laboriously built decades earlier, probably during the summers or holidays. It was six meters deep, with a crude wooden floor. On an old table were a dusty radio covered with cobwebs, two crystals, and a keying device which the Soviets had used a decade earlier. There was no antenna, no power supply. The radio had never been used. In the same musty cellar were a few wooden spears, a few pieces of African raffia, a Masai shield, and some earthenware cups fired in a kiln along the lower Nile. Some candle stubs were stuck in crude earthenware plates; the dusty tallow was thirty years old, like the old *Geographical Journals* stacked in one corner. On the walls upstairs were the photographs of the Sudan, the Nile at Khartoum, and the wattle *banda* at Entebbe, the .500 cordite elephant gun, the Holland .303. There were no pictures of Compton-Bofers. There were photographs of the father, retired from the Sudan political service on a pitiful five hundred pounds a year; photographs of mother and stepfather; of friends at Oxford. There was one photograph which had been taken during Compton-Bofers's days in Berlin before the war—a yellowing snapshot of a young German girl, long limbed and blue eyed, taken under the chestnut trees of a sidewalk cafe near the old Karl Liebknecht house. No one knew who she was. Once the newspapers confirmed that Alan Compton-Bofers was the Soviet agent that Special Branch had been searching for, a photo did appear in the newspaper, but it wasn't furnished by either the family or his friends. It was given to a journalist by the ex-husband of one of Compton-Bofers' stepsisters. It had been taken more than thirty years earlier on the terrace of the Hotel Carlton in Cannes at the hour of the aperitif and showed mother, stepfather, and stepsisters smiling in the apricot sunshine. Compton-Bofers was there, in the far corner, a strange smile on his lips, looking slightly away from the camera, as if he wasn't really there at all.

"What did you chaps expect him to do?" Beresford Perse exclaimed bitterly to Ivor Simpson the afternoon after the inquest. They were in Compton-Bofers's study at the house on Campden Hill Square. Ivor had stopped to express his condolences to Mary Compton-Bofers, and to ask a few questions. "What did you expect? Did you want him to renounce Leninism as the fount of his inspiration! To reject Stalinism, dogma, and bureaucratism forever! Good God, couldn't you leave him at peace? What did you think—that he was off with his trollop that night at Heathrow to some disgusting Borstal on the banks of the Moscow! Did you actually believe that!"

"I regret what happened as much as anyone," Ivor said.

Beresford Perse turned from the decanter, a drink in his hand. "I understand Roger Cornelius is here from Washington. I suppose he had a hand in this dreadful affair." Ivor didn't answer, waiting for Mary to join him. "Where is he, that abhorrent man? I should like to have a word with him."

"I don't think that would be wise," Ivor said calmly.

367

"As far as I'm concerned it's a matter of the utmost insignificance. The press accounts are wholly misleading and vicious in inference. Was it Roger that arranged this frightful affair?"

Ivor studied Beresford's cold white face without replying. "What are you staring at?" Beresford asked shrilly.

"I was trying to think of a decent answer I might give you."

"I should rather imagine that it would take more time than either of us have. I can think of an answer to give you." He put the drink on the mantelpiece. "My grandfather warned the Conservatives in nineteen thirty-one and again in nineteen thirty-eight, 'Pray God that we can keep the Americans out of it.' I consider those words prophetic. Yet no one wants to listen. They've smashed us to atoms with their power and the tyranny of their freedom is driving the world to their dungeon."

Ivor said nothing. "Are you listening to me?" It occurred to Ivor that Perse had drunk too much at luncheon. "The Americans, the dreadful Americans," Beresford muttered in a voice not wholly his own. "Do you remember that?"

Ivor thought he did. It was Compton-Bofers's imitation of one of his Marxist dons at Oxford, an imitation he had done extremely well, and which everyone recognized. One evening at the Dorchester, Roger Cornelius had heard it and had misinterpreted it. He had protested, and Compton-Bofers, too drunk to argue, had thrown a drink in his face.

The door opened and Beresford quickly crossed the room. "Here you are, my dear. Can I get you something?" Mary Compton-Bofers was in black, but was no longer wearing her veil. She gave Beresford a pious bread-and-water smile, and came to the couch where Ivor stood. She sat down slowly, her eyes fastened to his face. She was smiling courageously. For a moment, Ivor thought she was sympathizing with his own embarrassment. But in the silence which followed, he knew that this wasn't the reason at all.

"I suppose it's a matter of conscience now above all, isn't it?" she said. When he didn't answer immediately, she put her hand on his. Her hand was quite cold. The smile was still on her lips. Looking into those cool blue eyes, he found he had nothing more to say.

Strekov was already in flight—over Kent, the Channel, eastward over the continent towards Switzerland. A few days later MI5 and Special Branch began their fictitious search for Strekov. They located the shop in Ealing with the small sign on the door:

Herman Cook, Ltd.
Scientific and Surgical Instruments

They found the furnished flat nearby, once occupied by a Swiss or German national who, after his arrival in England two or three months earlier, had traded in surgical instruments imported from Europe. He had led a quiet life. "Oh, he was an odd mixture, all right," his landlady told the visiting press, "but a proper gentleman, too, if you know what I mean." She was a plump, chainsmoking woman in her early fifties with carrot-colored hair. She sat in her littered flat in a cotton peignoir, smoking their cigarettes, and telling them all she knew of the man who had rented the flat several months before. When she saw the publicity she was receiving, she realized that she was getting nothing in return, and found an agent. She refused to talk to the press after she had signed a contract with a London tabloid. It was pretty thin gruel. She'd only met Cook on three occasions. The tabloid gave her a single story splashed over the front page and she dropped out of sight.

Roger Cornelius and others were still optimistic. They would wait. Days, weeks, and months would pass before they would know whether or not they had been successful. And finally on a quiet autumn or winter night, in a small crowd leaving the Baltic station or the Dynamo Stadium in Moscow, or on a chilly afternoon along the paths of Sokolniki Park, or at a crowded state reception blue with cigarette smoke, glittering with flashing miniatures and lifted glasses, shrill with the latest gossip about the Middle East, Vietnam, Laos, *détente*, or the opacity of Chinese intentions, a signal would be given, a wire tripped; and from that moment on a curious silence would isolate a few obscure offices in London and Washington. Lights would burn all night in a silent wing of the old Agency building on Twenty-third Street across from the State Department and at Queen Anne's Gate. For a time the Agency's morning brief to the White House would provide new facts where no detail had been previously, give assurance where doubt and hazard had been the rule, and supply confidence for decisions which had once been conjectural. Only a score of men would know the identity of the new source. They would be locked in a solitude as deep as that of astronomers waiting out their vigils for that mysterious light which may come once in a generation and no more, pulsating from a darkness where no light had ever been.

But it wouldn't last. Even Roger Cornelius recognized that. It would dim and expire, the way all lights do. Certainty would again be puzzled by doubt. A handful of men in Washington and London would again sit in obscurity in gray offices on gray afternoons, alone again with the questions their time couldn't solve.

THIRTEEN

He had been in Geneva for two days. The desk clerk at the small hotel where he was staying thought him English; the French bartender, a German businessman. He was wearing a soft gray tweed suit, a dark-blue overcoat, and a pair of rubber-soled English shoes. In the small bar in the basement stocked with American whiskey miniatures and English port casks, French wine bottles and German lager steins, he listened to a young pianist play Aznavour and Beatles instrumentals, drank only whiskey-soda, and tipped well. His luggage had been ticketed from Brussels. Near evening on the third day he met a man at a small German restaurant near the *Rue de Rhone*. They had coffee together and walked through a side street to where a Mercedes with Swiss plates was waiting. The car dropped him at a street corner near his hotel. When he left the Mercedes, he was no longer carrying his briefcase. In the hotel room he opened the sealed envelope given him in the car and found a dark-blue East German passport with gold lettering. Inside were a Swiss immigration cachet, Polish and Czech visas, and an airline ticket for Warsaw for the following morning. Why not a Polish passport, then? Had his documentation been prepared in Geneva, Berlin, or Moscow? He packed his remaining bag, checked out of the hotel, and took a taxi to the *Gare de Cornavin*. He left the bag in a metal locker inside the train station, bought a paper and some postcards, and left the station by a side entrance. Fifteen minutes later he found a second taxi and was driven to a small obscure pension across the river near the university.

The room was ready for him at the top of the narrow stairs. It was clean and warm, the single bed was turned down, and an orange fire was burning on the grate to take the chill from the air. Over the white cast-iron mantel was a pair of green tourist prints of a Geneva cathedral. The faded lemon wallpaper was embossed with small white roses. It was a plain room, commonplace and sterile, a room where one needn't remember the past or anticipate the future, where nothing of consequence would ever occur, and where emptiness itself was as ubiquitous as the diurnal drift of dust through the sunlight evaporating through the stiff curtains.

It was the dacha Strekov thought about, perhaps because of the gaslight, perhaps the isolation, perhaps because Geneva was a city she had never seen but would have enjoyed. He stood at the window, remembering again the smell of wood smoke and the morning sunlight warm on the kitchen floor of the dacha after they returned from bathing in the river. The wind blew high in the trees where the sunlight was splintered like grapeshot. How far had it traveled? Awakening on autumn mornings, they saw the sharp shadows of the blowing leaves moving across the white sheets and the pine wall beyond. He remembered the chair where she sat in the evening, reading aloud.

That evening in Geneva he found a small restaurant near the university and ate dinner alone. Afterwards he walked along the quiet streets, looking into the shop windows and the small flats where students and professors lived. As he climbed the stairs to his room, the concierge opened his door a crack and told him that breakfast would be ready at half past six. He must be on time, he told him. He studied Strekov through the crack and shut the door. In the room on the third floor Strekov read the paper and later sat at the window looking out into the darkness. It was after eleven when he sat down at the desk in the corner and began a letter to his wife. It was an old habit.

After the war he had been at Minsk during the Party purges and one evening sat down at his billet and wrote a letter to a cousin. The face of a young girl in the street that day had reminded him of her. After he'd completed the letter and was addressing the envelope, he realized that his cousin was dead. She'd died in 1938. Mystified, he'd carried the letter with him for over a month. He reread it while returning to Moscow on the train. The letter's meaning was no clearer to him then than it had been in the billet. He watched the yellow light from the coach windows reflected against the snow banks along the track, still puzzled. In the hours after midnight the train had stopped and the passengers waited in a small rural station while the work train and the snowplow cleared the tracks ahead. He sat at a bare wooden table with an old army colonel, his wife and granddaughter. An old man in soft leather boots brought them tea. The room was gray with the smoke of the fire; the cold floor was littered with straw which smelled of the barn; peasants, soldiers, and young children, just awakened from sleep, crowded the noisy tables. Strekov drank the tea and sat apart, looking through the cold pane of window towards the darkness where the train was waiting. Each time he moved his head from the pane back to the table and his teacup, something moved in the darkness outside. He would look back and nothing moved at all. Turning, something moved again. An old samovar sat steaming on a table nearby, as old as a patriarch, and as he watched it he identified a thin trickle of hot air rising from its surface. Almost invisible in the brightness of the room itself, it was clearly identified against the black mirror of window. That was what he had seen. Thinking of the letter, he thought again of the trickle of steam. He thought about it that night returning to Moscow. It seemed to him that his letter was from a dead soul speaking to the dead. Perhaps his mind had known that. But this wasn't the full answer, since his cousin was very much alive to him when he wrote his letter. He threw the letter away in Moscow and stopped thinking about it. When his wife died, he continued to write to her, not only because it was a habit long established, but because only in writing to her did he find the solitude that he needed to know his own mind. That evening in Geneva, Strekov wrote:

> I've never trusted myself with boredom, the most toxic of all poisons. Anything that I've ever done amounts to no more than a victory over that.

Was that what he thought? He continued:

> Few understand this, I suppose. Boredom is a disease. At the dacha in the woods after her death, I was capable of anything which might hide its emptiness—to stop the sounds of the river,

the ice melting, the leaves tapping at the window. Boredom is as mindless as the sea; its monotony bred in time a will to leave it, to crawl from its boundless emptiness and lift itself, a single sperm of animate ego. That was the original treason, wasn't it? The mind's will to separate itself from this unspeakable mindlessness. So this accounts for this poor creature's native faithlessness. How could it explain this to the sea itself? With words. No. Our words are only our final corruption, the speech of our difference and our squalor, when we are finally civilized to no greater truth but the knowledge of our own decay.

His eyes ached. Words again. Only words. He folded the letter in disgust and put it in his pocket.

He dreamed that night of the dacha lying in the rain-thick woods. He had come up the path after years of absence, carrying an old breechloading gun, his twill coat and trousers heavy with the water flushed from the drooping boughs along the path. In the damp chill of the room he couldn't light the lamp or the kerosene cooker. His fingers were stiff and cold. The matches came apart in his hands like crumbs of earth.

A young peasant girl with a wet face and wet yellow hair sat in a cane-bottomed chair near the old stove. A damp shawl lay over her shoulders and she was trembling convulsively. Her father had beaten her when he'd discovered that she'd slept with him during the week after his wife's death. But now her father had forgotten and had sent her with eggs and cheese in exchange for several of the ducks Strekov had shot on the river that day. She went to the kitchen to get the ducks, but when she came back she whispered, "The dogs have gotten them. The dogs." She began to cry, afraid that her father would beat her again. Strekov lifted the wet shawl from her trembling shoulders, untied the loose smock she wore, and led her into the bedroom. He told her to warm herself under the covers. She stripped away her damp skirts and petticoat and crawled naked across the bed, her breasts and arms blue with the cold. He crawled after her across the muslin sheets, but they clung to his skin like a damp shroud. She was shivering. He tried to warm her with his body. Her breath was like frost. She hadn't bathed since she had last slept with him; her damp hair smelled of wood-smoke, as it had three days after his wife's funeral.

The dacha was empty and cold. He went outside and down the path towards the river. He stood on the jetty, looking out over the darkness of the Dneipr. To the south a bright string of colored lights shone through the mist on the river. Music and laughter drifted across the river from the excursion boat. He untied the skiff and pushed out across the black water, but near midstream the skiff swung about violently and began to gather speed in the slough of the current. He stood up and tried to steer the skiff with the weight of his body, but the boat reeled under him and he fell backwards into the icy current. When he revived, the skiff was gone, and he was on his hands and knees, crawling up the riverbank and back along the narrow path towards the dacha. But the water followed, trickling over his hands, flooding the path beyond, and racing in torrents into the orchard and wild strawberries. He saw it rising in the woods beyond. Through the rain he saw the dacha beginning to drift in the wild water, spinning slowly as it lifted from its foundations, like a matchbox in a winter gutter. The current plunged over him and carried the dacha away into the darkness of the river. *No*, he cried out, *No, no*—

The gray light emptied, as cold as death, draining the room where he had been sleeping, and he heard the footsteps outside before the knock came, and, afterwards, the voice.

"Time."

In London the days had begun with the mist touching the window and the light touching the rust-colored flock wallpaper, the smell of burnt toast and browning bacon trickling up the stairwell from the basement kitchen. Now Strekov dressed in the chill Geneva light and went down to the dining room, where he drank a cup of weak coffee. The car was waiting for him beyond the front steps, its parking lights on. "Cold this morning," the young Russian said. He was of medium height with light brown hair. Strekov nodded and settled beside him in the rear seat, his breath showing on the air of the sedan.

At the air terminal a third Russian was waiting for them. He was short and muscular, wearing a new raincoat and a gray trilby hat. He spoke to them in German—an undisciplined, ungrammatical German of the kind learned in a prisoner-of-war camp. His face was round and muscular; his pale eyes had an insolent vulgarity to them. They shone like pieces of mica in the early morning cold. He looked curiously at Strekov's tie, at his coat and shoes, but said nothing. He told them the plane would be late. They waited in the corner of the terminal, staring out across the nearly deserted room. The short Russian stared at Strekov, who didn't seem to notice. He examined his suit, his tie, and his shoes. The shoes seemed to fascinate him the most. At last he looked at his own shoes, studied them critically, leaned down and scratched a crust of mud from the thin sole, then pulled up his pale green socks. When the restaurant opened Strekov crossed the waiting room and entered. He drank a cup of tea and the other two Russians joined him. Strekov watched a plane lumber down the runway, its engine vibrations throbbing against the window, the long fusilage thrust upward as it rotated, like a swan beginning its flight. The younger Russian watched the plane disappear and asked Strekov if he knew Geneva well. Strekov said he didn't.

"London?"

"Yes," Strekov said. "London."

To the younger KGB officer Strekov seemed like a man of taste and privilege, a man at home in the cities of the West, a man who smoked their cigars, who knew their music, their cinema, their brandies, and perhaps their women. In certain ways he was groomed like a Western diplomat or businessman. The smaller Russian drank his coffee noisily, holding the cup with both hands. "London is different, I suppose," the young man said.

"Every city is different," Strekov answered. The smaller Russian got to his feet, wiping his hands on his coat, and crossed the room to the door.

The younger Russian said that the other was a Lett who'd arrived from East Berlin three days ago, traveling with a group from Karlshorst. "He's crude," he said. "He has no manners at all."

They left the restaurant and crossed into the waiting room. The Lett was standing at the ticket counter. Nearby a few travelers were lifting their suitcases from the floor and turning back towards the entrance. "The Germans don't fly today," he said. "The flight has been canceled."

"They can't cancel it," the younger man said.

"Dogs must shit," the Lett said. "Sometimes dogs shit on your shoes. This one has shit on our shoes."

"When is the next flight?"

"Ask the comrade lady there," the Lett said, nodding towards the ticket agent. He took a coin from his pocket and moved towards the bank of phone booths. When he returned, he was perspiring from the heat of the booth and his tightly buttoned overcoat. "*Nichego*," he muttered. "Okay. We fly tonight. To Prague. Prague is better anyway."

Strekov returned to the same third-floor room at the pension. The same chairs, the same desk, the same emptiness. Nothing had changed. Nothing remained of his occupancy the previous night. The Lett followed him silently up the creaking stairs and entered the room behind him. He stood at the window, looking suspiciously down into the street. Strekov told him to go downstairs and wait. The Lett, still lighting his cigarette, didn't seem to hear him. A plume of yellow smoke curled away from his flat nose, like a silken spider web broken in passing. Strekov remembered the brilliant morning sunshine of the Dneipr and the path to the river. The Lett turned and looked at him. Strekov looked back at the bright, hard eyes and the small, vulgar fascist face. "You got into an English cunt," the Lett said. "Between the legs and someone found you there."

"Get out."

The Lett smiled and went out.

Strekov took a walk in the early evening. He found a tobacco shop and bought a few packages of English cigarettes. A small radio was playing Haydn on the shelf behind the tobacconist. Strekov stood at the door listening to the music. The tobacconist lifted his head. "Do you want something?" The shop was empty. He was waiting to close. Strekov went out. He felt relieved on the street outside, and he realized that it was on account of the music. How long could one listen to it? He was leaving it. It was like an old room being closed for the summer, the furniture covered with dust covers, the piano shrouded over, doors and shutters drawn, flowers and books packed away. Europe was now such a room to him. He would never return. Would others come? He'd miss none of it.

He sat in the room on the third floor, waiting for the car. When the room was full of shadows, like a shady stream full of somnolent trout, he washed his face and shaved, returned his toilet kit to the suitcase, and put on his coat. He was tired. Since he'd first known that he was returning to Moscow, he'd thought only of that—the dacha and the nearby woods—remembering the days he'd isolated himself in solitude there, listening to the sound of the snow melting in the woods. How would he explain it to them?

He remembered the moment he'd seen the sudden burst of color through the small window, the sun splashing mysteriously through the trees; and near dawn the following day the sound of the bird singing—once, twice, three times, then a fourth. An insipid lyric, almost like a whippoorwill's. The sun fell again through the trees that morning, fell into the thick green leaves as if through a lyre, and gave back the sound of a bird singing. He was bored. He felt the weight lift, seeing only the splash of color from the monotony of the woods beyond.

That was when he had first decided. He'd had the access—the details from Lake Balkhash, the cables he'd monitored, the briefings he'd attended during the Presidium visits, the crash of the helicopter after which each secret briefcase and its contents had been assembled in the single room in Moscow for collating and recording—what had been recovered, what compromised, what was still missing. Nothing had been inaccessible. The camera work was child's play. But was he still ill? Was he still feverish the night he'd found Bryce's broken body in the stone cell, still bored with their mindless universalism, their obscene hypocrisy? The films were already in his possession then, a personal triumph, a secret joke. Maryna would have understood it. It was Bryce's death that had made him angry. But it wasn't the anger. What was it? He remembered the sunlight splashing through the trees, the fierce bud of light that restored the will to think about the future. But now he had begun to believe that it hadn't been the sun at all but some cyst exploding silently at the back of his brain or within the optic nerve, full of some flagellant toxin left by the fever, reproducing the counterfeit plumage of the leaves and swimming against his sick heart with the sound of the pine and fir needles dipping against the window and weaving their shadows against the walls. If that wasn't the reason, what was?

Boredom. I was bored. Your mindlessness bored me. All of you.

He stood at the window. The car was at the curb. He would let his father-in-law have the dacha.

An hour later he was aboard the Prague-bound flight. As the jet lifted soundlessly above the city, he looked down at the archipelago of lights that circled the mirror of lake, looked down and saw for the last time not the city at all, but his own reflection in the dark circle of glass, already beginning to fade from the darkness.

There had been time that afternoon. He knew what he faced in Moscow. He could have changed his mind at any time since the meeting at Paddington. He could have found refuge in England or the US. They had told him to think about it carefully, but there was nothing to think about.

I can remember everything you said

Better to accept what you are. Life was short. Better to take it while you can, take it at full grasp. She had taught him that at a time when he'd thought he had nothing left to learn. He had no sympathy for the faded souls who limped soundlessly into oblivion—the great Russian grandfathers lost among the shades of history, the senile patriarchs who entertained their madness with elegent witticisms and sterile tautologies, like the music of the elderly Haydn in the tobacco shop, or the emasculated White Russian or Trotskyite pedants and bards in the Western literary salons and the bourgeois lecture rooms, writing their private histories at Oxford or the British Museum, moving stiffly at closing time: old men, old passions, old trees full of dead leaves, muttering banalities among the shades of Marx, Guizot, or even Metternich—"L'erreur ne s'est jamais approchée de mon esprit"—On a gray winter day with the gray sky rolling like surf overhead, the dead leaves flying, and the clip-clop of the cabs, the yellow streetlamps coming on through the fog. No, not exile. He had found his own in the dacha with his wife long before, in the notebooks, in the endleaves of his books.

The plane landed at Prague. They waited in their seats for the passengers to depart. When the last had left the cabin, five men came quickly down the aisle.

"Strekov?" the first demanded.

"Strekov," he said calmly. They seized his wrists, pinning his arms against the seat rests while a third man moved his hands through the pockets of his jacket and brought out the letter. "It's a letter to my wife," Strekov said.

"His wife is dead," the Lett said.

The Russian put the letter in his pocket. Then he lifted Strekov's hands abruptly, pulled him upright, and shackled the wrists behind his back. "My cigarettes?" Strekov asked. The package was on the empty seat beside him.

"He's mad," the Lett muttered. One of the Russians picked up the cigarettes, turned the package carefully in his hand, studied the printing, finally the cigarettes themselves, and put them in his pocket. In the car at the foot of the rear stairs two more men were waiting. They pushed Strekov into the first car. Four men got in with him, and the two cars sped towards the corner of the airfield where the plane was waiting, its jet engines already flaming in the cold night air. The Lett looked through the windshield in surprise. "Not even one night in Prague?" he grunted.

"Not even one night," said the man beside him. "Tomorrow they'll put you back in your kennel in Moscow."

Everyone laughed, but the Lett resented it. "A bigger kennel," he said. "Bigger than yours."

The sky was gray overhead when the sedan sped into the courtyard on Dzerzhinskay Street. Strekov was still shackled. He was brought through a side door and down a long corridor. In a large, official room at the end of the corridor Orlov was waiting with a senior official from the state prosecutor's office. Other officials stood nearby. Zhilenkov and Chernyak stood behind Orlov. The lights were very bright; Strekov was sleepless and unshaven. His hands were still behind his back. He stood between two of the KGB officers who had brought him from Prague while the state prosecutor's representative read the official indictment against him. He was charged with treason and murder. Despite the bright lights he tried to focus his eyes on the face of the state prosecutor's representative as he spoke, but the indictment was very long. He found himself looking at Zhilenkov instead. The angle was less painful. He saw nothing there he recognized. Suddenly he was jolted from the side and realized that the state prosecutor's vice-minister was looking at him. He had stopped reading. Again he asked Strekov if he had anything to say.

Strekov shook his head. They took him away to Lubyanka prison. It was late afternoon when he was finally moved to a solitary cell deep in the basement. They had taken away his watch. His head was shaved. He wore a pair of thin cotton coveralls and the cell was cold and damp. In the corner was a straw pallet. He lay down, curling his knees against his chest, trying to retain his body heat. He had no socks, only a pair of prison shoes without laces. He had walked miles through the prison corridors, and already his ankles and toes were chafed from the worn leather whose last owner had flexed folds and creases in the iron boot which cut across his tender feet like steel. He tried to sleep, but within twenty minutes he was taken from the cell and down the endless corridor to a stone stairwell which led to the floors above. His defense counsel was waiting in a bright, overheated room without windows. The lights were as bright as the lights in the formal room on Dzerzhinskay Street where he had been charged. The defense lawyer was a large, balding man with pebble-lensed spectacles on his nose. He sat at one end of a long baize-covered table. The guards put Strekov at the other. Between them six men sat, three on each side of the table. Strekov knew none of them. The lawyer read the charges against him while he listened, but his feet had been rubbed raw, and he found himself thinking more of them than of the indictment. The defense lawyer asked Strekov how he intended to plead. "To which charges?" Strekov asked.

"Treason."

"Not guilty," Strekov said.

"You provided state secrets to a foreign power," the defense attorney said. The room was terribly hot. They waited.

"I gave documents of a certain type to a foreigner," Strekov said.

"So you plead guilty."

"No," Strekov said.

"But you admit passing documents to foreigners?"

Strekov had moved his feet from beneath the chair to relieve the pressure of his right shoe. He looked at the odd shoes and the naked white ankles. They weren't his feet at all. "I gave documents of a certain type to a foreigner," Strekov repeated.

"State documents?" The defense lawyer waited. A gray-haired Russian leaned over and whispered to the defense lawyer. "Documents which originated in or were controlled by a state ministry?"

"Documents under my control," Strekov said.

Two of the men seated to Strekov's right nodded. Again the gray-haired Russian whispered to the lawyer, who leaned forward and listened. He sat up. "So it is true, then. You betrayed to the Americans certain affairs of state in which you were associated in Berlin and in London. You betrayed your comrades at Karlshorst, as well as certain individuals in London. One in particular, an Englishman."

"Not true," Strekov said.

"You were in contact with the American intelligence services in Berlin," the gray-haired man said to Strekov. "Do you deny that?" His voice was calm, his blue-green eyes studying Strekov, who didn't answer for a minute, trying to remember the face. He couldn't. He thought that the man addressing him was from Orlov's office, a KGB adviser to his defense counsel whose duty was to protect the KGB and to advise the defense lawyer of matters of great sensitivity.

"No," Strekov replied.

"You were in contact with the Americans in London. You betrayed the man known as Solo to the Americans."

"No."

The lawyer said, "You admit that you passed documents?"

"Yes. Documents under my control."

"The prosecution will claim that you were cooperating with American intelligence officials in East Berlin, that you provided them with certain information concerning operations at Karlshorst, that you betrayed the Englishman with whom you were associated in London, that you participated in the murderous assault upon Comrade Bykov at Treptow. . . ." The voice droned on. The Uzbek had died in the alley behind the Treptow warehouse, where he had been sent with Bykov at Zhilenkov's orders to bring the American in for questioning as to his association with Strekov.

"I knew nothing about it," Strekov said. "The charges are not true as written."

"You admit you passed documents," the lawyer cried, his bald head gleaming under the fierce white lights. "You admit it. If that is true, you must plead guilty!"

Strekov said, "The charges as written are false."

"This is sheer pedantry—bureaucratism!" the lawyer exclaimed. The gray-haired Russian waved his hand and the guards led Strekov away. He hobbled between them, iron soles clattering on the stone floor, limping painfully on his bleeding feet. The corridor in the basement was bitter cold after the dry, prickly heat of the interrogation room. His cotton shirt lay like ice against his spine. He wrapped the thin blanket over his shoulders and collapsed on the straw pallet. He tried to sleep. He wasn't conscious of his hunger so much as the cold, whose edge sent involuntary shudders through his body. His teeth chattered. The chattering stopped. He was almost asleep when he heard loud voices in the stone corridor. "This won't do," he heard a voice protest. "This won't do at all! Who made this idiotic mistake!" The cell door opened. A tall Russian with close-cut blond hair stood in the doorway. The guards lifted Strekov to his feet, but he pulled himself free. The blond Russian said there had been a mistake. They took him to a cell on a floor above. The new cell was painted gray, with an iron-gray cot, a small wash basin in one corner, and a wide, barred window high on one wall. Strekov could see the dark Moscow sky. On a small wooden table were a pair of worsted trousers, neatly folded; a cotton shirt; socks, underclothes, and a woolen jacket hanging over the back of the chair. Strekov recognized them. They were his clothes. The blond Russian asked him what he needed. Strekov said he wanted his shoes.

They left him alone in the gray cell and he changed his clothes. A few minutes later a guard returned with his shoes. He had just put them on when the door opened again and two different guards took him to a large room on the main floor. The state prosecutor sat at a large table in the center of the room, flanked by his senior staff. Strekov sat alone at a small table facing him. It was a small amphitheater; the gallery was dark. Klieg lights illuminated the state prosecutor's table and his own; somewhere to Strekov's right a motion picture camera was whirling away.

The state prosecutor read the statement of charges. From time to time he drank from a water glass on the table in front of him, leaning away from the microphone. There was no microphone on the bare table in front of Strekov, who sat in silence, listening to the statement. The warmth of the room brought his hunger to life; his mouth was dry; and sleep tugged at the edges of his mind like a drug. When the state prosecutor finished reading from the text in front of him, he hesitated, looked to one side, pushed back his chair, and stood up. Other chairs were pushed back as well, and from the darkened gallery beyond the klieg lights Strekov heard the rustle of movement, a loud suspiration of breath, the lifting of cramped bodies and limbs, and realized that the gallery was full.

He sat at the table, contemplating the darkness. Whose faces? Did he know any of them? The state prosecutor was staring at him fixedly. Someone nudged Strekov from the rear. He stood up, waiting to answer the state's charges. But at that moment the state prosecutor turned, his aides turned, gathered up their papers, and left the table. The klieg lights dimmed. Strekov was taken through the shadows and out the rear door. He was led to the overheated interrogation room where his defense counsel and his staff waited. Since Strekov had last seen them, they had eaten their dinners, perhaps shaved, changed their jackets or their shirts. Their faces were the same.

"We would ask you again how you will plead," the defense lawyer began. "You betrayed state secrets. You've admitted that. Let us review the charges once more."

Strekov said, "We are wasting time. The charges are false." The defense lawyer ignored him and began to read. "Giving information regarding sensitive operations at Karlshorst—" He lifted his eyes.

"Not true."

"The compromising and betrayal of your comrade in London—"

"Not true."

"Divulging secret information regarding the operation of the Illegals Directorate of the—"

"Not true."

"You admitted you provided documents!" the defense counsel shouted angrily. "Yet you sit there like some imbecilic parrot."

"These are not the charges I'm guilty of."

His defense counsel knew nothing except what Orlov's office had supplied the state prosecutor. He turned to the gray-haired Russian who sat at his side, watching Strekov. "It's impossible!" he said. "He pleads guilty to the crime, but not to the charges. The state prosecutor has written the charges. Am I to tell that state prosecutor that's he right but for the wrong reasons, that he's incompetent? That his staff are fools?"

The gray-haired Russian lifted his hand, still watching Strekov. "You supplied documents," he said calmly. "You admit that."

"I admit that."

"Then you only have to tell us which documents you supplied."

"Weapons information," Strekov said. "Weapons delivery systems."

No one spoke. "Impossible," someone breathed from across the table.

"The Strategic Rocket Forces," Strekov continued. "ICBM dispersion, guidance systems, solid-fuel components."

"That's not possible," muttered the man with gray hair, his face colorless in the bright lights.

"You were at Karlshorst," someone said.

"Before Karlshorst, I was here in Moscow."

"You had no access."

"There were the helicopter crashes," Strekov continued. "The one at Tyura Tarn. Another at Lake Balkhash. Two missile engineers were killed, two chemists, three officers with the Strategic Forces. The briefcases were recovered. We assembled them here in Moscow; we photographed the contents—each document. Sabotage was suspected. Orlov remembers. I was in charge of the detail. Those were the photographs I passed. They were on film. I'd had them with me for eight months. I wasn't sure what to do with them." Strekov's voice wound down.

The room was silent. Abruptly one of the men to his left got to his feet and left the room. The gray-haired man stared at Strekov in disbelief. The room had become unbearably hot. Strekov removed his jacket. "These things are less than a man's life," he said. "I betrayed no one—not in London, not at Karlshorst." Another man got to his feet, still scribbling on his pad, and went out.

"Less than a man's life?" the gray-haired KGB officer said woodenly. "They safeguard the revolution, the Party—"

"These aren't the things that safeguard the Party," Strekov said.

The gray-haired man stood up. The defense counsel followed. Ten minutes later Strekov was led away. The guards took him to the the small cold cell in the basement. On the straw pallet was the thin, pajamalike prison garb he'd rid himself of in the gray-walled cell less than three hours earlier. Nearby were the hated shoes. He undressed without protest, sitting on the floor finally to take off his socks and rubber-soled walking shoes. When he stood up and handed the clothes back to the guard, they made him take off his underwear. Naked in the cell, he slipped the thin cotton shirt over his head and pulled on the trousers. The cold had driven the hunger from his body. He wanted only to sleep. When the colorless soup was brought, he sipped from the bowl only to feel its heat. But it was cooler than his body, and he put it aside and fell asleep instead.

Strekov's confession made no impression on the prosecution. The charges weren't altered. There were bureaucratic reasons for ignoring the truth, security reasons as well. The KGB *apparat* preferred to believe Strekov's admission was deliberately designed to slander its role in internal security at a time when its methods, its personnel, and its tyranny were under attack from within. If the military, most especially the Strategic Rocket Forces—the bulwark of the Soviet Union's strength—joined the internal assault against the KGB, made common cause with the liberals, the poets, and painters, as well as the constitutional reformers, where would the anarchy end? The KGB preferred to try Strekov for crimes committed within the seclusion of its own bureaucratic estate—the betrayal of its own agents, spies, and informers. The Strategic Rocket Forces were uneasy with Strekov's confession, but found a certain utility in the KGB's explanation of Strekov's behavior: that it was a plot fabricated by criminalistic elements abroad to sow internal discord, demoralize the Russian military, weaken confidence in Russian defensive capability, and lay the groundwork for political opportunism abroad. The Soviet Rocket Force elite were also dubious that a KGB officer like Strekov, adept at political thuggery and bureaucratic hooliganism, could bring order to a thousand flame-scorched documents scattered over a remote wilderness. No man could, even if he had possessed the technical and scientific education of their most senior scientists.

The prosecution maintained the indictment as it had been originally prepared. The trial was held *in camera*. Strekov sat at a bare wooden table, surrounded by white lights. "Where was the initial approach made?" the prosecutor asked him the first day. "London or Berlin?"

"No one approached me in either city."

"A radio was found in your flat near Karlshorst. Where is the crystal for the radio?"

"I used no radio, no crystal."

"Why did you have the radio?"

"For personal reasons. I listened to it occasionally."

"Speak up! Why did you have the radio?"

"For personal reasons."

"What was the frequency of the crystal?"

"I had no crystal," Strekov said.

"Did you use the radio to betray Comrade Bykov?"

"No."

"Yet you say you listened to the radio."

"I listened to the radio, yes."

"To what frequencies?"

"Many frequencies."

"To all of Europe?"

"Yes, to all of Europe."

"To everything moving in the ether, to the stars, to the music of the spheres?" The prosecutor laughed and there was a murmur of laughter from the dark gallery.

The judge said that Strekov didn't have to answer the question, but he answered it anyway. "To everything moving in the ether, yes."

"You were identified at a London railroad station in the company of two American intelligence officials."

Strekov said, "Only one was American."

"You admit that you met with them, that you passed secret documents to them."

"No. That is incorrect."

"You betrayed your comrades to them."

"No."

At the end of the day the prosecutor said, "You're lying. You've been lying from the beginning—about the radio, the death of your comrade at Treptow, the murderous assault on Comrade Bykov, the betrayal of the Division Directorate in Moscow! But in the end we'll know. We'll know what you know, and when we do, it will come freely. All of it! We'll know all there is to know, and nothing will be left. Nothing! We'll know much more than you've ever told us, do you understand?"

Strekov said nothing. At the end of the third day the judged ruled that Strekov was ill and the trial was adjourned. Two psychiatrists from a forensic medicine team were brought in. He was interrogated in private during the days that followed. Time no longer meant anything to him. When the trial reconvened, he had forgotten what he had said or done, and even when it was read back to him, it made no sense. It was as if he were listening to a congress of madmen. He would listen silently, knowing that the trial had nothing more to do with him, nothing to do with his life at all. He had nothing left to admit or give up. It had all been taken from him and what they were harvesting were the last dead leaves from boughs already long dead themselves.

In the courtroom they had reinvented his treason, but they hadn't yet discovered the reasons for it. There was no reason, no reason at all, and this was the irrationality that haunted them, that brought the prosecutor back again and again to the final question. Why? Why had he done it? They were simple Party men—fathers, husbands, grandfathers, patriots, veterans of the Great War, civil servants, *apparatchiki*, and employees of the state—as he had been. Why had he done it? The question shone unanswered in the eyes of the prosecutor, like dead scales across the faces of the KGB advisors and the drawn face of Colonel Orlov, who sat like a ghost in the first row.

He'd gained nothing from it—nothing at all. Why? It was this question which led Strekov back again to the interrogation room after the day's trial was completed, which was repeated again the morning following as the prosecutor pored through the endless pages of official transcript. What was he betraying? Who was he betraying? Why? Why had he done it?

He told them for the last time that he had nothing left to betray. In time the aminazine they had been administering began to claim his body and he was no longer capable of answering the simplest question. His defense counsel said that he'd lost his mind, but the judge continued the trial. The prosecution witnesses were recalled, one by one. They waited for Strekov to confirm their testimony, to tell them why he had done it, but they had waited too long. Having been unable to subdue his will, their medicines at last took away his voice, and as the days passed, his eyes grew dimmer too, and he followed with less and less clarity the events which shaped themselves about him. So in time he was no longer a party to the proceedings at all, but merely their nameless hostage, sitting with his shaved head turned to one side, listening to distant voices, staring blankly and without comprehension at the ugly tumors which had begun to appear on his arms and chest.

In the late afternoon of the final day he was sitting at the table, his head to one side, looking towards the windows, not thinking about the trial at all, trying to remember where he was. The prosecutor was talking, and the room was as white as snow. Through his narrowed eyes he filtered out the black figures there, and heard the quiet hush of the hillside, the light gauze lying under his bootsoles.

"The fox in the woods," he said suddenly, but his voice failed him. The prosecutor turned. The judge asked:

"What did he say?"

He tried to say it again, but the sound wouldn't come. With great effort he brought his hand up, holding his one wrist with his fingers. The room was silent. He lifted his two fingers and held them apart, bending the shaking fingers to show the ears of the fox, and how he had stood under the apple boughs at the edge of the meadow. He held the fingers aloft, but the prosecutor and the judge saw only the thin, trembling hand. The trial was over.

In the days of solitude that followed, waiting for their final judgment, sitting half naked in the stone cell with only a straw pallet in the dark corner, he squatted for hours staring at the single recessed grill where the electric light shone above the door. He breathed the open sewer drain, and the suppuration that oozed from the sores on his body, thinking again of the fox, trying to bring his hand up. "He's mad," the prosecutor had said.

With his cracked lips he tried to understand it: mad, madness, mad, but when he heard the first harsh sounds forced from his throat, as ugly as two stones scraped together, he realized what his voice could no longer say, and that in the physical sense he was already dead, his mind drifting away like smoke from bones and flesh already as lifeless as ash. He prayed without words that he was not mad and then to die, prayed that it had been the fox, and the sunlight he had seen, the raindrops glistening among the pine needles along the Dneipr; prayed that it was the sun, river, and pine, and not the bright nebula of some pathological fistula exploding in his brain or optic nerve. If in dying he could know that, its knowledge would be enough and he would be free of that suffocating shroud his body had become.

With little time left, he prayed that there were other reasons for what he had done, prayed to understand his faithlessness as she might have understood, prayed to empty their poisons and to free his spirit as she had once freed it. In the end he found it. They'd driven from him everything but that, and what remained they could no more lay hands to or deny him than they could deny the long, cold sunlight that had once lain across the floor of the dacha, the melted snow dissolved in the fabric of his shooting jacket, the smell of woodsmoke, his wife's shimmering tea leaves, or the shadow his mind had made against the endleaf of one of their books—words which gleamed like frost on a winter pane and would once again tell him of his substance. They were words written in pencil in the chill silence of the sitting room, words written on a cold night the year following her death with the ice thrashing in the woods, the snow steep on the riverbanks, and the wind touching the flue—words written when he'd come back to

the guttering lamp after a second night of searching for her in sleep
through the empty dacha:

> In my study where the cold lamp waits
> I come to lay my furious resolve

He had not known what they meant at the time. Now he knew.

> The coals meanwhile have threatened to expire
> Leaving one last thought:
> From what we serve each creature takes in kind.
> Stunned by cold the dead wasp lifts upon its barb;
> The mind takes poison from its own.

It was there, in the moldering pages on the bookshelf at the dacha—
the truth their own had failed to find. It was enough. They had taken
from him everything but that; and finally they took that, too. It went
up fiercely as he died, the last thing his mind remembered as it hag-
gled with his broken body at first, a cold wind slamming through an
empty house, and then soared with a rush through the bloody aper-
ture of his skull, like the angry lifting of ashes flaring from a flue, glowing crimson and red for an instant against the ice-blue Russian dawn.